Kate Hardy has alway[...] read before she went to [...] Mills & Boon books w[...] decided that this was what she wanted to do. When she isn't writing Kate enjoys reading, cinema, ballroom dancing and the gym. You can contact her via her website: katehardy.com.

Michele Renae is the pseudonym of award-winning author Michele Hauf. She has published over ninety novels in historical, paranormal and contemporary romance and fantasy, as well as writing action/ adventure as Alex Archer. Instead of writing 'what she knows' she prefers to write 'what she would love to know and do.' And, yes, that includes being a jewel thief and/or a brain surgeon! You can email Michele at toastfaery@gmail.com, and find her on Instagram, @MicheleHauf, and Pinterest, @toastfaery.

ONCE UPON A SECOND CHANCE

KATE HARDY

MICHELE RENAE

MILLS & BOON

First published in Great Britain 2025
by Mills & Boon, an imprint of HarperCollins*Publishers* Ltd,
1 London Bridge Street, London, SE1 9GF

www.harpercollins.co.uk

HarperCollins*Publishers*, Macken House, 39/40 Mayor Street Upper, Dublin 1, D01 C9W8, Ireland

Once Upon a Second Chance © 2025 Harlequin Enterprises ULC

Forbidden Kiss with the Prince © 2025 Pamela Brooks

Reunion with Her Highland Rival © 2025 Michele Hauf

ISBN: 978-0-263-41762-3

12/25

This book contains FSC™ certified paper
and other controlled sources to ensure responsible forest management.

For more information visit www.harpercollins.co.uk/green.

Printed and Bound in the UK using 100% Renewable Electricity
at CPI Group (UK) Ltd, Croydon, CR0 4YY

FORBIDDEN KISS WITH THE PRINCE

KATE HARDY

MILLS & BOON

For Gerry—one day we'll get back to Greece…

CHAPTER ONE

IN ANOTHER LIFE, Niko thought as he walked round the edge of the dig site, he would've been here. Working with the team of archaeologists who were excavating the Temple of Amphitrite, just outside the capital of Amphithos, looking at the heritage of the island, being part of all the discoveries as they happened. He would've loved every second.

But the sailing accident last year that had killed Leo, his elder brother, had changed everything. It meant that Niko was no longer the little brother who spent all his time with his nose in a book—well, he still read, but most of the time nowadays it was state papers rather than anything else. He was no longer the 'spare', the backup in case anything happened to Leo: he was the heir to the island kingdom. And everything he'd planned to do with his life had been whisked away, like the grains of sand that tumbled over the top of the beach on a breezy winter morning.

He *missed* Leo. Missed his brother's sunny nature, his terrible jokes, his infectious grin. Missed his certainty. Leo had been the perfect Prince Charming, who put people at their ease and would've made a brilliant king when their father was ready to step down from the role. And Niko had adored his elder brother. He'd been perfectly happy to live in Leo's shadow: to be a private support rather than the public face of the monarchy.

Except, now Leo was gone, Niko had to take over and live the life Leo should've had. He needed to prepare for becoming the King of Amphithos, learning how to rule the island and balance any diplomatic tensions on the world stage. Instead of being the best man at Leo's wedding, the nerdy and academic uncle to Leo's children, the one who kept away from all the razzmatazz... Now, Niko was going to have to marry for duty's sake, produce the next heir to the kingdom, and lead his country.

He didn't even have a breathing space to come to terms with his new role properly, because losing Leo had aged both his parents dramatically. His father's physician had advised that, for the sake of his health, Leonidas III should step down and let his younger son—now his only child—take up the mantle.

Of course Prince Nikolaos would do his duty. Of *course* he would. Hadn't he done that from the day he'd identified his brother's body, stepping down from his role at the university and exchanging his history books for legal briefings and budgets? He'd swapped poetry and art for in-depth reports on wine, olives and tourism. He'd learned to be a statesman and stuffed all his emotions and his dreams into a little box, putting the needs of the island before his own. He was going to marry a princess from a list chosen by the Palace Council and his parents—a dynastic marriage for the sake of Amphithos.

Though Niko was struggling to live up to Leo's legacy. It made him feel guilty, because he found it all a pressure rather than a pleasure, the way Leo had. He was living the life his brother should have had, but it wasn't the life he'd wanted for himself. At all.

'Just snap out of it and stop wallowing, Niko,' he told himself roughly. 'There isn't a choice. You have to step up. Be the king.'

But it wouldn't hurt just to take a *tiny* look at the dig that should've been his, would it?

It didn't get better than this, Gemma thought as she walked across the site. She was a week into the job of her dreams, excavating a previously unknown temple to Amphitrite—the goddess of the sea and Poseidon's wife. Her team would be staying on the island kingdom of Amphithos, just off the western coast of Greece, for the next six weeks. She'd already fallen in love with the island; it was full of lush vegetation, olive groves and bougainvillea. The capital city, Vrachos Delfinion—meaning 'Dolphin Rock'—was gorgeous, from the Venetian-built ancient palace through to the fishermen's cottages in the harbour with their white walls and blue painted shutters. The beaches had plenty of soft golden sand, and the turquoise Ionian sea lapped lazily at the shoreline.

Summer in paradise.

How much life could change in a few short months. A year ago, Gemma had been knocked sideways by her fiancé jilting her at the altar. Andy hadn't turned up to their wedding: not because he'd fallen in love with someone else, but because he'd fallen out of love with her. He hadn't even had the guts to tell her to her face, or to call the wedding off before the actual day; instead, he'd asked his best man to tell her at the church door, while he left the country to travel to India and 'find himself'.

At the time, Gemma had been devastated. She'd loved Andy and she'd believed he loved her all the way back. He'd been the one to propose. He'd been the one who wanted the big party to celebrate their nuptials. Gemma would've been just as happy with a quiet, simple wedding and a reception in a village hall with a home-made buffet and their friend's band supplying the music. In her view it was the wedding itself and having the people you loved there that counted, not expensive clothes and gourmet menus and fashionable party favours.

With the help of her parents, her brother and her friends, Gemma had sorted out the mess Andy had left behind him. During the course of the past year, she'd picked herself back up and she'd come to feel grateful that she was single. The wedding-day-that-wasn't had been a horrible experience, but she realised now that marrying someone who wasn't truly committed to her would've been a huge mistake and taken much more time and pain to unpick.

Since then, she'd avoided relationships and concentrated her focus on her work; and now she had the reward of working on her dream dig, on what they hoped would be a unique temple in the Mediterranean. Better still, their entire team had been put up in one of the university's student accommodation blocks rather than having to camp out in tents for the duration of the summer dig. With a beach where she could swim every morning before work, a café nearby which sold excellent coffee and even more excellent pastries, and a taverna across the road from the dig site offering simple, beautifully cooked and locally sourced food for dinner, the location was perfect.

She'd already sent the students off to Theo's Taverna, and she'd just set the alarm and was about to lock up the little building where the finds were being stored when she noticed a man walking through the site.

'Excuse me!' she called.

Either he hadn't heard her or he was in a world of his own, because he didn't reply. Well, she couldn't leave him wandering around out here.

Sighing inwardly, she locked the door, shoved the keys into the pocket of her jeans, and headed over towards him. '*Kalispéra. Miláte angliká?*' She only knew a smattering of Greek right now; although she was learning a little more each day, with the help of the students on her team, she didn't know enough yet to have a lengthy conversation with someone. If the answer to her polite question was no, he didn't speak English, she'd have to resort to her phone to help her translate.

'Yes, I do,' he said.

Gemma was surprised to discover that he had barely a trace of an accent, given that he looked like a local.

He was dressed casually in faded jeans, a white T-shirt and canvas shoes. His dark hair was slightly wavy and cut short; his beard was close-cropped; and his eyes were the colour of amber. She judged him to be a couple of years older than she was, maybe on the cusp of thirty, and he was one of the most beautiful men she'd ever seen. Had Gemma's mother Cassie been here, she would've nudged Gemma and murmured that this guy reminded her of a young George Michael, her crush as a teen, and then burst into a chorus of 'Wake Me Up Before You Go-Go' and made Gemma sing along with her.

Gemma suppressed both the amusement and the sudden wave of homesickness. She needed to look and sound professional, right now, because this man shouldn't be here and she needed to ask him to leave. Pushing George Michael to the back of her head, she said, 'I'm very sorry, but I'm afraid the dig isn't open to the public.'

'And you are…?' he asked, challenging her.

She drew herself up to her full five feet five inches and removed her sunglasses. 'Dr Gemma Stone, lead archaeologist on this project, from the University of London,' she said crisply. 'And you are…?'

She didn't know who he was.

And it made Niko want to punch the air, because it meant that Dr Gemma Stone would have no preconceptions about him. She wouldn't curtsey to him, or address him as 'Your Highness'; she wouldn't rush to offer her condolences on the loss of his brother. She'd see him as just an ordinary man. And, with her being an archaeologist, she'd be able to talk to him about the things he'd been missing so badly. Win, win, win.

'Niko,' he said. 'Just Niko.'

And then he made the mistake of holding his hand out to shake hers. The second her skin touched his, it felt as if he'd been struck by lightning.

Oh, help. This wasn't supposed to happen. He wasn't in the market for a relationship—well, not unless she was secretly the Crown Princess of Somewhere-or-other, someone his mother would be happy to add to the list of suitable potential brides for the king-to-be of Amphithos. And that wasn't likely.

The problem was, he hadn't felt that zing of attraction towards anyone for a long time. He knew it wasn't something he should act on, either. But Gemma Stone was irresistible. Her strawberry-blonde hair was pulled back at the nape of her neck with a scrunchie, protected from the sun by a leather fedora that made him think of both Indiana Jones and an English TV archaeologist he'd had a secret crush on for years. There was the cutest sprinkling of freckles across her nose. Her piercing blue eyes were full of challenge and, he suspected, a sense of humour; and her mouth was as beautiful as that on any statue of Aphrodite he'd ever seen.

'And you're here, Niko, because…?' she asked.

He could hardly tell her that he was about to become the king of Amphithos, her excavation was on land that just so happened to belong to his family, and—until he'd needed to resign from his job at the university to join the family business—he was actually the person who'd originally suggested they should excavate the site. He'd also been the one who suggested her team should come over to help. He'd sat through a few lectures by her professor, eighteen months ago, and he'd liked what he'd heard. 'I'm just interested in the dig,' he said.

'Journalist?' she asked.

'Mmm-hmm.' It was a mumbled noise, not a proper word, so it wasn't a *complete* lie, he told himself.

'I'm afraid we're not really in a position to report anything to the press at the moment,' she said. 'If you'd like to leave me your business card, I can make sure you're on the list for any press releases as soon as we're able to talk about our finds.'

Niko felt the colour stain his face. 'Sorry. No business card,' he said. Telling her who he was would make it obvious why he didn't need a business card, but he didn't want to do that. He wanted to enjoy these few moments of feeling he was still part of the academic world. Admitting that he was the prince would make things way too complicated.

'How about your email address?' she asked, taking out her phone and clearly ready to take a note.

Awkward. Then again, he was pretty sure he could talk his way round this one. 'Niko@palace.amphi.com,' he said.

Her eyes narrowed. 'You're connected to the palace?'

'I work with the press office,' he said. Which was true, up to a point. She didn't need to know that they worked for him, or that he worked with other departments at the palace as well. Plus she'd been the one who'd suggested he was a journalist. He'd simply gone along with it rather than correcting her.

'I already have a contact at the royal press office,' she said. 'Yiannis.'

His private secretary, who also oversaw PR. 'That's fine,' Niko said. 'He'll forward any relevant information to me.' If Gemma Stone assumed that Yiannis was his boss, instead of the other way round…well, he hadn't actually *said* that, had he?

Her eyes narrowed. 'Then, Niko, thank you for your interest in the site, but perhaps you'd be kind enough to let me finish locking up? My students will be wondering where I've got to, and it would be a shame if they had to come back from the bar across the street and check up on me.'

Amphithos had a very low crime rate and Gemma was perfectly safe, but even so Niko rather thought at least one of her students should've stayed behind to help instead of them all rushing off for a cold beer after a hard day's work. 'All right, Dr Stone, I'll let you get on,' he said with a smile, stuffing down the disappointment that he hadn't been able to get even a peek into a trench. 'Thank you for your time.'

'You're very welcome, Niko,' she said with a polite smile. 'Sorry I couldn't be of any more help.'

CHAPTER TWO

THE FOLLOWING MORNING, just after sunrise, Gemma went for her habitual swim before work, enjoying the peace and quiet. How amazing it was to swim in the ocean instead of jostling for space in the university swimming pool, with just the sound of the waves swishing onto the shore and seabirds calling overhead.

Everything was fine until she felt a sudden pain in her right calf.

Cramp.

She knew better than to try to swim through it; she needed to stretch out the muscle. Thankfully she wasn't too far from the shore; when she tried standing up, she was relieved to discover that the sea came up to her chin. If she'd been just a few more centimetres deeper, out of her depth, she would've really been in trouble.

It was a bit of a struggle, but she made it to the shore and finally managed to sit down on the sand. She flexed her right foot, trying to pull her toes in as hard as possible to stretch the muscle, and massaged her sore calf.

She was just at the point of standing up again and trying to work out where she was when she realised two soldiers were walking towards her. As they reached her and she stood up, one of them said something to her in Greek.

'I'm sorry,' she said, frantically racking her brains for the words she needed. The combination of cramp and shock at seeing the soldiers—men with actual guns, not what she was used to seeing on the streets back home—had flustered her completely. *'Anglikà,'* she said, hoping it was the right word so they'd realise she needed help and she wasn't some kind of master criminal with nefarious intentions who should be dragged off to the dungeons at gunpoint.

'We speak English,' the first soldier said. 'What are you doing here, madam?'

'I was swimming,' she said, gesturing to her swimming costume and bare feet. 'I got cramp. That's why I had to get out of the sea and onto the beach.'

'This beach is private. It's out of bounds to the public,' the second soldier said. 'We have to ask you to leave.'

Despite the warmth of the morning sun, she shivered. 'I'm so sorry, but I really don't want to risk swimming in the sea again, in case the cramp returns.'

'You need to leave the area,' the first soldier said. 'We'll escort you to the gate.'

'I apologise for trespassing,' she said, starting to panic slightly. How could she walk back to the university on the road, when she didn't have shoes? She gestured to her bare feet. 'But—look, as I already told you, I was swimming.' The panic deepened, making her gabble. 'Please can you help me? I don't have my phone on me or any money. I can't call anyone to bring me a towel and some clothes and pick me up, because I can't remember anyone's phone number, and anyway I doubt if any taxi would agree to take me anywhere dressed like this, and—'

A third man joined them and spoke in rapid Greek. Then he added in English, for her benefit, 'Good morning, Dr Stone.'

Then she really looked at the stranger who'd just joined them—a man in a very expensive-looking suit. Someone she'd met before. A man who could vouch for her. She could've wept with relief.

'Good morning, Niko,' she said. 'I'm so sorry. I was swimming and I got cramp. These gentlemen tell me I'm trespassing.'

'Strictly speaking, you are. This beach is private and belongs to the royal estate,' he said. He turned to the two soldiers and spoke again in Greek.

They inclined their heads.

Niko looked at Gemma. 'I just told Géorgios and Petros it's fine; I know who you are and you're working on the dig with the university. I told them I'll take it from here,' he explained.

'Thank you. I appreciate your help. But won't you get into trouble with Yiannis?' she asked.

'I very much doubt it.' He smiled. 'We'll find some dry clothes and footwear for you at the palace, and I'll take you back to your team.'

Considering she'd more or less marched him off the dig yesterday, he was being kinder than she deserved, right now. 'Thank you,' she said. 'I really—'

'—shouldn't swim on your own,' he cut in dryly.

'Not that you're likely to be accosted or hurt by anyone, because the island's pretty safe, but the sea can be very unpredictable. Does anyone know where you are?'

'No,' she admitted. 'I mean, I've talked about how much I enjoy swimming before breakfast, so one of the students would probably have guessed I'd done exactly that and gone looking for me. They would've seen my towel and shoes on the beach and raised the alarm when they couldn't see me anywhere.'

'Had you got into difficulties,' he said, 'then they might've been too late when you were found. Plus, with no phone and no means of identification on you, how would the emergency services know who to contact? Or, if you were still alive but unconscious, how would they know if you had any severe allergies or medical conditions they'd need to be aware of when treating you?'

Right at that moment, Gemma felt like a stupid child. And she couldn't argue with Niko, because she knew he was absolutely right. She'd been thoughtless. Reckless, even. All she had on her was the door key she'd pinned to the strap of her swimming costume. She'd been so carried away with the idea of being able to swim in the sea before breakfast that it hadn't even occurred to her to carry some form of identification. 'I'm sorry,' she said again.

'Never, ever take risks with the sea,' he said softly. 'Come on. I'll take you to the palace.' He shrugged off his jacket and made as if to place it round her shoulders.

'No,' she said swiftly. 'You'll ruin your jacket. I'm covered in sand and seawater.' Though she was awkwardly aware that she was very underdressed, in bare feet and a red swimsuit that she'd fallen in love with but had to admit clashed a bit with her hair. She could hardly go walking into the palace dressed like this.

'Then give me a moment, please, Dr Stone. What size shoes do you take?'

Clearly he was going to borrow something for her, she thought with relief. 'An English five,' she said.

'OK.' He took a phone from his pocket and made a swift call. A couple of minutes later, a young woman in a smart uniform arrived carrying a hooded towelling robe and a pair of beach shoes. Both looked brand new.

'*Efcharistó*,' she said gratefully to the young woman, donning the robe and putting on the shoes as the woman melted away into the background.

'You said earlier that you had cramp. Can you walk?' Niko asked.

'Yes.'

'Good. Come with me,' he said. 'I'll get you a cup of coffee to warm you up before I take you back.'

'I don't want to be any trouble,' she said. 'Really. If I could just borrow your phone to call a cab, I'll sort out the fare when I'm back at my accommodation.'

'There's no need. I'll arrange transport,' he said.

'Thank you for rescuing me,' she said. 'I appreciate it. Especially as I was a bit—well, I was rude to you, yesterday, and I apologise for that.'

He smiled. 'I didn't have an appointment with you and I was a complete stranger. You did absolutely the right thing, asking me to leave the site.'

When they reached the palace, he took her through to

a back entrance and unlocked the door with a security fob. Then he shepherded her into a small but comfortable sitting room that she assumed was part of the press office, and gestured to her to sit on a rich upholstered sofa.

'Coffee?' he said. 'And I assume you didn't eat before your swim.'

'I didn't,' she admitted, 'but there's really no need to put anyone to any trouble. I'll eat something when I'm back at my accommodation.'

'I'm having breakfast. You might as well join me,' he said. 'It's not putting anyone to any trouble. Any allergies or dietary restrictions?'

'None,' she said. 'Thank you. I'd really love some coffee.'

Before she knew it, there was a plate of delicious-looking Greek pastries on the coffee table, along with a jug of coffee.

'Milk? Sugar?' he asked.

'Just a splash of milk, please.'

He smiled. 'Help yourself to something to eat.'

The coffee was fantastic, as were the still-warm *baklava*, and they did a lot to revive her. She was about to ask him if he'd like to have a proper tour of the dig, as a way of thanking him for rescuing her, when there was a knock on the door and the press officer came in.

'*Prinkípas* Nikolaos, Petros was telling me that there was a secur–' He stopped dead as he noticed Gemma sitting on the sofa. 'My apologies, *Vasilikí sas Ypsilótita*.' To Gemma's surprise, he actually bowed to Niko. 'Sorry for interrupting your meeting, Dr Stone,' he added.

Vasilikí sas Ypsilótita. She didn't know what it meant, but Yiannis had actually *bowed* to Niko. And was it her imagination, or had he just called Niko 'prince'?

Yiannis was the only person she'd met so far from the palace; he'd had a courtesy meeting with her at the university when she'd arrived, where he'd asked her to give him a daily email briefing on the dig and said that she could contact him if there were any issues that the university couldn't sort out. Gemma had known that the dig site belonged to the royal family, but she'd assumed that the king would be far too busy to have any kind of contact with her. She'd researched the history of the site, but it hadn't occurred to her to research the royal family as well.

Now it looked very much as if the man who'd rescued her—the man she'd escorted off the premises yesterday—might just be the king's son, and she knew almost nothing about him.

Embarrassment made her toes curl, followed sharply by the realisation that Niko had lied to her. He'd told her yesterday that he was a journalist, not a prince. Lying was her personal big red flag: something she absolutely refused to countenance, since Andy had broken their engagement and shattered her world last year.

'Good morning, Yiannis,' she said. 'You haven't interrupted anything. I was just leaving.'

Some of her feelings must've shown on her face, because Niko did at least have the grace to flush. 'Dr Stone, please give me a moment,' he said, and switched to rapid Greek.

Yiannis listened, nodded once, and looked curiously

at Gemma for a moment before leaving the room without another word.

'Sorry about that,' Niko said.

'You lied to me,' she said quietly.

'About what?' he asked.

'Who you are. You told me yesterday you were "just Niko". But you're not "just" anything, are you? Yiannis called you "prince", didn't he? I don't know what *Vasilikí sas Ypsilótita* means, but I'm guessing that's connected.'

'Your Royal Highness,' he translated, wincing.

'So you really *are* a prince.' And she'd made a huge gaffe. The sort that could not only make her lose her job, but could have knock-on effects for the rest of her team.

He looked awkward. 'Telling you that I was the son of the king would've made you feel ill at ease. And I didn't particularly want to behave like some has-been actor and demand, "Don't you know who I *am*?".' He hammed up the phrase and rolled his eyes. 'Besides, it wasn't a complete untruth. My family and friends call me Niko.'

'You also said you worked for the palace press office,' she reminded him.

'Actually, I said I worked *with* them,' he corrected. 'Which is also true.'

'Up to a point. You deliberately misled me.'

'Yes, I did, and I apologise for that. Yiannis is my private secretary, and he also oversees the palace PR team.' He looked awkward. 'I didn't mislead you to make you feel foolish.'

She folded her arms and raised her eyebrows, waiting for him to give her a proper explanation.

'It was because, had my brother not died in the yachting accident last year, I would've been working in that team with you,' Niko said. 'I'd had a day stuffed full of paperwork and meetings and people talking at me until my ears bled. Was it so bad to want to escape for five minutes and see something that's important to me—to be who I am as a person, rather than acting in my official role?'

Put like that, his behaviour sounded much more reasonable. And Gemma supposed that it must be difficult, living your life in the public eye. Every word you said would be dissected and analysed, every movement speculated over. You'd have to be so careful what you did and said, every second of every day; it must be *exhausting*.

Then she realised what he'd said. 'You would've been working with me?'

'Leo—my elder brother—was meant to be taking over from our father. I was going to support him. I'd planned to handle the heritage of the island,' he said. 'My first degree was in history, I did a masters in archaeology, and my doctorate was on the mythology of the island.'

'You have a doctorate,' she said, surprised.

He shrugged. 'Look up Dr Niko Spiridon. Until last year, I was a lecturer at the university. I worked with ancient documents and maps. And I would've been working on this project because it's possibly the only known temple in the Mediterranean dedicated solely to Amphitrite.'

'There are the foundations of the joint temples of Poseidon and Amphitrite on Tinos, but that's about it,' she agreed, still trying to come to terms with the fact that Niko had worked at the university. 'But you're the son of the king. How could you have been a lecturer?'

'Plenty of royals have ordinary jobs,' he pointed out. 'I believe your late queen's cousin worked as a primary school music teacher for years.'

'There's a fair bit of a difference between being a minor royal and being the king's son.' One who was second in line to the throne.

'I was the *younger* son,' he emphasised. 'Although the plan was for me to support my brother when he became king, until then it was agreed that I could do the job of my choice. And I was interested in the mythology of our island.' He smiled. 'There's not that much about Amphitrite in Greek mythology, apart from Poseidon falling in love with her when she was dancing at Naxos. She fled to the ends of the sea to escape him, but Poseidon's dolphin talked to her and persuaded her to marry Poseidon.'

'And Poseidon turned the dolphin into a constellation as a reward,' she said. Even though it still rankled that Niko had lied to her, a bigger part of her was enjoying having an academic conversation with him. 'Is that why your capital's called Dolphin Rock?'

'That's my theory, yes,' Niko said. 'There are various mentions in historical documents of a temple being established near here. Given the name of the island, I suspected it could be Amphitrite's temple. I know there's the legend about Poseidon's palace being built in the blue caves at Antipaxos, a bit further down the coast, but I still thought there was a good chance that something important is here. I narrowed things down on the maps, and the archaeology team at the university did some geophys on what I calculated was the most likely site. It looked promising, so we did some test pits.'

'Which brought up personal objects decorated by dolphins and seahorses—creatures linked with Amphitrite, so they might have been votive offerings,' she said, having read translations of all the reports.

He nodded. 'If I'm right and it's her temple, I'm seriously hoping there's some kind of mosaic—a floor, I think, rather than something like the glass wall-covering of Neptune and Amphitrite at Herculaneum.'

A little burst of joy bloomed inside her. Prince Nikolaos was also Dr Niko Spiridon, whose reports she'd read and enjoyed. A nerd, at heart. He loved the same kind of things she did. How could she not respond to that? 'Are you thinking something like the floor in the House of Dolphins at Delos?' she asked.

'Yes, but I'm hoping it's Amphitrite driving a chariot with her *hippokampoi*, the fish-tailed horses of the sea,' he said, and his voice was slightly husky with suppressed excitement.

She found it sexy as hell.

If she was honest, she found *him* sexy as hell.

Niko had looked gorgeous enough in simple faded jeans and a T-shirt, yesterday; today, dressed in that beautiful suit teamed with a crisp shirt and understated tie, he reminded her of a film star. His metal-framed round glasses made him look like the intellectual he was—and that was the most irresistible thing, to her. A beautiful, clever mind.

Unable to stop herself, she said, 'I found some tesserae yesterday. I think you could be right about there being a mosaic floor. Give me a proper number I can reach you on, and I'll message you the second it looks as if we've found it.' In his shoes, if she'd worked on finding the site and then someone else took over investigating it, she'd have found it unbearable to have to give everything up, the way he had. Which was why she blurted out, 'Because I think you need to be there to help the team uncover it.'

'Thank you,' he said. 'That would be…'

And then he stopped. She could guess what he'd been about to say. It'd be a moment out of time for him, away from the pressure of taking over as the king. Yet his daily reality was a mixture of politics and paperwork. Strictly speaking, he didn't have time for this. He'd had to bury his passion for history and archaeology, for the sake of his duties. Because, since his brother's death, he was now the heir to the kingdom.

His brother.

She'd been so carried away at finding out that he was a historian and had links to her project that she'd forgotten her basic manners. 'I'm sorry about your brother,' she said quietly.

His face tightened and the light in his eyes dimmed. 'Thank you.' He inclined his head in acknowledgement.

'I have an older brother,' she said. 'If anything happened to Ed, I'd be devastated. It must be doubly hard for you, because everything you do is in the public eye.'

He raised his eyebrows. 'Show emotion—as a man—and you look weak. Don't show emotion, and you're a cold fish.'

Whatever he did, he couldn't win. Her heart ached for him.

Her sympathy must've shown in her face, because he said, 'It is what it is. But thank you for letting me be Dr Spiridon again for a little while.'

'If you'd told me who you actually were yesterday—I mean Dr Spiridon, not Prince Nikolaos—I would've taken the time to show you round properly,' she said. 'I knew you'd been corresponding with John, my head of department. I'd expected to work with you, but before I came out here he said you'd had to resign from your post for family reasons.'

'I did,' he said, those beautiful amber eyes darkening.

And now she knew what they were. His brother had died, and now he had to take on his brother's role in the monarchy. He'd had to give up a career he loved. She knew how devastated she'd feel if she had to give up her career, and her heart ached for him.

'Without a watch or my phone, I have no idea what time it is,' she said, 'but if you have time to visit now, I'd be more than happy to show you round. Or whenever is convenient for you. My schedule can be flexible.'

She was responding to him as an academic, not a prince, Niko thought. As a colleague who loved the same kind of things that she did. And he suddenly realised how much he would've enjoyed working with

Gemma Stone. They might've sat on the beach together with a glass of wine at the end of a day's dig, watching the sun setting over the sea and the sky turning to flame, talking intensely about the people who'd lived here thousands of years ago and speculating what their lives had been like. They would've talked about art and poetry and the constellations gradually appearing as the sky turned ink-dark. About Amphitrite and the women who'd worshipped her, millennia before. And maybe, as they'd talked animatedly, enjoying their conversation, their hands might've brushed together. Their fingers might've entwined. They might've drawn closer together. Leaned in for a kiss...

He shook himself mentally.

He couldn't go back to his old life. Even if Gemma felt the same pull of attraction towards him that he felt towards her, there was no point in starting any kind of relationship with her. There could be no future for them. Not when he had to marry for the sake of his country. And that made her completely off limits.

'I'll have someone drive you back to your accommodation, Dr Stone,' he said. 'I would offer to take you myself, but I have a meeting in—' he glanced at his watch '—less than twenty minutes. But thank you for your offer of showing me round the dig. I'll take you up on that at some point.' He'd keep it vague so he didn't risk having to break a promise.

'You gave me your email address yesterday,' she said. 'I'll send you photographs of the tesserae when I get back to the dig. If I find any more evidence of a mosaic, I'll email you.'

Niko just about stopped himself scribbling his private number for her on the back of a palace business card. That would be way too tempting. 'Thank you, Dr Stone,' he said instead. He wanted to call her Gemma, but keeping things formal between them would maintain the little bit of distance he needed. 'Good luck with the dig. I'll send someone to escort you back.'

'I'll get the robe and shoes cleaned and returned to the palace,' she said.

'No need. Keep them. We hold supplies of essentials here, in case guests forget something.' He gave her a small smile. 'But if you really want to do something in return, then promise me you won't take any more risks by swimming on your own.'

The expression in her eyes told him that she realised what he meant. He'd lost his brother to the sea; he didn't want any more accidents or deaths.

'I promise,' she said softly. 'And I keep my promises.'

'Of course. *Kaliméra*, Dr Stone.' He didn't quite dare shake her hand, not after the way her touch had affected him yesterday, so he stood up, gave her a small bow, and headed towards the door.

'*Kaliméra*, Dr Spiridon,' she said.

CHAPTER THREE

NIKO MANAGED TO compartmentalise his thoughts and concentrate on his meetings and his work for the entire morning, but at lunchtime he checked his email and there was one from Gemma.

It was a photograph of half a dozen tesserae: red, black and white. Along with the message: I'm hoping these are from a wave. GS.

His thoughts precisely. A wave was one of the most common borders for a Greek mosaic: black for the sea and sky, with a series of regular-shaped white waves curling over themselves towards the right, and a line of red outside of the black tesserae. Inside the square, there would be further motifs. In high-status rooms, there might be a circle or an oval containing a picture—polychromatic, as if it had been painted—and in the four curved corners there might be more designs relating to the central picture.

Thank you. Fingers crossed the next ones are green. NS, he emailed back. He knew Gemma would know what he meant; if there was a picture like the one they'd talked about this morning, Amphitrite's horses would have green fins for their manes as well as their tails.

He thought about it all afternoon, between meetings.

Actually, no. He thought about *her* all afternoon. Not only was Gemma the first woman he'd been attracted to since before Leo died, she was also the first person in months who'd talked to him about something that made him feel all lit up inside.

If he had any sense, he'd avoid her—because this feeling was dangerous to his peace of mind. He definitely wasn't going to drop round to the dig site this afternoon after his last meeting.

Absolutely not.

Absolutely, *definitely* not.

'*Prinkípas* Nikolaos, is everything all right?' Yiannis asked at the end of the afternoon, walking into the office where Niko was sitting at his desk, making notes.

'Of course,' Niko said, fibbing hugely.

'It's just that you seem a little…distracted.'

'I was paying attention,' Niko said, and reeled off a list of things that had been agreed in the meeting.

Yiannis smiled. 'I wasn't questioning you, *Prinkípas* Nikolaos. Everyone knows you're bright enough to do three things at once.'

'Thank you for the compliment,' Niko said, 'but, Yiannis, would you please stop using my title when we're not in a meeting?' Until last year, Yiannis had been happy enough to call him 'Niko'. This new formality was one of the changes that grated most. It made him feel as if he were in a cage.

'I've known you since you were a small child, Niko,' the private secretary said. 'Something's bothering you.'

It was, but Niko couldn't burden either of his parents with the truth. He shouldn't be admitting to it at all. But the kindness in Yiannis's eyes was enough to break through his defences. 'Just sometimes I miss my old life,' he said quietly.

'Of course you do. Anyone would, in your shoes,' Yiannis said. 'But remember that a good king has interests outside budgets and paperwork to keep himself grounded. Some play sports, some tinker with cars, and some find solace in the garden or a vineyard.'

Niko smiled at the reference to his father's hobby vineyard—the one King Leonidas had taken over from his own father. Yiannis was very good at spin. 'Shall we just take the direct route to what you want to tell me, Yiannis?'

'All right. There's no reason why you can't still pore over maps or wield a trowel from time to time. Especially on a dig where you were the one to pinpoint this particular site in the first place,' Yiannis said. 'And I think Dr Stone might be good company for you. She's *filikí*.'

Simpatico.

Yeah.

That was another part of the problem. He'd liked Gemma Stone instinctively, and he just didn't have the space in his life to let that feeling develop the way he might've done, a year ago. Before Leo's death, he could've dated anyone he wanted. He could've made a case for marrying anyone he wanted, even a non-royal. Now...he had to put his duties first. Perhaps it would be more sensible to keep temptation at a distance.

'Since you asked me to be direct, I'd like to remind

you it wasn't your fault that Leo died,' Yiannis said. 'And I think your brother would be furious with you for giving up everything you love for the job.'

That was true, Niko thought. Leo would've sat him down and asked what the hell was going on in his head. But what choice did he have? His parents were in pieces. They needed his support. He had to do his duty and step into Leo's role. And he needed to be the kind of king his brother would've been. Anything less would mean letting his family down. Letting Leo's memory down. He'd loved his elder brother too much to allow that to happen. 'There's no other way,' he said. 'As the younger son, I could have worked part time at the university and part time for the palace when Leo became king. As the only son, I can't.'

'Cutting yourself off completely from the things you love will only make you miserable,' Yiannis said. 'You need a safety valve—you need to make time for *you* in your schedule. And there's no reason why you can't spend a little time at the dig.'

Niko thought there was a particular reason why he probably shouldn't. A reason with strawberry-blonde hair and piercing blue eyes. But he gave Yiannis a polite smile. 'Later.'

And he really did intend to stay away from Gemma. Until an email dropped into his inbox. Did you have this colour green in mind?

She'd sent him a photograph of a tessera. A green one. The sort that might come from a finny tail or mane.

How could he resist?

Gemma's email signature included a mobile phone number. He texted her from his private phone. On my way now. NS.

Dr Niko Spiridon also happened to be Prince Nikolaos of Amphithos. Which meant he was completely out of her league. And the attraction she felt towards him needed to be suppressed, Gemma thought. She probably shouldn't have sent him that email this morning; she should have sent it officially through his private secretary or the palace PR team instead. And that went double for the photo she'd just sent him of the green tessera.

But she'd seen the longing in his eyes. It was obvious to her how much he missed his old job. If their positions had been reversed, she would've wanted him to keep her in the loop. This was merely a professional courtesy to the person who'd discovered the site in the first place, she told herself. And she tried not to be too pleased when he texted her to say he was on his way.

This time when Niko walked through the site towards her—again after everyone else had finished for the day and gone for a beer and something to eat at Theo's Taverna over the road—she walked over to greet him with a smile.

Should she call him Your Highness? she wondered. But she rather thought he might prefer a different title. One he'd earned for himself rather than been born to. '*Kalispéra*, Dr Spiridon. Welcome to the dig,' she said.

'Thank you, Dr Stone.' There was a little gleam of

pleasure in his amber eyes that told her she'd struck exactly the right note.

But then she made the mistake of holding her hand out to shake his. It was supposed to be a professional gesture; instead, the contact made her knees feel weak, and his smile made her heart give a weird little kick. Hoping he couldn't tell how flustered she was, she took him over to the trench where they'd found the green tessera earlier that afternoon. 'There's the base of a column over here, which I think is a tufa core dressed with a marble facade,' she said. 'I'm hoping we've found a corner of the temple. And if we go down another thirty centimetres I reckon we'll find the floor.'

'And then uncover the *hippokampoi*,' he said.

She gave him the bag containing the tessera. 'Take a closer look.'

'Beautiful,' he said as he took it out and inspected it. 'And to think the colour's still so rich after nearly two and a half thousand years.'

'This is the sort of thing I love to find,' she said. 'Things that connect us to the past. I don't care about gold and jewels: it's everyday life that draws me. The tweezers and make-up pots and combs, the spindles and the loom weights, a child's shoe, a cooking pot. Things we'd still use today.'

'The more things change, the more they stay the same,' he quoted softly.

'Let me show you round the site,' she said. 'I assume you have a bodyguard and he needs to be with you?'

He smiled at her. 'Stephanos, my security detail, is with me, yes.'

His bodyguard was already there? But she hadn't noticed anyone with him.

Clearly her thoughts had shown on her face, because Niko said, 'He's very discreet. Strictly speaking we're on palace land, plus the security team says you're not a concern.'

Of course the palace would've had her checked out. Niko was the heir to the kingdom. They couldn't take risks about whoever approached him. This was no different to the security checks made to clear people for working in a school or with vulnerable people, she reminded herself.

But a background search also meant his team would know everything about her. The mess of her wedding-day-that-wasn't wouldn't have been reported anywhere, but then again, someone might have put something on social media and that might've come up in a search. Or maybe she was just being paranoid because the way Andy had jilted her had hurt so much. But the fact his security team might know about it felt *personal*.

The awkwardness she felt must've shown in her expression, because he said gently, 'It's a routine thing, Gemma. They haven't told me any details, just that you're not a problem in their eyes.'

'OK,' she said, relieved he didn't know everything. She didn't want him thinking that she was a complete fool. She'd made a huge mistake with Andy, yes, but it could've been worse.

She took him round the site, talking him through the dig plan, then showed him some of the finds they'd logged so far.

'This is fantastic,' he said. 'Everything you've shown me fits in with what I'd expected to see here. Votive offerings—*personal* ones.'

'And it's so nice that the temple seems to be just for Amphitrite, not Poseidon as well. These are the women of the island asking the Queen of the Sea to look after their menfolk when they're out on a boat and bring them home safely.' Then she remembered that Niko's brother hadn't made it home safely from the sea. 'Sorry.' She bit her lip. 'I didn't intend to...' Her words trailed off awkwardly.

'I know you didn't,' he said quietly. 'It's not a problem. And you're right. Poseidon had a bad temper— it's why they called him the Earth-shaker, because he'd whip up storms and earthquakes with his trident. Amphitrite was gentle, the mother of all the seals and all the fishes. Of course the women would put their trust in her, rather than in an unpredictable god who liked stirring up trouble. And they'd encourage their men to do the same.'

They continued looking through the finds together, with Niko asking questions and also giving her more information about related finds in the capital's museum. And she was shocked to realise they'd just spent an hour and a half together. He was probably supposed to be at some important dinner function or political meeting, and she'd made him late.

'Sorry. I didn't mean to keep you quite so long,' she said.

'Actually, I think I'm the one who's kept *you* here late,' he said.

'I never mind talking about my work.' She smiled at him. 'It's third time lucky, then.'

'Meaning?' he asked.

'The first time we met, I threw you out. The second time we met, I was the one trespassing. *This*,' she emphasised, 'is how it should've been, all along.'

'The first time, I was dishonest with you and deserved the brush-off; the second time wasn't your fault, though I do hope you're not going to risk swimming on your own again; and I agree completely,' he said. 'This is how it should be. Two professionals. I think we could probably talk all evening and not run out of conversation.'

Even though the sensible side of her knew she shouldn't say it, the words tumbled out anyway. 'Niko, if you're not busy tonight, why don't you come over to Theo's and let me buy you dinner? I assume the students from the university here already know you, so they'd be delighted to see you—and my students from London would be thrilled to meet Dr Spiridon, the man who worked out where we should dig.'

Dinner. Talking with students, something that always energised him. He'd missed that so much since he'd resigned his lecturer's post.

It also gave him the chance to spend more time with Dr Gemma Stone. In public, with plenty of people surrounding them, he reminded himself: not quiet and just the two of them. Which would be much safer, because being in public would stop him being tempted to act on the crazy suggestions popping up in his head right now.

And he just so happened to be free, that evening.

'Let me talk to Stephanos,' he said, and called his security detail.

When he finished the call, he smiled. 'I accept your invitation to dinner, Dr Stone. Provided I can cook dinner for you later in the week.'

She blinked. 'You cook?'

He rolled his eyes. 'Do you think my background means I automatically have no domestic skills?'

'Doesn't it?' she challenged.

'I admit, nowadays my laundry and most of the housekeeping is handled by the palace staff, and a lot of what I eat is made in the palace kitchens,' he said. 'But I learned to cook before I became a student—and I've done my share of chores, in my time.'

'Right,' she said, sounding as if she didn't believe a word he said.

He grinned. 'I look forward to making you eat your words, Dr Stone. Literally.'

She grinned back. 'You're on, Dr Spiridon.'

Oh, he could fence with this woman all evening, he thought. She was a delight.

The students were all thrilled to see him and he could barely get a word in edgeways between the ones he'd taught and the ones who were a bit starstruck because they'd read one of his textbooks. They bubbled over with infectious enthusiasm. And he'd forgotten how much he enjoyed sharing a simple well-cooked meal and a glass of red wine with people who shared his passions. The students practically fell over themselves, wanting to show him photographs of their favourite sites and tell him stories of their favourite finds. And Gemma didn't hold any of them back or try to put a dampener on their enthusiasm; she encouraged them to talk and ask him sensible questions.

When they'd finished dinner, he said his goodbyes. 'I'm buying you all a couple of beers or glasses of wine,' he said, to cheers of, '*Yamas*!'

'I'll put the money behind the bar,' he continued, 'but it's on strict condition you all stay the right side of sober and turn up on time to the dig tomorrow.'

'Technically,' one of them said, 'if we don't, that would count as treason and you could stick us in jail.'

He laughed. 'Something like that. And don't let Dr Stone here swim on her own. For that matter, I don't want *any* of you in the sea on your own, OK?'

'Got it, boss,' one of his former students said.

'And it was so good to see you again. We miss you,' one of the others said.

'I miss you lot, too,' he said, meaning it. They were like a litter of eager puppies, full of the kind of bounce that could easily be overwhelming, but he'd loved his job working with them. 'I'll drop in on the dig later in the week and catch up with you.'

'We can lend you a trowel and a hard hat between us,' one of the English students said. 'Gemma reckons we'll find the mosaic floor, this week. You can't miss us doing *that*.'

'I won't,' he said, smiling.

'I have paperwork to sort out,' Gemma announced, 'so I'll see you lot in the morning.'

Followed by a chorus of 'goodnight' and '*kalinýchta*', Niko and Gemma left the bar.

'Thanks for indulging them,' Gemma said.

'It was my pleasure,' he said, meaning it.

And he really had intended to say goodnight. Except the words that came out of his mouth instead were, 'Shall we walk by the sea?'

She stared at him for a long, long moment, her expression impossible to read. Clearly she knew it was a bad idea, too. Then she smiled, and it felt as if something was blooming inside him. 'I'd like that,' she said.

They both slipped off their shoes and strolled across the soft sand, which had changed from gold to silver in the moonlight. The turquoise water of the day was now the same inky blue as the sky, with just a hint of silvery foam when it swished onto the shore. The moon hung as a low crescent, tracing a lightly silvered path across the waves. It was a scene Niko had seen hundreds of times over the years, and yet tonight it felt brand new. As if he'd stepped into a moment out of time.

They didn't need to talk: just walking together was enough.

His hand brushed against hers as they moved down the beach towards the shoreline, and the light contact gave him goosebumps. Another brush of skin against skin, and this time it felt like lightning. The third time their hands connected, his fingers tangled with hers. Caught. And just like that, by a mutual unspoken agreement, they were walking with their hands loosely linked.

A few more steps, and all Niko could hear was the

regular hiss of the sea against the sand. Or was it the roaring of his own blood in his ears? Whatever. It didn't matter. Nothing mattered other than her closeness and the warmth of her skin against his.

It wasn't enough.

Nowhere near enough.

Knowing he shouldn't be doing this, and completely unable to make himself stop, he halted. Turned towards her. Dropped his shoes, uncaring where they fell. Their fingers still entwined, he raised his other hand to her face and tucked a strand of hair behind her ear. He cupped his palm against her cheek and stared at her. The moonlight darkened her eyes to the same inky blue of the sea. How could he resist lowering his mouth to hers?

His lips tingled as they brushed against the corner of her mouth, then travelled across the softness of her lower lip. Somehow—and he had no idea how it had happened—she'd dropped her shoes, too. Her hands were tangled in his hair, his arms were wrapped around her waist, and the kiss had deepened to the point where he was dizzy. Nothing existed except this moment: the moonlight, the song of the sea, the vanilla scent of her hair and the intoxicating feel of her mouth moving against his.

When he broke the kiss, his heart felt as if it were racing at a million miles an hour. She looked as dazed as he felt.

And somehow he had to fix this.

'I'm sorry,' he said. 'I shouldn't have done that.'

'*We* shouldn't have done that,' she corrected, disentangling her hands from his hair. 'I apologise, too.'

For a nasty moment, he thought she was going to call him 'Prince Nikolaos' or 'Your Royal Highness'.

But then she looked him straight in the eye. Unflinching. Facing the situation head-on. 'Let's blame it on the moonlight, Dr Spiridon.'

He let out the breath he hadn't even been aware of holding. So she *did* still see him for himself, not for his title. That was a relief.

'Or we can blame it on us being overexcited because we both think we're going to find that mosaic floor this week,' she added.

'We could,' he agreed. Honesty compelled him to continue, 'But I think we both know it wasn't that.'

'You're a prince,' she said quietly. 'And I'm an ordinary woman.'

There was nothing ordinary about Gemma Stone, he thought. And, even though she saw him for who he was, she clearly also realised that his life was complicated. That he couldn't do whatever he wanted. That his title came with responsibilities and expectations, and he was completely hemmed in.

'You're learning to rule, to take over from your father,' she said. 'My life's in England. I'm here in Amphithos for the summer, but when the dig finishes I'll be going back to London to teach my students. I admit, you're right. What just happened between us wasn't the moonlight or the excitement of discovery. But neither of us is in a place to let it go any further.'

He couldn't help asking, 'You have someone waiting for you at home?'

'No. Though you don't need a partner to live a valid life,' she said coolly.

He winced. 'That's true. I apologise. I didn't mean to...' He couldn't think how to express what he meant. 'Be a mansplainer,' he finished, knowing it wasn't the right term, but not quite able to think straight when he could still remember what it felt like to kiss her.

She smiled. 'You're not a mansplainer. And I don't think you're the regressive type.'

'I'm not. I'm very pro equality,' he said. 'My parents aren't regressive, either.'

'But they have to be practical. You have responsibilities. You don't have time for a distraction, right now,' she said.

'So, what? We communicate strictly via Yiannis?' he asked. 'You'll send him photographs and ask him to pass them on to me?'

'And insist that he accompanies you on any official visit?' She wrinkled her nose. 'That would be the sensible way to do things. Put some barriers between us.'

'You're right. Absolutely right,' he said. It would be eminently sensible. *Except that isn't what I want.*

She raised an eyebrow. 'Did you mean to say those last few words inside your head?'

He felt tell-tale colour wash into his cheeks. 'Oh. Did I say them out loud?'

'I'm afraid you did,' she said. And there was a flicker of amusement on her face.

'I apologise,' he said. 'Which I seem to have to do a lot, around you.'

'In another world or another time,' she said softly,

'it might have been different. Very different. But we're in this time, this world. You're a prince, and I'm not looking for a relationship.'

For a moment, there was a shadow on her face, and he knew instinctively that someone had hurt her. Badly.

He would let her set the pace. 'So where do you think we go from here?

'In your shoes,' she said, 'I'd want to be involved in the dig, as much as possible. So I think…we agree to be friends while I'm on Amphithos. And we stay strictly as friends and colleagues.'

'No more moonlit walks by the sea, listening to "moaning Amphitrite" who nourishes the fish,' he said.

'The *Odyssey*,' she said with a smile.

Niko was ridiculously pleased that Gemma had recognised the quote. It was obvious that their minds worked along similar lines. He'd love to get to know her as a friend. Just because the rest of what he wanted wasn't possible, it didn't mean that he had to behave like a toddler and refuse what she could offer—or what he could offer her. 'I think I absorbed Homer as I grew up,' he said. 'And my favourite room in the palace is the library.'

'Does that make you the male version of Belle?' she teased.

He laughed. 'Sort of. In de Villeneuve's original, Beauty was a secret princess. My background isn't a secret. But I'm like Belle in that I've always been a bookaholic.'

'*Beauty and the Beast* was always my favourite fairytale,' she said. 'Not because I thought I was beautiful, but Belle always has her nose in a book and I identified with her. I wanted a library of my own when I grew up, whether someone gave it to me as a very special present or I built it for myself.'

In another world, he thought, things would have been very different. He and Gemma could've been soulmates, bound together by their love of books and history and mythology. He would *definitely* have given her a library as a present. 'You can use the palace's library any time you like,' he said, which was about the nearest he could get to fulfilling both their dreams. 'I'll ask Yiannis to sort out official clearance for you.' He paused. 'My personal library would also be open to you. And I hope that as my *friend*—' he emphasised the word '—you'll come to dinner tomorrow night to see it for yourself.'

'As your *friend*,' she said, giving the word as much emphasis as he had, 'I would be delighted.'

'Then it's a *not*-date,' he said. 'Ask for Yiannis at the gatehouse. I'll make sure they know to expect you.'

'All right,' she said.

'Good. I'm glad that's settled. I'll walk you back to your accommodation.'

He kept the conversation light and about archaeology on the way back to the university block where she was staying. And he managed to restrain his impulse to kiss her goodnight. Just.

'See you tomorrow,' she said. 'If anything happens with the floor, I'll keep you posted. Otherwise, what time would you like me to arrive?'

'Seven?' he suggested.

She nodded. 'Dress code?'

He spread his hands. 'Whatever.'

'Great,' she said with a smile. 'Until tomorrow, Dr Spiridon.' Her smile turned mischievous. 'I would say *hasta mañana*, but that's the wrong language.'

He couldn't help smiling back. 'It's *méchri ávrio*, in Greek,' he said. 'Goodnight, Gemma.'

'Now that one I *do* know,' she said. '*Kalinýchta*, Niko.'

'*Óneira glykà*,' he said. 'And your homework is to find out what I just said.'

She laughed. 'Challenge accepted.'

And, even though part of him regretted that he couldn't do what he really wanted—to pick her up, carry her off somewhere private and kiss her until they were both dizzy—that laugh and the warm feeling it gave him stayed with him all the way back to the palace.

CHAPTER FOUR

BACK IN HER FLAT, Gemma sat down with her laptop. *Óneira glykà* meant 'sweet dreams'.

Yeah.

They'd be very sweet indeed, if they were of Dr Niko Spiridon.

Except there were so many reasons why she shouldn't dream about him. It'd taken her months to pick herself up and dust herself down after the way Andy jilted her. She wasn't ready for another relationship right now, if ever. And even if Niko did tempt her—and if she were honest, she'd admit he did—there was still a huge barrier between them, because he was no longer the university lecturer who just happened to be part of the royal family. Since his brother's death, he'd become the heir to the throne of Amphithos; and he'd be the king when his father stepped down in a few months' time. Plus he was supposed to marry someone of royal blood. Even if there was a way of getting round that particular issue, and Niko was permitted to date a commoner, she wasn't sure he'd see her as Ms Right For Now, let alone anything more. After all, if she hadn't been enough for Andy to marry, how could she possibly be enough to capture a prince's heart?

No. It would be much better to be practical and grounded about this. Their agreement to be just good friends was definitely the right one. There would be no risk of heartache. She'd stick to talking history and archaeology with him, and find a way to dampen down the attraction she felt towards him. That way, there wouldn't be any misunderstandings.

The next morning, Gemma was thoughtful as she opened up the dig site. Mindful of the risk she'd taken, the previous day, she hadn't gone for a swim before breakfast; but a couple of her students offered to swim with her in future, when they turned up to start work. 'That'd be wonderful. Thank you,' she said, touched that they'd obviously listened to what Niko had said, the previous night.

During the morning, they found some more green tesserae in the trench, but the mosaic floor itself remained elusive. Gemma took a phone snap of the tesserae and sent it to Niko with a message saying she'd catch up with him later.

As she did a quick tour of the site, checking how all the groups were doing, she noticed that the London students were all talking animatedly about Niko: how nice Dr Spiridon was, and how amazing it was that an actual prince would bother to sit and chat with students. His former students chipped in with stories of what an inspiring teacher he'd been and how his lectures had had them all wanting to rush out and do some fieldwork and search through the dustiest corners of the library, all at the same time.

'He's so nice. Not to mention gorgeous,' one of them said.

Yes, he was, Gemma agreed silently, but as far as she was concerned he was off limits.

Another said, 'It doesn't seem fair that he has to marry some princess or other just because she has royal blood. He ought to be able to marry whoever he wants.'

'Definitely someone who loves history as much as he does,' one of the students from Amphithos agreed.

Gemma knew she shouldn't be commenting, but she couldn't help herself. 'Has his marriage been agreed?'

The student regarded her seriously. 'I guess it'll be sorted out between the government and the palace. I think his mother, Queen Elena, is in charge of finding him a shortlist of suitable brides. I really do hope she finds him someone who loves the same things that he does, or he'll be miserable.'

Gemma hoped that whoever they chose would make Niko happy. She wasn't going to allow herself to wonder what it could've been like between herself and Niko, because she knew she wasn't even a suitable girlfriend for him, let alone anything more. She didn't have blue blood, she'd made the kind of mistake in her past that the media would seize on and use to drag his name through the mud, and it would all be a hideous mess.

With that firmly uppermost in her mind, she concentrated on her job. One of her colleagues from the Amphithos team had agreed to lock up, that evening, and she was able to leave the site a few minutes earlier than usual so she could wash her hair and change before going to Niko's for dinner.

He'd said the dress code was 'whatever', but jeans didn't feel like the right choice to visit the palace. She chose her smartest pair of trousers and a pretty top with long chiffon sleeves, and wore her hair loose instead of in the usual plait she braided it in for work.

The local taxi dropped her at the palace. On the journey, Gemma was struck again by how pretty the capital was, with bright pink bougainvillea spilling lushly over the white-and-cream-coloured walls of the houses. The palace itself was gorgeous, an ancient structure of honey-coloured stone, with tall windows and a colonnade running around the building.

At the gatehouse, she asked the guard to call Yiannis; a few minutes later, Niko's private secretary came to collect her. He shook her hand warmly. '*Kalispéra*, Dr Stone. The prince is ready for your meeting.'

She regretted the pretty top, then, wishing she'd chosen a plain white shirt or something that looked a bit more businesslike. Maybe she should've worn her hair tied back, after all—and borrowed or bought a pair of heels instead of wearing polished but low-key flats. But she supposed it was a bit better than the last time she'd been at the palace, in bare feet and wearing only a bright red—albeit modestly cut—swimming costume.

At least Yiannis didn't look disapprovingly at her.

She followed him down a marble-floored corridor lined with gilt-framed paintings and statues on pedestals; gold and crystal chandeliers hung from the ceiling. The further into the palace they went, the more out of place and awkward she felt. Niko really did live in another world.

At last, Yiannis stopped by a door, and pressed an intercom.

'Prin–' he began.

Niko interrupted him with a pointed cough. 'Yiannis?'

'Niko,' Yiannis said, rolling his eyes, 'your guest is here.'

'Thank you for bringing me here safely, Yiannis,' Gemma said, and held out her hand to shake his.

'My pleasure, Dr Stone,' Yiannis said.

'Please call me Gemma,' she said gently. 'We're sort-of colleagues, after all.'

He looked at her and sighed. 'My generation is much more formal than yours—but all right, Gemma. If that makes you more comfortable.'

'It does,' she said gratefully.

The door opened, at that point. Yiannis bowed, and strode down the corridor.

'Come in,' Niko said, smiling at her and standing to the side. 'Dinner should be another ten minutes. Let me get you a drink, and then I'll show you my library.'

'Something smells delicious,' she said.

'*Psari plaki*,' he said. 'Greek fish stew, with potatoes and roasted broccoli. And Greek orange cake with frozen yoghurt for dessert.'

She handed him the box of chocolates she'd bought during her lunchbreak.

'You didn't actually need to bring anything, but thank you,' he said. 'I love chocolate.' He ushered her through to the kitchen, which was ultra-modern with a grey marble floor, pale granite worktops and acres of matte grey cupboards. At the far end of the room was a small dining table, set for two.

'Wine?' he asked.

'That would be lovely, thank you,' she said.

He opened one of the cupboards, which turned out to be the fridge, took out a bottle of white wine and poured them both a glass. '*Yamas*,' he said, lifting his glass.

She didn't dare risk clinking her glass against his; it was way too delicate and she was terrified of breaking it, so instead she smiled and lifted her glass in a toast. 'Cheers.'

She took a sip and discovered that the wine was perfectly chilled. 'This is absolutely delicious,' she said. She took another sip. 'Is it Chablis?'

'Close,' he said. 'It's Robola.'

'Sorry—I've never heard of it,' she said.

'It's an ancient variety—around a thousand years old, maybe more,' he said. 'It has a similar flavour profile to Chablis, though: flinty and zesty.'

'Is it produced in Amphithos?' she asked.

'Yes. It's from my grandfather's vineyard,' Niko explained. 'We know that wine was produced on the island a couple of millennia ago. Archaeologists found various wine jars at a site excavated when my father was a child, and pottery decorated with vine leaves. One of the horticulturalists found the oldest varietals on the island, and my grandfather decided that he wanted to try producing a modern version of ancient wine, using traditional methods and low intervention. After he died, my father took over the hobby vineyard, and he's experimenting with other varietals—there's an even older red grape that was nearly extinct, which my father helped to rescue. The first harvest was last year and he can't wait to try it.'

'So it could be like the wine that was offered at Amphitrite's temple?'

He laughed. 'I think the wine back in those days was rather rougher than what we produce now. All the records suggest they had to mix it three parts water to one part wine.'

'Got you,' she said, smiling back. 'If I ever talk to your father about wine, I promise not to insult him by saying his wine's like the one they drank thousands of years ago.'

'Good. Come and see my library,' he said.

The room was her absolute dream, with a high ceiling and tall shelves that definitely needed the stepladder tucked neatly next to one of the bookcases.

Glancing across the shelves, she could see that the books were in a mixture of languages—French, German and Spanish as well as Greek, Latin and English—and Niko had clearly organised it in the same way as any academic library was organised, so he could lay his hands on what he needed very quickly. There was a comfortable chair for reading and a small table next to it, the perfect size for a mug of coffee or a glass of wine. Tucked into the corner there was a desk with a laptop on it, and next to it was a large table with a map cabinet underneath it; on a shelf above were the kind of weights you usually found in archives, and a pair of white gloves. It was the perfect room for reading and working, and she loved it.

'It's *stunning*,' she breathed.

He looked pleased. 'Thank you.'

He talked her through the shelves; and then an alarm rang on his phone.

'That means dinner's ready,' he said. 'When I was a student, I burned way too many meals because I was busy with research and forgot the time. I learned to set a timer to remind me when something was ready.'

She loved the fact he was so practical. 'Good idea,' she said. 'I tend to use a slow-cooker, or I prep meals that don't take long to cook—either a stir fry or something I can stick bake in the air fryer.'

'Good call,' he said. 'So you don't waste research time.'

She laughed. 'I should get you to say that to my mum, next time she nags me about eating properly!'

Back in the kitchen, Niko ushered her to the table. He refused to let her help as he brought the dishes to the table. 'Help yourself,' he said.

He'd cooked cod in a tomato sauce; there was a side dish of potato wedges and another of roasted tenderstem broccoli.

'This is fabulous,' she said after her first taste. The tomato sauce was spiked with chilli, capers, olives and paprika, and the cod had been finished with a squeeze of fresh lemon juice; the potato wedges had been cooked with herbs, lemon and feta.

'It's very quick and simple,' he said. 'Locally produced food, prepared without fuss.' His amber eyes twinkled. 'Though I'll admit the dessert comes from the palace kitchens. Baking isn't my thing.'

'Nothing wrong with that,' she said with a smile. 'And I'm more than happy to eat my words, especially if it means a second helping of this. Even though you're a prince, you can cook.'

He laughed and raised his wine glass to her. 'I'm glad that's settled.'

Niko was good company, and Gemma thoroughly enjoyed chatting with him over the main course; he told her about the history of the island and drew her out about her favourite parts of her job.

The orange cake and frozen yogurt were as wonderful as he'd promised, as was the coffee he made to serve with the chocolates she'd brought. Maybe it was the bitterness of the coffee that made her feel slightly melancholy, but it must've shown in her expression because he said quietly, 'What's wrong?'

She wrinkled her nose. 'We're becoming friends.'

'But?'

'I know you have a dossier on me.' And friends didn't have dossiers on each other, did they?

'My security team has a dossier on you,' he corrected. 'I don't intend to read it.'

But Yiannis probably knew what was in that dossier, and even though he was discreet he might decide that the prince needed to know the truth about her. And she'd rather get the messy stuff out of the way. Especially if it was something that had been picked up from social media and there was an unkind spin to it. She hated the way that people poked fun at others online, and didn't seem to know when to stop. Snarky comments weren't clever, in her view; they said more about the commenter's lack of kindness than they did about the commentee. 'I'd prefer you to hear it from me. And, once I've told you, I completely get it if you decide I'm not a suitable friend.' She swallowed hard. 'A couple of years back, I made a really bad judgement call.'

'Everyone makes at least one of those in their lifetime,' he said lightly. 'What did you do? Drink too much at a party and throw up over the host's shoes?'

Way, way worse than that. 'I fell in love,' she said. 'I met Andy at a party—a friend of a friend of a friend kind of thing. We got on well, he asked me out, and we dated for a year. Then he asked me to marry him. I said yes, but he wanted a big, splashy wedding and it—well, before I knew it, everything was booked. Huge dress, flashy car, swish hotel for the reception, ridiculously expensive bridal favours... It felt as if things were spiralling out of control.'

Had she broken off the engagement? Niko wondered. If she had, it had probably been the right thing to do. If you had doubts before the wedding, you needed to put things on pause and talk it through until you'd ironed out the problems.

'But he said he loved me, and I knew I loved him, and I thought it'd be all right,' Gemma said, and looked away.

So she'd gone through with the wedding after all, and then things went wrong? That, too, happened all the time. Several of his friends had been unhappily married and then divorced. He gave her what he hoped was an encouraging smile, and gave her space to continue.

'The day of the wedding, I got ready with my mum and my bridesmaids. I went to the church in the car with Dad. And Andy's best man was waiting at the church door.' She took a deep breath. 'He told me Andy had changed his mind about marrying me.'

Her fiancé had jilted her at the altar? What a horrible thing to do to someone. If Andy had changed his mind, why on earth hadn't he talked to Gemma before the wedding day and helped her cancel everything if they hadn't been able to work through their problems? And, more importantly, why hadn't Andy told her himself? Why had he left it to someone else to give her the news? 'I'm sorry. That's a really horrible thing to do,' he said.

'I could've understood it maybe if he'd fallen for someone else,' she said. 'It still would've hurt, but you can't help who you fall in love with.' She still didn't meet his eyes. 'But it wasn't that. Nobody else was involved. He'd simply fallen out of love with me. *I* was the problem. I wasn't enough for him.'

'No.' Niko shook his head emphatically. '*He* was the problem. He wasn't honest with you, and he left someone else to tell you. That's a coward's way of doing things. I agree, it's a mistake to get married if you don't feel the same way as your partner, but you don't hurt them by just not turning up to the wedding. You talk to them, you decide on the way forward together, and if you cancel the wedding then you do your fair share of the work. You don't just walk away and leave everyone else to clear up the mess.' No wonder Gemma had been so definite that she didn't want a relationship. In her shoes, Niko rather thought he'd feel the same. 'I'm sorry he treated you so badly. But it's on him, not on you.'

'It took me a while before I could start thinking it wasn't my fault,' Gemma said. 'I mean, I'm an archaeologist. I've learned to read evidence and make sensible conclusions. If I can do that, why didn't I see that things were going wrong between Andy and me? It made me wonder if I ignored the warning signs because I didn't want to see them.' She grimaced. 'Though, when I look back, there really weren't any warning signs. His mum and his best friend didn't have a clue, either, so I wasn't the only one who was taken in. But the whole thing has left me finding it hard to trust anyone. I haven't wanted to date anyone since then.'

That was understandable, Niko thought. In her shoes, he'd find it hard to trust, too. 'I'm sorry you had such a horrible thing happen to you,' he said. 'He let you down very badly.'

'He did. And for a long time I thought it was something lacking in me.'

He shook his head. 'It wasn't.'

'My head knows that, now,' Gemma said quietly. 'But the rest of me still doesn't feel it.'

Niko understood that feeling, too. His head knew that he was doing the right thing, stepping into his brother's shoes; but his heart mourned the life he'd really wanted and he felt like a fraud.

She shrugged. 'Maybe I'm a coward, but I'm not looking to pick myself up, dust myself down, and put my trust in someone else. I'm not ready to take the risk of being let down again or being dumped just when I thought it was for the long term. I'd rather stay single and focus on my work, my family and friends.'

'You're not a coward,' he said. 'Someone breaking off your relationship is a hard enough thing to deal with, but for it to happen in front of your family and friends, on your wedding day, without a proper explanation…' He blew out a breath. 'That's rough.' She'd been hurt so badly. How could you trust that love would be long-lasting, once someone had treated you like that? It'd take a lot for her to risk giving her heart away again, Niko thought.

Not that he had any business thinking about her heart or who she might give it to. Despite his attraction to her, he couldn't be her future partner. His duties lay elsewhere.

'When it happened, I wanted to curl into a ball and howl,' she said. 'But then I thought about it. The people waiting in the church had travelled from all over the country to come and spend the day with us. Everything had been paid for. Sending everyone away again and scrapping everything would've been such a waste. So I talked to my parents, my brother, Andy's parents, the bridesmaids and the best man, and we agreed we'd ask everyone to take back their wedding presents and we'd turn the wedding into a party for family and friends— pretty much what we'd planned for the day anyway, just without Andy or any presents. My brother offered to face everyone for me and tell them, but I wanted to do it myself instead of wimping out. I didn't want to be like Andy and leave it to someone else to clear up the mess.' She lifted her chin. 'I still had my pride. I wasn't going to let him take that away from me, too. So I stood at the altar and explained that my fiancé had changed his mind about marrying me.' She grimaced. 'I felt like a worm, telling everyone that he'd jilted me. I could see all the pity in everyone's faces and I hated people feeling sorry for me. So I reminded them that families often only get to see each other at weddings and funerals. They'd all made the effort to get here, so rather than waste it we wanted everyone to enjoy themselves as much as possible. We'd have the party without the wedding. I told them I didn't want anyone to feel sorry for me, and I'd see them all in an hour's time at the reception. And then my bridesmaids and I went home with my mum and we changed our dresses before the party.' She smiled. 'It was a bit awkward at first when we got to the wedding breakfast and everyone sat down. But my dad and my brother had moved all the places around so it wasn't obvious that the groom was missing. Dad stood up and said everyone might be getting away with not having to listen to the speeches, but we were still doing some of the toasts. He did a toast to family and friends. And my brother stood up and nearly made me cry when he made a toast to the best and bravest little sister ever. I mean, I wasn't *that* brave. It wasn't like rescuing someone from a burning house or saving someone's life.'

'It still takes a lot of courage to stand up and face people in a situation that you know will make them gossip and speculate about you,' he said.

'Maybe, but what was the alternative? Sit in the dark, sobbing into a box of tissues and pretending it hadn't happened?' she asked, shrugging off his compliment. 'It took a couple of glasses of wine, a good pudding and some music, but eventually everyone relaxed and made the most of the day. The photographer did little groups instead of formal wedding photos. I texted everyone who was coming to the evening reception to let them know that the wedding bit was cancelled but we were still having the party anyway, without Andy. A few of Andy's friends and colleagues said they felt too awkward to come, even though I'd made it clear they were very welcome, so I asked the hotel to deliver half the evening buffet to the local homeless shelter. I couldn't face going on the honeymoon on my own, but cancelling it at that late notice would've meant we wouldn't get a refund. Luckily, the travel agent was lovely and sorted everything out so my parents could take the holiday instead.'

Niko wasn't surprised that Gemma had taken such a practical attitude. Or that she'd tried to make life better for other people.

'It's put me off relationships,' she said. 'I'm not planning to risk my heart again. But if I ever do meet someone who can change my mind about that and asks me to marry them, then I'll insist on a quiet ceremony with only those closest to us there, and no fuss.'

Which sounded perfect to Niko. It was what he'd hoped for, once. 'You're lucky you have the no-fuss option.' The words came out before he could stop them.

She looked at him. 'I assume that yours will have to be a full state wedding?'

He nodded. 'Once the Palace Council has chosen my bride.'

'You really have to have an arranged marriage?' She looked shocked. 'You don't have any say in it at all?'

He raked a hand through his hair. 'A year and a half ago, I had free choice of my life partner—well, up to a point. I still would've had to choose someone acceptable to the monarchy. But there was room for negotiation, and it would've been fine to have a quiet wedding.

Now, the situation's different. I'm not the "spare" any more. My future bride will be marrying a king-to-be. So she needs to be someone who can cope with the job; practically speaking, that means someone with a royal background who's grown up with the pressures. The Palace Council—with advice from my mother—are vetting suitable brides, and I get to choose from their shortlist. So I suppose there is a *bit* of choice.'

'That's positively medieval,' she said, her eyes full of sympathy. 'And it's tough on both you *and* your future bride.'

'Emotions don't come into a royal marriage,' he said. 'It needs to be sensible and businesslike. The kingdom needs stability. It makes sense for me to marry someone who's been brought up in the same kind of environment as I have. Someone who's used to what it's like being a royal and can cope with the lifestyle. It's not all parties and glitz and glamour, the way it might look like to the rest of the world. You're on public display all the time, and anything you do or say is reported in the press. There's no such thing as privacy. If the paparazzi don't spot you, then someone with a smartphone will, and the pictures will go viral. If you're not smiling, or if there's any obvious tension between you, it'll be spread through the media and everyone will be speculating about the cause.'

'It sounds exhausting. Like living in a goldfish bowl,' she said thoughtfully, 'whereas you're used to the life of an academic.'

He shrugged. 'I'll learn. Don't think of me as a poor little rich boy, because I'm not. I'm well aware of how privileged I am. But the other side of that particular coin is that I have responsibilities. I need to do my duty, and do it well.'

'I think,' she said, 'you have a lot of strength. You didn't get to choose the life you really wanted, but you're stepping up to do your duty anyway.'

'There's no other choice. It's me or me,' he said simply. 'I'm part of the family firm. Although everyone knows I would've much rather stayed working as an academic and being in a support role to the new king, I'm not going to walk away and leave the job to a very distant cousin I've never met and who's never even visited the island. That wouldn't be fair to anyone—not to my people and not to my family.' Though he still worried he wasn't going to live up to Leo's legacy. He intended to make sure he did—even if that meant working twice as hard, and giving up everything he'd always wanted. He'd do right by everyone.

'Was your brother like you?' she asked.

Niko smiled. 'No. Leo was much more outgoing than me. Everyone who met him was charmed by him. And I don't mean that he was as shallow as a puddle, more that he was good with people. He *connected* with them. I loved him very much, and I was glad to be his supporter rather than the star of the show.' He spread his hands. 'But everyone in this role needs a pressure valve. Mine's history; Leo's was fast cars and sailing. He was a good driver and a good sailor, and although I think some of his friends encouraged him to take risks, he knew what he was doing and always calculated the risks first. That storm blew up out of nowhere. He was in the wrong place at the wrong time. Sadly, the sea won. And we weren't the only family who lost people we loved; none of his friends survived, either.'

'I'm sorry. You must miss him,' she said.

'I do. Horribly. He's always been here, my whole life. Losing him feels as if the ground under my feet isn't safe any more. How can he be gone? He was thirty years old. He was a good man. He would've made a brilliant king. He would've done so much good.' He shook his head. 'How can all that promise be snuffed out like that?'

She said nothing, simply squeezed his hand briefly in sympathy. And that kind, quiet support was enough to make him confess something he'd never told anyone else. 'Sometimes I sit on the balcony and look out to sea, and I talk to him as if he's still here. It helps.' He blew out a breath. 'And I'll stand in his shoes and try my best to do as good a job as he would've done.'

Niko was the kind of man who considered things and put other people first, Gemma thought. Not like Andy, who did what he wanted and left other people to make his excuses. Niko had integrity.

And his situation meant that he was very firmly off limits. She hadn't been brought up in his world. She didn't have a clue what it was like to have be watched every minute of every day.

'Do you have a time limit?' she asked instead, wondering how long he had to get accustomed to his new role.

'My father wants to step down next year. So the wedding will take place first—that's all the pomp and ceremony bit, and it's really aimed at giving our people something to celebrate. The wedding's not so much mine and my bride's as the kingdom's,' he said.

'What about the coronation?'

'That's much simpler—I swear an oath in Parliament.' He smiled. 'Actually, my grandfather's the one who slimmed down the pomp and ceremony. He thought there were better things to spend the kingdom's money on than a day of parades—education and healthcare, for a start.'

'Your grandfather sounds like a sensible man,' Gemma said.

'He was. I had a lot of time for *Pappoús*,' Niko said. 'We were close. He was the one who started my love of history and culture—the one who taught me all the Greek myths, who bought me my first copy of Homer. My father's the same kind of man; he thinks about things and he notices details.'

And Niko was like them, too, she thought. 'I was close to my granddad as well,' she said. 'He took me to the British Museum and told me all about the mummies. Ed—my brother—loved them as well, but for me it went a lot further than that. I wanted to know all about the way people lived, back then, and I wanted to discover things people hadn't seen for years. I used to dig in my granddad's back garden.' The reminiscence made her smile. 'I was always so pleased with myself when I found little bits of broken china, and Gramps was always so patient with me—even though obviously all I'd found was rubbish.' She raised an eyebrow at him. 'Now, if I'd been like you and grown up with a Greek temple in my back garden…'

He laughed. 'If you'd found a Greek temple in England, I think you'd have stunned the world of archaeology! But yes, you're right. I was really lucky. We didn't know about Amphitrite's temple back then, and *Pappoús* would've been thrilled to bits—as well as wanting to know if there was any evidence of the wine used for libations and whether the grape varietals were related to the ones he grew.'

'I imagine you and your father would be interested in the same thing,' she said, 'so I'll be sure to let you know if we find anything.'

'Thank you,' he said.

'Can I do the washing up?' she asked.

He wrinkled his nose. 'Now that's where you have me. When I shared a house as a student, I did my share of the chores. In the palace, I don't. The first time I cooked for friends, the palace kitchen was upset—our main chef has worked here for years, and she thought she wasn't doing her job properly because I hadn't asked her to cook for me. Leo warned me I'd caused a problem, so I went to see her and explained it was just my way of relaxing rather than any slight on her work, and I would always, *always* ask for dessert prepared by her because my baking would never be as good as hers.' He winced. 'I apologise if I come over as an entitled brat.'

'You don't,' she said. 'I was brought up to do chores and to offer help with the washing up. You're used to banquets being catered.'

'We have simple family suppers when we can, maybe once a week,' Niko said. 'But, yes.'

'And if you're hosting someone, your duty as host is to pay attention to your guests, not do the washing up,' she said.

His eyes crinkled at the corners. 'Exactly. And I've noticed your coffee cup is empty. May I?'

'And my duty as your guest is to be polite and accept gracefully, not offer to help you make it, right?'

'Right,' he said.

They ended up sitting at the table and just talking over another pot of coffee, this time decaf. When Gemma glanced at her watch, she was shocked to realise how late it was.

'I'd better call a cab,' she said.

'No need. I'll drive you back,' Niko said.

'I can't ask you to do that. And there's your security detail to think of.' He might be discreet, but his job was to be there for Niko. 'It's not fair to drag someone out at this time of night.'

'It'll only be for a few minutes,' he said. 'And I'll make sure Stephanos gets extra time off in lieu.' He smiled. 'Anyway, you're not asking. I'm offering. There's a difference.'

She couldn't argue with that. 'Then thank you,' she said.

In the end, Stephanos drove her back to the university and Niko sat next to her in the back of the car. Although part of Gemma felt awkward about talking to Niko and not including Stephanos in the conversation, Niko reassured her. 'Chatting to us both would distract him from doing his job. He knows you're not being rude.'

'As long as he really does know that,' she said.

And at least having Stephanos there meant she wouldn't be tempted to do anything stupid, like holding Niko's hand or kissing him, the way they had the previous night at the beach. Though, at the same time, she wished it could be different—that Niko had still been the lecturer whose research had pinpointed the temple's location. And maybe, just maybe, they could've started seeing each other over the summer. Just casually. See where things went.

But Niko's destiny lay elsewhere, and she wasn't going to repeat her mistake of losing her heart to someone, no matter how tempting she found him.

'I'll keep you posted on the progress with the dig,' she said. 'Goodnight, Niko.'

'Goodnight, Gemma,' he said quietly.

She noted that the car stayed there until she'd let herself safely in to the block where she was staying before Stephanos drove away. Niko was polite and thoughtful to the last.

In another life, she could really have let herself fall for him.

In this life, she had to resist the temptation. They could enjoy each other's company, maybe even become proper friends—but as soon as she left Amphithos it would have to be over. He needed to marry a princess, and there would be no room for even a friendship with her—let alone anything else. And she couldn't quite suppress the little voice in the back of her head that reminded her she hadn't been enough for Andy, so how could she possibly be enough for a prince?

CHAPTER FIVE

OVER THE NEXT few days, Gemma fell into a routine: a morning swim with a group of her students before work, the day spent working on the dig, lunchtime updating Niko on progress via Yiannis and catching up with her paperwork, and then Niko would join her at the dig when his meetings at the palace had finished and her students and colleagues had gone over to Theo's Taverna for a beer and some food. Sometimes she and Niko joined the students; sometimes he'd drive her back to the palace and cook for her.

But Friday was the crunch day: the morning when one of her students uncovered part of the mosaic floor in the innermost cell of the temple.

'You have to tell Dr Spiridon,' the student insisted. 'He can't miss this.'

Gemma agreed. She took a snap of the bit that had been uncovered, then sent it to Niko's private phone with the message, We've found the floor.

Clearly he was in a meeting, because he didn't respond.

Everyone left their positions in their own trenches to join the excavation in the centre of the temple, and together they continued to work on uncovering the mosaic. Just as Gemma had hoped, the wave pattern flowed around the entire rectangle. She sent Niko more pictures when it became clear that there was an oval within the rectangle, and in the corners of the rectangle there were seals and fishes.

Still he didn't answer.

She really couldn't let him miss any more of this. Not when they were so close to finding the very thing she knew he wanted to see. She called Niko's private secretary. '*Kalispéra*, Yiannis. Can I speak to the prince, please?'

'I'm afraid he's in meetings all day, Dr Stone,' Yiannis said.

Protocol said that she should just shut up and wait for Niko to finish his meetings. But this was something he wouldn't get a second chance to do—and she knew how much he wanted to be part of it. He'd hate to miss such a key moment. 'Yiannis, I appreciate that the prince is busy, but we're in the process of uncovering the mosaic floor and the middle bit's the really important bit. He's the one who actually discovered its existence. The students and I all feel he needs to be here with us when we actually finish uncovering it.' Or maybe she was being too pushy. It wasn't her place to insist that he should be allowed to follow his heart for a few hours, was it? Besides, his private secretary knew how Niko felt about the temple, and she didn't need to point out that if Niko followed his heart for a few hours, it would help him keep going with the duties he'd had to take on. 'If he can spare the time,' she added swiftly. 'Could you perhaps get a message to him and let him know the situation, please?'

'All right. They're due a coffee break. I'll mention it.'

'You,' she said, 'are wonderful. Thank you. I owe you cake.'

Yiannis unbent enough to laugh. 'No need, Dr St— Gemma,' he corrected himself.

Ten minutes later, her phone pinged with a text from Niko. *Yiannis passed on your message. Thank you for giving me the heads-up. Might need to borrow a trowel. Be with you soon as I can.*

Trowel no problem, she texted back, thrilled that he was prepared to interrupt his work for her. No, for *the dig*, she reminded herself. It was the mosaic he was coming to see, not her.

He wasn't long. And when she looked up from the trench to see Niko striding towards her, clad in jeans, boots and a dark blue long-sleeved shirt, plus a sun-hat similar to her own, her heart skipped a beat. He was every sexy movie archaeologist rolled into one, and then some.

Not that she should be noticing this. They were *friends*, she reminded herself. Sort-of colleagues. And his destiny lay on a different path from hers. Whatever she felt about him, she needed to keep it to herself.

'Yiannis told me you asked him very nicely to spring me from the meetings so I could be here for this,' Niko said, joining her. 'Thank you.'

'It wasn't just me. The students all said the same. You couldn't miss this,' she said.

'Definitely. And thank you for sending the photos. They're amazing.'

'Pleasure,' she said. 'Let me show you what we've uncovered so far.'

'That wave border,' he said. 'And in the corners, those are definitely seals rather than dolphins. Look at their little faces.'

He looked incredibly moved. Gemma wanted to fling her arms round him and hug him, but it wasn't appropriate. Instead, she said, 'Amphitrite, mother of seals, fishes and dolphins.'

'I really hope we find her in the centre, driving her chariot with the *hippokampoi*,' Niko said, and his voice was full of longing.

'Do you think they'll be like the ones in the mosaics at Bath, Dr S?' one of the students asked. 'With a horse's head and front hooves, and a curly fishtail?'

'Maybe,' he said. 'Except I hope we'll have green fins and a tail with these ones, because they're Amphitrite's. Plus these will be a Hellenic design rather than Roman.'

The students shifted round so Niko could work next to Gemma on the central part of the floor. As more and more of the mosaic was uncovered, the tension at the dig grew palpable. Usually the students had music playing; today, they worked in silence, all focusing keenly on what was appearing before them.

Finally, Gemma uncovered a piece of mosaic that made her catch her breath. 'This looks like curly hair to me,' she said quietly.

'I agree,' Niko said. 'I think we might have found

Amphitrite, right in the centre of her temple. There would've been a statue here, but that's no doubt long gone. Though the mosaic's still here.'

His fingers accidentally brushed against hers every so often as they worked methodically to uncover the mosaic; each time, it sent a little shock of pleasure through her. Although Gemma tried to tell herself it was simply the excitement of being part of the discovery, she knew it wasn't that making her heart beat faster. It was Niko's nearness that had all her senses on full alert. It really wasn't appropriate and she knew she had to batten down her feelings, but how could she not respond to him?

Finally, Niko brushed away the last little bit of soil to reveal the full picture in the centre of the floor.

'Just what I'd dreamed of finding. Amphitrite, on her chariot, drawn by four *hippokampoi*,' he said softly. 'With finny manes and tails—and is that seaweed?'

'This must be what it felt like when Howard Carter first looked inside Tutankhamun's tomb,' one of the students said.

'Or when they found the ship at Sutton Hoo, and that amazing gold buckle with all the garnets,' another said.

'It's given me goosebumps,' Gemma admitted. 'This is—well, *history*.'

Niko's fingers tangled with hers and squeezed, just for a moment—a private show of gratitude, she thought. 'Thank you—all of you—for letting me be part of this,' he said.

'Without the work you did on pinpointing the site last year, Dr S, we wouldn't be digging here,' one of the students pointed out. 'For you not to be here today would've felt so wrong.'

'We need to get photographs,' Gemma said. 'And I want a snap of all of you together. My team.' She beamed proudly at him. 'You've done really well.'

'You need to be in the photo, too,' Niko said.

'So do you,' Gemma responded.

'I'll take the photos,' said Stephanos, Niko's security detail, coming over to join them.

He took photos on Gemma's phone as well as Niko's, and another with Niko's camera.

'If I could ask you all not to post about the discovery until Monday,' Niko said, 'I'll get the palace PR team to work with the university to send out a press release over the weekend. I'll clear the draft with you first, Gemma.'

'Or we could write it together.' The words came out of her mouth before she could stop them.

'And you're definitely having dinner with us, Dr S. We'll buy the beers, this time,' one of the students said.

How could he resist? Right at that moment Niko was part of the team, the way he'd once been, and he wanted that feeling to last a little longer. Even more, he wanted to spend time with Gemma. The more he got to know her, the more he liked her. And even though he knew there was a time limit on this—she was going back to London, and he had duties to fulfil—he wanted to spend these few precious weeks with her. Weeks where he could be a man, not a prince; time where he could choose to spend with the people he wanted and enjoy the informality of their company.

'Let me make a couple of calls, first,' he said, and had a short conversation with Yiannis while the students helped Gemma put a cover over the floor. He waited for her while she locked up, then walked over the road to the taverna with her. He kept his hands in his pockets so he wasn't tempted to take her hand, and kept the conversation light while they all ate and celebrated their find.

After a cup of strong coffee to go with the sticky pastries Theo served for dessert, Gemma smiled at him. 'If we're going to get that press release written tonight, we'd better leave our students to it.'

'Agreed.' He smiled at the students. 'Thank you for dinner. I'll leave money with Theo for some drinks.'

They lifted their glasses in a toast to him; he sorted out everything with Theo, then went to join Gemma at the door.

He knew they really ought to write the press release at a desk. Preferably with a little distance between them. He needed to resist the urge to take her hand, press a kiss into her palm and fold her fingers over the spot. Resist the urge to slide his arm round her shoulders and draw her against him. *Resist the urge to brush his lips against the corner of her mouth and tease her into kissing him back...*

But, as they stepped outside, the moon and the waves called to him. 'Why don't we write the press release on my phone at the beach?' he suggested.

The argument for common sense was written all

over her face: they were supposed to be just friends and semi-colleagues, and anything they wrote together should be done safely at a businesslike desk rather than in the place where they'd ended up kissing, only a few nights before, with the soft sand tempting them to fall into each other's arms.

When she said, 'It's much easier to write on a laptop,' he knew she'd been thinking of that kiss, too. 'And my flat has a desk.'

A student flat would also have a bed in very close proximity to said desk. Which would be way too tempting, especially as Niko's control was hanging by a thread. 'The car's right here. It'd be quicker to drive back to the palace than to walk over to your flat.' And his library was safe. Professional. He remembered their conversation about *Beauty and the Beast*. 'Plus if we need any books we'll have them to hand.'

Of course they weren't going to need any books. They both already knew all the background stuff they were going to talk about in the press release.

She gave him a sidelong look, as if she knew exactly what was going on in his head. As if it was going on in hers, too, because her pupils were huge. OK, so everyone's pupils looked bigger in low light…but he knew perfectly well that there was another reason for pupil dilation. Attraction. Desire. No doubt his own pupils were just as huge, right now.

In his own library, surrounded by reminders of his position as heir to the throne, he might have a chance of keeping that desire in check. Being businesslike.

'All right,' she said.

They didn't speak as Stephanos drove them back to the palace. They didn't speak as they walked through the corridors with the gilt-framed paintings and the statues and the chandeliers. They didn't speak as Niko opened the door to his apartment, switched on the light and let her enter the hallway first.

She took her boots off and placed them neatly together in the hallway, next to her hat and the rucksack where he knew she carried paperwork and a steel water bottle.

'Coffee?' he asked, aware of how cracked his voice sounded and hoping she wouldn't notice.

'That would be lovely, thanks,' she said politely—but there was a bloom of colour on her cheeks. She clearly wasn't immune to this thing between them, this pulsing excitement, either. Maybe bringing her here had been a mistake. He'd thought that being at the palace would remind him of his responsibilities and do something to suppress all the crazy longing, but it wasn't helping anywhere near enough.

Using the bean-to-cup machine to make the coffee gave him a tiny space to rein his feelings back under control.

'Shall we go through to the library?' he asked, handing her the mug and making quite sure there was no skin contact, because he knew it would snap his control again.

'Sure,' she said.

And it was meant to be business. It really was.

Except when he walked through the door he saw his reading chair, and a picture slid into his head. Himself sitting there, reading a book. Gemma sitting on his lap, also reading a book. He'd have one arm round her waist, and her fingers would be tangled with his. And the curve of her neck would be within kissing distance; all he'd need to do would be to move his head, just slightly, and he'd feel her pulse beating hard against his mouth...

Oh, God. He really had to stop this.

But the picture in his head wouldn't budge. It stayed there, singing a siren's song. What if they could steal a few moments from time? What if they had a mad fling, even though they knew they couldn't have a future? What if they acted on the pull between them and just let it happen?

The sensible side of him reminded him it wouldn't be fair. It'd be dishonourable, and he didn't want to be the type of king who just took whatever he wanted and to hell with the consequences. Gemma had already been hurt by someone who'd claimed to love her and then broken her heart in front of her family and friends on their wedding day. She deserved more than a fling; she deserved much more than he could offer her. He needed to put the brakes on.

Now.

Like, *really* now.

'Niko?'

'Sorry,' he muttered. 'Just thinking.' And he didn't dare meet her eyes, in case his thoughts were as obvious as he feared they might be.

'We have a press release to write,' she said.

'Uh-huh.' Mechanically, he set his mug on a coaster

on his desk, then took his laptop from the drawer, switched it on and opened up a new document.

'Would you prefer the office chair or…?' His mouth dried as he looked at his comfortable reading chair again and his head was suddenly full of that little fantasy on an endless loop, the two of them curled up together on that chair and kissing.

'Whatever works best for you,' she said. 'Maybe I should sit back here while you sit at your desk.'

Was it his imagination, or was there a slight wobble in her voice? Did she, too, harbour fantasies of the two of them sitting together in that chair, wrapped in each other's arms and lost in the magic of a forbidden kiss?

'Good idea,' he muttered. Putting distance between them was *definitely* a good idea. It was about the only way he'd be able to concentrate. And maybe her self-control was better than his, because she sat down. He did the same, keeping his back to her.

He had absolutely no idea how he managed to type a press release about the discovery of the mosaic floor, because the only thing he was aware of was her nearness. But somehow there seemed to be words on the screen, and he was reading the document aloud to her. Though, for all he knew, he might be speaking complete gibberish. His mind felt completely disconnected from his senses—and from his common sense. For pity's sake, why was he even thinking about this? He knew perfectly well he couldn't even ask her to date him, given that he needed to marry for political reasons. An unexpected love match was completely out of the question.

Though, if he'd still been Dr Spiridon and had that choice, he would definitely have asked her to date him.

He really, really liked this woman. He liked the way her mind worked. He liked her sunny nature and her cleverness. The physical attraction between them was the icing on the cake.

But things had changed. Leo had died. Niko didn't have his old freedom any more. And part of him felt he'd already lost too much—his brother, his freedom, the job that had suited him perfectly. He didn't want to risk losing his heart as well. Especially to someone who might find the crown too much to bear and would walk away.

The problem was, his common sense and his sense of need were completely at war, and he was being ripped between them.

'Do you mind if I read it for myself?' she asked eventually.

Oh. So he *was* speaking gibberish, then. He just hoped she didn't want an explanation, because he didn't want to tell her he was distracted by thinking about her and how he was trying to untangle the mess of feelings he hadn't expected and didn't quite know how to deal with it.

'Just that I work better visually than listening to something,' she added.

Ah. Maybe he was reading too much into what she'd said, because he was thrown off balance. She sounded sensible and academic and in full control of herself. Which was a good thing. Maybe some of it would rub off on him. 'Sure,' he said.

Though he regretted agreeing when she came to stand beside him. He could smell vanilla—whatever shampoo or shower gel she used—and he was very, very aware of her bodily warmth. If he spun his chair ninety degrees towards her, he could scoop her onto his lap and...

'Niko?'

He had no idea what she'd just said to him, and he wasn't even going to attempt bluffing it. 'Sorry. Thinking about Amphitrite,' he mumbled. Which was a total fib. He wasn't thinking about an ancient goddess at all; he was thinking of the clever, pretty, *fascinating* woman who was standing right beside him.

'Can I just change this little bit?' she asked. 'I'll put the document on track changes.'

'Yes.'

She leaned across him ever so slightly so she could reach the laptop's keyboard. So close, but nowhere near as close as he needed her to be. His heart rate went up a notch. She deleted a couple of words and typed others. He could barely breathe. Every nerve-end was screaming out, telling him to hold her.

She saved the file and moved his laptop to the side. And then, shockingly, she was leaning against the desk opposite him, right where the laptop had been. So close that his knees were actually touching her legs. She looked him straight in the eye, that piercing blue gaze seeing through every excuse he'd been making to himself.

'How are we going to manage this, Niko?' she asked.

'Yiannis will liaise with the university,' he said.

A corner of her mouth quirked. 'I wasn't talking about the press release.'

'Oh.' And then he felt even more stupid, because he didn't know what to say. For pity's sake, he was supposed to be taking over as the King of Amphithos next year. Right now, he was an incoherent *lump*. He couldn't find any of the right words. He couldn't find any words at all. All he could focus on was the longing he felt.

'You and me,' she said. 'It's a seriously bad idea.'

'Yes,' he agreed. But his heart was saying otherwise.

'You're going to be king. I'm going back to my job in London.'

All true.

'Anything else would be a complication that neither of us needs,' she added.

He knew that. His common sense knew that. The very few unscrambled brain cells currently working in his head knew that.

But the rest of him disagreed, practically yelling that this was a complication he *did* need. Something he wanted desperately. Something he rather thought she wanted, too, because her tone definitely didn't match her words. When he looked her in the eye, he could see that same longing there, too. He wasn't imagining it.

She was right: this would be a seriously bad idea.

But, now she'd broached the subject out loud, how could they go back?

He reached out and took her hand. Looked at it. Small and feminine; yet also incredibly capable. Short, practical, unvarnished nails. Soft skin, despite the fact that he knew half her day was spent with her hands covered in dirt when she was in the middle of an excavation.

Irresistible.

Unable to stop himself, Niko brought her hand to his lips and kissed each fingertip in turn, exerting the lightest possible pressure. His lips tingled where they touched her skin; the tingling grew more intense when he pressed a kiss into the centre of her palm, the way he'd fantasised about before, and folded her fingers over his kiss.

'How do *you* think we should manage this?' He echoed her earlier question.

She didn't pull her hand away; instead, she laid the palm of her free hand flat against his cheek. 'I don't know. Tell me to go.'

He couldn't, because he wanted her to stay. Mutely, he shook his head.

'I don't want a relationship, Niko,' she said. 'I'm not looking for love.'

'I know,' he said, equally softly. 'It's the same for me.' He couldn't have love. His future held a dynastic marriage. He took a deep breath. 'But I can't stop thinking about you.'

'I can't stop thinking about you, either,' she admitted.

'I'm going slowly crazy,' he said.

'Me, too,' she said, and his pulse leaped crazily.

'So what do we do?' he asked.

'We can't just have a mad fling to get it out of our systems, the way we might've done if you were a normal person.'

'*Normal.*' That stung. Hugely.

She winced. 'I didn't mean that the way it sounded. Sorry. It came out wrong. I meant…not royal. Your life is in the public eye, Niko. People will *notice* if you and I… They'll gossip. It'll make life difficult for you politically.'

But she hadn't moved away. If anything, she'd moved just that little bit closer—like him, unable to resist the pull. One hand was still stroking his cheek, and the other was curled in his hand. He twisted his head so he could press another kiss into her palm. 'I could always go on a royal visit to… I don't know, Australia. The Arctic. Somewhere. Anywhere.' He shook his head, trying to clear it and concentrate. 'Wherever the furthest place from here is.' He couldn't think where that actually was, right at that moment. 'But I'm pretty sure it wouldn't make any difference, Gemma. However much physical distance we managed to put between ourselves, it wouldn't stop me thinking about you.' He raised his eyebrows. 'We can keep saying that we're just sort-of colleagues, that we're starting to become friends—but it's not quite true, is it?'

'I'll go back to London,' she said. 'I'll try to find a colleague to take over from me here.'

'If you were in London, would it stop you thinking about me?' he asked.

'No,' she admitted. 'I'd still remember how it felt when you kissed me on the beach. That's been replaying in my head for *days*.'

He'd been replaying it, too. 'If you went back to London, I'd still be thinking about you. I've been imagining kissing you here in my library.' He couldn't stop the breathy longing in his voice. 'Both of us sitting on my reading chair, you sitting on my lap and your hands in my hair,' he said.

She glanced over his shoulder at the chair she'd vacated, and her pupils expanded that little bit more. '*Ohhh*. Yes.' The word hissed between her teeth. And it wasn't just agreement, he knew. This was consent.

Her lower lip was full and inviting, and that sexy little rasp in her voice was his undoing. He stood up, scooped her up and carried her back to the chair, settling her on his lap. 'This isn't supposed to be happening,' he said. 'I know it's wrong. Forbidden, even. But I can't resist you, Gemma. I want to take your hair out of that braid and see it spread across my pillow. I want to kiss you. Make love with you. Even though I shouldn't be doing this because I can't offer you anything honourable. That's not who I am. I don't want to be a selfish, grasping taker.'

'I don't have crazy flings,' she said. 'I'm a boring, staid archaeology lecturer who's happy with her life exactly how it is. Quiet. No waves.'

But her arms were wrapped round him, just as tightly as his were wrapped round her.

'You're not boring,' he said. 'You're like a sunrise.'

'With my orange hair, you mean?' Amusement lit her eyes.

'Your hair isn't orange. It's beautiful.' Unable to stop himself, he kissed the tip of her nose. 'It's not just how you look. It's *you*. Everything about you. It makes everything feel all lit up.'

'And you. You're like a Greek god,' she whispered. 'I could imagine you rising up through the waves and walking out of the sea, like…' Her eyes narrowed. 'Not Poseidon, because you're not bad-tempered. One of the clever gods, I think.' She leaned forward and kissed the tip of his nose. 'Maybe Apollo, the god of music and poetry and medicine. Not just because you're beautiful.'

She thought he was beautiful? His pulse leaped again. 'I can't think straight enough to be sensible,' he said. 'I know I don't have the right to ask, but stay with me tonight, Gemma. Please?'

She took a deep breath, and for a moment he thought she might manage to find the strength he didn't have to resist the idea.

But then she said, 'Yes.'

And he was completely lost.

CHAPTER SIX

NIKO STOOD UP, still with Gemma in his arms, and carried her to his room. Then he set her on her feet, kissed her lightly and closed his curtains. She wasn't sure which of them had done what, but the end result was that they were both naked, lying on the most luxurious and soft sheets she'd ever experienced in her life. Kissing. Touching. Exploring.

Everywhere he touched her, it felt as if she'd turned to flame. He made her feel like the goddess whose mosaic they'd uncovered, all powerful.

'Your hair,' he said huskily. 'I need to see it loose. Can I unbraid it?'

She nodded, sitting up, and he removed the elastic from her braid. She could feel him undoing the plait, slowly and carefully so he didn't pull her hair. He combed through her hair with his fingers, letting it fall over her shoulders. 'Beautiful,' he said, burying his face in it. 'So soft. So silky. Strawberry-blonde— yet your hair smells of vanilla, not strawberries.'

'And you smell of limes,' she said, twisting round so she could draw her fingers through his own wavy hair.

He traced the line of her collarbones, then dipped his

head so he could kiss the hollows. And then he looked at her, his eyes widening. 'We need a condom.'

She stared back at him, looking as shocked as he felt. 'I don't carry any. And I'm not on the Pill.'

'I do have some condoms,' he said, wincing, 'but whether they're actually in date, I couldn't tell you.'

She couldn't help laughing. 'Niko, that's crazy.'

'Yeah, you're right,' he said ruefully. 'Carrying you off to my bed like a caveman, when I might not even have protection. How stupid is that?'

'Not stupid,' she said. 'Firstly, you remembered before it was too late; and secondly, that tells me you're not taking this for granted.'

'I hadn't dated anyone for a few months before Leo died,' he said, 'and I haven't had time to date since then. I haven't thought about protection, because I haven't needed any.' He grimaced. 'Sorry.'

'It's fine,' she said, and traced his lower lip with the pad of her thumb. He responded by drawing her thumb into her mouth and sucking it hard, making her shiver. 'I think you need to check that expiry date,' she said huskily.

'Hold that thought.' He kissed the tip of her nose, then climbed off the bed, took a small box from his bedside cabinet, and checked the box.

'The good news is,' he said, 'they're in date.' He looked at her, his expression pained. 'Though I've pretty much killed the mood now.'

She liked the fact that he was so self-aware. 'Actually, you haven't,' she said. 'We both needed to know. And it wouldn't have really mattered if the condoms *had* been out of date, because we could've...' She licked her suddenly dry lips. 'Improvised.'

'Improvised?' he asked, his pupils darkening.

'I'd say you're better-read than I am, with that incredible library in, what is it, five different languages?' she said. 'And I read a *lot*. So don't try to tell me you don't know how to improvise, Dr Spiridon.'

He grinned, and it felt as if the sun had just come out from behind a cloud. 'Well. Now. Perhaps we can do both. Improvise...and take things further.'

Weird how that made her feel shy and bold, both at the same time. 'Show me,' she invited, and he pulled her back into his arms.

Much later, when they'd finished exploring each other and were sated, Gemma lay wrapped in his arms with her head on his shoulder, 'So what happens now?' she asked.

'It's late. Let's go to sleep,' Niko said. 'I'll make you breakfast in the morning, then we can talk, and I'll run you back to the university.'

'Thank you,' she said. 'Hopefully before anyone spots me and asks awkward questions. And I've arranged to go swimming with a couple of my students.'

'I'll get you back in time,' he promised.

'Thank you.' She paused. 'We need a believable cover story.'

'We worked late and you were exhausted, so you stayed in a guest suite at the palace?' he suggested.

'I'm not sure anyone would believe that one,' she said.

'We'll think about that cover story tomorrow,' he

said. 'For now, I want to ignore the real world and enjoy going to sleep with you in my arms.'

'And you've set a relatively early alarm?' she checked.

'I have.' He chuckled. 'I love that you're so practical.'

'There's no point in being anything else,' she said.

'True.' He snuggled closer, and gradually his breathing slowed.

It was a long, long time since Gemma had spent the night with anyone, though she was under no illusions that this crazy summer fling with Niko had any kind of future. But it wasn't hurting anyone. Maybe they both needed this time, this space, to move on with their lives. In a way, she'd been stuck since Andy had jilted her, not wanting to trust anyone with her heart again. Maybe Niko could teach her to be open to trusting again. And she could teach him that he had the strength to be the king his country needed—that he could still be himself as well as being the king.

Liking the idea that they might be healing each other, she relaxed enough to fall asleep in his arms.

The following morning, Gemma woke with a start. She wasn't sleeping on serviceable cotton sheets on a narrow student mattress; this was a wide, comfortable bed and the sheets had a luxuriously high thread count. And there was a delicious aroma of coffee.

She opened her eyes, realised that Niko must be in the kitchen, and dressed swiftly before going out of the bedroom to find him.

'Good morning,' he said when she walked into the kitchen. 'I was about to bring you some coffee.'

'I'm here, now,' she said with a smile.

And he'd set the table for breakfast: a loaf of bread, a jug of freshly squeezed orange juice, bowls of thick Greek yoghurt, dark honey, blueberries, walnuts and pumpkin seeds.

'I can do you eggs, if you like,' he said.

'No, it's fine. This is all lovely,' she said, gesturing to the table. 'Thank you. This is very civilised.'

'And not far off what they would've had for breakfast at the temple you're working on,' he said. 'Barley bread dipped in wine, or a kind of pancake made from flour, oil, honey and a form of yoghurt, with fruit.'

'That's the bit that fascinates me most about my job,' she said. 'Not the treasure—the human stories.'

'It's why I like the desk research side. Maps, documents, books and oral history,' he said.

They really did see things the same way, she thought. If only they'd met earlier. Or if only he wasn't a prince.

But it was as it was, and they needed to be sensible.

The conversation stayed light until they'd finished their breakfast, and Gemma was aware of the concern in his eyes—concern that was no doubt matched in her own. Time to deal with the elephant in the room. 'So how are we going to deal with this?' she asked. 'You're supposed to be dating princesses.'

He gave her a rueful smile. 'Not *quite*. The Palace Council—and my mother—are making a list of suitable candidates for the future queen. I'm not dating anyone right now.' His amber eyes were serious. 'I would never have even kissed you, let alone asked you to stay with me last night, if I'd been dating someone.'

She nodded, knowing he had a strong sense of honour. 'But you can't date me.' Because she wasn't a princess and there was no way she'd ever be considered as a candidate on the Palace Council's list.

'If I had the choice,' he said, 'I'd ask you to date me properly. And that's not me trying to flatter you.'

'Thank you.' She gave him a rueful smile. 'I guess we can date *im*properly.'

He smiled back. 'I like your thinking.' He grew serious again. 'Last night wasn't enough for me.'

'It wasn't enough for me, either,' she admitted.

'But it feels sleazy and dishonourable, offering you just a—well, a fling.'

It made her feel better that it was throwing him off balance, too. And that he wasn't taking her for granted, the way Andy had done. 'Take the royal stuff out of it,' she said. 'Neither of us is in a place to consider having a proper relationship. We both know that. But this thing between us—I don't think we can ignore it, either.' At least, not without making themselves miserable. 'Which leaves a fling as our only option.' She paused. 'A *discreet* fling, because I don't want to cause any political hassle for you, or for you to get pilloried by the media.'

'Discreet,' he said thoughtfully. 'So how do we manage that?'

'We carry on doing what we've done, this past week,' she said. 'I send you updates on the dig. You drop in to say hello to the students, and sometimes eat with us. When you leave Theo's, I go to do my paperwork.'

'Except maybe you do it here in my apartment rather than at your flat,' he said.

She nodded. 'I can't invite you to my flat, because it's basically a bedsit and you'd need your security detail to sit outside the door. Apart from the fact that it would be the complete opposite of discreet, I wouldn't want to make life difficult for Stephanos—it's not fair to make him sit in a corridor all night.'

'Technically, it's his job—but I agree with you. That's not how I want to treat my staff. And I like the way you think of other people, not just yourself,' he said. 'OK. So we're colleagues in public. And more than colleagues here.'

'And, at the end of the summer, we wish each other well,' she said. 'I go back to London and you finish preparing to become king.'

'That sounds a bit clinical—but you're right. We need to be clear about things. We can have each other, but not in public and only for this summer.' He raised an eyebrow. 'It's very *Casablanca*.' He did his best Bogart impersonation. 'We'll always have Amphitrite's temple.'

'Works for me,' she said with a smile. 'Being together—in private only—means we're giving each other a breathing space. Time to come to terms with…' She thought for a moment about how to put it diplomatically. They both knew what they'd been struggling with. 'Things we've found difficult to come to terms with.'

'Having our plans turned completely upside down,' he said. 'You're right. We can help each other handle that change.'

'It's mutual and it's equal.' She raised her almost empty coffee mug. 'To us.'

He clinked his own mug against hers. 'To us. And I'd better get you back to the university.'

'Or maybe a driver from the palace can take me,' she suggested. 'If anyone sees you in a car with me at this time of the morning, they'll put two and two together and work it out very easily. I could call a taxi, but that risks a leak.'

'A driver from the palace it is,' he said. 'I'll organise that. Feel free to grab a shower or anything you need from the bathroom.'

'A spare toothbrush would be wonderful, please,' she said. 'I'll have a quick shower and change back at my place.' She'd already pulled her hair back into a low ponytail, planning to comb it back at her flat.

He told her where to find the spare toothbrush; by the time she'd finished in the bathroom, a driver was waiting to take her back to the university. And by the time she'd changed into her swimming costume, ready to meet up with the students who were joining her for an early morning swim, he'd emailed her a revised press release for review.

She read through it swiftly. Works for me, she messaged back. Happy to talk to any journalists.

And then she headed out for her swim, feeling as if the sun was just that little bit brighter.

CHAPTER SEVEN

THE NEXT WEEK was one of the happiest Gemma could ever remember. Paradise, even. She spent her days doing the job she loved and discovering more items at the temple, her evenings with the students and stealing time with Niko, and every other morning she woke in his arms.

Life was perfect.

Until the following Monday afternoon, when a visitor arrived. Gemma hadn't met her before; but, given that she looked to be in her early sixties and she looked very much like Niko, Gemma was pretty sure that she was Niko's mother. Particularly as she was accompanied by someone Gemma *did* know: Stephanos, Niko's usual security detail.

'*Kalispéra*, Your Majesty,' she said, trying her best to execute a decent curtsey. 'I apologise for being rude and saying it in English, but I'm afraid my Greek vocabulary still isn't very wide.'

'*Megaleiótitá*,' Elena said. 'My son should perhaps be teaching you a little better.'

Gemma felt the colour flood into her cheeks. Oh, no. Queen Elena clearly knew about her fling with Niko. Rather than this being an unscheduled, spontaneous tour of the dig, it was more likely to be a way for the queen to meet the woman who was leading her son astray…and perhaps to warn her to back off.

The queen's expression was totally unreadable and Gemma really wished that Niko was here to help her. She glanced at Stephanos, hoping that maybe he could give her a steer, but his expression was equally impassive, and she couldn't see his eyes behind his sunglasses. It looked as if she was in this on her own. And she knew she needed to tread carefully.

'I'm sorry. *Signómi, Megaleiótitá*,' she added swiftly, stumbling slightly over the pronunciation and hoping she wasn't making life even more difficult for Niko. She gave another awkward curtsey.

This time, the queen smiled. 'It's not a problem, Dr Stone. I speak English. Perhaps you could show me round the dig.'

'Of course, *Megaleiótitá*. And if you have any questions on the way, please ask. If I don't know the answer, I'll make sure I find out and get the information to you,' Gemma promised.

'*Efcharistó*,' the queen said, giving a brief and very regal nod.

Gemma took the queen through the dig, showing her the precious mosaic and answering her questions. All the time, she was sure that the queen had another motive for this visit. When would Niko's mother ask what she *really* wanted to know? And Gemma knew that she had to be careful with her answers, to avoid making life difficult for Niko.

'Talking about history really makes you light up,' the

queen said at the end of the tour. 'Just as it does for my son—and it used to be the same with his grandfather.'

'Dr Spiridon told me how his grandfather taught him all about Homer and mythology,' Gemma said.

'Did he, now?' The queen looked thoughtful. 'Well, he has been spending rather a lot of time with you.'

Gemma winced. This was the crunch moment. The queen was clearly aware of the exact nature of their relationship, despite their public cover that Niko was solely interested in the academic developments and she was updating him. 'I'm sorry, *Megaleiótitá*. I realise it looks…complicated,' she said, feeling her way and hoping she wasn't making a mess of things. 'I know that Niko has duties to fulfil. He and I are friends.' Which was true, up to a point; they were friends. Though she could feel the colour seeping through her cheeks because they were more than friends, and she had no idea of the etiquette here. How did you tell a queen that you were having a fling with her son? There wasn't a way to put a good spin on it.

The heat in her face heightened when the queen said dryly, 'That would be "just good" friends?'

Had they really been so obvious? Or so oblivious that everyone knew what was really going on? Though Gemma didn't want the queen to think she would do anything to hurt Niko, or damage his reputation in the media. 'I'm very aware of Niko's responsibilities,' she said quietly. 'I'd like to reassure you that I would never knowingly do anything that would cause him difficulties.'

'When we lost Leo, the light went out in Niko's

eyes,' the queen said, looking solemn. 'And it stayed out until he met you. You've given him that light back.'

Was this the queen giving her approval? Or was it an acknowledgement of the situation and a warning that it needed to stop?

Gemma decided that honesty was the best policy. 'We're friends. We share similar interests. If I had discovered this site but couldn't work on it, I hope someone would've kept me up to date on any developments in the dig. That's what I'm trying to do for Niko. There are no strings. I know—' she stumbled over the words '—about Yiannis's dossier.' And she was also embarrassingly aware that the queen would probably know all about the mistake Gemma had made with Andy. 'I realise I would never be suitable for anything more than friendship with your son, and I would never seek to distract him from—' *the misery of an arranged marriage to a princess he barely knew and didn't love* '—his duty to the kingdom.'

Elena regarded her closely. 'He spends every evening with you.'

And that was the warning Gemma had been half expecting: in his mother's eyes, she was distracting Niko and it needed to stop. 'I apologise, *Megaleiótitá*. In future, I'll tell him I'm too busy to update him personally, and I'll send all information through Yiannis.' Which was what she knew she should've been doing all along.

'That isn't what I meant,' the queen said. 'Come for supper, this evening. It will be informal—just Niko, my husband and me.'

What?

The Queen of Amphithos had just invited her to supper?

With Niko's father?

She was going to be eating with the royal family?

Gemma was aware that her mouth was hanging open slightly, and the queen was waiting for an answer. She was being incredibly rude. Flustered, she dipped in a quick curtsey. 'That's very kind of you to invite me, *Megaleiótitá.*'

'I think,' the queen said, 'we can drop the formality. Call me Elena.'

'Yes, *Me*—Elena,' Gemma said.

'I think we understand each other, Gemma.'

No, they didn't. At all. Gemma didn't have a clue what was happening here.

'We'll see you at seven. Thank you for showing me round the site.' She stood up and smiled at the security detail. 'Time to go back and let Dr Stone get on with her work, I think, Stephanos.'

Stephanos bowed. 'Of course, *Megaleiótitá.*'

Gemma saw them both to the entrance of the site, and then glanced at her watch. Her mum had recently gone part time at work, and with any luck she'd catch her mum at just the right time. She grabbed her mobile phone and called home.

Cassie answered instantly. 'Is everything all right, darling? This isn't the usual time you ring home.' She sounded concerned, and Gemma suddenly felt really homesick. She could really do with a hug, right now.

'It's fine,' Gemma said. 'Well, no, actually, it's not.' She explained the situation. 'And I don't have a clue what to wear tonight, and there isn't time to go shopping anyway, and I don't know why she invited me, and—' She stopped, aware that she was gabbling, lost in a spiral of panic. 'I'm terrified, Mum. What if I mess everything up?'

'Of course you're not going to mess anything up. She said it was an informal family supper, so don't worry about being too dressy.'

'All I have with me is one little black dress, in case we had a formal dinner at the end of the dig,' Gemma said gloomily.

'That would be fine. Or wear black trousers and a pretty top, something that makes you feel comfortable and relaxed,' Cassie advised. 'Obviously not jeans.'

'Trousers and a pretty top. I can do that. But what do I take as a gift? I can't take wine—I mean, apart from the fact that they're probably used to the kind of vintages that would cost me a week's salary per bottle, Niko's dad has a hobby vineyard. You can't take wine to a winemaker.' Gemma bit her lip. 'And I can hardly take flowers to a queen, can I? The palace is bound to have a massive garden, and there will no doubt be formal arrangements all over the palace. A normal bunch of flowers will make me look like a cheapskate, and an expensive bouquet will look as if I'm trying too hard and it'll still be pathetic compared to the flowers at the palace.'

'Stop panicking. A simple bouquet of roses works in most circumstances. But I'd say you can't go wrong with taking some good chocolates,' Cassie said. 'Keep it simple and don't overthink things. You've been invited to an informal meal with Niko's parents. He'll be there, too. Just be yourself.'

An ordinary woman. A lecturer and archaeologist. Someone who'd never even met anyone royal until Niko had turned up at her dig. Ice slithered down Gemma's spine. She hadn't been enough for Andy, so how could she possibly be enough as company for a king and queen?

'Stop worrying. It'll be *fine*,' Cassie said.

'I know. You're right. Thanks, Mum,' Gemma said, not wanting to worry her mother further, but she wasn't convinced that it would be fine at all. Had she already passed some kind of test and the king and queen would be welcoming her as Niko's friend? Or would she be in for a second grilling—one where she could fail and make life difficult for Niko?

And what was an informal supper, anyway? At her own house, or anywhere her family or friends invited her, she knew it would mean sharing simple food around the kitchen table. But her family wasn't royal. Niko was the only royal person she really knew—and she rather thought he might not be very like other royals because he'd spent years seeing himself in terms of his job as a lecturer rather than as a prince.

'Call me if you need me, later, Gem,' Cassie said.

'I will,' Gemma promised.

She texted Niko, next. Just in case he didn't yet know of his mother's plans. Your mother invited me to an informal supper with your dad and you tonight.

Duh. Niko was her son. He was the best person to ask what to bring. What kind of chocolate does she like?

Clearly he was busy in meetings with his phone on silent, because he didn't reply. And she only just made it to the specialist chocolate shop a couple of minutes before they closed. On the way back, she received a text from him. You don't have to bring anything. But she likes all chocolate.

That was a relief. If he'd said that his mother hated chocolate, she'd really be in trouble. The only other thing Gemma could think of to take with her—albeit something she couldn't actually *give*—was one of the fragments of the pottery winecups, because she hoped it might interest Niko's father. She signed it out of the finds area, showered and changed back in her room, then took a taxi to the palace.

Yiannis met her at the gatehouse, just as he had when she'd first had dinner at Niko's apartment; this time, he took her to a completely different part of the palace. There were chandeliers, marble sculptures and floors, and gold-framed paintings everywhere: it reminded her of the kind of museum she loved visiting, but she absolutely couldn't imagine what it was like to live in this kind of place and be surrounded by priceless antiquities. 'Have a pleasant evening, Gemma,' he said, giving her an encouraging smile.

She appreciated the way Yiannis had tried to bolster her too-obviously flagging confidence, but she felt completely out of her depth. Even when Niko opened the door to her, she couldn't relax.

Clearly her nervousness showed, because Niko smiled at her. 'Don't worry. They won't bite. My mother wouldn't have invited you for supper if she hadn't liked you.'

That was a good thing. She hoped. Or was he just trying to soothe her nerves?

And the fact she was tied up in knots over an invitation to dinner just proved how unsuitable she was for Niko. A princess would simply take it in her stride.

'Should I leave my shoes here, by the door?' she asked.

'No, it's fine. Keep them on,' he said.

She wished again that she'd thought to ask him about a dress code, because she noticed that he was wearing a formal suit. Who wore a suit to an informal family dinner—especially someone she knew wore jeans outside the palace? Right at that moment, she felt incredibly underdressed.

But she summoned up her courage and followed him through to a reception room, where the king and queen were sitting on a sofa.

'Welcome to the palace, Gemma,' the queen said, smiling at her.

'*Kalispéra, Me–*' Gemma began.

'"Elena" is fine,' the queen reminded her. 'This is Leonidas, my husband.'

I'm being introduced to the *king*, Gemma thought. On first-name terms. How surreal was this?

'And you already know my son, Niko.'

'I, um… Yes.' Awkwardly, Gemma handed Elena the box of chocolates she'd bought earlier. 'These are for you. Thank you for inviting me, this evening.'

'You're very welcome, Gemma. And thank you for

the gift.' She smiled. 'You didn't need to, but it's appreciated. I recognise this packaging. Leonidas will pour you a glass of wine, and then we can eat.'

'Is this wine from your vineyard, *Megaleiótate*? The Robola?' she asked, curtseying as the king came towards her with a bottle of white wine and a glass.

He smiled. 'It is, and you may call me Leonidas. And you are here as our guest. Tonight, we're informal. You don't have to curtsey.'

'Thank you,' she said. 'I was worrying that I'm not suitably dressed.'

'You're an archaeologist. If you wore a business suit, it would be ruined by lunchtime on the first day,' Elena said. 'And you were expecting to spend most of your days on the dig. Of course your wardrobe would be your working clothes.'

Her mother was right. She *had* been overcomplicating things. 'Thank you, Elena,' she said quietly. 'I brought something to show you from the site; we found it this afternoon. I thought you might like to see it, Leonidas, because it's a fragment of one of the drinking cups we think was used for red wine at the temple. We're not sure if it was used for drinking or pouring as a libation.'

'Cups, plural?' Niko checked.

She nodded. 'This fragment's decorated. One of the other fragments contained wine lees, so we've sent that one for testing.'

Leonidas looked interested. 'Will you be able to tell what kind of wine it is?'

'I hope so,' she said. 'And we might even be able to

tell the varietal and whether it's related to anything in your vineyard. The lab is a lot more sophisticated now than it was even five years ago.' She took the marked plastic bag containing the fragment from her handbag.

'And I may handle this without needing cotton gloves?' Leonidas asked.

'Yes.' She smiled, and took the fragment from the bag for him.

'It was decorated with vine leaves,' he said, studying it closely. 'My father would have been fascinated by this. He helped to save one of the old varietals. As did I,' he said. 'It's important to remember our island's history.'

'I'm very grateful for the opportunity to work at the temple,' Gemma said. 'And when we finished uncovering that mosaic floor—I think all the students had goosebumps.'

'Elena tells me it's spectacular. Perhaps I shall visit,' Leonidas said.

'You'd be most welcome,' Gemma said.

'Please, come and sit with us in the kitchen,' Elena said. 'We should eat.'

Gemma discovered that the queen really had meant an informal supper. The kitchen was similar to Niko's, with a table big enough for four set by the window overlooking the garden. There were *meze* laid in the centre of the table—olives, hummus, vine tomatoes, salads, fluffy bread, stuffed vine leaves, fresh fish and tender lamb—and everyone passed dishes to everyone else.

And suddenly it really was an informal family supper like the one she was used to at home, instead of the ordeal she'd been expecting. Yes, the cutlery was solid silver and the plates were Sèvres porcelain and the glassware was expensive crystal, but the warmth of their welcome dissipated the formality and stopped her from feeling completely out of place.

Niko's parents asked her about her job, about her family, but it didn't feel like a grilling; it felt as if they were interested. Even though they clearly knew her background from the dossier, they made her feel at ease. Niko chipped in from time to time, and she could see the sadness mingled with the love in their expressions when she talked about her brother and they talked about Leo.

'I'm so sorry you lost him,' she said, meaning it.

'He'll always be here in our hearts,' Elena said. 'We still have difficult days, but we have our memories to sustain us through them. And we have things to help prop us up. Leonidas has his vineyard.'

'My wife,' Leonidas said, 'indulges me.' He took her hand and kissed it. 'When I am out of sorts, she lets me sulk among my vines with my secateurs, and then when I come back she plays the piano to soothe my soul. She plays like an angel.'

'Hardly,' the queen said, but she was smiling. 'Leonidas has his vines; I have my piano. Niko has his books and his history. We manage.'

Gemma knew exactly what the queen was telling her. She knew how hard this was going to be for Niko, who'd never wanted to be king and felt as if he were taking over his brother's life; but he would manage. *Without her.*

'Play for us tonight, *kardiá mou*,' Leonidas urged.

'All right. Let's go through to the drawing room,' Elena said.

Gemma would normally have asked if she could do the washing up, but Niko had explained to her before that the palace staff handled everything. It wouldn't be like home, where her parents used the dishwasher after family meals and bickered over how to stack it.

'Niko, would you make the coffee?' Elena asked.

'Of course, *mamà*,' he said. Obviously realising that she'd offer to help him and that wasn't what his mother wanted, he said, 'Go with them, Gemma. I won't be long.' And his smile reassured her that everything would be just fine.

Although the furnishings were clearly high quality, this felt like a home rather than a palace: the king and queen's private space. There wasn't the overpowering gold and burgundy of the formal rooms she'd seen in the palace, but soft velvets in deep blue and green. There were framed family photographs on the mantelpiece, just as there were in Gemma's parents' own living room: weddings, christenings, graduations.

Elena sat down at the grand piano in the corner of the room, and played Debussy's *Clair de Lune*—without any sheet music, Gemma noticed. She couldn't help closing her eyes, letting the music wash over her. Elena played very well; it felt like having her own private recital.

'That was beautiful,' Gemma said when Elena finished. 'I love Debussy.'

'He's my favourite, too,' Elena said.

'My mother was a concert pianist when she met my father,' Niko said, coming in with the coffee.

Gemma felt her eyes widen. Was he telling her that his mother hadn't been a princess? Was this the reason Elena had invited her tonight, to let her know that her background might not be the barrier she and Niko thought it was? 'A concert pianist,' she said. 'That explains why you didn't need any music, Elena. And why it felt like being in the front row at a proper concert.'

'Elena has quite the repertoire,' Leonidas said proudly. 'And I've seen her play in concert halls across Europe. Including the Royal Albert Hall in London.'

A concert pianist. And yet she was the Queen of Amphithos?

'Leonidas wasn't supposed to choose me as his bride,' Elena explained. 'Nina, my elder sister, was on the Palace Council's list. But she was in love with someone else, and she begged me to change places with her. She said that because I was the younger sister, he wouldn't bother choosing me and I'd just be sent home again.' She grimaced. 'I felt so out of place when I came here. I got lost, and somehow I ended up in a room with a piano. So I did what I always do when I'm out of sorts: I sat down and played.'

'I was walking down a corridor when I heard this wonderful piano music,' Leonidas said, going over to his wife and standing with his hands resting on her shoulders. 'I wanted to know who was playing. I entered the room and saw her playing with her eyes closed, and I thought her the most beautiful woman I'd ever seen. It was the moment I fell in love with her.

We talked and talked all the rest of that day, and I knew she was the one I wanted to marry.'

'He gave me the choice,' Elena said. 'He said he wanted to marry me, but he didn't want me to feel I had to give up my music. It was my choice. Being his queen would take up much of my time, but if I married him he'd always try to find a way to let me play. Though obviously I wouldn't be able to tour any more.'

'She turned me down,' Leonidas said. 'She left me with the other princesses—none of whom were even one per cent of the woman she was, and none of whom interested me in the slightest.'

Other princesses? Ah. So Elena *had* been a royal before her marriage.

'She went to play her concert tour,' Leonidas continued. 'Athens, Rome, Paris, London.'

'And he sent me roses at every concert,' Elena said. 'Except on the final night, when he delivered them in person.'

'In London,' Leonidas said. 'I have very, very happy memories of London.'

'Seeing him again made me realise how much I'd missed him,' Elena said. 'So when he proposed to me again, backstage at the Royal Albert Hall after the performance and carrying the biggest bouquet of white roses I'd seen in my entire life, I accepted. And every time I play Debussy, I remember the first moment I met him.'

'That's so romantic,' Gemma said. She glanced at Niko, who had clearly heard the story many times before, and he was smiling fondly at his parents.

'Sadly, neither of my sons took after me when it came to music,' Elena said.

'I don't play, either,' Gemma said. 'Though I love music. My mum and I sing together in the kitchen. All the Eighties stuff she grew up with.'

'I'm a similar age to your mother, then,' Elena said. To Gemma's surprise, the queen played a few bars of Wham's 'Wake Me Up Before You Go-Go'.

'Don't let her sing,' Leonidas begged, laughing. 'She plays the piano like an angel, but singing? She can never hit the high note on this song.'

Gemma grinned. 'Neither can my mum. Actually, neither can I.'

'Ah. So we know what we have to do now, child.' Elena laughed, played a few more bars, sang a little and motioned with her head to Gemma to join in.

Gemma did so, singing flat. They both missed the high note, and the four of them ended up in peals of laughter.

'I'm glad you joined us tonight,' Elena said privately to Gemma at the end of the evening, when Gemma thanked her for the invitation. 'I see why my son enjoys your company so much. You *shine*.'

It put a lump into Gemma's throat. She'd worried so much about this evening, and yet the king and queen had treated her as a special guest who was very welcome, rather than an interloper who needed to be driven out. 'Thank you. But Niko shines, too,' Gemma said. 'And that's because of you and Leonidas. You let him do what he loves for all those years. And he has your example to help him step up to his duty.'

'I hope so.' Elena nodded. 'Goodnight. And we will see you here again.'

Gemma wasn't sure whether it was a command or a promise, but she was glad they'd found a connection.

'I'll walk you out to the car, Gemma,' Niko said, coming to join them.

In the entrance hall to his parents' apartment, he wrapped his arms round her. 'Thank you for tonight. I haven't heard my parents laugh like that for a long time. Not since…'

Gemma knew what he wasn't saying. 'They're lovely,' she said simply, and stroked his face. 'Nowhere near as scary as I expected.'

'Oh, they can be scary when they go full-on royal,' Niko said. 'But tonight they relaxed enough with you to be themselves. And it was lovely to see them just being my parents again. I wish…'

He wished what? That he didn't have to marry a princess? Or that she was royal, so they wouldn't have to give each other up at the end of the summer?

She was starting to feel that way, too.

But.

'Things are as they are,' she said softly, and kissed him. 'In another world, it would be different. But we'll both do the right thing.'

'When we have to,' Niko said. 'Until then…' And he kissed her lingeringly.

CHAPTER EIGHT

NIKO STARED AT the page on the report, not really seeing the words before him. His thoughts were full of last night and the meeting between Gemma and his parents. It had definitely been a turning point. He knew his parents were still grieving for Leo, and probably always would be, but Gemma's warmth had drawn them out for a few hours and reminded them that life still had its bright moments. She'd done the same thing for him, too. He felt different when he was with her. As if he'd found a space to breathe.

It made him wonder if maybe he could bend the rules. What if he didn't have to marry a princess? His parents had told Gemma the story of how they'd met; although Niko had heard it countless times before, last night had raised different questions in his head. Would his father still have married his mother if Elena hadn't been of royal blood? Would Leonidas have broken the rules for her?

Niko didn't necessarily think that rules were there to be broken, but he did think that laws, rules and regulations needed to adjust with the times. What had been appropriate a century ago wasn't necessarily appropriate for today. And plenty of other European royals had married people who weren't from a royal background, hadn't they? Yes, the crown was a pressure; but it would be manageable if they dealt with it together.

It made him think about what he was looking for in his life partner. Someone who was kind, thoughtful and able to connect with people. Someone who believed in mutual support—someone who'd be her own woman, and they'd juggle their responsibilities together. And, most of all, someone who made his world seem brighter just by being at his side.

Someone like Gemma.

This was crazy. They'd known each other for a matter of weeks. He shouldn't be thinking about her in these sort of terms. He couldn't possibly have fallen in love with her—could he?

Yet his father still maintained that he'd fallen in love with Elena on the first day they'd met—when he'd heard her play the piano and they'd talked and talked and talked.

Niko had definitely been attracted to Gemma from the first time he'd met her, the day she'd politely but firmly asked him to leave the dig site. But it was the third time they'd met—when they'd talked properly—that he'd realised how much he liked her. His feelings had grown stronger every day. And that evening he'd cooked for her, when he'd asked her to stay the night… He'd felt more alive than he had in years. Felt as if they *fitted.*

Could Gemma fit in with his life here? And, even if they could overcome any barriers set up by the Palace Council, would she want to be here with him? Would she want to be his future queen?

He thought about it. What was the difference between Gemma and a princess who'd been brought up in royal circles? She was used to talking to all kinds of people in her work, from nervous first year students up to senior professors and university chancellors. When she'd thought he was an ordinary member of the public, she'd been nice even as she'd asked him to leave. Last night, she'd been respectful to his parents, but she'd treated them as human beings, rather than as the rulers of Amphithos. They'd responded to her warmth. He was pretty sure Gemma would find a way to connect to other royals and dignitaries.

The press? He knew she'd dealt with them in the past, albeit in her role as an academic. She was definitely bright enough to learn how to deal with them where the royal family was concerned.

The people of Amphithos? He was pretty sure they'd take her to their hearts. They'd recognise her warmth and sincerity.

The sticking point, he thought wryly, was Gemma herself. Even if she felt the same way about him as he realised he felt about her, he knew she'd think herself unsuitable to be his partner. The way her ex had dumped her had shattered her self-esteem, and he knew that she still doubted herself. She'd even said that if she ever found someone who tempted her to risk getting married, she'd want a super-quiet wedding. As Prince Nikolaos's bride, she'd end up with a full state wedding, a massive affair that would be televised and celebrated around the entire island. Could he really ask her to put herself through that for him, making herself the centre of attention when she was used to being private?

He'd fallen in love with her—something he really hadn't expected to happen. But maybe that love meant he should let her go at the end of the summer, so she could find happiness on her own terms. A quiet academic life with someone who loved her and supported her. Last year, he could've made that choice; he could've found an academic job in London, had the quiet wedding of her dreams and lived a happy, private life with her. This year, he was in training to be the King of Amphithos, destined for a very public wedding—to a princess—and a very public life.

There was no middle way.

Unless he could show Gemma over the next few weeks that there could be moments of compromise. That they could still find a quiet and private life together, even while he fulfilled his public duties. They'd manage to strike a deal with the press so they weren't completely in a goldfish bowl.

The question was: how?

That evening, when they'd finished having dinner with the students, Gemma went for a walk with Niko along the edge of the sea. The waves swished into shore, brushing over their feet; the water still felt warm, even though the sun had gone down and the moon was out. Although they'd started off just walking side by side, their hands had brushed against each other and they'd ended up holding hands. Funny how such a little thing could mean such a lot; holding his hand and walking together in the moonlight made her feel as if the whole world was at their feet.

'My parents really liked you,' Niko said. 'They asked if you could make space in your diary on Monday nights from now on, and join us for family suppers.'

'I liked them, too,' Gemma said. 'Yes, please. And thank them for being so kind.'

'You're the one who deserves thanks,' he said. 'I haven't heard my mother sing since Leo died. And my father rarely laughs nowadays. It was so good to see them like that with you.'

The relief in his eyes made her wonder whether easing the weight of their grief was one of the main reasons why he was willing to give up everything he loved and had worked for, to do his duty. Being a good son, a good heir, meant supporting his parents and stepping into Leo's shoes without giving anyone a hint of how much it was costing him inside.

'I'm glad I could help,' she said.

'Sometimes…' He stopped.

She squeezed his hand. 'Talk to me, Niko. You know it won't go anywhere else.'

'I know,' he said. 'Of course I trust you. I just don't want to burden you.'

'We're friends,' she reminded him. 'Friends support each other.'

'I guess.' They walked a few paces more in silence. 'Leo dying absolutely shattered their world,' he said eventually. 'And mine. I can cope with my own feelings, but it's hard to watch how diminished my parents are. They carry on as normal in the public eye, because that's what you're supposed to do as a royal—but when they're in private, the weight of their grief just squashes them. And I can't lift it on my own. I don't know how to make things better. All I can do is try to be as good an heir as Leo was—and I worry that, because I was self-indulgent and did what interests me, I didn't learn enough to do Leo's job as well as he would've done it.'

Should she tell him what his mother had confided in him? Then again, if she broke that confidence, Niko might think she'd break his confidence, too.

'You're doing better than you think,' she said.

'That's kind,' he said, 'though not necessarily true.'

'Oh, it's true,' she said. 'Though I can't tell you how I know without breaking a confidence.'

He blinked. 'I'm not with you.'

She squirmed. 'Your mum talked to me. I'm not going to say what she told me—that's up to her if she wants to share with you. But let's just say she knows you're finding it hard to step into Leo's place. And she appreciates your strength.'

His frown deepened. 'I hope I'm not adding to her burden.'

'You're not. It's empathy,' she said. 'Think about it. I didn't know your mum was a concert pianist, but she gave it up willingly for your dad. Just as you've given up your academic career for your parents. She understands what it means to sacrifice something important to you.'

'I never really looked at it that way before,' he said. 'Thank you. It helps, knowing I'm not making it harder for my parents. I just wish I could do more.'

Did he feel that he wasn't enough? She knew that feeling only too well, especially since her public jilting. 'You're enough,' she said.

His fingers tightened round hers. 'Thank you for the vote of confidence.'

It would be oh, so easy to stop dead and hold him tightly. But they were in public. They shouldn't even be holding hands. 'We need to be careful,' she reminded him. 'This is just a moment out of time, for both of us. When the dig's over, we'll be going back to our real lives.' She ruthlessly suppressed the wish that things could be different. They needed to be sensible, and they both knew it.

'I know,' he said quietly. 'In another world, it'd be different.'

'But we're in this world, not a parallel universe,' she reminded him.

'Yeah.' He stopped, and spun her into his arms, just as she'd thought about doing to him. 'I know this is a risk, but the beach is deserted. If the students see us, they won't tell a soul. They're on our side.' He brushed his mouth against hers. 'Right now, I want to kiss you in the moonlight.'

When he put it like that, how could she possibly resist? When he kissed her again, wrapping his arms round her, this time she kissed him back, her hands tangling in his hair.

When he broke the kiss, he stroked her face tenderly. 'Gemma Stone, you're so special. Always remember that.'

'You're special, too,' she whispered. This felt almost like goodbye, and she wasn't ready for it. She wanted to treasure every minute of the few weeks that were left to them.

'I'd better stop distracting you from your work.' He paused. 'Tomorrow night at my place?'

'I'll cook,' she said.

He grinned. 'Can you?'

'I can do anything,' Gemma said. With Niko by her side, she really felt that she could.

'Want a sous-chef?' he asked.

The idea of cooking together really appealed to her. 'If I can afford his salary,' she teased.

'I was thinking payment in kisses,' he said.

She laughed. 'Deal.'

He kissed her again, this time lingering. 'I'll see you back safely,' he said. 'And then tomorrow. Seven?'

'Seven's great,' she said. 'I'll bring the food.'

He coughed. 'The palace kitchens have a pretty good stock of food.'

'But if I raid it for ingredients, then it still counts as you providing dinner,' she said, 'and I want this to be *me* treating *you*—and I'm only using your kitchen because using a shared student kitchen here would be awkward.'

'Equals,' he said. 'OK. If that's what you want.'

'It is,' she said.

'If you're worrying I think you're a gold digger, because I have a royal background and you don't,' he said, 'then let me assure you that I don't think of you that way at all. You're my equal.'

And how good that made her feel. His equal. Even if it was only for a little while.

On Wednesday evening, Gemma arrived at the palace with the ingredients for dinner. She got Niko to chop the vegetables while she browned cubes of chicken breast in a sauté pan, then added the veg to the pan with stock, smoked paprika and sundried tomatoes. Andy had never cooked, leaving it to her or ordering a takeaway; Niko was the perfect sous-chef, doing everything she asked and then paying attention to what she was doing.

She added orzo pasta to the pan.

'I like the fact you're doing this the Greek way,' Niko said. 'Cooking it with other ingredients rather than treating it like soup pasta.'

'It's almost like a risotto, this way,' she said, allowing him to claim his sous-chef payment in kisses.

Once the pasta was cooked, she wilted spinach in the pan, added a couple of tablespoons of cream cheese to finish the sauce, then split the contents of the pan between two bowls and added a sprinkling of parmesan and chopped basil.

'This is gorgeous,' Niko said. 'I'm so going to steal this recipe from you.'

'Not my recipe,' she said. 'I found it on the internet. If you look up "marry me chicken", you should find a version of it. I add more veg so I can do it as a quick one-pan dinner after work.'

'Marry me?' Niko said.

For just a moment, she thought he'd actually asked her to marry him, and her heart skipped a beat.

Marry him...

No. Of course he hadn't meant that. He wasn't free to marry her. He had to marry someone chosen by the Palace Council. No. He'd been asking her why the dish was called that. 'I think it's from a magazine or some-thing—when the recipe was first invented, the person who taste-tested it said it was so good they'd ask the cook to marry them on the spot.' She smiled. 'I have no idea if that's true or not.'

'It's a nice story,' Niko said.

Even though she kept telling herself to be sensible, she still thought about it when they walked on the private beach by the palace after dinner, and again when Stephanos had dropped her home that evening. The simple domestic task of cooking together had felt so comfortable, so right.

But things were as they were. There was an end date to their fling. They could snatch moments like this evening and pretend, but it wasn't going to happen in the real world. She'd just enjoy this, store up the memories, and concentrate on her work when she got back to London, she decided.

The next morning, she was busy at the dig when Calliope, one of her students, came up to her. 'Gemma, there's a bunch of press here asking to talk to you.'

She frowned. 'I'm pretty sure the press release told them to ring either the university or the palace to make an appointment rather than just turn up. Still, if they want to take pictures of the mosaic, that's fine. I don't mind showing them round.' She straightened up, brushed off the worst of the dust and followed Calliope to the huddle of press at the site entrance.

'Dr Gemma Stone?' one of them asked.

'Yes.' She smiled. 'From the University of London.

We're running a joint dig with the University of Amphithos—Calliope's one of my students from the university here. Would you like me to show you round? All the students have signed release forms, so it's fine for you to take photographs of them working.'

To her surprise, they took several pictures of her.

'Hey. I'm just part of the team,' she said lightly. 'I'd prefer my students to be credited in the photos. They've all worked really hard on the project. And the mosaic is really special. Follow me.'

She took them over to the mosaic, but before she had a chance to tell them about it, one of the journalists leaped in with a question. 'How long have you been seeing Prince Nikolaos?'

What? But nobody knew about that. The journalists were here because of the historical find, weren't they? She blinked. 'I beg your pardon?'

The journalist repeated the question.

Oh, help. She'd better explain their professional relationship. 'Hang on,' she said. 'You do realise that when the prince was working at the university—as Dr Spiridon—he was the one who pinpointed the site? Of course I see him regularly. It's because I keep him up to date with all the developments on the site.'

'That's not all you do, though, is it?' one of the other journalists said.

She frowned. No way could they know. She and Niko had been discreet. Nobody at the dig would've leaked the fact they were seeing each other, because the students all adored Niko; she thought she got on well with them, too.

The journalist took pity on her obvious confusion. 'You've not seen the news?'

'News?' Her frown deepened.

He took out his phone and showed her a newspaper website. There was a picture of them kissing on the beach, the other night, with a headline in Greek. She didn't have a clue what it said. Or how to explain the picture without making things difficult for Niko.

'May I put this in translation mode?' she asked, playing for time.

At his nod, she touched the Greek flag on the screen and switched it to the English flag.

The headline slid into horrific view. *Who's that girl?*

She scrolled down to see the speculation about who the prince was kissing.

And then there was her official photograph from the university website, captioned *Dr Gemma Stone, University of London.*

Oh, no.

She continued scrolling. And just skimming the headlines told her where the focus was. *Digging bones or digging gold?*

Oh, dear God. They thought she was a gold digger? That she was interested in Niko's family's position and their wealth?

From jilted at the altar to dating a prince...

She'd thought the first few stories were bad enough, but the journalists had clearly done some effective digging on social media—not just her own, but that of friends, and they'd clearly managed to piece together what Andy had done on their wedding day. Even though it felt as if someone was rolling her in a bed of nettles and her skin felt hot and sore and prickly, she forced herself to read the story.

Just as she'd dreaded, they were judging her. Asking what was so wrong with her that she'd been dumped at the altar. Part of her wanted to curl up in a ball and weep. Those were the same questions she'd asked herself, over and over, and still hadn't found an answer.

But the newspaper had suggestions. From the number steadily ticking upwards on the comments box even as she looked at it, clearly the readers had suggestions, too.

And then the shock and horror turned to molten anger. These people had muck-raked and judged her without even bothering to talk to her and find out her side of the story. As far as the press here was concerned, she was a gold digger and not good enough for their prince. They clearly saw her as dragging Niko down; another article even questioned the prince's judgement. According to them, if he couldn't even do his duty and find a royal bride, what damage would he do to the kingdom during his reign?

That wasn't fair. Niko would be an amazing king.

Even though the sensible part of her knew she should say nothing and get Yiannis to help deal with this, her outrage at their behaviour outweighed her common sense.

'I hope,' she said crisply, 'you all speak excellent English, because my Greek isn't up to what I want to say. Unless you'd like me to call on one of my students to translate for me?'

The journalists looked taken aback.

'We speak English,' one of them said. 'So how long have you been seeing the prince?'

'That's none of your business.'

'Isn't it?' one of the others demanded.

She saw red. Didn't they have any kind of fellow feeling at all? Couldn't they put themselves in his shoes, think how they'd feel if they lost someone they loved so much, and see how hard he was trying to do what was right for his country, no matter the cost to himself? He was vulnerable, and they were a pack of vultures, picking and picking and picking at the sore spots. And it wasn't OK. At all. 'No, it isn't,' she snapped. 'I guess I'm fair game because I'm only here temporarily. I can walk away at the end of the dig, so you can amuse yourselves by having a go at me. But don't you dare have a go at Niko. He *lives* here. He's one of you. He's supporting his parents—both as their son and as their heir. Have any of you stopped to think about how his life has changed, this last year? He loved his older brother. And not only does Niko have to deal with his loss—and deal with seeing how losing Leo has affected his parents, too—he's had to stop doing the job he loves and step up in Leo's place as the heir to the throne. His whole life has changed.' She warmed to her theme, wanting them to see the reality of Niko's life and relate to it. 'How would any of you feel if that happened to you? How would you feel if you'd made a huge discovery and someone else was the one to see it through? Wouldn't you want someone to keep you in the loop?'

A couple of the journalists muttered and looked guilty, but one of them called out, 'Yeah, but that's not all you were doing, was it?' His words were followed by a burst of salacious laughter from several of the others.

'Is Niko really entitled to no privacy at all? Is he supposed to live every single minute on public display, as if he's in a fishbowl? Do you think that kind of pressure is healthy? Or helping him adjust to his new role?' she demanded. 'And how do you think this sort of gutter-sweeping is affecting his parents? How would *you* feel if you'd lost one of your children in an accident, and the other was pilloried in the press when they'd done nothing wrong?' She folded her arms and glared at them. 'You should be ashamed of yourselves. This isn't proper journalism. If any of you did your job properly, you'd ask to talk to him and do a proper interview instead of printing gossip and speculation. And you'd think about his position. How you'd feel in his shoes, if you had no choice in who you dated or who you married because of your job.'

They all stared at her in silence.

She clicked on the comments and scrolled through another bit. 'This is gutter media, the lowest of the low. Obviously I'm reading a translation, but this is the sort of nonsense you see in my country, too. Letting people "have their say"—you're giving airspace to keyboard warriors who hate everything and want to complain about things, but behind an anonymous nickname. It's *clickbait*. And what are you getting out of it? Money? A feeling of popularity because you've got so many "likes"?' She shook her head in disgust. 'What happened to your morals?'

'Ask yourself why your students are filming all this,' one of the journalists bit back.

'We're filming it so when you start printing lies, we have proof of what Dr Stone really said and we'll release it to make sure people know the truth,' Calliope, one of the students who was filming, said. She said something in Greek, and then said to Gemma, 'Just so you know, I told them the same thing in our language, so they can't pretend they didn't understand.'

'Dr Stone is a brilliant teacher and she's doing an excellent job here,' Petros, another student, said. 'She's a guest on our island. What kind of hospitality is this, to let people who don't know her and who've never met her attack her?'

'The prince is meant to be finding a royal bride, not screwing around,' one of the journalists said coarsely.

'Dr Spiridon—as we knew him—was an inspirational teacher,' Calliope said. 'He's set his gift aside and stepped up to do his duty. Who are you to criticise that? Why aren't you supporting him instead of pulling him down?'

'He has to put our country first,' the journalist said.

'Which is why he stopped teaching when his brother died and he's been supporting the king ever since,' Petros pointed out. 'He's put his family and his country first, and himself last. So what if he's been—' He clammed up abruptly, clearly realising what he'd been about to admit.

'—talking to Dr Stone about the dig,' Calliope put

in smoothly. 'If you're here to see the mosaic, any one of us will be happy to talk to you. But if you're here to be nasty to Dr Stone or Dr Spiridon, then you're not welcome and we'll call security to have you removed.'

They didn't actually have security, but the press couldn't be sure of that. And, right at that moment, it seemed that actually the palace security had already been informed about the situation, because Yiannis—for once, unsmiling—pushed his way through the journalists, shouldered by two of the palace security team, who began to clear the journalists away from the site.

'Dr Stone, would you come with me, please?' Yiannis asked.

Was this an official royal summons? Facing Niko's parents wasn't going to be easy, especially knowing that they must've seen all the horrible things written about Niko because of her involvement with him. But Gemma wasn't going to let the journalists see she was rattled by Niko's private secretary asking her to go to the palace. 'Of course, Yiannis,' she replied. 'Callie, Petros—could you keep everyone going on today's plan, please? I'll be back as soon as I can.'

'Yes, Dr Stone,' they chorused.

Calliope squeezed her hand in sympathy. 'It'll be all right, Gemma,' she whispered. 'The palace will help.'

But, now that burst of anger had died down, Gemma was full of trepidation.

She and Niko hadn't been careful enough. They'd been photographed in a clinch.

How much damage had that caused—and how was she going to fix it?

CHAPTER NINE

'ARE YOU ALL RIGHT, Gemma?' Yiannis asked when they were both safely in the back of the car.

No. She wasn't all right. At all. But she was more worried about Niko than about herself. She winced. 'I'm sorry, Yiannis. I just lost my temper with the press.'

'I'm sorry I didn't get a chance to warn you. You didn't call me back, so I assumed you might not have seen the media this morning. I did try to call you to tell you what was happening. So did the prince,' he added gently. 'But you didn't answer your phone.'

'I didn't get any calls.' But when Gemma glanced at her phone, she could see a long list of notifications of missed calls and texts. 'Oh, no. I'm sorry. My phone must've been on silent.' She bit her lip. 'I did wonder why the press turned up in a pack like that. I assumed they'd had the press release and were all excited about the finds and the potential for tourism on the island, so I took them to see the mosaic. But instead of letting me tell them about it, they asked me about the prince and showed me what the media was saying about us. I'm sorry. I've made life difficult for Niko. I'll…' She blew out a breath. 'Actually, no. I can't say I'll fix it, because I don't know *how* to fix it. I've probably made it worse, because I lost my temper with them.' She gave him a rueful smile. 'You know the stereotype about having red hair and a hot temper? I really lived up to it. Stupidly. I gave them a lecture.'

'A lecture?' Yiannis asked.

She nodded. 'Some of my students filmed it. They're not planning to leak anything—my students, I mean. Callie—Calliope—said they were filming in case the journalists try to lie about what I said, and she wanted to make sure we have proof of what I did actually say to them.'

'It would be helpful,' Yiannis said, 'to have a copy of that.'

'All right. I'll ask Callie if she can send it to you,' she said. 'Give me a second and I'll text her now. I assume it's OK to give her your email?'

'It's fine,' Yiannis confirmed. 'Thank you.'

Gemma flicked into her messaging app and quickly asked Calliope to send the video to Yiannis. 'I'm not sure when she'll pick up the message,' she warned Yiannis, 'but when she does she'll send the video to you.'

He nodded. 'What did you say?'

She told him the gist of it. 'I'm sorry for making things worse. I'll take my direction from you, from now on.' She shook her head in frustration. 'I've had media training because of my job, and I should know better than to argue with the press. I should've said "no comment" and moved on, not even looking at the guy's phone. I know I shouldn't have taken the bait. But it made me so angry.'

'That they'd dragged up your past?' he asked gently.

'No, though that was bad enough. That just made me feel ashamed of how naive I'd been.' She grimaced. 'What I really hated was the way that they were all judging Niko so unfairly. I told them to put themselves in his shoes and think about how they'd feel. To think about his parents.'

'That's a perfectly reasonable thing to say,' Yiannis said.

'But all those horrible comments by readers on the stories—why do people think they have a *right* to sit in judgement? Most of them have probably never even met Niko. If they had, they'd realise he's going to be a really good king—he'll be fair and honest, and he'll do his best for the country. But they seem to have these set ideas of what a prince or a king is allowed to do and what's forbidden. Clearly I'm unacceptable to them for all sorts of reasons—I'm not royal, I'm not Greek, and I've been engaged before.' She ticked them off on her fingers, but she couldn't bring herself to say the one that broke her, because she didn't want to see Yiannis trying to be polite about it. Though she knew the truth: she hadn't been enough for Andy, so how could she possibly be enough for Niko and his kingdom? How could their prince fall in love with a woman whose judgement was so poor that she'd fallen for a man who jilted her at the altar and got someone else to break the news?

'Social media can bring out the worst in people,' Yiannis agreed, 'but it can also be a force for good.'

'It's going to need a lot of spin,' Gemma said. 'I feel horrible that I've made life more difficult for Niko.

And then there's his family. His parents have been through enough, without having to put up with all this nonsense.'

'Every kingdom has to deal with sticky patches,' Yiannis said.

This one felt a lot stickier than any situation Gemma had encountered before. And it was way out of her experience. But she was sensible enough to know that she needed advice from someone who knew how to deal with these things. She'd listen to Yiannis and Niko, and then she'd step up and do whatever had to be done.

Even if that meant never seeing Niko again; and the thought made her heart feel as if someone had just put a vice round it and squeezed.

Finally, the car pulled up to the palace gatehouse. Yiannis had a word with the security guard, and then the car took them round to a side entrance.

'The prince is waiting for us in his office,' Yiannis said.

Gemma hadn't even apologised to him, yet, or answered any of his texts. Still, she'd rather make her apologies face to face.

Yiannis used his keycard to enter the palace, and shepherded her through to Niko's office.

Niko looked up from his desk as the door opened. 'Gemma! Are you all right? I'm so sorry.'

At exactly the same time, she said, 'Niko, I'm so sorry. Are you all right?'

They stopped and stared at each other, realising they were gabbling over each other's words.

'I'll give you a moment,' Yiannis said. 'I'll go in

search of coffee and pastries. I think we're going to need caffeine and sugar to help us sort this out.'

'Great idea,' Niko said, appreciating his private secretary's tact. Right then, he needed some time alone with Gemma. 'Thank you, Yiannis.'

When the door had closed behind Yiannis, Niko stood up and leaned against his desk. 'Are you all right? I'm sorry I couldn't protect you from the press this morning.' He'd been horrified to see the reports in the media, and when Gemma hadn't answered her phone he'd asked Yiannis to check on her. He would've preferred to do it himself, but he knew the media would've scented a juicy story as soon as they saw him and they would've gone after her even harder.

'It isn't your fault,' she said.

'Actually, it is,' he said wearily. 'I kissed you on a beach without triple-checking first that nobody was there to notice.' Because he hadn't been able to resist her. Because he'd been selfish and let his feelings override his normal caution. Because he'd put his own desires before the needs of his country. 'It was careless of me—and you're the one who's caught all the flak. I'm sorry. It's hurtful, seeing your past dragged up and twisted.' Particularly when it was for entertainment.

'I think you came in for as much flak as I did,' she said wryly. 'More, actually. Your suitability as king is being called into question.'

They both knew that a year ago, it wouldn't really have mattered that Prince Nikolaos had dated a non-royal and kissed her. The media wouldn't have been as invested in the relationship. Now, with the weight of Niko's duty on his shoulders, it mattered so much more.

'I'm sorry that your parents have had to put up with all this, too,' she said. 'I'll write them a proper letter of apology.'

How typical of Gemma to think of other people before herself, Niko thought. 'You really don't have to, though I think they'd appreciate that,' he said. 'They know it's not your fault. My mother's view is that the press is having a slow news day and that's why they're making a fuss. Yiannis agrees. If we don't give them anything to write about, then it'll die down quickly.'

Niko knew the monarchy had faced difficult press stories before. A couple of years previously, one of Leo's former girlfriends hadn't been happy about him ending the relationship and had decided to give the press a kiss-and-tell story to get her revenge. Leo hadn't even needed the advice their parents and Yiannis had given him; he'd instinctively known how to handle it. Ignore it, even when the press weren't telling the truth, because discussing it would only give them more material.

Oh, Leo, he thought. You'd charmed the press back onto your side within a couple of days. I'm going to have to work twice as hard to do what you did naturally—and I'll do it, because I won't let the country down, I won't let our parents down and I won't let you down. I promise.

He forced himself to smile at Gemma and adopt a far more upbeat tone than he actually felt. 'Don't worry. They'll soon find something else to chase after.'

She winced. 'I might have messed that one up already.'

'How?'

'I, um, lost my temper with them. Not because of them dragging it all up about Andy,' she said. 'It was the way they were talking about you. And I wasn't letting them get away with smearing you. I, um, gave them a bit of a lecture,' she muttered, her cheeks bright red. 'Which probably gave them more ammunition. I'm sorry.'

She'd stood up for him?

But how?

Gemma had never had to face this kind of thing. Gossip among people who knew her, about her wedding-that-wasn't, was one thing; having strangers rake over your life and judge you unfairly because they didn't know who you really were, was very different.

But she'd taken the journalists to task. For him. 'You stood up for me.' He tipped his head to one side. 'That's…'

'Politically, probably the worst thing I could've done,' she said. 'I gave them more material to use against you.'

'Actually, that's probably one of the nicest things anyone's done for me,' he corrected. 'You took my side and you told them off.'

'Callie filmed it so I have proof of what actually happened.' She winced again. 'I called out the journalists on bullying and they won't take kindly to that.'

Niko wanted to hug her—except, given that this whole row in the media was about his inappropriate behaviour, he needed to keep his distance. 'The palace press office will help you if they attack you. We're not giving in to the bullies, Gemma.'

'I think,' she said, 'it might be better if I get on the next plane to London. As you said, if they don't have anything to write about, it'll all die down and they'll forget about me. If I stay here until the end of the dig, I'll just be fanning the flames.'

Niko walked over to her, then, and wrapped his arms round her. Distance be damned. She was feeling bad, and he was here, so he was going to comfort her. 'No. We're not letting them drive you away. You're here to do a job, and you have a right to do it.'

'The longer I stay, the more they'll criticise you. My leaving is the only real way to stop them talking.'

'Maybe there's another way,' he said. Everything that had been in his head, these last few days—how he felt about her, how he didn't want a marriage based on business interests, how he wanted *her*—felt as if it was bursting out of him.

She was talking about going back to London. He didn't want to lose her. He'd already lost too much he cared about. He wasn't going to stand by and risk losing Gemma, too.

She was everything he wanted in a partner. Everything. She understood who he was, seeing beneath the surface of the prince. Despite never having to deal with the press like this before, she'd stood up to them—for his sake. And she'd made him realise that he didn't have to be perfect to step into his brother's shoes: he just had to be himself. With Gemma by his side, her love supporting him, he'd be a far better ruler than he would if he did what everyone expected and entered into a loveless marriage with a princess.

Because he'd be happy.

And that made all the difference.

He pulled back slightly so he could look her straight in the eye and hoped she could see his sincerity. 'Marry me.'

'What?' She shook her head, as if she didn't quite believe what she'd just heard and was trying to clear her thoughts.

'Marry me,' he repeated. 'Instead of fighting the attraction between us and telling ourselves we can only have a temporary fling, maybe we should give in to it.' He remembered what she'd told him about feeling she wasn't good enough for Andy. He needed to make very sure Gemma knew he thought she was good enough for him. 'I think you'd make an excellent princess. An excellent queen.'

'That's insane, Niko. It can't possibly work, and you know it,' she said, and wriggled out of his arms. 'You're supposed to marry a princess. I'm not a princess. Not even close. Even if you could get away with marrying someone not royal, your country will expect you to choose someone who's at the very least Greek and understands your country's way of life. I'm a foreigner. The press is right about me. I'm not suitable for you, even as a fling. I'm definitely not bride material.'

'I think you are,' he said softly. 'I know Andy hurt you, and I realise it'll be hard for you to put your trust in another wedding, but I'm not Andy and I'd never treat you the way he did. Right now, I think you're letting your past get in the way of the solution that'd work for us both.'

She narrowed her eyes at him and took a step back, inserting space between them. 'Insulting me isn't going to get me to agree to doing what you want. And just because you're going to be the king, it doesn't mean you can tell me what to do.'

'I apologise. I didn't mean to insult you or boss you about.' He raked a hand through his hair. This was all going badly wrong. 'I l—' No. Perhaps he'd better slow this down. Given her reaction to his proposal—telling him that it was an insane idea—if he told her he'd proposed because he'd fallen in love with her, he was pretty sure she'd panic and back away. It was too much, too soon. 'I like you,' he amended, hoping that he'd somehow find the happy medium between showing her he wanted her, but without putting too much pressure on. 'I like you a *lot*. And the way we've worked together over the temple site makes me think we can be a good team. Yes, everyone's expecting me to marry someone royal—but that's simply because of tradition. It's not actually the law.'

She stared at him, as if not quite able to take it in.

'If anything,' he concluded, 'I think you not being a royal would be an advantage, because my people will feel that your background is like theirs and they'll take you to their hearts.'

He liked her, Gemma thought.

A lot, he'd said; but at the end of the day it was still *like*, not love. Her last relationship had been built on love, yet it had fallen apart at the altar. How could she possibly expect a relationship built on mere liking—plus convenience—to last through a wedding and beyond?

Doing what Niko suggested, announcing their engagement and then actually getting married, would be the quickest way to get her heart broken again. If she hadn't been enough for Andy, an ordinary man, how could she be enough for a prince and his entire kingdom?

And yes, she'd been falling in love with Niko over the last few days, wondering what life might have been like if they'd met when he was still an academic. Wondering if they could've had a real future together. But that had been a fantasy. Now, she had to face the reality. She wasn't future queen material. This morning was proof of that. Despite her media training, she hadn't coped well when things had gone wrong with the press. Instead of being cool and calm and collected, and discussing things rationally, she'd lost her temper over the way they'd treated Niko and she'd argued with them. She'd made enemies instead of doing a charm offensive getting them to work with her.

They'd never accept her as Niko's wife—and, from the look of the comments on the news stories, neither would the people of Amphithos.

Didn't the prince already have enough to deal with, coping with his brother's death and having to give up the career he'd built for himself? Wasn't it going to be hard enough for him, stepping up to the royal duties he'd never expected to have to fulfil? She wasn't going to make it worse by agreeing to marry him and then watching it all fall apart when he realised she just wasn't enough to be the Queen of Amphithos.

Giving up on Niko made her feel as if someone had just filleted her heart, but it was the only possible way forward. She needed to stay away from him—away from temptation. Even though she desperately wanted to hold him close, kiss him, and tell him that she liked him a lot, too, that in another world she would eventually have overcome her fears and said yes to his proposal, she knew that couldn't happen.

From now on, their relationship was going to be strictly business.

'I can't marry you,' she said. And then, before he could open his mouth to try and persuade her to change her mind, she added, 'I don't want to marry you.'

And then, while she still had the strength to move, she added, 'I'm sorry.' Putting one foot in front of the other took every ounce of her concentration, not to mention her coordination, but she made it. She paused at the door. 'I'm sorry,' she said again. Sorry that she couldn't be who he needed. Sorry that they'd never stood a chance. Sorry that she was hurting him, but she couldn't see any other way.

His amber eyes were full of misery, and she hated herself for pulling a rug from underneath him. But what other choice did she have? If she agreed to his plan, it'd end up in more heartache for them both, in the long run. It was much better to end things now.

'Goodbye,' she said softly, and left the room.

CHAPTER TEN

I CAN'T MARRY YOU.

Niko could maybe have worked with that.

But then Gemma had said the line that had floored him. *I don't want to marry you.*

He'd thought—hoped—that they'd got closer. That her feelings mirrored his own. That they were coaxing each other out of the shadows and into the light.

Clearly he'd been wrong. Very, *very* wrong.

And he was shocked by how much that hurt. So shocked and hurt that he couldn't utter a single sound.

He'd meant every word he'd said to her. They would make a good team. He really liked Gemma as a person—no, *more* than liked her. Liked the way she saw things. Liked the way she treated people. She'd make an amazing queen, empathetic and thoughtful.

But that was only part of it. In the short time they'd known each other, Niko had fallen for Gemma completely. All the ancient philosophy he'd read by Plato that talked about two people being two halves of one whole: with her, it finally made sense. They *fitted*. He wanted to be with her. He wanted to be by her side, support her in her career—and to know she was there for him, too. It didn't matter that it had all happened so quickly; he knew it was real.

Yet she'd just told him to his face that she didn't feel the same way.

He wasn't enough to make her want to stay here.

She didn't want to marry him.

Total rejection, from someone he'd felt such an affinity with—and it was all the more of a shock because he'd been so sure she felt the same way about him. They'd been able to talk for hours at a time and could still find yet more to talk about, the next time they'd seen each other. He'd thought they were in tune: intellectually, physically, emotionally.

How had he managed to get it so wrong?

'God, Leo. I wish you were here,' he muttered, staring at the framed photograph of his brother that sat on his desk.

Ironically, if Leo had still been there, this situation wouldn't have happened in the first place. Niko wouldn't have been struggling to be someone he'd never expected to be, the heir to Amphithos. And maybe he would've taken it more slowly with Gemma, got to know her over months rather than days.

Or maybe he was kidding himself. Her words echoed in his head: *I don't want to marry you.*

You couldn't get clearer than that, could you?

'I've lost the plot, Leo,' he told the photograph. 'Completely. I thought Gemma and I saw things the same way. We have so much in common. I thought we had a future, and all we had to do was be brave about it and reach for what we both wanted. But I panicked at the idea of her going back to London. I said the first thing that came into my head to try and change her mind. And obviously I got it completely wrong, because she told me she didn't want to marry me.'

In his mind's eye, he could even see his elder brother's rueful smile.

'Yeah. I'm an idiot,' he said. 'In all sorts of ways. And I'm trapped. Right now, I'm falling short at everything. Our parents are in bits, because they miss you even more than I do—you were their firstborn, and for a parent to bury a child is just the worst thing. I can't make things right for them. I can't fill the gap you left behind. Not that I ever want them to forget you, but I want them to remember you with smiles instead of having that yawning abyss of pain they don't think they'll ever manage to cross. I'm trying to learn to be the kind of king you would've been, but every day I'm working harder and harder yet I'm ending up further and further away from where I need to be. And I've managed to mess it up with the one woman who's made the world feel as if it makes sense for the first time since you died. It's all a mess, and I don't even know where to start fixing it.' He sighed. 'Maybe I shouldn't even try. Maybe I should love her enough to let her go and find happiness without me. Someone who doesn't have all the complications I do. Someone who can love her all the way back without the press whipping up rumours or keyboard warriors trumpeting their outdated views and hurting her.' He blew out a breath. 'Maybe I should just go with what the Palace Council want and marry a princess off their list. Someone I can rub along with.'

But it wouldn't be the same as marrying for love, the way his parents had. The thing he realised now he'd wanted for himself, too.

But as there was a knock at the door—Yiannis, he presumed—he knew he had to assume the persona everyone wanted to see. Prince Nikolaos, the serene and sensible heir to the throne. He'd just have to work a bit harder at getting it right and making sure the hot mess underneath it all didn't escape again.

Despite the action plan Yiannis had come with and persuaded Gemma to agree to—not responding to the press, referring all questions to the palace press office, and having some of the palace security team protecting the dig for the next week—the press, the next day, was a bloodbath. There were photos of Gemma at the dig, covered in dust, her strawberry-blonde hair gleaming in the sun—for once, she wasn't wearing her hat—and looking furious, her red face clashing with her hair.

And they mocked her. Just because she had red hair, they said, did she really think she was like Athena, the goddess of war? She'd practically declared war on the journalists. Shouted at them like a fishwife. How did she possibly think she could ensnare their prince?

Niko wanted to storm round to the pack of them and shake them until their teeth rattled. How dared they treat her like this?

He couldn't have a hissy fit and refuse to deal with them, because that would only be fuel to them and they'd treat her even worse; plus he needed to work with them, for the sake of Amphithos. But there was surely *some* way he could persuade them to see her for who she really was, and stop this relentless pursuit.

Yiannis walked into Niko's office and put a mug of coffee on his desk. 'If you don't stop grinding your teeth,' he observed mildly, 'your dentist will have a lot to say at your next checkup.'

'I...' Niko blew out a breath. 'Sorry. I should know better than to read the media. But I hate that they're going after her. They're *sharks*.'

'Maybe you need to see Calliope's video,' Yiannis said. 'May I?'

At Niko's nod, Yiannis took over the laptop's keyboard, and brought up the video from the folders he shared with the prince.

Niko watched it in silence.

Gemma's impassioned speech really made his heart squeeze. She saw right to the core of him—how he was trying so hard to be the prince the island needed, how he was struggling to leave his old life behind but he was determined to do it for his country's sake. She was standing up for him and for his parents, making the point that they weren't just the royal family, they were also human beings. She was asking the press to put themselves in his shoes and think how they'd really feel.

Fishwife? No.

Courageous? Absolutely.

But the thing that struck him most was that she'd stood up for him. *Really* stood up for him. The words she'd used, the passion on her face—they belonged to someone who loved him all the way back.

And then it hit him.

Given that Andy had jilted her at the altar, was it *marriage* that was the sticking point, rather than him? And in particular was the problem the kind of wedding he had to offer? Had she been put off by the idea of having to suffer all the pomp and glitter that the country expected of a royal wedding, televised and beamed round the globe, instead of the quiet family wedding full of heart that she wanted?

If that was the case, more importantly, could he find a way around it?

'She's magnificent,' he said. He looked at Yiannis. 'She's the one I want,' he said. 'I love her. I don't care that she's not royal. I don't care that she hasn't been born to the role. When I'm with her, I feel truly alive—truly myself. And I think she'd make a terrific queen. She can connect with ordinary people because she's one of them—even though at the same time she's very far from ordinary. She's special.'

'Your parents,' Yiannis said, 'happen to think the same. They were very touched by her letter.'

The one she'd written by hand instead of by email, apologising for making life difficult for the royal family with the press, and apologising even more for needing to turn down their invitation to supper on Monday nights. His mother had shown him. And she'd said quietly that this was the kind of strength a ruler needed: an ability to put themselves into someone else's shoes, kindness, and humility.

'But?' Niko asked, seeing the word written on his private secretary's expression.

'You need to give it time,' Yiannis said. 'Wait for the press to settle down again. Keep your distance from each other until then.'

Niko knew it made sense. He couldn't even send her a text saying he was thinking of her because it was too much of a risk—after all, how many people had had their messages hacked and spread all over the media? Yet, if he didn't send her a message to let her know she had his support, would she think he didn't care? Would she think he was a spoiled playboy prince who'd taken a fancy to her, on a whim, and then abandoned her to the less-than-tender mercies of the press?

As the week dragged on, he felt more and more miserable. It didn't seem as if the press would ever back off, and missing Gemma was a visceral ache that wouldn't go away. Even though he worked long hours, trying to tire his brain out so he didn't have the energy to think, it didn't work. In the still of the night, he missed her. Desperately. And there was nothing he could do to change it.

Gemma stared at her paperwork.

She was on top of it. Completely. But it was an effort to concentrate, because she really missed Niko. The work she loved wasn't an escape, either, because she associated the site so much with him.

Did he miss her? Or had he believed her when she'd said that she didn't want to marry him?

Well, she didn't want to marry him. Not in the big, fancy wedding that would be expected of the King of Amphithos.

But she missed Dr Niko Spiridon, the man who'd walked hand in hand with her along a moonlit beach and kissed her until her knees were weak. The man whose dream library was so close to the one of her own dreams. The man she couldn't stop thinking about and *wanting*.

Yiannis had spoken to her after she'd left the palace and talked her through the PR plan. She knew he was right: it was the safest way. All communications would go through him, and everything between herself and Niko would be strictly business. Nothing personal.

But it left Gemma with a huge gap in her life. She missed his ready smile, the light of interest in his eyes when he listened to her, the way they could talk for hours. She'd never met anyone she'd felt this in tune with, even Andy.

How had he become so important to her, so quickly?

Especially as they'd both known right from the start that they didn't have a future. They'd agreed that their fling was temporary, which made it safe. Yet it hadn't been safe at all, had it? When he'd walked on that moonlit beach with her, all her defences had dissolved into the sand. She'd fallen in love with him.

No. Worse than that. She actually *loved* him. It wasn't just the heart-thumping, exciting part of falling for someone—the thrill of the chase, or whatever you wanted to call it. This was something deeper. He was everything she was looking for. He had integrity and he thought about the needs of others. He appreciated things instead of taking them for granted. He listened when she shared ideas, said things that made her look in directions she hadn't thought about. Niko was the closest she'd ever met to someone who fitted the description of a soulmate. Plato's 'other half', made real, she thought wryly—and he was about the only person she knew who'd get that reference and tease her about it.

He'd actually asked her to marry him.

For his sake, she'd said no.

But what if she'd said yes?

She shook herself. It was pointless speculating, because she knew his country would never accept her. Even a week after the news had broken, the press were still panning her, claiming she saw herself as the Greek goddess of war simply because she had red hair. Yesterday, they'd even altered the photos they'd taken of her at the dig, adding a shield, a sword and an ancient Greek helmet.

But Athena wasn't just the goddess of war. She was the goddess of wisdom. Of knowledge. Of learning. Of arts and crafts. Associated with justice. Anyone from this part of the world would know that. But the media were clearly enjoying themselves poking fun at her, depicting her as a wannabe-warrior, and their readers had joined in the mockery.

Except jokes stopped being funny when one person was the sole butt of them.

By the middle of the following week, she was thoroughly miserable, and tired from sleepless nights where she missed Niko's company. Reading late into the night didn't help. Even the nice note that the queen had sent her—telling her 'this too shall pass'—didn't help, because then she'd made the mistake of listening to the Debussy piece the queen had played for her, and it had made her cry. She'd cried even more when she remembered that evening at the piano, singing together and laughing with Niko and his parents, as if she were one of them—which she knew she never could be.

Gemma forced herself to concentrate on her students. And on the Wednesday afternoon she was crouched by a trench, talking to a couple of her students about what they'd just found, when there was a loud rumble, followed by a yell.

She looked up to see that Petros, who had been kneeling at the edge of another trench, had disappeared. There was a hole in the ground where he'd been working. Clearly he'd fallen through it—but how far had he fallen? Was he hurt?

She went quickly over to the trench, and lay down so her weight was dispersed across a greater surface area; the ground was clearly unstable, and lying down meant she was less likely to cause another hole to appear. 'Petros? Are you all right?' she called. 'What happened?'

'The trench just gave way beneath me,' he called back. 'I think I'm in some kind of cellar.'

'Are you hurt?' she asked.

There was a scuffling noise, followed by an 'ow'. 'I can't put any weight on my left foot,' he told her. 'I landed awkwardly when I fell.'

That wasn't good. 'Did you hit your head at all?' she checked.

'No, but my left wrist and hand hurt as well.'

Which stood to reason, since he'd clearly fallen on his left side. At least his head was OK, she thought. Hopefully he didn't have concussion. 'Have you got any light down there?' If he could see what his surroundings were like, it might help them work out a rescue plan.

'Just what's coming through the hole,' he said.

'Right. First, we need to know what's down there and if the ground beneath you is stable. Then we need a rope so we can tie it round you and people up here can haul you out,' she said. 'Hang on. You're not going to be down there for long, I promise.'

The students had crowded round her, but to her relief they were sensible enough not to get too close to the hole. She directed one of the students to call the emergency services—an ambulance because she suspected Petros's foot and hand might be fractured, and firefighters in case they couldn't get Petros out. She asked another student to fetch some ropes and ladders, so they could spread their weight across the surface, and to collect the strongest members of the team to help haul him up.

'Shouldn't we wait for the fire brigade, rather than try to get him out ourselves?' one of the students said, looking anxious. 'That hole opened up out of nowhere. It's dangerous.'

'I know, but I don't want to risk more of the floor caving in and landing on Petros while we wait for the emergency services,' Gemma said. 'At least he's talking, so hopefully his injuries aren't serious.' He'd said he hadn't hit his head, but what if he *had*, and he'd blacked out for a second so he didn't remember the impact? They needed to get him checked out by the medics as soon as possible. 'We need to know what the situation is down there so we can sort out the rescue.' Fortunately there was a ball of twine in her pocket. She attached one end to the small and very bright flashlight she carried, switched the torch on, then started to lower it down through the hole. 'Petros, my flashlight is on the end of the string. What can you see?'

There was a tug as he grabbed hold of the flashlight. 'I was right—I'm in some kind of cellar. There are what look like storage jars down here. I'm not sure how stable the roof is,' he called back, a few moments later. 'There are a few little piles of earth dotted about on the floor.'

Meaning that the ground wasn't stable and had been crumbling away for a while, then no doubt the rain had weakened the area even more, seeping into the gaps. The hole would've opened up anyway; digging the trench had just forced it to happen a bit sooner. 'OK, Petros. Don't worry. We're going to get you out.' She'd been thinking about how best to do that. 'If we feed a rope down to you, will you be able to make a harness and tie it round yourself?'

'I don't think so,' he said. 'I think I might have broken my wrist because I can't move my fingers very well. I definitely can't grip well enough to tie a knot.'

'OK. We'll go for Plan B,' she said. She looked at the students who'd come over with rope and ladders to haul Petros out. 'We need to position the ladders round the hole to spread our weight, so we'll be less likely to make more of the earth around the hole collapse. Then I need you to lower me down so I can sort out a rope harness for Petros.'

'We can't lower you down. You're the boss,' one of them protested.

'I'm also probably the lightest person here,' she said, 'so it makes sense for me to go down. Plus do any of you know how to tie a rope harness?'

They looked at each other. 'No,' one of them admitted.

'Well, I do. Once I've got Petros in a rope harness, you can pull him up between you, and then you can lower the rope down again to get me out.' And hopefully the roof of the cellar would be stable enough not to crash into the hole and bury her.

It seemed to take for ever, but finally they lowered her down into the hole. The rope caught the edge of the hole when she landed, causing a little shower of dirt to fall.

Petros gasped. 'Is the roof going to fall in?'

She hoped not. She used her best lecturer voice, hoping she sounded a lot more confident than she felt and that it would reassure him. 'I'm sure it will be fine. The emergency services are on their way. Let's get this harness on you.'

She managed to support Petros to a standing position and tied the rope harness round him. It had been a few years since she'd last done this—in her last year at uni, when one of her housemates had taught her—but, although it took longer than she would've liked, she managed it.

'OK. Ready for you to pull Petros up,' she called.

It was worrying that the emergency services weren't here yet. Had it been just the cellar ceiling giving way, or had there been some sort of tremor affecting the whole island? What if the road was blocked and they couldn't get Petros to hospital to get him checked out properly? What if he had concussion, or worse?

Petros had left the flashlight with her; she shone the beam upward to watch him going up, then wished she hadn't when more earth fell from the edges of the hole. Should she move out of the way in case the ceiling caved in and buried her? Or were other parts of the ceiling even less stable?

Time seemed to slow, as if the seconds were ticking through treacle. And it was *dark* down here. Was that scrabbling she could hear? Rats? Or a trickle of earth that could turn into a roar?

She shivered. It was cold here, too.

Stop being pathetic, she told herself fiercely.

But she couldn't help wishing Niko was here. She'd felt brave, above the ground, when she'd come up with the plan to rescue Petros; but now her courage was starting to fail. What if the ceiling collapsed and she ended up choking to death beneath the rubble? What if she never got the chance to tell Niko how she really felt about him?

He'd been brave enough to ask her to marry him, and she'd hurt him—when she'd answered, he'd looked as if she'd just pushed him into an icy lake. Why hadn't she had the courage to be honest, and give him the answer she'd really wanted to give him? Why hadn't she said yes instead of no? Why hadn't she realised that doing the right thing didn't mean walking away—that it meant facing the press with him, as a team?

She could hear more scrabbling...or was that more earth trickling down, the precursor to a rumble and a huge fall? And why hadn't she heard any sirens yet?

She shone the light around—and then as the light shone on terracotta she remembered what Petros had said was down here in the cellar. Even more, now, she wished that Niko was with her. This was something he'd definitely want to share with her.

Carefully, she took her phone from her pocket and took several photographs.

Niko would definitely want to see these.

And she wasn't going through anyone else to show the photographs him. This was her excuse to see him again. A very, very valid excuse. And then maybe she could apologise, and they could—

A siren broke into her thoughts; a few moments later, one of the students called down. 'Dr Stone, the fire crew are sending a harness down for you. They want you to buckle it up, make sure the rope's attached, and tug the rope twice. Then they'll pull you out.'

She shone the beam of the flashlight up towards the hole; she could see a harness being lowered down on the end of the rope—and, ominously, another trickle of earth.

'I see it,' she called. 'But more earth is falling through the ceiling. You need to be careful up there.' What if the ground around the hole crumbled further? The fire crew could be pulled down with her, and badly hurt.

But she followed their instructions, buckling herself into the harness and tugging the rope twice so they could pull her up.

Swinging on a harness on the end of a rope definitely wasn't her idea of fun. But eventually she was back on the ground, standing on her own two feet.

'The paramedics think Petros has broken his wrist and his ankle, and they're not sure if he has concussion or not,' Calliope told her. 'They want you to go to hospital, too, so they can check you over.'

'I'm fine. I wasn't hurt and I don't need checking over,' Gemma said. 'The most important thing is to make this area safe, and to get some experts out here to check whether there are any other weak spots we need to avoid.'

'Are you refusing to go to hospital?' Calliope asked.

Gemma smiled. 'Yes, Callie, I am.'

'I'm beginning to think we should call you "Indy" instead of "Gemma",' Calliope teased.

'My hat and I are quite happy with what we're called now,' Gemma teased back, laughing. 'Now, we have work to do.' And then, with any luck, she could call Yiannis and arrange a private meeting with Niko.

CHAPTER ELEVEN

'AN ACCIDENT AT the site?' Yiannis asked into his phone.

Niko lifted his head and stared at his private secretary. Site? Was he talking about the temple? What kind of accident? Was Gemma all right?

'I see,' Yiannis said. 'And what does the hospital say?' *Hospital?*

Had she been hurt?

And that changed everything. The risk of press intrusion didn't matter any more, not if she was in physical danger. He needed to be with her, to be sure she was safe, and he wanted to sort out any help she needed. Worried, he went over to Yiannis's desk. 'What's happened?' he demanded. 'Is Gemma all right?'

'There's been an accident at the temple dig,' Yiannis said, putting the phone down. 'Gemma's not hurt. One of the students has a broken wrist and a broken ankle. Apparently, a trench collapsed unexpectedly— they didn't realise they'd dug it over the top of a cellar—and he fell through. Gemma got the students to lower her into the hole to rescue the student.'

She'd asked them to lower her into a hole where nobody knew what was at the bottom of it, and put herself at risk? 'She did *what*?' Niko asked, his eyes narrowing.

'That was the university calling. They said Petros—the student—is fine. Rather, he will be, once they've checked him over at hospital and put the fractures in plaster. And you can stop worrying about Gemma. The fire crew pulled her out. She's unharmed.'

'I need to hear that for myself. From her,' Niko said. 'I'll call her.'

'You're supposed to be keeping your distance from each other so you don't stir up any more scandal,' Yiannis reminded him.

'This takes precedence,' Niko snapped. Then he winced. 'I apologise, Yiannis. I'm worried about Gemma, but I shouldn't be taking it out on you.' He sighed. 'If I ring her she won't answer, because she'll stick to the rules. But you're her contact at the palace. She'll talk to you.' She sent Yiannis daily updates. Niko had read every one of the efficient and business-like communications. They'd made him miss her even more. The sparkle in her eyes as she talked about the job she loved. Her smile. The way she made the day feel brighter just by being in it. 'Can you ring her, then pass her straight to me, please?'

'Of course.' Yiannis gave a small nod, then made the phone call.

'Gemma? It's Yiannis at the palace. We've just heard the news. Are you all right?'

Oh, for pity's sake, would he just shut up and hand the phone over?

Before Niko could say it, Yiannis rolled his eyes. 'The prince would like a word.'

Niko forced himself to take the phone gently from

his private secretary rather than snatching it, the way he wanted to. 'Gemma, are you all right?' he asked urgently.

'I'm fine. Don't fuss.'

'What happened?' he asked.

'There's a cellar we didn't know about beneath the temple. When Petros took another layer out of the trench, the ground became unstable and he went through the floor. He's being patched up in hospital. I'm going there in a few minutes to check on him for myself, but in the meantime we've blocked off that part of the site until we can make sure the edges of the hole are shored up properly and the ground is stable.'

Relief made him sharp. 'What if the floor had fallen in while you were in the cellar? You could've been badly hurt—even killed!'

'Well, I wasn't,' she snapped back. 'I'm going now, Niko, because I need to sort out my students and make sure they're all OK.'

'I… Call me,' he said. 'Call me later tonight. Please.'

'We're supposed to be keeping away from each other,' she reminded him.

'I don't care.' He almost growled in frustration. 'You could have been hurt. I need to know you're safe—and I'm here if you need anything. Just call me. You're way more important than any nonsense from the press.'

'I'm fine. Don't fuss,' she said again, though this time her tone was gentler.

'Give Petros my best wishes,' Niko said. 'And please let me know how he is.' Just to make sure she knew it wasn't just an excuse to talk to her, he reminded her, 'He was my student, last year.' Which meant he still had a duty of care towards the younger man.

'All right. At the moment, we think it's a broken ankle and a broken wrist. And he's gutted that he won't be able to go down into the cellar and explore what's down there. I lowered my flashlight before I went down, and he left it for me when they pulled him out of the hole.'

'And you explored the cellar?' Unbelievable. She'd been in danger from a falling roof, could've been killed by a lump of masonry or buried under a suffocating heap of earth, yet she'd explored?

'Not quite. I stayed where I was, in reach of the rescue team,' she said, 'but I shone the light around.' She paused. 'There are storage jars. Big ones. But *don't* get any ideas,' she warned.

He knew she was thinking exactly the same thing that he was.

This was like when Knossos had been excavated, more than a century ago, and large storage jars had been found. Specifically, one with an octopus painted on it. What if these jars, stored for centuries underneath the floor of Amphitrite's temple, were painted with the kind of sea creatures associated with the goddess? And were there remains of anything inside the jars? Oil, grain—or even wine?

'If there's wine in any of those jars, my father will want to see it,' he said.

'Your father is *not* taking the risk of being attached to a flimsy harness and going down into an unsafe cellar. And neither are you.' Her voice was slightly croaky. 'Niko, if anything happened to you…'

The emotion in her voice gave him hope. 'That's what I was thinking when I heard you'd gone down the hole to rescue your student,' he said softly. 'I needed to talk to you, to hear for myself that you were OK.' Despite the fact she'd broken his heart by telling him she didn't want to marry him, he'd needed to know she was safe.

'I'm fine. Really, I am. And we're not supposed to be in contact. Not until the press back off.'

Which would be when? This week, next week, sometime, never? Niko wondered. 'I don't care about the press.' She was more important to him.

'I need to go and see Petros,' she told him.

'I know.' He took a deep breath. 'And I know we're not supposed to be in contact—but I just needed to hear your voice.' More than that. He needed *her*. But he wasn't going to pile on the pressure by telling her.

'When I was down in the cellar, I thought of you.'

She had? The hope flared a little brighter.

'I wished you'd been there with me. Not because I was scared—well, I was, a bit,' she admitted, 'but because I wanted to share the discovery with you. Talk to you about Knossos and whether the cellars mean there was a palace nearby.' She paused. 'I took photographs from where I was standing—obviously I wasn't going to risk poking around until the ceiling was made safe. I haven't shown anyone else, yet.'

The flare turned into a blaze. This wasn't solely business, was it? She wanted to share her discovery with him, and not just because he was the prince or even because he was the one who found the site. It was the connection between them that mattered.

Maybe they could use this as an excuse to see each other...

'I'll call you later this evening,' she promised. 'By videocall. I'll have downloaded the photos to my laptop by then.'

Meaning he'd be the first person after her to see those photos.

'I'll look forward to that,' he said.

But knowing that he was going to see her—even if it was only on a screen—thrilled him more, much more, than the idea of learning about the secrets of the hidden cellar.

'Happier, now?' Yiannis asked when Niko ended the call.

'Yes. She's definitely OK. She snapped at me,' Niko said. And he was aware that his smile felt a mile wide. Because she was safe. Because she worried about him, too. And because she was talking to him again.

Over the next couple of hours, the media picked up the story of the rescue. Photos—obviously taken via drones—showed the hole in the middle of the trench. A couple of enterprising journalists had managed to visit Petros and photographed the casts on his wrist and his ankle, as well as interviewing him about precisely what had happened.

And suddenly all the hostility the press had shown towards Gemma vanished. They recognised how brave she'd been, putting Petros's needs before her own safety and getting herself lowered into that hole to rescue him.

'Well, well,' Yiannis said. 'Look at the comments on these stories. There's been a one-hundred-and-eighty-degree turn on what the public were saying about her earlier. Now, they're saying that she's brave and honest.

They're saying that she puts others first.' He paused dramatically. 'And they're saying that she'd make the perfect princess.'

'She would,' Niko said. 'I know it. My parents know it. You know it. And now the people admit it, too.'

'You look as if you think there's still a problem,' Yiannis said.

'There is. Gemma doubts herself,' Niko said. 'I'm assuming you know from that dossier what happened with her ex.' Niko still hadn't read it, and had no intention of reading it. Gemma's word was enough for him. 'In her shoes, I'd be wary, too. All I can do is hope that I can prove to her what I see and make her see it, too.'

Though he rather thought that what she needed was for him to step up for her. She'd rescued Petros, despite the fact she knew it was dangerous and the roof of the cellar could've fallen in on her. Maybe he should take an emotional risk that matched her physical bravery, and tell her the truth about his feelings for her. Maybe he was kidding himself that she returned those feelings, but the least he could do was to tell her the truth. Let her know that he hadn't asked her to marry him because she was merely a convenient choice, but because she was the *only* choice he wanted.

Because he loved her.

That was something that needed to happen face to face. Even a videocall wouldn't be enough.

He sent her a text. Can I send a car for you this evening? I think we need to talk properly, face to face.

Though if she thought he meant talking in his apartment, she might back off. I was thinking we could talk in the palace gardens, he added. Where we'll be in full view of anyone in the palace, but we'll be able to talk with some privacy.

That got a reply. Very Jane Austen of you, my dear Prinkípas Nikolaos.

?? he responded, not quite getting her drift.

What you're suggesting is a bit like having a chaperone at a Regency ball. You'd need to be in public view to prevent any scandal spreading—in a garden, say, rather than on a secluded balcony or in a room with a closed door. But if you were walking at a distance from everyone else, you'd be able to talk privately without being overheard.

Ah. Now he understood. The Jane Austen way works for me, he replied. Shall I send a car for seven?

Eight might be better, she said. It's been an unusual day, and I think my students need a bit of reassurance from me. I'm having dinner with them at Theo's.

This time, it wasn't an invitation for him to join them. Understood—I'll send the car to Theo's at eight, he texted back. How's Petros?

Enjoying having people making a fuss of him, she said. But he's seriously fed up that he won't get to be the one bringing up the contents of the cellar he crashed into. He was too shocked from the fall and in too much pain to really see what was around him. I'll let him record all the finds so he doesn't feel left out.

Good solution, he agreed. See you later.

And knowing that he was going to see her tonight made all the misery of the last few days feel as if it was worth it.

CHAPTER TWELVE

IT WAS UTTERLY RIDICULOUS that she felt so nervous, Gemma thought as she climbed into the back of the car Niko had sent for her and fastened her seatbelt. For pity's sake, she'd been to the palace plenty of times before tonight. Even on her very first visit, when she'd accidentally trespassed, she'd been made welcome.

Though the last time she'd been at the palace had been tough. The day when the news had broken that Niko was seeing her. His people and the press had reacted so badly that they'd been forced to stay apart ever since.

He'd made it pretty clear that he'd missed her as much as she'd missed him. When he'd thought she might be injured, he'd ignored all the potential problems with the press and spoken to her directly, telling her to call him if she needed anything at all and making it very clear that he was there for her. The complete opposite of Andy.

Or was she hoping so hard that this was what he meant, she was missing the real purpose of him wanting to see her face to face? Had she got it wrong?

They both knew he didn't have the freedom to do whatever he liked. If the press got wind of them seeing each other tonight, they'd react badly. As the heir to the kingdom—the man who'd be stepping up to the kingship next year—Niko had to put the crown first. Which meant keeping his distance from a non-royal and very foreign distraction.

Maybe, she thought with a sinking feeling, over these last few days of their separation, Niko had thought about her suggestion that she should leave the island. Maybe he'd realised she was right, and tonight he was going to ask her to go. He had too much integrity to leave it to a minion to give her the news, especially as he knew about the way Andy had jilted her. He wouldn't put her through something similar a second time. He'd tell her himself. Face to face.

She didn't know the car driver, and he hadn't tried striking up a conversation with her, the way a taxi-driver usually would. Or maybe drivers who worked for the palace were trained not to converse with guests. Either way, the quiet journey made her nerves tighten even more.

Yiannis was waiting for her at the gatehouse. 'Good to see you, Gemma. Let me take you through to the gardens,' he said with a smile.

'Thank you, Yiannis.' She forced herself to smile brightly at him. Fake it until you make it, right? If she pretended she was cool, calm and collected, then maybe she wouldn't feel twitchy any more.

She had no idea whether she was overthinking things or not. She could ask Yiannis, but she didn't think he'd enlighten her. He'd welcomed her, but at the end of the day he was still Niko's inscrutable private secretary.

'I'll leave you to talk to Niko,' Yiannis said, when he'd let her through a gate into the most gorgeous garden. Many of the plants had silvery foliage and blueypurple flowers. She recognised lavender, salvia, oregano and thyme, but there were other plants she'd never seen before; the sheer gloriousness of the flowers made her want to go over and smell them. There was a creamy-white rose rambling all over a low wall; and, best of all, the garden overlooked the sea and the setting sun.

In another world, she would've loved the romance of the setting and enjoyed the view. In another world, she and Niko could've stood together to watch the colours shimmer across the sky, hearing the birds sing and enjoying the sweet scent of the flowers.

But this was reality. The end of their fling. And Niko had clearly planned to do this face to face, because he wasn't a coward who'd make other people handle the difficult stuff for him.

He was sitting on a wrought iron bench, looking out to sea; when the gate clicked behind her, he looked round, saw her, and stood up.

'Thank you for coming to see me,' he said.

'You're welcome,' she replied, matching his formality.

What now? Was he going to shake her hand? Every nerve in her body wanted him to wrap his arms round her, kiss her until they were both dizzy, and tell her he'd missed her. Maybe he wanted that, too. But she knew that wasn't why she was here. This was going to be a formal goodbye.

In private, yet still in public, just as she'd suggested.

The prince was going to tell the commoner who'd fallen in love with him that it simply wasn't possible for them to be together.

'Please. Take a seat,' he said, gesturing to the bench.

'Thank you.'

He waited politely until she'd taken a seat, then sat next to her.

'This garden's amazing,' she said. 'All the blues and purples—and you overlook the sea as well.'

'It's my favourite view in the world,' he said.

One he hadn't shown her before. Then again, they'd been in too much of a hurry to explore each other. There hadn't been time for him to show her round the palace gardens.

'I see there are lots of herbs,' she said, trying to stifle her nervousness with small talk.

'The bees like it,' he said. 'The thyme honey from the palace hives is spectacular.'

She took a deep breath. Time to be brave and face the truth. To rip off the sticking plaster. 'Why did you ask me to come here?' she asked.

Instead of answering, he asked, 'Have you seen the press today?'

Half of her was tempted to point out that it was rude to answer a question with a question, but that would only drag things out. Instead, she gave him a truthful reply. 'I've been avoiding it, actually, in case they've made up any more memes about me,' she said. 'Those horrible photos where they added Athena's battle-helmet, shield and sword… But I knew they were trying to annoy me and they would've mocked me even more if I'd reacted, so I had to suck it up and ignore it.' She gave a huff of wry laughter. 'They really don't know their mythology, do they? She's not just the goddess of war.'

'No. She's the goddess of wisdom, associated with

justice and creativity,' he said. 'All of which describe you. You're wise, you're fair and you're creative.'

But she wasn't wanted around here, was she? Or he wouldn't be bothering with all this small talk. He'd be holding her close, telling her he'd worked out a way to fix everything and they could be together.

The fact he wasn't doing any of that told her pretty much where she stood. 'Thank you for the compliment,' she said coolly.

His beautiful amber eyes regarded her steadily. 'You did the right thing, not rising to the bait. But the press—and their commentators—have rather changed their minds about you, this afternoon.'

She frowned at him, not understanding.

'They're all thrilled by how you rescued Petros. How brave you were,' he explained. 'You didn't know how unstable the land was, but you still went in after him. You tied a rope harness for him. You got him out safely.'

'It's my job to look after my students.' She flapped a dismissive hand. 'I was the lightest one on site, and I know how to tie a rope harness—I had a flatmate at uni who was a climber and was on the local mountain rescue team during the holidays, and she taught me some basic techniques,' she explained. 'So it made sense for me to be the one to go into the cellar.'

'It was dark,' he said, 'and you had no idea what was down there.'

'Here be dragons?' she suggested, thinking of the way medieval map-makers had marked unknown territories. She gave a wry smile. 'Callie says the students are thinking of changing my name on the site to "Indy".'

Niko hummed the Indiana Jones theme tune and grinned. 'Actually, that's not so far off. Some of the commenters have compared you to Indiana Jones,' he said. 'And a sizeable chunk of them have decided that you're actually better than a princess—you're brave and capable, more than just a pretty face. Though you're that as well,' he added.

And oh, that smile. It made her heart feel as if it had done a somersault. A triple somersault, even. Niko thought she was pretty. And he'd told her before that he liked her 'a lot'.

But that wasn't enough to build a relationship on.

Not even close.

Her feelings must've shown on her face, because he grimaced. 'I apologise. That was incredibly patronising. And that's not who I am or who I want to be.' He shifted to face her. 'Gemma. When you threw me out of the dig, I thought you were the most amazing woman I'd ever met. But I'd barely scratched the surface. The more I got to know you, the more I liked you.'

She waited for the 'but' to drop. But he was a prince and she wasn't royal, so they should never have started their fling?

'But it isn't just liking,' he said, throwing her off balance. 'It's a lot more than that. And it's everything about you. I love you, Gemma. We haven't known each other for very long, but it's long enough for me to be sure that you're the one I want to spend my life with. The one I want to be my queen.'

He loved her?

But he couldn't.

It wasn't allowed.

She focused on the one bit she could argue about. He'd asked her to marry him a week ago—a knee-jerk reaction. Convenience. 'Your *convenient* queen,' she said.

'No. You're not the convenient choice. At all. Actually, you're the only choice,' he said.

Oh, for pity's sake. What happened to honesty? Of course she wasn't a proper choice! She narrowed her eyes at him. 'That's rubbish, and you know it. You're supposed to marry a princess and produce an heir to take over the country from you,' she said. 'I'm not royal. And even if I was, my job as your wife would be to provide an heir.' What if she couldn't live up to those expectations? What if she wasn't enough? 'What if I couldn't have children? What would happen then?'

'You're making mountains out of molehills, Gemma,' he said softly. 'Instead, you could always ask me what I've been doing while we've been staying away from each other and waiting for the press to calm down.'

She had no idea where this was going, but she'd humour him. For now. 'What have you been doing?'

'Checking the constitution. Very thoroughly,' he said. 'And it seems that, actually, I don't have to marry a princess. Traditionally, the heir to the throne has married someone of royal blood, but it's not actually written in the constitution that my bride has to be a princess or even the most minor of royals. Which means I'm free to do what other royal heirs in Europe have done—I can marry the person I want to marry, regardless of

their background. And you're right. We need to produce an heir. But if we can't, who's to say you're the
one at fault? It might be me.'

She hadn't thought of that. She'd just panicked, feeling insecure and remembering how she hadn't been
enough for Andy.

'There are other possibilities,' he continued. 'We
could foster. Adopt. This is a modern monarchy and it
needs to move with the times. If we need to change the
rules, then we can petition Parliament to make those
changes.'

'Right,' she said, but she couldn't quite believe him.

'I also talked to my father,' Niko said. 'I asked him
what he would've done if my mother hadn't been of
royal blood. And he said—I quote—"I would've married her anyway. I've only had eyes for her since the
moment I saw her playing the piano." Which is pretty
much how I feel about you. I love you,' he said again.
'I've only had eyes for you since you showed me round
the temple site. When I realised I could talk to you
about the stuff that matters to me. When I realised that
you see me for who I am—the nerdy historian—and
you still seemed to enjoy my company.'

'I do. I did,' she corrected herself, because she still
thought he was in cloud cuckoo land—thank you, Aris-
tophanes—and this wasn't going to end well.

'Dr Stone,' he said. 'Gemma. I want to spend my life
with you. I want to grow old with you, learn to run this
country with you by my side, grow our family if we're
lucky, and support you in your career.'

Her career? Apart from the fact that she was convinced he'd got this all wrong, if by some crazy means they did actually get married, no way would she be allowed to continue as an archaeologist. She'd be the queen. Her job would be to produce an heir and do whatever the king wanted.

It must've shown on her face, because he said quietly, 'Just because I'm going to be the king, it doesn't mean you have to give everything up. You won't be able to work full time, admittedly, because I'll need you to help me host visitors, but we'll learn to juggle things.'

He seemed to have an answer for everything; but there was one thing he couldn't change.

'But your people need to approve your bride,' she pointed out. And his people had made it clear they didn't approve of her. The newspapers had been full of how she'd turned his head and ruined his judgement, and how he'd be a failure as a king.

'Actually, they do approve of you,' he said. 'That's why I asked you if you'd seen the news today. Look.' He grabbed his phone from his pocket and found the newspaper's website. 'I'm switching the website to translate it all into English,' he said, 'so you can see it for yourself and be sure I'm not just trying to sweet-talk you by translating it and spinning it at the same time. Look at the comments.'

Trying to ignore the trepidation, she read the page and scrolled down further. The words stunned her.

Worthy of our prince.
Brave.
Honourable.
Strong.

'See?' he asked gently.

'What about your parents? What if they don't approve?'

'Oh, they do. They like you very much,' Niko said. 'And they appreciated your letter, by the way.'

The heartfelt apology she'd written by hand. 'I...' She couldn't think straight.

'If you're stuck,' he said, 'let me be your prompter. This is the bit where you're supposed to say that you love me, too, and you'll marry me.'

'You haven't asked me to marry you.' At least, he hadn't asked her *today*. The last time he'd asked her, she'd been sure it was a knee-jerk reaction and said no.

'Then let me ask you now,' he said. He dropped to one knee in front of her and took her hand. 'Gemma Stone, you dazzle me. I love everything about you. Your warmth. Your spirit. Your mind. I want to wake up with you every morning, and feel your pulse beating against mine as we fall asleep. I want to make a family with you, if we're lucky. I want to do nerdy stuff with you. I want to kiss you stupid in my library. I want you to help me fill the palace with love and laughter, make it feel like a home again. Will you marry me?'

It was all so extravagant. Like Andy's proposal had been. All the pomp and the noise.

She hadn't realised she'd spoken aloud, until Niko got to his feet again, scooped her up, and sat on the wrought iron bench, settling her on his lap.

'It doesn't have to be all pomp and noise,' he said. 'There will be some—unfortunately, it goes with my job. But we'll be grounded. Dr Stone and Dr Spiridon.

That's who we are and who we'll always be. Just…we'll also have a bit of a side hustle.'

'You mean, we'd be the King and Queen of Amphithos, which is really *not* a side hustle,' she said. 'I'm not sure I'm worthy of being queen.'

'Oh, but you are,' he said. 'I saw that video Callie took of you when you called the press out on their behaviour. You were magnificent.'

She felt the colour heating up her face. 'You saw it? Oh, no. Please tell me it wasn't leaked online.'

'No. Yiannis showed me the copy Callie sent him. And I showed my parents,' he said.

She groaned and hid her face in her hands. 'That's hideously embarrassing,' she muttered.

'No,' he corrected. 'You were brave. You stood up for me. You stood up for my parents.' He paused. 'My dad said the press had a point about you being like the goddess Athena—a warrior when you're angry, but for the most part you're actually the other bit of her. The goddess of wisdom and associated with justice.'

'That's…kind of him.' Her toes curled with embarrassment.

'No. My dad doesn't say things he doesn't mean,' Niko said. 'Gemma, I love you. I want you as my queen. My parents want you as my queen. My country wants you as my queen. Why can't you see how perfectly you'd fit?'

She thought about it.

Could she fit?

He'd said he loved her. He loved her spirit and he loved her mind.

Which meant he loved her for who she was.

She was *enough*.

'If I say yes,' she said, 'that means we'll have a flashy wedding.'

'It goes with the territory,' he said. 'Actually, all Greek weddings are flashy. Everyone celebrates and it's not like English weddings where you invite some people to some bits only. Everyone does the whole lot. You don't walk down the aisle on your father's arm to be given away—you walk with your whole family and you meet me at the door.'

That hadn't occurred to her.

It wouldn't be an English wedding. It'd be here in Amphithos. A Greek wedding.

'It's the chance for everyone to have a party and celebrate love,' he said. 'But we can work round it. We can have a quiet wedding, first. A private service, not televised. You, me, family and close friends only. And then we'll have a public blessing of our wedding. It doesn't even have to happen on the same day. We can change things to make them work however you want them to. Whatever makes you comfortable and happy.'

He was prepared to argue her case against the Palace Council and maybe his parents?

Obviously her worries must've shown in her expression, because he said. 'Just as you stood up for me, I'll stand up for you. I want you. I love you for who you are. And if that means having a quiet wedding in your parish church first, or a civil ceremony in a museum in London after closing time, then we'll do it.'

'That'd be cheating your country,' she said.

'No.' He brought her hand to his mouth and kissed it. 'They'll be disappointed, but they'll learn to accept that some things need to be private. If you want a private ceremony, then that's what we'll do.'

He'd go against tradition for her.

Because she was still letting the past hold her back.

But if she was brave enough to let herself be lowered through an unstable hole into a cellar, she could be brave enough to face another big, splashy wedding. Because Niko wasn't Andy. He'd never let her down. And she thought about what he'd said. The service would be totally different.

'Yes,' she said. 'I'll marry you. And we'll do the public ceremony. If you can be brave enough to marry a commoner, then I can be brave enough to walk with my family and meet you at the church door.' Even though she rather suspected what he meant by 'church' might actually be the cathedral.

'Sure?' he asked.

'I'm sure,' she said.

He coughed. 'I was looking for two other little words.'

'Two?' she asked. 'Isn't it three?'

'In English, yes. In Greek, it's two.'

She smiled. 'You need to expand my vocabulary. Teach me.'

'*S'agapó*,' he said.

'*S'agapó*,' she repeated. 'I love you.'

His whole face lit up with joy and love.

And then he kissed her.

CHAPTER THIRTEEN

The following spring

LEONIDAS HAD ABDICATED in January, and Gemma had been by Niko's side as he swore an oath in Parliament, then was proclaimed King Nikolaos II by the Prime Minister. Although the coronation was a quiet affair, there were still crowds in the square outside the palace, waving flags and waiting to see the new king; they'd cheered as Niko appeared on the balcony with the Prime Minister. The cheers had been even louder when Niko had beckoned to Gemma to join him, and kissed her on the balcony. 'My first duty as King—to kiss my wife-to-be,' he'd told her with a smile.

And now today was their wedding day: a perfect Greek spring day, with flowers everywhere, blue skies and sunshine.

Gemma had butterflies in her stomach, but she knew this wasn't going to be like the disastrous wedding day she'd had with Andy. The structure of the ceremony would be different, and the bridal traditions were different, too. And, most importantly, her future husband wasn't the kind of man who was too much of a coward to face his own decision—the kind of man who'd dump her at the altar and get someone else to tell her.

Greek weddings—even royal ones—were family affairs. Her entire family had come to stay at the palace for a few days before and after the wedding: her parents, her brother and sister-in-law, her niece and nephew, her aunts and uncles, her closest friends and their partners. It had been lovely to catch up with them all, introduce them to Niko's family and friends, and to show them round the island that had become her home six months ago, when the university where she worked had sent her on secondment to Amphithos with a view to the university offering her a permanent part-time role at the start of the next academic year. And her favourite part of the evening had been when Elena had played the piano for them, and insisted on all the women joining her in singing Wham songs—Elena and Cassie, Gemma's mum, had bonded over their shared love of George Michael and their shared inability to hit one particular high note, as well as teasing Gemma's dad, Michael, that Cassie had fallen in love with his name before she fell in love with the man himself. Meanwhile Leonidas and Michael had commiserated with each other on their wives' musical choices, rolling their eyes but teasing them affectionately.

Other royal guests had arrived, the previous day, including Elena's sisters and their families. Last night, Elena and Leonidas had held a formal family dinner at the palace to give everyone a chance to meet and mingle.

And Gemma couldn't wait to marry Niko today: the first day of the rest of their lives together.

'Can you run us through the day again, darling?' Cassie said. 'I don't want to make any mistakes.'

'OK. We walk to the church as a family,' Gemma said, 'and we meet Niko and his family at the church door. He gives me my bouquet, and then we walk down the aisle together. Everyone else walks behind us and takes their seats.'

'So your dad isn't walking you down the aisle and giving you away?' Daisy, Gemma's sister-in-law, checked.

'That's not how they do it here. There isn't a best man or a ringbearer, either, at least not in the way we'd do it in England,' Gemma explained. 'Instead, we have "sponsors" who help during the ceremony. They're usually someone older than the bride and groom, and they both have to be members of the Greek Orthodox church or we would've asked Ed to be Niko's. Elena's oldest sister Nina is Niko's godmother and she's agreed to be my *koumbara*, and Leonidas's best friend, Konstantin, is Niko's godfather and will be his *koumbaro*.'

'I assume the service will all be in Greek?' Cassie asked.

'Yes, but we've translated everything to English on the order of service, and explained what's happening in all the rituals,' Gemma said. 'After the service, the photographer will take photographs, and we give everyone the wedding favours we made yesterday.' Although the palace event planners had organised everything, Elena had said it was traditional for the family to make the wedding favours themselves. Gemma had enjoyed the production line of putting five white sugared almonds in gold organza bags and tying them with a ribbon, with everyone chatting and laughing; it had felt like a proper family affair. 'Niko and I will do a circuit of the city in an open horse-drawn carriage while everyone else goes back to the palace, and then we'll join you for the wedding breakfast, cake and dancing.' The idea of the carriage ride felt slightly daunting; would the press switch back to mocking her again, the way they had when the news of her relationship with Niko had broken, or would they be happy to celebrate Niko and Gemma's love for each other? And, although Niko's people seemed to have taken her to their hearts since she'd rescued Petros, what if they changed their mind again and greeted her with boos instead of cheers?

She shoved the worries away. Whatever happened, Niko would be right by her side. They'd make it work—together.

'Are we still doing the "something old, something new" tradition?' Daisy asked.

'Absolutely. The something old is my necklace—the one Mum and Dad gave me on my twenty-first,' Gemma said. 'Something new is the dress. Something borrowed is my tiara—Elena lent it to me, and I'm not even going to *think* about how much the diamonds are worth, or I'll be patting my head all day to make sure it's still in place! And Lily—' Gemma's best friend '—gave me a blue ribbon to be sewn into the hem of my dress.'

'Everything's sorted, then,' Cassie said. 'You'll get your bouquet at the church door, and we all have corsages.'

'Which will be delivered any second now,' Gemma said, glancing at her watch.

'Your dress and veil are both hung up, ready for you to change. Where are your shoes?' Daisy asked.

'Ah. Apparently Konstantin brings them over to me while Niko's getting ready,' Gemma said. 'In Greece, the bride's shoes are a gift from the groom.'

'Please tell me it's not going to be like that reality TV show where the groom sorts out the wedding and the bride doesn't get any say in it—or a chance to try the shoes on to make sure they at least fit,' Cassie said, looking slightly anxious.

'Apart from the fact I'd trust Niko to get it right, I chose the shoes myself. They're comfortable, and I tried them on with my dress to make sure they work with the hemline,' Gemma reassured her. 'Niko paid for them and took them for safekeeping. When Konstantin gets here, we need to write the names of all the single women at the wedding on the bottom of my shoes.' She smiled. 'Apparently, according to tradition, the ones that get rubbed out are the ones who'll get married next.'

'Is that instead of throwing your bouquet to see who catches it?' Daisy asked.

'It is,' Gemma confirmed.

Nina, Niko's aunt who was to be Gemma's *koumbara*, came in to check whether anyone needed anything.

'We're just waiting for the hairdresser and make-up artist to arrive,' Gemma said with a smile. 'And you look beautiful, Nina.'

'Thank you, *louloúdi mou*,' Nina said with a smile. 'But you will be the most beautiful one of all, today. As you should be.'

She bustled round sorting out coffees and pastries for everyone, including for Konstantin when he came over to drop off Gemma's shoes.

When everyone's hair and make-up had been done, and the hairdresser had fixed the tiara in place, finally it was time for Gemma to get dressed. Her wedding dress was simple, a confection of locally-made lace and tulle with a sweetheart neckline and lace shoulders and sleeves. Most of the lace was floral, but there was a tiny dolphin at the centre of her neckline as a nod to Amphitrite—whose temple had brought her and Niko together.

'Beautiful,' Nina said, and took photographs with everyone's phones when the official photographer had finished.

Finally, Nina's phone shrilled with an alarm. 'Time to go,' she said. 'Even though I'm part of Niko's family, from today our family will also be yours, Gemma, and yours will be his. Plus I'm your *koumbara*, so it's my job to get your side of the family there on time,' she added with a smile.

Because the palace was right next door to the cathedral, they'd dispensed with cars and carriages, planning to walk from the front door of the palace across to the cathedral. There were barriers to mark off the walkway for the bridal party, and beyond that were throngs of people waiting to catch their first glimpse of the bride, many of them wearing crowns and waving flags.

Several people called out to her, and Gemma had learned enough Greek to know they were wishing her good luck.

'*Efcharistó!*' she called back, waving. '*Kali sas ygeia!*'

The fact she'd used their own language to say thank you and wish them well made the crowd roar with approval. And suddenly all Gemma's worries melted away. Because today she was outrageously happy. She was marrying the true love of her life, and nothing else mattered.

She could see an amazing arrangement of flowers twining round the two pillars outside the cathedral door, and then cascading down the steps. In between the pillars, Niko waited with his family and Konstantin, holding the very simple bouquet Gemma had chosen. It was made from lily of the valley, the royal family's flower, combined with olive leaves; the stems were tied with a white silk ribbon.

'*Kaliméra*, my gorgeous wife-to-be,' he said, smiling at her as she reached him.

'*Kaliméra*, my gorgeous husband-to-be,' she said, feeling ridiculously shy and as if she'd burst with joy all at the same time.

His beautiful amber eyes were full of love as he looked at her. He gave her the bouquet, then took her father's hand and kissed it as a sign of respect. 'I promise I will make your daughter happy,' he said softly.

'I know you will,' Michael said, smiling at him. 'Just as she'll make you happy. I couldn't be prouder of you both.'

The crowd watching in the square outside cheered; Niko took Gemma's hand, and together they turned and waved to the crowd—Niko with his free hand, and Gemma with her bouquet.

Then they walked through the open doors of the cathedral and down the aisle together, Niko on the right, towards the altar in the centre where the archbishop was waiting to marry them. Their families followed them inside and sat in the pews.

The archbishop was dressed in magnificent gold and white vestments, wearing a gold mitre. He welcomed them warmly, then spoke a few sentences in Greek before translating into English. 'Welcome to our church. We are here today for the wedding of King Nikolaos to Gemma. Not everyone is of our faith or familiar with the rites of our services, so I hope you will find the explanations useful in the order of service booklet. Welcome. And let the betrothal begin.'

He started with prayers and blessings, and then moved to the exchange of rings. In keeping with the Greek tradition, both Gemma and Niko wore a plain narrow gold band on the ring finger of their left hand that had been blessed by the archbishop when they'd got engaged. Now, Konstantin in his role as *koumbaro*, removed the rings and placed them on their right-hand ring-fingers. Gemma remembered Niko telling her that in the Greek tradition the wedding ring was worn on the right hand, which was traditionally seen as the hand of truth and strength.

At the nod from the archbishop, Constantin then swapped the rings between them three times, each time fitting the rings on the top joint of their fingers, to symbolise the intertwining of Niko's and Gemma's lives. Finally, the rings were slid into their correct place on the right hand—the equivalent of saying 'I do', Gemma remembered, because there were no vows spoken in the Greek ceremony. Marriage was a spiritual union of two people in love, according to the Greek church, rather than a contract. And Niko really felt like her other half.

Prayers ended the first part of the service; then came the crowning service. After psalms and more prayers, the archbishop lit two long candles, the *lambades*, from a single flame, and presented one each to Niko and Gemma. After more prayers, the archbishop joined their right hands together. When the archbishop had blessed the *stéfana*, the wedding crowns, Nina placed them on Niko's and Gemma's heads to symbolise them being the head of their new household. Instead of using the heavy royal *stéfana*, Niko and Gemma had decided to go back to the origins of the tradition as a nod to their shared love of history, and their crowns were woven from olive branches, lemon blossom and vine leaves. The crowns were tied together with a white silk ribbon, and Konstantin exchanged the crowns on their heads the traditional three times.

After more prayers, Niko and Gemma took three sips each from the common cup of wine. Then the archbishop led them in procession around the altar table three times to seal the union, with Nina following them to hold the ribbon joining the crowns: symbolising their first steps together as a married couple.

Finally, the archbishop congratulated them on their wedding and Konstantin removed the crowns.

'Congratulations. You are now man and wife,' the archbishop said in English. 'Although it's not customary to kiss the bride in a Greek Orthodox church ceremony, of course Gemma is English, so I believe it is now that that your priest would say, "You may kiss the bride". I think it appropriate to keep to that tradition.'

'I agree,' Niko said with a broad grin, and kissed his bride with gusto.

Everyone clapped and cheered.

'Congratulations,' the archbishop said. 'And the whole country wishes you ever happiness.'

Niko and Gemma walked hand in hand down the aisle to the door of the cathedral, and stood on the steps between the flowers to let the press take photographs. The wedding guests came out behind them, showering them in rose petals and then posing for their own photographs before collecting the bridal favours.

'According to tradition, the almonds' sugar coating is to keep life sweet for the married couple, and the coating is hard to symbolise the strength of marriage,' Niko said softly.

'I read that there had to be an odd number in the favours so it couldn't be evenly divided, just as the bride and groom shouldn't be divided,' Gemma said.

'And five is a good number because it represents what people wish for the bride and groom: health, wealth, happiness, family and a long life together,' Niko said. 'That's everything I want for us.'

'That's everything I want, too,' she said.

He helped her up into the carriage, and arranged her dress before sitting next to her. 'Ready for me to introduce you to our people, my queen?' he asked.

'Yes,' she said. Because the flutter of nerves didn't matter, not when he was right by her side. They were a team. Together, they could handle anything life threw at them.

Everyone cheered as the horses trotted through the streets. People had their phones out, taking snaps of them as the carriage passed and chanting loudly.

Niko grinned. 'They're telling me to kiss my bride.'

'In that case, I really think you need to follow the will of the people,' she said.

'I quite agree,' he said, and kissed her lingeringly to the cheers of everyone around them.

His people really had accepted her—not just as Prince Niko's girlfriend, but as King Nikolaos's queen. She smiled until her face hurt, filled with joy as she waved back to them.

Finally, the horses brought them back to the palace and through the archway into the private courtyard. Niko climbed out of the carriage and helped her down.

'And now,' he said, 'let the party begin...'

* * * * *

If you enjoyed this story, check out these other great reads from Kate Hardy

His Strictly Off-Limits Ballerina
A Fake Bride's Guide to Forever
Wedding Deal with Her Rival
Tempted by Her Fake Fiancé

All available now!

REUNION WITH HER HIGHLAND RIVAL

MICHELE RENAE

MILLS & BOON

CHAPTER ONE

ALLEGRA STARK PULLED her rental car to a stop before the drive that wound up toward a majestic eighteenth century castle perched on high rocky landscape overlooking the Sound of Raasay, hugged by the islands of Skye and Raasay. The sign posted at the drive read: Private Property, Not a Tourist Destination.

For all the castles she'd seen on the short drive from the Lochalsh ferry landing this was not the largest, oldest, most well-kept or even most valuable. But it was the prettiest. And the most famous. She knew because she'd spent a lot of time in this very castle twenty-five years ago when she'd filmed six seasons of *Clan MacKenzie*, a romantic drama with a paranormal twist set in the early 1900s.

As she stared at the castle now, framed by a moody periwinkle-gray sky that promised rain this weary afternoon, so many emotions gripped her heart. Happiness, to see the castle's pinkish-ochre stone exterior remained virtually the same in appearance, including the sparse shrubberies, apple trees and flowers on the property. Longing, for the simple life of living on a Scottish island far from the bustle of a busy American city. Melancholy, for the good times she'd experienced filming here. Dread, over what repressed emotions may rise once she walked the castle floors.

But that was one of the reasons she was here. To face those

past memories, embrace them and then shove them out of her life for good.

The other reason was that she—along with one other bidder—had been given an exclusive opportunity to make an offer on this castle. The owner was selling. And Allegra wanted this place to repair and glam up so she could then add it to her company, Glamcations, roster of vacation B&Bs that offered a glamorous yet mentally relaxing stay amidst a cozy international setting.

Turning onto the private drive, she spied a woman waving wildly as she circled the rocky area before the castle entry. Had to be the owner, Miranda Donaldson. Clad in wellies, a bright yellow rain slicker and a wool cap boasting cat ears, the woman made her way from the garden where she'd been cutting flowers (abandoned on the ground at the sight of Allegra's approach).

Knowing she was expected, but not wanting the woman to think someone had ignored the posted sign, Allegra parked and quickly slid out of the car. She tugged at her fitted red pantsuit. She'd overdressed for the misty Scottish spring, but her go-to mode was career woman. Of course, she'd packed more practically for a few days' stay.

Offering her hand to shake and a big smile, she said, "I'm Allegra Stark."

"Of course you are!"

The woman, quite tall and wearing a bit of extra weight, lunged toward her for a hug. Allegra was squeezed by powerful arms and even slightly shaken. Then, released, she wobbled for her balance.

"Oh, Allegra Stark is here," the woman announced. "At my home! Oh!" She patted her chest as if out of breath. "But it was your home once too. Such joy!" She grabbed Allegra's hand and clasped it with glee. "You know I'm your biggest fan? Of course you do, I spoke to you just last week on the mobile. I can't believe you're actually here. How does it look?" She swept a hand behind her to encompass the front of the castle.

"Lovely." Still a bit shaken by the gregarious greeting, Allegra allowed her gaze to take it all in.

For a moment she saw the rigging and film crew hustling about, setting up shots. Her dressing trailer to the left and Finn McGregor's trailer beside hers. The costume and makeup trailers had always had a stream of extras moving in and out. That had been in another lifetime, it seemed.

A lifetime she was going to relive if the memories came as freely as this one did now.

"But you must be tired from your trip." Miranda looked her over, taking in Allegra's hair. She no longer sported the coal-black hair of her twenties; platinum was a better word than gray (at least to her). "Let's go inside and have a drink. Come along." Miranda hooked her arm in Allegra's and led her toward the side door.

"I am surprised how exhausted I am," Allegra admitted as they entered the boot room lined with shelves, coats and assorted outdoor gear. Miranda eased off her wellies. "It's been a long day of layovers and delayed flights. I'm hoping to hit the sack early."

"You'll stay here?" The hope in the woman's eyes reminded Allegra of those years she had done the Hollywood-star thing. So much admiration from people who idolized her simply for pretending to be something she was not. "I've had one of the guest rooms prepared for you."

Yes, the woman had offered a room for as long as Allegra wanted to stay. The closest town was Portree, and to judge the inns and hotels she'd seen while driving through earlier, they were quite touristy. She preferred a quiet place to relax and—honestly, now that she was back in Scotland she wanted to soak in the air, sea and land and just…be.

"I will," she said. "For a day or two?" Miranda had said she wanted a little time to consider the bids. Understandable.

"Well, I should tell you about the convention. Come along." Miranda gestured as she walked down the long stone-walled hallway that eventually deposited them in the kitchen. "Do you like the remodel? This was the one room I couldn't leave—" she made air quotes "—period correct."

The castle had been chosen as the filming site for the reason that it had been preserved with nineteenth-century furnishings. But also, it had once been owned by the Mc-Gregor family. Finn McGregor had been her costar in *Clan MacKenzie*. He'd grown up here, and, rumor told, when the casting director had learned of that connection, the young actor had won the role.

Allegra took in the ultra-modern kitchen design, the clean white cabinet facings, the stainless steel and marble counters. It was a tremendous upgrade from the original design but she was pleased to see that the hearth was still there.

She pressed a palm to the cool limestone that had been quarried from the island. How many scenes had been shot with her brewing an herbal concoction in a cast-iron pot? Ha! "As beautiful as I remember."

"I didn't change much," Miranda offered as she poured lemonade from a pitcher for them. "I couldn't! This place is a treasure. I could hardly rip out Connor and Madeline's bedroom!"

The names of their characters. Allegra had played Madeline Williams, a plucky young American naturalist and explorer who had come to the island in search of real fairies. Finn had played Connor MacKenzie, newest clan leader and proud defender of his family. (And suspected fairy.)

"Come sit and have refreshment," Miranda declared grandly. "I'll take you on a tour of the castle as soon as the other bidder arrives. He should be here soon."

Allegra slid onto a barstool before the counter. The lemonade was tart but appreciated after a long day of travel. "You said something about a convention?"

"Oh, yes! Oh, my goodness, I'm so excited for it. Oh." She pressed a hand over her heart. "I'm so thrilled my heart stutters!"

And very demonstrative. She'd gotten a hint of what to expect over their phone call. And from their email communications when Miranda had introduced herself as the president of the *Clan MacKenzie* fan club. Had been since the first episode.

"Perhaps you should sit as well," Allegra suggested as she noticed a flush on the woman's cheeks and neck.

"Oh, I can't. I'm buzzing with excitement having *the* Madeline Williams sitting in my very home. Such joy!"

Allegra assumed there would be things to autograph before she got out of this situation. She was fine with that. While she'd set acting and anything related to the series aside, the occasional revisitation wasn't so much horrifying as wistful.

"Do you know I've never had the thought to put together a convention for the series?" Miranda leaned across the counter. "After all these years!" With a wince, she clasped a hand to her chest again. Must be the tart lemonade. It did register at the base of Allegra's throat with a sharp bite. "It occurred to me that I couldn't let the castle go into someone's hands without first honoring the series in the grandest manner possible. So, in a just over a week, over a hundred of the series' biggest fans will gather here to celebrate. I've a list…" She patted a clipboard that sat near a basket of fragrant oranges. "Things to finish fixing up. Rooms to tidy. Chairs to be received. Sound system to be set up. Lighting. This next week will be a bustle."

"Sounds exciting."

"Oh!" Miranda suddenly straightened and looked out the

window as if a stork trying to see above high grasses. "The other bidder has arrived!"

She hustled around the counter and toward the hallway. "I must go out and greet him!"

"Who is it?" Allegra called as she turned to eye the motorbike and rider parking next to her rental car.

"Why Finn McGregor, of course!" Miranda called just as the side door slammed shut.

"Finn…"

Allegra set her glass on the counter, then gripped the cold marble countertop. Her breaths gasped. Heartbeats jumped.

She hadn't thought to ever see him again. Not in person.

And not by surprise like this.

She swore inwardly.

Finn McGregor was the last man she wanted to see. He had…stolen her heart. She'd been madly in love with him when they'd been filming. Hadn't been able to separate her fictional love for him from a real and genuine attraction and desire. Yet, when the series had wrapped, he'd walked away from her and hadn't looked back. And she hadn't been the same for a very long time after.

And yet, she thought now as her shock subsided a little, she had put the love she'd carried for him for decades in the past where it belonged.

Yes, it was quite a fitting thing to happen, after all, she told herself, ignoring her still shaking hands. She had returned to the castle to put old memories to rest and it was only right that it would allow her to consign all thoughts of him to the past forever.

CHAPTER TWO

FINN RECEIVED THE bodacious hug, that was more a running full-body slam, like a pro.

"Oh, Finn McGregor! I'm so happy you're here. The other bidder has also just arrived. Did you have a good trip?" Mrs. Donaldson stepped back, gasping. It was to be expected from such a vigorous hug. "How do you like being back at your family home? Is that the famous motorbike they featured with you on the cover of *Scotland Life*?"

"Aye, she's my trusty road steed." Finn owned a cottage on the mainland just out of Inverness that he rarely used and had taken this opportunity to pull his bike out of storage. "It's good to be back in the place I called home when I was growing up."

The castle stirred up memories; most of them good. They'd filmed here six years. Good times. But before that, he'd been born here and lived through his early teen years. Of course, when his mother had passed, his dad, inconsolable, had sold the castle within a year following her death.

So not all good memories.

"Thank you, for inviting me to bid on the castle. I think you'll be thrilled to hear my plans for it. But we should get you inside." He touched Miranda's arm. "You're shivering?"

She waved him off. "Just feeling a bit off-kilter today. I think it's the excitement of meeting my two favorite actors! Come along and I'll let you get reacquainted with Allegra!"

She began a half-run/wobble toward the castle doors.

While Finn stood riveted to the ground. "Allegra?"

Had he heard the woman right? Allegra Stark was…here? He hadn't seen her in decades. Though he'd thought of her often. Hard to get such a smart, compelling woman out of his mind. Really? She was the other bidder?

Miranda held the door open. "Come along, Connor MacKenzie! I've your bonny bride awaiting ye!"

She'd quoted a line from the series. It swept him back to the time when he'd played a young clan leader who fell in love with an American field researcher. Allegra had embodied her character, giving her a heart and soul that he felt sure had been the major draw to the series.

Acting and the experiences surrounding the profession were always super weird. And in his many decades as an actor he'd not always handled his personal life well. But he had matured. (Unfortunately.) He knew his craft, had been one of the top actors for decades and won all the awards.

Yet now. He was no longer being offered the action or leading man roles. The current script he'd been offered cast him as a former '80s porn star who was trying to come to terms with aging out of the profession. Unbelievable.

So when he'd been offered the chance to bid on this castle, it had felt like the stars were aligning. The clouds were clearing. Because he wasn't going down without a fight. A script for a new television series he had created was in revisions at the moment but his agent had already sent it out to a few studios he thought would want immediate eyes on it. Now, to obtain the filming location. Along with the script, they would make an irresistible package he could take to any producer and, once again, Finn McGregor could stand with his head high in a leading man role.

As well, standing before his childhood home? He hadn't thought he needed this return but his smile was irrepressible.

A call to his dad was necessary. He and old man McGregor hadn't seen one another in years.

"Finn?"

He nodded to Miranda. "Yes, right behind you. Just taking in the scenery."

He hadn't forgotten that Scottish springs could be brisk and windy. That never dulled the enjoyment of getting back on the motorbike and speeding down the single-track roads. Everything about returning here excited him. It was as if he were that twenty-something acting prodigy all over again. But even more? A younger Finn McGregor laughed and skipped across the field, no cares, only happiness.

He entered the castle and a cozy warmth braised his chilled cheeks and neck.

"Allegra!" Miranda called as they entered a bright kitchen that didn't look at all as it once had. "Here's Connor MacKenzie in the flesh!"

Eager to see the woman he'd worked with nearly daily for six years. Side by side, falling in love for the cameras, going on adventures, marrying, raising their family. They'd been fictional husband and wife. A fiction that many in the press had wanted to be literal. It had only ever been playacting.

After filming had wrapped for the day, Finn had learned to keep Allegra at a distance. Best for both of them. Especially his wild rogue heart.

A beautiful woman with thick long wavy silver hair stood before the bay window where he had once napped as a child. Couldn't be his Allie. When filming, she'd had hair as dark and shiny as raven wings.

As he entered the room, she turned. Her smile was soft, genuine and so familiar. Her face was still narrow and her cheekbones as high as the Hebridean cliffs. A few lines frayed from the sides of her eyes, but wrinkles were few. "Allie?" He checked his voice. His best asset as an actor; it had gasped.

"Finn."

When she held out her hands, he took them because it felt as though the director had just called "action" for a scene. Dreamy, yet at the same time undefinably strange. Her hands were narrow and warm. The cuff of her smart red suit jacket brushed the back of his hand. Her eyes were still a piercing blue that he had once fancied resembled the center of an iceberg. Cold yet so intriguing, even a little otherworldly.

"I had no idea you were the other bidder." She tugged from his grasp. A gentle tug, but still, she ended the hold before he wanted it to end. Course, his hands hadn't warmed yet from the ride here. "Who would have thought we'd meet after so long in the very castle that brought us together?"

"Crazy. I had no idea either. A surprise reunion. Sounds like something out of a movie script."

She chuckled softly. "I was thinking the same thing. Very…coincidental."

He followed Allie's glance to Miranda, who stood ten feet away, her hands clasped gleefully before her. The woman could barely contain her excitement and blurted, "I brought you together! It was me! All my idea!"

So this reunion had some underhanded pre-plotted tones to it? Sneaky. He supposed he should have expected nothing less from the president of the *Clan MacKenzie* fan club. Finn had contacted her six months ago, asking if she'd be interested in selling. She hadn't been then. But two weeks ago, she'd called him back. Their phone conversation had detoured into a raving summation of her following the series over the years, detailing costumes, settings, all the characters and their backgrounds, etc. She knew her stuff. He'd call her fanatic, but never to her face.

"You want this castle?" he asked Allie.

"The offer to make a bid couldn't have come at a better

time for my business. And you? What reason do you have for wanting the castle?"

"You know I grew up here." It came out more accusatory than he wanted, but it suddenly felt like a bargaining chip he hadn't thought he would need.

"Of course, but I had no idea you were the competing bidder. You've a desire to return to your childhood home? I thought you had homes in New York and LA?"

So she'd kept tabs on him? Fair. He knew she lived in Arizona and owned a B&B business. Difficult not to want to know what she was up to throughout the years. But as well, with the new series script in the works, he had considered contacting her to reprise her role.

"I do have a few homes," he said. "But as for the castle, well. I've big plans."

That he may not reveal just yet. First he needed to settle into the idea of standing in front of Allie. They had been so close. And yet, so far apart. And she smelled soft and sweet. She'd never worn scent while filming. He liked it. Subtle. And intriguing. It felt as if they'd never parted while also as if they'd been reunited after being lost at sea for decades.

So he had a wild imagination. It was his moneymaker.

"Isn't this delicious!" Miranda clapped a few times. "I had hoped your reunion would go off splendidly. I'm so pleased to see the two of you together again. Oh, we must toast!"

She spun around the counter and produced a bottle of champagne. Just conveniently to hand? Even more suspicious.

"I'm sorry, but I don't drink," Finn quickly said before she could pop the cork. "I've been sober twelve years."

Miranda's face went bleak. She clutched the champagne bottle. "Oh. I did know that. I'm so sorry!"

"No worries. Maybe Allie would like a bit?"

"I'm good." She walked over to the counter and took the

bottle from Miranda to set aside. "Why don't you show us around the castle before it gets dark?"

"Oh, of course. And then you've to place your bids. And we'll discuss the convention as well."

"Convention?" Finn looked to Allie, who shrugged and nodded.

"Yes, I'll tell you all about it while we walk the castle. I'm so happy for us all!" Miranda slapped a palm to her chest and winced. "Whew! The ticker is getting a workout today. Come along, my dears! I want to show you Connor and Madeline's bedroom that I've kept in exact condition as when you were filming."

Finn caught Allie's heavy sigh. Same. But he would placate Miranda because he wanted her to view him as the best one to own the castle. And really, wasn't he the most deserving? It wasn't as though Allie had grown up here, put down metaphorical roots in this very soil.

"It's really good to see you, Allie. I missed you."

"You did?"

"You're one of the most memorable women to have ever passed through my life. Of course, I did."

"That's kind of you to say." She fiddled with the ends of her hair. "I, uh… I've thought of you over the years."

"Thinking of you always makes me smile," he said before he could stop himself. If he was going to win this castle, he needed to keep his personal feelings out of the mix.

"MacKenzies!" Miranda called out from around the corner. "Let's get this tour on the road while Allegra can still keep her eyes open."

With a sweep of her fingers through her long hair, Allie said, "I am dead on my feet with all the travel today. Let's make this quick."

Finn offered his arm for her to take. "My lady."

She stared at his offering for a moment. And when he began to feel a niggling sting of rejection, she finally took it and they followed their host.

The castle looked much as it had when they'd been filming. None of the stone walls had been framed over to modernize it. All the antler chandeliers—which Finn noted had been there since before his family owned it for seventy years— still hung everywhere. The tapestries used during filming had even been the originals the castle owners had hung in the mid-eighteenth century.

Allie followed Miranda and Finn through the various rooms, finding memories flashed into thought, but left as quickly as she was distracted by...him.

Finn looked almost as he had when they'd filmed twenty-five years ago. While some leading men tended to lose their sex appeal as they gained years, Finn seemed to have come into a deeper more grounded version of himself. He'd always possessed a vibrant smile that could instantly lift her spirits. Still had it. And his light green eyes were delving when they needed to be and sensual at other times. His hair hadn't faded from its natural dark brown, though some silver strands streaked above his ears. The crow's feet hugging his eyes gave him a distinguished gravitas. And she did like the fine stubble he wore along his jaw and mustache, which gave him a seasoned, gritty appeal.

The man could still make her swoon. If she allowed herself that floundering descent into adoration. But she would not do that now. She was beyond such silliness.

Emotionally, she had taken a one-eighty from her twenties. She'd gained wisdom regarding her appearance. A new wrinkle here and there? She didn't care what anyone thought of her looks. If someone didn't like her, that was fine too.

No two people were going to hold the exact same opinions about anything. Especially when it came to romance and the accompanying swirl of crazy emotions. No longer would she stand aside and harbor an unrequited longing for a man— any man—who didn't care for her feelings. Such longing was a waste of time and energy. She treated herself much better now.

But that didn't mean she couldn't appreciate a handsome man. And Finn McGregor embodied his charming appeal.

Their tour returned them to the living area, a large study with an oversized leather sofa, tweed chairs and plenty of ancient iron decorations. Miranda directed them to sit before the low table made from a salvaged tree trunk. Dashing off, their host then quickly returned with pens and paper.

Miranda displayed a brown envelope. "I've decided I'd like to do the bidding this way. You'll write your offer on those slips of paper. We'll put them in the envelope. And then…" Her giddiness had fled as she'd led them through the castle. Now she appeared as tired as Allegra felt. "Well, I'd like to wait until the convention to reveal the winner of the bid."

"Oh." Finn picked up the pen. That *oh* had been more of an annoyance than acceptance.

"That's the way it's going to be done," Miranda said with uncharacteristic firmness. "Which leads me to one more request I have of the two of you."

Allegra met Finn's gaze. Unexpected plot twist?

"I'd like the two of you to appear at the convention. Pretty please? Just for an autographing and photo op. Also—well, I have scheduled a questions-and-answers session."

She'd already scheduled them in? So much sneaky plotting packed into one seemingly ingenuous woman. And yet, if she wanted to ingratiate herself to the one who would ultimately choose the winner of the bid…

Finn cleared his throat. Picked up the blank paper. "I'm not sure, Mrs. Donaldson. I'll have to check my schedule."

"Oh, of course, Finn McGregor. I completely understand. This is a very last-minute request. What of you, Allegra?"

"I'd love to," came out as easily as if she'd had weeks to consider the offer. "Seems like a fitting farewell to *Clan MacKenzie*'s fans. I don't have to get back home right away. I'm sure I can find a place in Portree to stay until then."

"But you'll stay here!" Miranda rushed in. "I mean, your guest room is free for you to use. I won't bother you or get in your way. But I'd love it if you'd enjoy your stay here. You as well, Finn."

It was a generous offer. And she wouldn't mind wandering the grounds for a few days, stopping into Portree, even going on the touristy hikes that offered gorgeous views of the island's mountains, trails and fairy pools.

"I'll think about it. Thanks." She picked up her pen, and knowing what her budget was—and who her opponent was—she…went a little higher.

Finn stuffed his folded bid into the brown envelope, then handed it to her. "May the best man win?"

"Or woman." Allie slid her bid in the envelope.

"Lovely!" Miranda clapped.

"Can you tell me why you are selling?" Allie asked. "This castle is such a landmark."

"Oh, it is a lovely castle. Indeed. But…" Miranda gesticulated wildly as she talked. "I've decided I want to travel the world. And since my husband passed four years ago, this place is much too big for me. And Scotland. Well! The weather here is so terribly…" she shivered and patted her heart "…moist."

Allie caught Finn's grin as he bowed his head. That grin reminded her of the occasions they'd share a private laugh while waiting for the director to call "action." So rare. But unforgettable.

"So terribly moist," Miranda reiterated. "Oh." She patted her forehead with the back of her hand. "It is hot in here, yes?"

"It's actually a little chilly with that window open," Allie noted. "Are you feeling well?"

The woman had gasped as they taken the stairs and even now she steadied herself with both hands to the back of the sofa.

"Perhaps I need a cool drink. If you two will excuse me a moment? I'll be right back!" She bustled off toward the kitchen.

Finn stood and paced to the massive window that over-looked the sound. The scenery alone would attract vacation-ers to this sight once Allie refurbished the place and glammed it up. But as well, the history, not only of the TV series, but the centuries of Scottish Highlands history, were a draw.

"So you own a vacation service?" Finn asked. Allie looked surprised for a moment. Had he been keeping tabs on her too?

"Yes, it's called Glamcations."

"I've heard of it. Don't you do a lot of charity work?"

So he *had* been keeping tabs on her. Interesting. "Twice a year we offer the locations we currently own to a woman or women's group in need. We're particularly fond of the Can-cer Crones. They're an amazing bunch of survivors."

"We?"

"Me and my partner, Savanah Wilton. She's our social media guru. I don't even understand Facebook, really. I'll never figure out TikTok."

"My people do that for me." He tossed that out without a thought.

Entitled actor? She'd watched him grow from an inexperi-enced young actor to burgeoning first-rate star as the show's seasons progressed. The man had hit it big in Hollywood. And he deserved all the praise for his talent.

"So what's your reason for wanting the castle?" she asked. "Vacation home? Don't you have a home on the mainland?"

"I do. A cottage just out of Inverness. Never spend much time there unless travel brings me close. And beyond childhood memories…" Finn leaned his hands on the back of the sofa. There was that boyish gleeful smile that won all the women's hearts and managed to grace the covers of virtually all the entertainment magazines. "I've a script written for a sequel to *Clan MacKenzie*."

"A sequel?" While Allie had left Hollywood behind and rarely bothered to turn on the television, she heard bits and pieces about what was going on with who, when and what studio.

"Yes, Connor and Madeline's children."

She'd given birth to three fictional children during filming. Oh, such times.

"Sounds intriguing," she said. "But don't you think today's viewers are over *Clan MacKenzie*? If they've even heard of it. That was so long ago."

"The historical long-run series is popular, especially on streaming services. I get fan mail to this day for the show."

As did she. She was always surprised that people still wrote letters when emails were much easier. Not that she had an email address anyone knew about.

"Has the script been optioned?" she asked.

"It's currently with a producer who said he may be interested. And that's where the castle comes in. That's a shoe-in for the studio if I bring the film site along with the script."

Possibly. Though much was filmed on lots nowadays, and CGI was so easy to use that recreating the setting digitally could possibly be cheaper than actually filming here. "I'm assuming you'd be in the series?"

"Of course. And you."

She shook her head. "That's not my thing anymore. I have zero interest."

"Why not? Allie, I'd really like to talk to you about reprising your role as Madeline."

Bother. She didn't want to get into the details of why acting had messed her up. Or pull him up on why he'd assumed she would be interested. And…she was so tired. Truly, the day had been long, what with the travel and the emotional surprise of seeing Finn. And…something was missing. "Where's Miranda?"

Finn straightened and looked toward the kitchen. "Not sure. It is rather quiet." He started toward the kitchen and Allie followed.

She saw Miranda's legs sticking out from behind the counter and rushed to find her sitting on the floor, slumped against the fridge, unconscious.

"Call for emergency," she said.

Finn tugged out his phone.

CHAPTER THREE

AN AMBULANCE RUSHED Miranda to the Portree hospital. The ambulance crew's initial assessment was that she'd had a heart attack. Her daughter, Dorothy, who lived in Edinburgh, had been called and she was on her way to the island. Allie and Finn had stayed at the castle, not wanting to be in the way, and not sure where they actually should be since Miranda was not a family member.

"We'll take care of the castle till we hear from Miranda's daughter," Allie had assured the paramedics. "If you could give my number to her daughter, I would appreciate it."

Now, hours later, exhaustion hit her hard. Allie shook her head when Finn offered her more lemonade. "I need a shower and to crash."

"You're still planning to stay here?"

"Yes, Miranda offered the guest room."

"She did the same for me. I wasn't sure I'd stay more than the night. But now…with what's happened?"

She hadn't considered that. On the other hand, her tired brain could barely see straight. Miranda had made the offer; knowing her, she'd insist they stay.

"I suspect it will be too late to find a room in Portree."

He leaned his elbows onto the counter, putting himself eye level with her. He didn't look tired or even mussed, while she felt as if the world were dragging her quickly downward.

"Well we don't need to stay for Miranda to make a decision on the bids, do we? What did you bid?"

"I'm not telling. What did you bid?"

He drew his fingers across his mouth to seal his silence.

"Fair enough."

"Let's hope for a positive prognosis for Miranda, aye? She's a good one."

"Yes, she is." And his kindness was a balm to her exhaustion. She yawned.

"You look wrecked. You should head up."

"So will you stay the night?" She realized it would be nice to have another body in the big empty castle. And staying alone didn't appeal, especially when she was a sort-of guest.

"I will. There was a room at the end of the second-floor hall that looked made up. Used to be my room when I was a kid."

Yes, he'd once called this very castle home. How could she possibly win in a bid against that?

He placed his hand over hers and squeezed gently. The reassuring touch was another kindness she hadn't realized she needed right now. "I don't have anything pressing on my schedule. I'm currently considering a role, but my agent told me to take my time, so I am. And if it means I get to spend some time getting to know you again, of course I'll stay."

Allie narrowed her gaze on him, wondering about his motives. Getting to know her? Why hadn't he had the same thought decades ago?

Oh, Allie, don't dive into those memories tonight. You really do want another body nearby so you're not alone in this big empty castle.

"You're half asleep already," he commented. "I remember you could sleep sitting up tucked away in a corner of the set. Stumbled over you a few times."

"It's a talent." Which had fled when menopause thundered in with hot flashes and brain fog. She slid off the stool and gathered her purse and car keys. "Do you know how to cook?"

"I, uh…" His surprise registered as adorable commas crinkling the corners of his eyes. "Is that a requirement for staying here?"

"No. But I do love it when someone makes eggs for me. I can roast, I can stir-fry, I can bake, but for some reason I can't scramble a decent egg to save my life."

"I can do that. I'll see you in the morning, then. Good night, Allie."

She waved as she wandered toward the stairs. Too tired to converse. Or maybe determined to avoid more alone time with the man who had once owned her heart.

Finn moved the eggs around the cast-iron skillet with a wooden spatula. Having lived alone most of his life, he could manage many dishes and actually found cooking for himself quite relaxing. It allowed his mind to wander.

That he was currently staying in the very castle he'd grown up in with the woman he'd once worked with was remarkable. And not just worked with. He and Allie had appeared close. At least on the surface.

Over the years he'd thought a lot about the relationship they'd had. Despite the time they'd spent together, they hadn't even begun to touch what he'd consider a friendship. Why was that? Certainly, he could have been much kinder. More open to her. A friend.

But did it even matter now? More than two decades had passed. Allie didn't appear any worse for wear for their lacking closeness. The woman had thrived. Created her own business that served others. And she still looked amazing. Her hair color was—all that palest silver-white—incredible. Combined with her gentle smile and iceberg eyes? She'd moved into a sort of silver-goddess mode without losing the sexy appeal of her younger self.

Whew! He was attracted to her. Still. And he had no current love interest in his life. Hadn't for over a year.

Finn liked to have someone in his life. But since entering his fifties, he'd noticed the usual surface relationships he'd once welcomed for their ease and short shelf life no longer cut it for him. He needed more. Something deeper. Lasting. Because, yes, he wasn't getting younger. And he did desire the constancy of a companion to walk through the rest of his life. He could act proud and unbothered by his single-dom status, but that was only an example of his acting skills.

"Wow!" Allie strolled into the kitchen, a gray wool sweater falling over dark skinny jeans. Shoeless, she had pulled thick socks up over her ankles. That goddess hair was braided to fall forward over one shoulder, with wisps that teased across her cheeks. "It smells like real food in here."

"You doubted me?" He winked at her. Standard McGregor flirtation tactic. An innate talent that had been pointed out by many media outlets. He couldn't stop it if he tried.

"Maybe? I didn't know you had a talent for domestic tasks."

"A guy's gotta feed himself." He plated the eggs and added a few wedges of fresh orange to each one. "I'm not merely a big-budget face. I can do more than act."

She sat at the round table and pushed aside the fussy arrangement of silk flowers that Finn would prefer ended up in the bin. He set a plate and fork before her. "What do you want to drink? There's water and lemonade."

"Water, please."

"Coming right up!" Toss in a bit of charm. The women were always fascinated by his easy smile and, as *People* magazine put it, 'kind eyes that made sexy promises'. "Did you sleep well?" He poured them both a glass and joined her at the table.

"Deliciously," she said with a lift of her shoulders that he recalled was something she did when she was pleased. "I've forgotten how nice it is to sleep in a humid climate."

"You mean…" he paused for effect "…moist?"

She laughed. "Oh, mercy, what is it with that word? But yes. Arizona is so arid. I'm going to take advantage of this weather while I'm here and tuck my moisturizer out of sight. Oh. These eggs are amazing. What did you put in them to make them so creamy?"

"Found some goat cheese in the fridge. Miranda must get it from the farmer down the road. I remember old Mac used to bring his fresh cheese to the set once in a while."

"Oh, yes! That was always a treat. You think he's still alive? He must have been pushing seventy back then."

"It's possible his son took over the goats. It's not often families sell their farms outright around here. The land is a precious commodity."

"But your family did?"

Had he told her why his dad sold the land and castle? Probably not. "It was tough for my dad after Mum passed," he said, then forked in some eggs.

"I'm so sorry. I didn't know that. I remember Sean McGregor. Such a kind man."

"Aye, he is. I'm going to call him if I'm to be here a day or two. Meet up at his favorite pub. So, you live in Arizona?"

"Yes, Sedona is my home base. I tend to stay in the properties we acquire for Glamcations while they are in rehab mode. Last year, Seville was my home for five months. I loved it."

"The land of matadors and flamenco dancers. I filmed there recently for a couple weeks. Met some young billionaires who own a VR company. One of their games is being made into a movie in which I hope to snag a role. So you don't miss acting at all?"

"Not a single moment of it."

Finn pouted. "Not even me?"

She paused with a heap of egg on her fork. "Well."

Not sure how to answer that one? Even if only to offer a polite reassurance? Hell. Practiced charm and bedroom eyes? Ineffective. He was already batting zero with her. Not a good way to start.

"It took me a while to get you out of my head," she suddenly said, setting down her fork and sitting back against the chair.

"You…what? I don't understand." Finn leaned forward, catching his elbow on the table and resting cheek against his hand. "What do you mean by that?"

"Honestly? We had a weird relationship for those six years."

Fair enough.

"It… Well, the whole acting experience messed with me emotionally," she said. "It's one of the reasons I didn't do much more acting after the series. I did those two movies and then decided to walk away. Clear my head."

"Of me?"

Allie rolled her eyes. "And other things. You know, the whole Hollywood machine. I'd been inducted into the glamour, the false ego, the self-aggrandizement. Such a strange costume to wear. It wasn't me. Even after I left, it was difficult to shrug off. It sticks quite deeply."

True. The Hollywood machine, as she put it, had permeated his bones. Though he didn't care for the way she described it. False ego? Very well, he'd rubbed up against that. A lot. Self-aggrandizement? Eh. But what was wrong with the glamour?

More troubling though: She'd had to get *him* out of her head? What had he ever done to her?

This was a huge conversation for breakfast. And for just getting back together. He wanted to learn more. Yet taking criticism had grown less and less easy for him. One of the reasons he strove to hold a producer credit on all his movies. Like selling this sequel idea. It wasn't going to happen unless he had complete creative and executive control.

Fine. So he had an ego. What actor could survive without an armor of emotional protection, entitlement and a touch of self-aggrandizement?

Allie's phone rang. "I think this is Miranda's daughter. I'll put it on speaker." She tapped the screen and said, "Hello," and once Dorothy had introduced herself, Allie introduced Finn. "How is Miranda?"

"She's had a minor heart attack," Dorothy said in a calm voice. "The doctors are very optimistic. They want to keep her in hospital for a few days to monitor her condition. I want you to know how thankful I am that you two were there. Had you not called emergency so quickly, it could have been much worse for her."

"I'm glad for that too. Please send Miranda our love." Allie moved the phone to the center of the table. "I hope you don't mind but we stayed the night in the castle. Wanted to make sure it was secure after all the commotion."

"I'm thankful for that too. And I've a favor to ask. I know Mum asked you to stay until the convention."

Finn tilted his head, catching Allie's wince.

"She did make the offer," Allie said, "but I have no intention of imposing. Especially with what has happened to your mom. It wouldn't feel right to stay under the circumstances."

"Oh, please, would you? I know it's a big ask but I need someone to be there at the castle in Mum's absence. There are deliveries to be received all week. You can make use of anything you need at the castle—vehicles too."

"You think it's wise to continue with the convention?" Finn asked quickly. "Shouldn't Miranda be resting?"

"We've had that very conversation and she is insistent the convention go on. She devoted months of work on this. And…she had a list of things…"

Finn widened his gaze at Allie. She could read his thoughts. *Really? Now they were going to ask for a favor?*

"Right, I've seen the list," she replied. "Just a few things that need tidying on the grounds and inside before the convention. If you insist we stay, I…would be happy to take a look at that list and see what I can do."

"Oh, would you? I would do it myself, but between my work and staying here in hospital with Mum…"

"Don't worry yourself, Dorothy. Between Finn and I, I'm sure we'll get this place the way your mum wants it for the big event."

Me? Finn mouthed at her.

"Finn is only too pleased to offer his help," Allie said.

He shook his head but could only smile. Of course he didn't really mind helping out. Not like he had anything else to do at the moment. And working alongside Allie might give him opportunity to soften her resistance to returning to acting.

"If you need anything," Dorothy said, "just give me a ring. And I'll update you on Mum's condition whenever I have a chance. When she's released from hospital, I'm taking her home to stay with me."

"Sounds good, Dorothy. Hug your mom for the both of us. Goodbye." Allie tapped the screen, then gave Finn a look of dread.

"Hey." He splayed his hands. "You and your niceness…" He let that hang. Ever the one to bring in baked goods for the crew or to compliment the extras, despite her obvious shyness, Allie had been loved for her generous spirit.

"You *are* going to help," she said with more firmness than her generous crown should wield. "It's the least we can do for the woman. She's had a rough go of it. You know her husband died four years ago? And now the heart attack?"

Staying a few days in a castle with the one woman he'd never felt he had a hope of truly understanding, despite the time they spent together, was going to be intriguing. Not only someone who was an enigma to him but someone he had acted out the fullest range of feelings toward, yet had never felt them for real.

Or had he? Yes, at times he'd wondered if they could have moved beyond the set to explore whatever might develop between them. But at the time he'd been too ambitious, set on making a career. His rogue heart had not been willing to allow another into his life for fear of losing his stride, his momentum. He'd fought so hard to be seen by the world—he couldn't lose himself in someone else.

And now? Allie hadn't changed much, beyond her hair color. And seeing her again stirred those feelings of wonder he'd shoved aside when they were younger. Dare he explore them now? Especially at a time when he longed for the closeness of a true and loving connection.

"What's on the list?" he asked. "I'm sure we can knock it all out in a day."

CHAPTER FOUR

THIS LIST WAS going to take weeks to complete. There were deliveries to be received, which Miranda had carefully marked day and time. Small yard cleanups and putting up posts to designate parking along the road. But as well, the hedgerow that demarcated the western edge of the property needed tending, a particular tree in the back needed a large broken branch removed (for safety's sake should a convention-goer wander too near) and a leak in the bathroom just off the ballroom where all the events were to be held needed fixing.

"Most of it can be handled by a professional," Finn said to Allie after she'd read off the list.

He set the last of the clean dishes back in the cupboard. The man had voluntarily washed the dishes after they'd eaten, *after* he'd cooked! What the…? But arguing against any man doing such tasks would have been even crazier, so Allie gleefully watched out of the corner of her eye as she browsed Miranda's list.

"We can't assume she would appreciate those bills," Allie said. "There's a utility shed out back. I'm sure the branch is an easy fix. I am not incapable. I know my way around tools."

Finn turned with a glint to his eye. Oh, that sexy come-on look she had swooned over when they'd been filming. Now? Admittedly, it still hit her right in the core. And lower. It wasn't true, the warning about menopause causing a woman to lose interest in sex. Not in her case, at least.

She stood, ignoring Finn's teasing look (and her still-active libido). "Yes, I can handle a *tool*," she emphasized the word. "I'm heading out back to the shed. Pick a task on the list and go for it."

"Be right behind you," he called as she left the kitchen.

He did not follow right behind. Which Allie appreciated as she entered the cool shed and flicked the light switch. Only now letting out the breath she may have held since Finn's flirtatious eye glint had caught her off guard, she leaned her shoulders against the back of the closed wood door.

The man had a skill, all right. An easy charm that she was well aware was practiced, even used purposefully to get his way. And yet, she fell for it every time. Even after not seeing him for so long, she quickly fell victim to his charm.

How strange to one moment be standing in the kitchen talking to Miranda, the next facing the one man she'd never thought to see again. She had come here prepared to face the memories of her past with Finn. But she'd never thought those memories would be embodied by the real man.

It was weird. She knew him. Well. And yet she hadn't felt compelled to greet him like an old friend with a hug. She almost felt like a shunned girlfriend whom he'd shrugged off as insignificant.

Why did she so quickly fall back into those heart-wrenching feelings? To even consider that the physical reactions in her body meant she still had a thing for Finn—it had been decades!

"Get it together," she coached.

Craving sex because of a sexy smile and craving the intimacy it brought were two very different things. She'd never been a one-night-stand person. But as well, intimacy was a tough one for her. Since her divorce, she'd not been so eager to open her heart to another man.

Been there. It hurt.

Alone worked very well for Allegra Stark.

A sigh was unavoidable. She had loved Finn. From a bone-deep place that superseded even her heart.

And Finn had pushed her away like all the other women she'd witnessed roll in and out of his life over the years. While a lauded Hollywood leading man, throughout his career he was constantly called out for his lothario ways. His never settling down with any woman more than a few months. Always having a sexy young thing on his arm for award shows and events.

Allie got it. An actor was never truly their own person. They belonged to the masses, the directors and producers, the fans. Expectations had to be met or jobs would cease to be offered. Which is why she'd escaped while she could. The sort of false veneer one had to wear for the cameras and fans wasn't sustainable. Not for her.

Still, it was truly unfair that the man had aged so well. Seasoned so perfectly even a five-star chef would cock his head and drool over the dish called Finn McGregor.

"Oh, brother." She shook her head. Already falling under his trademark charm when she should be practicing defiant avoidance of anything remotely flirtatious he cast her way.

And she would be around him until the convention now. What had she gotten herself into? On the other hand, helping Miranda was the very least she could do for allowing her to bid on the castle.

A rap on the shed door startled her.

"You in there?"

Be still her heart. It was going to be a challenge to not allow those old feelings of admiration and love to rise again.

Even as she felt them stir and begin their climb. But if ever there were a time and place to defeat them, it was now.

"Come in!" She grabbed a nearby tool. A gas-powered chainsaw.

Finn stepped inside and she shoved the trimmer at him. "I'm assigning you the tree branch. There's a ladder on that wall. Do you need me to hold it steady for you?"

He studied the tool. She would make a guess he might not have the first clue how to use it. Then again, she recalled he always did like to do his own stunts and learn skills, such as wood-chopping, using historical weaponry, even horseback riding.

"Point me toward the tree," he said, lugging the tool against a shoulder.

"Let me grab some garden tools and we'll go find it."

The old apple tree was dropping its faded blossoms into a wilting carpet at their feet. The branch in question, already broken, was still attached to the main trunk. It wouldn't require a ladder so Allie left Finn to go investigate the garden, which Miranda had noted on her list "needed tidying."

Tugging on her raincoat—she'd borrowed the pink one from Miranda's boot room; it was only slightly too big— she patted the pocket where she kept her phone. She'd check in with Savannah later, but she also wanted to be available should Dorothy call. Indeed, Miranda had been lucky that she and Finn had been here as opposed to being alone.

Allie had lived alone for twenty years. After her marriage had fallen apart, she'd taken her time before stepping back into the dating pool. There had been one man she'd enjoyed spending time with but he had been eager to have children and that wasn't on her list of possibilities. Most relationships had been fleeting; she'd had fun, learning new activities and even traveling, but none had truly touched her heart. No man had ever grabbed her by the soul. She needed that sort of connection now. An ineffable sort of knowing that he was the one.

She grew more independent with every year she aged. Was confident that she could do all the basic things to stay alive, keep her house in good condition, pay bills and understand contracts, and had even mastered tools and "rugged stuff" that most women ignored because they had a man to do it for them.

But *alone* did disturb her for the very fact that had Miranda been on her own, she may have been discovered too late. Her health severely damaged? Dead? A shiver trickled down Allie's neck to consider such.

She wanted *independence* but she also desired companionship. Was it possible to have both? Her five-year marriage to Jean-Louis had been a bust. At first it had been fun, passionate, jet-setting back and forth from Los Angeles (where they'd lived at the time) to Paris (his birthplace). And it was what she needed at the time—a way to put *Clan MacKenzie*…and Finn behind her.

Jean-Louis, a budding actor himself, had enjoyed the fast-paced Hollywood lifestyle. They'd met at the premiere party for her first movie following *Clan MacKenzie*. They'd hit the scene, attended all the premieres and awards shows, and had lived a luxurious lifestyle. But it hadn't been all roses and romance. Halfway through year four of their marriage, after an unexpected miscarriage, Allie had been devastated to learn she could never carry a child. Jean-Louis hadn't been interested in her suggestions about adoption and confessed he was relieved they would be childless forever. Rather than feeling comforted that Jean-Louis didn't want something she could never give him, Allie had begun to recognize the gulf that lay between them. Children or no children, Allie wanted a life away from the spotlight and Jean-Louis, well…didn't. They'd parted amicably in the end because both realized it had been fun for a while, but they walked separate paths when it came to their hopes and dreams.

Allie wanted her path to stay single track. And yet she wouldn't have minded someone else's path crisscrossing over hers. Friendship and socializing were necessary to good emotional health. Life was best lived in the company of others. And she had been ignoring that mental care too much lately. All business and no play could make for a repetitive and lackluster life.

But might she ever find a man interesting enough, or with whom she was comfortable enough to allow into her life? The one she would simply *know* belonged in her life? She was, frankly, set in her ways. Unwilling to budge too far to accommodate another. Call it selfish. Call it coming into her own.

Call it crone power.

"Allie!"

Turning and shielding her face against the sun with her hand, she saw Finn stood on the hilltop beside the tree, waving. She hadn't heard the chainsaw fire up.

With a self-congratulating smile, she set the rake against the garden fence and wandered across the lumpy moss and grass turf. "Need some help with the chainsaw?" she wondered.

"No." He pressed a button on the tool and it revved, quietly. One of those electric tools that hummed rather than growled. He gestured toward the tree branch laying on the ground She should have given him more credit. "I just need you to stand on that end over there and hold it secure while I cut it into pieces so I can haul it to the wood pile. You're light as a bird, but your weight should help."

She stepped on the base of the branch that had been cut from the tree, finding balance. He started to make a few cuts. "How do you know how much I weigh…" Oh, right.

He winked at her cheekily.

"Oh, yeah," she said. "You had to lug me in your arms and tossed across your shoulder more times than any twenty-first century man would even consider."

"That outfit you wore added twenty pounds for sure," he said with a smile. "I was much stronger then. But I'd still sling you over a shoulder if necessary."

"And what would constitute necessary?"

He held the chainsaw ready to cut, quietly humming, as he considered her question. "Zombie attack?"

She nodded grudging acceptance to that one.

"Wild goat loose on the grounds?"

She wobbled her head. Fair enough. Goats freaked her out. They'd had to call in a stunt double for a scene featuring a goat because she hadn't been willing to get too close to the wild—and possibly murderous—goat that a trainer had brought in for filming. Its eyes had looked demonic to her, and she still stood firm on that fear.

"The sudden desire to carry you to my bed?"

Allie's jaw dropped open. That had come out of nowhere. And she couldn't be sure if he were teasing or acting, or…

Finn winked again and placed the chainsaw blade to the branch. Sawdust flew as he cut sections in a meticulous manner.

While Allie balanced against the vibrations and movement, she struggled to decide whether she would run from a desirous Finn intent on carrying her to his bed.

Or stand waiting for him to sling her over a shoulder and take her away.

CHAPTER FIVE

AFTER THEY'D STACKED the firewood next to the older logs on the wood pile behind the shed, Finn removed his wool coat and tossed it over a fence post. He'd worked up a sweat. Felt good. It had been a while since he'd done manual labor. Not that some of his roles hadn't required physical work. But he did know when to step back and allow the stunt double to handle the dangerous stuff.

Allie flipped her long braid over a shoulder and smiled at him. "Ready for some lunch?"

He could always eat. And if served by a beautiful woman? "This feels very domestic."

"What? This?" She gestured between the two of them. "I don't know what script you're following, McGregor, but I will set you back to work after we've eaten."

"A hard-nosed boss. I can handle anything you dish out."

He made to put an arm around her shoulder, but she quickened her steps and dodged out of what might have been an embrace. All right, so they weren't besties, but he'd only wanted to give her a friendly hug for a job well done. She'd stacked as many logs as he had. And she hadn't looked winded either.

Once inside, Allie went about making something to eat, so Finn ran up to his room to wash up. Wiping the water from his face, he noticed a flake of wood bark in his hair and plucked it out. The last time he'd done anything that really counted as good honest labor was when he'd help his dad with the hedgerows as a teenager. The old man was a professional hedgelayer; he wove hedges into solid barriers that could keep even the heaviest and most cantankerous of sheep or goat from damaging it.

He hadn't seen his dad in a few years. Though he did text him once a month. Before his first acting job, they had been close. Never demonstrative in their affections. More like standing side by side, sharing a good joke over a pint. The old man was not overly emotional, but he didn't need to be. His kindness reflected in the way he treated people. Finn respected his hardworking dad.

He'd invited his dad to his first Grammy Awards show. Finn had been thrilled to win Best Actor. To see his dad's proud face in the audience had been the icing on top. Of course, the years following, dad had begged off. Sean McGregor wasn't much for traveling and he'd seen it once. He could watch it on the telly.

And Finn had stepped forward on his own, embracing the Hollywood lifestyle of fame, riches and excess. He'd moved away from the good solid values Dad had taught him. Away from family. Away from a simple life of muscle-building manual labor and a relaxing pint with friends.

Now? There was something about that anchor to the real, the solid, that nudged at him. A fine day in his homeland filled with physical labor, good food and wandering. That was the life Sean McGregor lived. It was an example Finn held dear to his heart, though he was sure his dad probably wouldn't think it of him.

He still needed to answer the call for one more movie, one more award, one more bit of tangible proof that he was still worthy, viable and capable of headlining. But he wasn't going to get that by playing Dirk Swagger, porn star. Ugh.

At Allie's call, he returned to the kitchen to find sandwiches, sliced apples and cheese waiting. Wasn't exactly the spread he'd expected.

"What?" she asked as she placed a square of cheese on a slice of apple and bit into it.

"Looks…like a snack."

"You expected a four-course meal?"

He sat and took a bite of the sandwich. Ham with mustard. Not terrible.

"I didn't want to raid Miranda's pantry too deeply. We are guests. We should tread lightly."

Fair enough. "Good thing Portree is close. We'll head there later for some provisions and a proper bite to eat, aye?"

"Sounds like a plan." She took him in, a hint of churlishness curling the corner of her mouth.

"What?" Finn wiped at his lips. "Do I have mustard on my face?"

"No. I just noticed that your Scottish brogue is more prominent than usual."

"It's being in me homeland," he said in exaggerated brogue. "Suits a lad well and fine. You've a problem with me spoken words?"

"Not at all. I love it—er…" She lifted her chin and straightened her shoulders. "Yes, a trip to Portree later. I need to pick up some better gloves if I'm going to be working in the yard more."

"You shouldn't be lugging around those heavy tools and getting dirty. I can handle the outdoor tasks."

"I don't mind. I'm not much for lying around and allowing others to do what I can do."

He didn't care for the accusation in her tone. "You think I'm a spoiled movie star?"

"Are you?"

Finn stacked the cheese slices carefully on the apple

wedges. "Maybe a little. Hard not to become what the media says I am."

"Why?"

He didn't understand what she was asking.

"Why do you have to become what others want you to be?" she clarified.

Because he'd been made that way. Molded from one film to the next, one contract to the next, one handshake and wink that said, *Yes, I will do your bidding so long as you continue to promote and support my career.*

"Allie, I like what I do. And you do know there's a certain expectation from fans and moviegoers that a star lives a glamourous lifestyle."

"I suppose. Wouldn't be interesting if our favorite movie star lived in a rambler and mowed his own lawn. So you quit drinking?"

"Twelve years ago. That was one expectation I took to ambitiously for a while. Hard to avoid alcohol when I was always invited to those brilliant parties. Whiskey was my drug of choice. But it made me foggy and cranky, and a bit of an arse at times, I'm sure you remember. I went to rehab twice before it stuck. But I'm clean and sober now and proud of it."

"Congratulations. Addictions are rough. What did you replace it with?"

Finn eyed her suspiciously. "You think I'm a coke fiend now?"

Her laughter was deep and quick. "No, not at all. I've always assumed that a person usually has to take up something else to replace that missing fix. Photography? Knitting? Reading?"

"Aye, I did lean even further into my passion for motorbikes. The Ducati out front is my baby. Keep her in storage in Inverness. I haven't ridden her for years. Don't get me started on her because I'll talk your head off."

"You can take me out and introduce me later. I don't mind a little bragging."

"Aye?" He took another bite of the sandwich and it tasted better. She wanted to hear about his passion? When was the last time a woman had shown interest in him for something other than his looks or his latest role? "What's on the schedule for this afternoon? Are you going to force me to do more hard labor?"

"Stacking firewood is hardly hard labor."

She got up to refill her glass and leaned over the list on the counter. Her braid had loosened and long strands spilled around her face. A sexy look that reminded of soft summer afternoons and silken fabric brushing skin. To brush those strands over her ear would allow him to touch her skin… He'd touched Allie so many times. On her mouth, her face, her arms, her breasts (yes, they'd filmed nude scenes). But had he ever really felt the texture of her skin? The softness of her hair?

"Wasn't your dad a hedge trimmer?"

Startled out of his daydream, he corrected, "Hedgelayer. Still does it."

"There's a messy hedge that separates this property from the neighboring one that needs tending."

"I noticed that on the list. I can give it a go. I used to help dad with the neighbor's hedges."

"Nice. You take a look at that while I start the dusting and sweeping in the ballroom. Apparently there's a delivery of chairs and tables arriving tomorrow."

"How many are attending the convention?"

"I'm not sure. A hundred? Two hundred? It'll be a tight fight."

"Were you aware Miranda wanted us to be guest stars before you came here?"

"Not at all. But I don't mind. Much as I came here to shove

all things *Clan MacKenzie* in the past, I think it'll be fun to do one last goodbye to the show."

"Why do you want to shove it in the past? I mean, it's already in the past. The work we did on the show was incredible. You should be proud of it."

"Oh, I am. It's just…" She teased a finger around the rim of her glass.

"You said something earlier about clearing me out of your head. What does that mean? And should I take offense?"

"It's nothing."

As a general rule, Finn was acutely aware that when a woman said it "was nothing" that it was, in actuality, a whole lot of something. "Must be something if you traveled all the way to Scotland to do it."

Teasing at the ends of her heavy braid, she shrugged up her shoulders and exhaled heavily. "I've spent the last twenty-five years creating a life *away* from acting, Finn. I don't want any part of the Hollywood experience left clinging as I move forward. And…it still does. Part of it, anyway. Mostly the parts involving you."

Way to make a man feel two inches tall. "Was it so terrible? Working with me?"

Her wince signaled to Finn it was time to offer what he'd considered many a time over the years. Because it honestly hadn't been great between the two of them. It had been a struggle between his innocent attraction to her and the pressures of fame that had shut him off from her completely. A foolish move. But he hadn't known any better then how to juggle those feelings. Now? She deserved his truth.

"Come sit down, Allie. I want to say something to you."

"What do you mean?" She slid onto the chair opposite the table from him and pushed her plate aside.

"You moved on from acting and changed your life and I think that's swell. A person should do what makes them happy. And I want you to know I've thought about us over the years."

"Us?" She set the glass down and curled both hands about it. "There was never an us, Finn."

Because he'd been so staunch in ensuring that *us*—even just a friendship—did not happen. "I know that. And… I'm sorry, Allegra. I've wanted to apologize to you for years."

"For what?"

"For not being there for you. For never allowing us to be in it together when we easily could have been."

She lifted her chin. Tugged in her lower lip with a tooth. He'd hit on something emotional in her. He felt the same reaction at the base of his throat. A tightening. But also the need to draw her in and show her what he'd been holding captive in his heart for so long.

"We were never friends," he said. "And while I didn't realize it at the time when we were filming, I can look back now and know that was the wrong way to do things. I should have been your friend."

She nodded, her focus on the glass of water before her. Her silence spoke so much.

"I know it sounds strange to label it like that," he continued, "because we worked closely for six years. Every day for the months of filming every season. We should have been friends. But I guess… I didn't try. I didn't know how to fit you in my life away from the job. Even while everyone assumed we were the best of friends. The interviews and all the media junkets, we were acting."

She nodded, agreeing. "It was a weird time."

"Super weird. And when I look back," he said, "and recall how tough it was for me, learning the ropes, being initiated into the Hollywood machine—even though we filmed here in Scotland—I realize it is always harder for a woman. Especially one young and so new to the business. You should

have had a confidant, a friend to lean on. Instead, after filming wrapped for the day, I walked away from you. Sheltered
in my trailer with the next day's script. Or worse, went out
partying. Can you forgive me?"

"I, uh…" She finally looked at him. Her eyes were so clear
and yet solid as millennia-old ice. God, he wished he'd done
things differently back then. But on the other hand, he'd been
protecting her from that part of him that had surrendered to
the crazy wild ride of stardom.

"Thank you for saying that," she said. "And, yes, I do wish
we could have been friends. Talked. Shared our problems or
even just chatted about the day.

"Connor MacKenzie I knew like the back of my hand. I
never really got to know who Finn McGregor was. And yet,
we were so close…physically. It was confusing sometimes,
for me."

"We've made out. A lot."

She nodded. A small smile from her softened the ache in
his heart. "I think I've kissed you more than I've kissed anyone else in my lifetime."

"Same. We've touched each other in ways only lovers do.
Hell, we've simulated sex."

"Those were some tough scenes. Physically and…" she
sighed "…emotionally."

"I'm sorry if it was awkward sometimes. At least we did
have a sort of makeshift intimacy coordinator on set."

"Yes, and I'm thankful she was there at a time when the
job didn't really exist. But doing things like that still messes
with a person's head. At least it did with me. I mean, you'd
kiss me, touch me…and then the director would call *cut* and
you walked away."

Finn nodded. It was what he'd had to do. To not lose himself in the woman who, if given the freedom to get to know
her away from the set, he might have fallen in love with. Of

course, he'd sensed she may have had feelings toward him. Yet he'd always told himself that it was only because she was such a good actress. She could convey true, deep love with a look. His intuition had warned him not to date her, to drag her into the new and adventurous lifestyle he was being handed on a silver screen platter. Because she wasn't like the other women who had hung on him simply because he was a star.

Since sobering up, he didn't like to talk about those years. He'd been wild. With the booze and the women. Thank goodness he'd not tainted Allie with that side of him.

"I'm sorry," he said. "If I could go back and change things, I know I wouldn't have the maturity to do anything differently. But now? This old man? I'm aware I made mistakes. Best I can do is apologize and move on."

"Apology accepted. And… I'm sure I could have tried harder too."

"You've nothing to apologize for, Allie. Whew! It feels good to put that out there. I hope you were able to find someone to talk to at that time."

"I had girlfriends I'd call on the weekends. I was fine."

He suspected from her tight expression that she hadn't been fine. She wanted to put the show and *him* behind her? No, she hadn't been fine and possibly still wasn't. But he'd leave it there for now. He did feel lighter now that he'd expressed that long-held concern. Now that they'd been thrown together to help out in Miranda's time of need, he intended to do what he could to find a friend in Allie Stark. And with luck, she could learn to trust him. And might she consider a role in the new series after it sold?

"Starting to rain," he noted. "I wonder if Miranda has extra rain slickers in the boot room?"

"She did have a few. The pink one's mine. I believe there's one with flowers on it that looks about your size."

"I can work the flowers with the best of them. I'll head out to survey the hedgerow. Unless you want me to help you dust?"

"I can handle a feather duster like a pro."

He took his plate and rinsed it in the sink and dried it off.

"Thank you," she said. "That apology meant a lot to me."

"Sure thing."

He left her sitting before the table. Because if he remained, he may have pulled her into a hug. And he wasn't sure how she'd take that. *He* needed the hug. But asking for forgiveness had been a big step for one day.

With hope, she'd soften to him and decide to keep his memory and, by proxy, *him* in her heart.

CHAPTER SIX

THE BALLROOM WAS surprisingly tidy. Allie figured Miranda must have a cleaning person come in on occasion. So she dragged the feather duster quickly over the stone walls where the dust tended to collect.

This room still looked as it had for filming. The massive hearth at center back and even the tapestry rug had been preserved. Heavy wood furniture formed a half circle before the hearth, while the majority of the room was empty. Dancing, anyone? She and Finn had learned many a dance for the show, all of it filmed in this room.

The vast side opposite the hearth was where the camera equipment had set up. And if one lit a fire in the hearth, the heat only carried so far, so having an active living space on the other side wasn't practical. The castle did have a modern heating system, but with a room so large, the fireplace was about the least-expensive form of heating.

Once she owned the place she might bring in a crystal chandelier to replace the deer antler chandelier. Not even might, it was a must. Glamcations did glamour, not dead animal parts. And she'd set up a yoga/wellness area beneath the high stained glass windows that featured scenes of long-lost dukes hunting deer or fox, bringing in heat lamps to keep it warm in the cooler months. If rented by a group, classes could be taught in the massive space. Add in a juice bar along with massage center?

Yes, that would be perfect.

As she dusted closer to the hearth, she recalled that one stone… In the show there had been a loose stone in the wall where Connor kept the MacKenzie family's valuables. As well, a magical crystal.

Tapping the stones with her fingers until she landed on a loose one, she discovered it hadn't been sealed shut. With a wriggle the stone came out to reveal a dark space. It had once been lit inside. The crew had set up a smaller special set featuring a narrow rock tunnel to film a container shot to show Connor looking inward as he would put his hand inside to grasp…

Allie reached inside, expecting that Miranda had already checked it out, but…she felt something…

She pulled out the prop stone that her character had once found in the fairy pool at the edge of the property. She'd brought it home to her new husband, Connor MacKenzie, excited that it could be magic, and he'd taken it away from her and admonished her never to go to the fairy pools alone again.

Of course, her character, brave and fiercely independent, had returned. Many times. She'd been an intrepid explorer in search of fairies. And that search had eventually resulted in learning Connor was half fairy.

The series story had centered around two feuding clans. The suspicion of anything paranormal had still been viewed as preposterous for the time period, yet also possible. Her character had communicated with Sir Arthur Conan Doyle during one episode in which Sean Connery had guest-starred as the writer/physician with a bent for the fantastical. She was proud to have been a part of the series. And to this day she would never dismiss the idea that fairies existed. She did live in Sedona, a hot spot for all things woo-woo and paranormal.

Finn's apology earlier in the kitchen had surprised her. Yet it had been spot-on. Miranda's fan club may be shocked to learn the show's main stars had never been friends. Not in terms of spending time with one another away from set, or even having conversations during breaks or lunches. Once filming had wrapped for the day, they'd returned to their respective trailers. Finn had had his life beyond work and would often spend weekends on the mainland where he had lived.

She… Well, she hadn't known anyone in that part of the world, and she'd been too shy to join in with the cast and crew when they socialized, or maybe you could say she was too gloomy over her feelings for Finn to put herself out there. Or to watch him hang on a local girl while he put back the pints? She was never much of a wild party person anyway. Instead she'd wander the moors and cliffs along the sea. Had, even then, felt a visceral connection to the land that, while best experienced alone, had still made her feel more than alone.

Not accepted by the one person she'd most been drawn to.

In hindsight she could understand Finn's avoidance of her. During the first season's run, their fame had exploded. Finn McGregor had become the hot new star on the scene. Of course he had soaked in all the media interest and instant fandom while she'd shied away from it. But his ignoring her had hurt at a time when she had been enamored of him.

Had loved him.

And, yes, she'd felt jealous when she'd see him with other women. How pitiful was that? Truly, she'd been infatuated.

Pressing her forehead against the cool stone wall beside the cubby hole, she closed her eyes and clasped the fake crystal against her chest.

No, she didn't want to go back and change things. Make Finn see her. Spend time with her. Be his girlfriend or lover (for real). Because she knew now it never could have lasted. They had been too young for real, lasting love. And with constant media scrutiny, romances between actors, especially those sharing an on-screen love story, had little hope for survival.

But what did she want from Finn now? Her intentions to allow the memories to rise and then kick them to the curb had been hijacked by his being here. It wouldn't be so easy to shove him aside now. His sure presence and sexy smile reminded her of how enamored she had been of him then. And the man had actually gotten sexier.

Not at all fair to her heart.

Now with his apology she felt as if she'd been firmly friend-zoned. No chance for a romance in his statement they might be friends. It was the best thing for both of them. So why did it sting like another rejection?

She studied the purple hunk of pearlescent glass that was shaped like a crystal yet glowed with an unnatural vibrance. It had held Connor MacKenzie's fairy power, a totem passed down through the ages by his fairy relatives. Once lost in the pool, after Allie's character had found it, it had restored Connor's magic, a magic he'd known he possessed and pined to someday use.

She clutched the stone to her chest. Holding it now returned her to those feelings of wonder she'd once acted out on screen. The stone, in the show, had bonded her and Finn's character.

And right now it felt like a little piece of magic she hadn't known she needed. "I have to show him this."

The floral rain slicker fit him perfectly. Quite a fashionista, aye?

With a chuckle for his silly thoughts, Finn studied the overgrown blackthorn hedge that marked the edge of the Donaldson land. Well-established, it had been there as long as he could remember. And he did remember the nights when his dad would call to accompany him out under the moonlight to go unloose the unfortunate bleating sheep that had attempted to jump the hedge only to land forelegs on one side and hind legs on the other. The neighbor's sheep had been daft like that.

He kicked the base of the hedgerow. A lot of vertical growth, and bramble at the ground, which was not what a properly laid hedge wanted. It would require some work to get it looking trim and neat. And while he'd seen tools in the shed to manage such work, an axe, billhook, pruning saw and heavy leather gloves, he could but shake his head at the immensity of the task.

Sure, one man could take to it and be finished in a day. A skilled hedgelayer. Sean McGregor could wield an axe to pleach a hedge like some kind of ninja shrub master. But for Finn? He might give it a go, but it could end up looking worse for wear and he may even damage some necessary growth. Not what he wanted should the future see this land once again the filming site for another *Clan MacKenzie* drama.

Tugging out his phone, he texted his dad. At the old castle for a few days. Want to get together? Some work needed on the hedge. Thought you might be interested. No reply. But then, his dad generally only turned his mobile on once at the end of the day.

Tucking away his phone, the afternoon mist decided him on inside work. He headed into the castle to check the toilet off the ballroom.

Allie was nowhere to be found. He assumed she was upstairs, perhaps wielding a feather duster. Had she taken his apology to heart? He hoped so. There was no way to turn back time. And he had cared for her. In his own manner. At least by shielding her from his increasingly reckless lifestyle.

There were two toilets in the room and a urinal. They had been installed during filming for the crew. The one in need of attention was making a weird gurgling noise. He was no plumber but after watching a few videos on YouTube and jiggling some of the inner workings and flushing a few times, it worked like a dream. The accomplishment was small but it still gave him a warm feeling in his chest.

"Master of so much more than fake spy stuff," he said with a satisfied nod.

His longest-running role as Jack Greystone for the *Code Grey* series of movies had cast him as an international spy utilizing all sorts of makeshift items for weapons and as means to escape tricky situations. But the toilet ranked right up there with using a corkscrew to defeat a machete-wielding villain. Good work for one day.

He found Allie in the kitchen sipping tea. The room smelled of sweet clove.

"Weren't we going to head into town for a real meal?" he asked.

"I'm ready when you are. But first, look what I found." She nodded toward something sitting on the table and he went to inspect.

The purple talisman made him smile. "You found—is this the real fairy stone? From the set?"

"I found it in the cubby safe by the hearth when I was dusting. Pretty cool that it was still there, huh?"

"I know they had dozens of these as props. Bound to have forgotten one lying about." He took the stone and rubbed the cool smooth surface. He pressed the crystal to his forehead as he'd done in the series.

"Do you feel your wings fluttering?" Allie asked.

"Nope. Calling all fairies," he mocked. "All fairies, come in."

"That's not how it worked."

He handed it to her and sat across the table from her. "I know. Some of those scenes were just plain silly though."

"I remember them as touching. You, as Connor MacKenzie, finally dared to reveal to a human you were half fairy and she trusted you." Allie patted her heart. "Such a tearjerker."

"I've avoided tearjerkers since."

"Why is that?"

Finn shrugged. "Mostly, I haven't been offered them. Save the one about the selkie. I did enjoy the romance in that one."

"Didn't you date your costar?"

"I wouldn't call it actual dating." She had only wanted him for one thing. Happy to oblige, that younger rascal Finn.

"Once *Code Grey* hit it big," he said, "I've since only been offered the action stuff. Action alpha man is my wheelhouse."

"*Code Grey* is a great series of movies. Not that I see many movies anymore. I'm just too busy. Yet you can take the actress out of Hollywood but you can never take the need for good entertainment out of my soul."

So true. He lived for stories of all kinds, told in all manner, from movies to books, even some of the gaming series had intricate and compelling stories. His agent had best stay on top of the prospect with the VR-gaming company in Seville. That could offer many choices roles.

"Why did you leave acting?" he asked. "Those two movies you did following the series were box office hits."

"What a weird ride, doing the press junkets and promotion for those movies." Allie leaned back on her chair and put up her bare feet on the nearby chair. "It didn't feel right with my soul. Everything was focused on the bottom line. Making money. Stuffing me into skintight costumes for the sake of sexual appeal. Getting the 'how much weight did you have to lose' question from reporters over and over while my male costars always got the interesting ones. I was never taken seriously. Much as I enjoyed the craft of acting, it wasn't me."

"You've always been an earth girl. I remember you'd walk

the cliffs after filming." He reached to toggle her biggest toe. "Barefoot."

She wiggled her toes, sexy as sin to him. "Feet were meant for grass and earth. I'm pretty sure that's why God invented grass."

"Don't get my toes in the green stuff much." His vacations were to places like Dubai or a luxurious private beach resort. "Didn't you marry right about the time of that first movie?"

"I met Jean-Louis at the premiere party. We dated four weeks before tying the knot."

"Wow. He must have been some kind of wonderful."

"He…was. And then he wasn't."

She fussed with the teacup on the saucer, not meeting his gaze. Of course he was delving but he did have a quest to know her better. And he was already feeling comfortable around her, as if they didn't have decades of time between them. It was almost as if they were sitting around comparing script notes. Relaxed. Confident. Just another day on the set.

"Our marriage lasted as long as it needed to," she finally offered. "He loved the acting world and I didn't. I suppose you could say we grew apart. It was an amicable parting."

"I'm glad about that. For you. Hollywood divorces can get nasty."

"I'm thankful as well. We went into the marriage with our own property and left with the same. And really, the residuals from *Clan MacKenzie* didn't last long. But they did help to start Glamcations and build me a little nest egg."

"I want to hear all about your business. But let's get on the road, shall we? I'm starving."

"Can we take your motorbike?"

"Wouldn't have it any other way."

"Let me grab a scarf and I'll be right down."

She dashed out of the kitchen. Finn couldn't imagine any man marrying that woman and *not* wanting to stay with her forever. But if her husband's interests had been opposite of Allie's, he was happy for her that it had ended on a good note.

Yet if he thought about it, he was much like her ex-husband. Both actors, and happy about it. So did that mean he'd never have a chance with her? And why was he thinking about another chance when he'd never taken a first chance?

CHAPTER SEVEN

THE MOTORBIKE RIDE into Portree was exhilarating. Finn had miraculously managed to find a dusty old spare helmet in the boot room for her. Allie had never been invited by Finn to ride with him while they'd been filming. It had been featured in many a magazine article about the up-and-coming young star. Of course he had taken others for rides. Costars, friends, random women who would sometimes show up on set, his latest fling.

To be honest with herself, she'd been jealous of those women. Not a good look on her. But now she knew better. And she was facing those memories, as planned. Time to kick the unrequited love she'd once held for Finn McGregor to the curb?

Sure. And to replace it with a new memory. A more mature Allegra Stark accepting a ride because it was an adventure she'd always wanted to try. Not because the driver was handsome and charming. Okay, maybe a little.

The roads were a bit wet so he drove slowly, which she appreciated, but also in her elation she wanted to yell "faster!" Thankfully, the rain had stopped. The air brisking her cheeks was nothing less than brilliant. As she leaned against his back, her arms around his waist, she tilted back her head and closed her eyes. What a rush! This is what she wanted life to feel like always. Free, unmoored, dashing off on adventure.

But also, with her arms around someone she cared about. Sharing adventure felt so wonderful.

She'd find her man someday. But she wasn't going to let go of Finn just because she felt she shouldn't have any contact with him. If she let go, she'd fall off. That was her story, and she was sticking to it.

Portree, capital of the Isle of Skye, overlooked a quaint harbor populated with seals and squawking cormorants and was surrounded by hills and mountains. Twilight burnished the gorgeous scenery with a golden glow. The town offered hotels and boutique bed-and-breakfasts, but not a lot of sights to see without hiking out or taking a guided tour. There were many restaurants, in all ranges of size, specialty and price.

It had been well over a decade since Allie worried about being recognized while out in public. Her silver hair had changed her appearance. One rarely guessed she was the raven-haired woman from the decades-old TV series. And that suited her fine. But as they parked the motorbike and Finn ran a hand through his helmet-crushed hair she had to ask, "Do you have a hat?"

He shrugged. "Is my hair such a mess?"

"No, I just thought…" She pulled off the scarf she'd tied over her hair to wear under the helmet. "Well, you are such a recognizable person."

He rubbed a preening hand along his jaw and looked around. "I don't mind it. The occasional autograph never hurt a guy."

And probably the occasional autograph is what the guy needed to feed his ego. Though she'd not seen it rise since they'd reunited at the castle. His ego probably kicked in when around a crowd. Fair enough.

They made their way to a midsize restaurant overlooking the harbor. The hostess did not recognize Finn, but they did luck out and managed a table in what looked like an obviously crowded dining room.

Allie noticed Finn glanced around as the hostess led them to their table. Not many people looked at them, and the few who did were younger faces who gave him a look of, *Is he? Nah, couldn't be.* If anything, they may recognize him from his *Code Grey* movies.

After they'd ordered and tea had been brought to the table, Allie leaned back in the booth, tucking up her legs, as was most comfortable. She sipped her tea and studied Finn. He glanced around, taking in their fellow patrons. A quiet bagpipe melody whispered from nearby speakers, competing with the clink of glass and silverware.

"Does it bother you when you are not recognized?" she asked.

"What makes you think that?"

"Just seems like you expect something that isn't coming."

"Am I that obvious?" He swiped a hand along his stubbled jaw and shook his head. "I suppose I am. I'm so used to dodging paparazzi and autograph hounds that when it doesn't happen, I wonder if I've stepped into a new dimension. It's disconcerting."

"Not refreshing? To have the peace?"

"I'm not sure I know what peace even is."

That made her sad. Her whole life she had strived for a perfect center, knowing herself and never stooping to please others. A peace that she could embrace. But had she wrapped her arms about that peace too tightly? Had it made it too difficult to contemplate letting others in, with all the mess that could involve?

"It's life-changing," she said. "But excitement has its place too. That motorcycle ride was exhilarating. I can't wait to get back on it."

"There is something to be said for loud and unrestrained.

I'll take you on a tour of the island, if you want. This is my old stomping ground, after all."

"Do you still have friends here?"

"A few of my friends from school are still around. I checked in with Crispin MacCreavy, my best mate when I was a teen, as I arrived at the airport. Left him a text to see what he's up to. And there was our neighbor who worked the fishery. He was a salty one. I based my character in *Seaswept* on him."

That movie had been about a fisherman who'd fallen in love with a selkie. It was one of Allie's favorites of his earlier work. Quiet, yet so romantic. Apparently, he'd shoved the romance scripts aside after that one.

Watching Finn's career unfold after *Clan MacKenzie* had shown her so much about him she'd not noticed while filming the series. He was often seen going out into the crowds to sign autographs and shake hands with young fans. He always posed for photos (once even arriving late for an awards benefit because of it) and he was linked to a charity that funded families who had lost their homes from natural disasters. Knowing that about him had deepened the love she'd felt for him, which of course had made it all the harder to handle.

She wondered now if she were being too harsh by wanting to erase the man from memory. There was nothing wrong with being friends, was there?

Why so indecisive all of a sudden? Hadn't she been determined to abandon all memory of Finn McGregor?

Their meals were brought and with an inhale of the seafood spiced with pepper and lemon and the rosemary potatoes, Allie dug in.

Finn smiled at her. "I remember how much you like to eat."

"Potatoes," she said, holding up her fork with a small buttery potato speared on the end. "All problems life throws at you can be solved with potatoes. Potatoes are my love language."

"I'll have to remember that one. So tell me about your Glamcations venture. How did it get started? What's it all about?"

After a few bites, Allie set her fork aside. "After my divorce, I kind of curled in on myself for about a year. It was my mother who stopped by one day, shook me by the shoulders—literally—and told me it was time to stop pouting. She suggested I start taking care of my soul."

"Sounds like one of those New Agey, woo-woo kind of moms."

"I adore my mother, sage, crystals and all. So, I went on a glamping vacation in Sedona. It was a group of women focused on finding themselves. That part was weird, even for someone raised by a woo-woo mom. But I did find a friend for life in Savannah. She's ten years younger than me. Is gorgeous. Has a brain for business and marketing. And never met a crystal she couldn't use to heal, manifest or stuff in her bra. But also she'd come off a bad relationship and was there in search of something more.

"After some discussion we agreed that we women often don't know how to spoil ourselves. We both loved the idea of camping in glamourous surroundings and wanted to take it to the next level. The original idea was to find locations set in or near major cities. Because you have to do the tourism thing while on vacation. But after a long day of visiting the sights, you return to a fabulous loft or home or even a castle that's got a masseuse waiting to change your religion. And a chef to lure you into his cult. All the spoily things we women love but never do for ourselves. Within five years, we'd acquired six properties across the United States, which are always booked. Our first international property was in the South of France. We added a Paris loft two years ago, and one in Seville last year."

"So it's only for women?"

"We don't rule out men. But we've found women are more apt to want the escape. Most bookings are just one woman, or a pair of friends. Some are groups. We've taken remote settings, scruffy and wild on the outside, and glammed up the insides and the experience. A five-star chef, a masseuse, a closet full of designer clothing for photo ops because, you know, if it's not posted on Instagram, did it really happen?" She chuckled. "Just a fun stay away from real life. We bring in lifestyle teachers for group events. And married couples use it as well. Sometimes all it takes to reboot a floundering marriage is a weekend away from the kids and being spoiled, treated to luxury."

"Sounds like something I could use."

Allie laughed, then caught herself. He was serious. "Oh?" She sipped her tea. "Well, you've an open invitation to use any of our locations whenever you want to. But I would think you live a glamorous and spoiled life already."

"It's not the glamour or the high-end lifestyle that appeals. I like the idea of being alone in a place far from the busyness of the world. And the paparazzi."

"Really? This coming from the man obviously let down because no one recognized him tonight? You're a dichotomy, Finn."

"Better that than boring, eh?" He lifted his teacup for a toast and she met him with her cup. "To discovering oneself."

"I'll drink to that."

"The castle would make a nice location for Glamcations," he said. "Do you think you won the bid?"

She'd almost forgotten they were competing for the castle. Already, she felt as though she were dusting, trimming and cleaning her own place.

"I hope so," she said. "Is there anything I can do to make you decline the place?"

"It *is* my childhood home, Allie."

She screwed up her lips. "Are you going to use that against me as a bargaining chip to win the bid? I didn't think the castle meant that much to you when we were filming. Just a place you once lived in."

"Hey now, I have great childhood memories. But don't worry. It's not my principal means to wanting the place. I really believe having the castle will be the key to selling the series."

She nodded. "Probably. So we're battling against one another."

"Not unless you come on board and consider reprising your role."

"Pass. But good try."

"All I can do is try. But if this series sells, I'll have producer credit, and I promise you'll be treated like the queen you are."

"Still passing. And still determined to come out the winning bidder." She tugged the fairy stone out of her jeans pocket and held it to her eye. "If there's any magic left in here…"

"You do know that's just a piece of glass?"

"Of course. But what's life without a little wonder and magic?"

"You always were the one with the fantastical soul," he said. "You made the show."

"I don't think so—"

"It's the truth. Everything you did seemed so effortless, as if touched by magic."

"Oh." She didn't know how to take that compliment. It felt great to hear but coming from a man she had always pined to hear a kind word from—and not scripted—it was unusual. But also, she reminded herself, people could change. And maybe she would be wise to accept the new and kinder Finn McGregor.

She tucked the stone back in her pocket and dug into the remainder of her potatoes. "Do you want my fish? I'm not crazy about it."

"For sure." He grabbed her plate while she was still eating and scraped the fish onto his plate. Then, realizing what he'd just done, he apologized. "That was rude."

"Not at all. It's..." What a friend would have done. "Get that last bit, will you?"

They arrived back at the castle as the sun set. The half-moon sat low and bright in the navy sky, surrounded by stars. As Allie started toward the front door, Finn called after her. "Do you want to check out the moon from the cliff?"

She paused, spinning with a smile, almost as if on cue for a scene, but her genuine happiness was unmistakable. Joining him, they strolled around back of the castle. The cliff overlooking the sound was not far from the low stone wall that fenced in the yard. A well-worn path led the way. Finn brushed at a few midges, though he noticed Allie wasn't bothered by them at all. Must be her sweet scent. He'd learned early on that a lemony oil tended to fend off the biting critters.

She walked to the lookout spot where they could take in the finest artwork in the world. Spreading her arms wide, she tilted back her head. "This is better than I remembered."

"That's because there are no intrusive camera riggings or yelling directors. We've the moon all to ourselves." But his attention fixed on Allie. "She is a beauty."

"It's always such a treat to stand in the air and feel the moon on my face."

He'd never spent much time staring at the moon, but the

romance of the moment did strike him. Finn debated whether to take Allie's hand. Something inside him needed to feel… anchored. Attached to a grounded being.

After brushing strands of hair from her face, she looked aside at him, noticing his distraction. "What is it?"

Why did he suddenly feel like a young lad who'd never kissed a girl? Even his acting skills fled. He was left with a thudding heart and shaky voice. "I—I was thinking I'd like to hold your hand."

"Oh?"

"I'm not trying to be sweet… Well, yes, I am. It's been a long time since we've held hands, Allie. And never without a camera crew present."

He held out his hand. *Please take it. Don't shun this nervous lad's wanting heart.*

"Yes, all right." She clasped his hand.

They had held hands many times for the show. But this wasn't an act. And for the first time Finn really experienced the feel of her skin against his. They stood side by side, eyes to the moon, hearts pounding. Instead of anchoring him, as he'd wanted, this handhold buoyed him. Lifted his senses and made him feel floaty. If he looked down, he might see his boots leave the scruffy ground. It was as if the fairy stone in Allie's pocket really did hold some magic. And he wasn't going to argue that.

"Look at that!" She pointed to the sea.

Finn spied the silvery glint of moonlight on the back of a surfacing dolphin. Pods of them frequented the narrow sound. "Mermaids come to greet the moon."

"Oh, yeah? Who sounds woo-woo now?"

He squeezed her hand and bowed his head sheepishly. It wasn't an act. His words were not studied or scripted.

"We had our first kiss here," she said wistfully.

"I remember." He…did not.

They'd kissed so many times. The first few times had been awkward. Learning their way around one another. In front of a full camera crew. After a while their kisses had become…functional. To kiss before a crew of dozens was never romantic. And always mechanical.

"You don't remember." She nudged his ribs with her elbow. "That's okay. Those kisses were so…"

"Not private."

"Not at all. But, man, Connor and Madeline did like to make out. I wasn't sure what I'd gotten myself into that first time we had to kiss. To have to look romantic and sexy before the crew? It was discombobulating."

"Like I said…" He squeezed her hand. "I should have been there for you."

"Maybe, but you were new to acting as well. I'm sure you were as frightened as I in the beginning."

"True. Kissing before a camera never gets comfortable." He pulled up her hand and kissed the knuckles. Then he clasped it to his chest. Could she feel the thunder of his heart? "We didn't know what we had, Allie."

Her mouth parted. Surprised? Or sadly in agreement?

"I did." She pulled her hand from his and shoved it in her back jeans pocket.

The sudden loss of her touch stuttered his heartbeats. Had he said something wrong?

"I should get inside. It's chilly out here. Thanks for dinner!" she called as she hurried back to the castle.

Finn followed her rushed departure. He'd meant what he said. He hadn't been aware of how wonderful having Allie in his life was at the time when they'd been filming. Of course he'd considered that she might have had the hots for him back then, but his arrogance had always been tempered by a little voice in the back of his head that reminded him that she was too good for the likes of him, and she probably knew it. She was just a good actress, that was all. He had missed the truth of it, that strength of feeling that still made her skittish around him now. Made her want to flee him as if she'd just been burned.

He wanted her to embrace him. To welcome him into her life. Because more and more he believed he'd been given a chance to finally do things right with Allegra Stark.

CHAPTER EIGHT

THE EVENT SUPPLY company truck arrived at 8:00 a.m. with a load of folding chairs and tables. Finn was not awake so Allie, fresh out of the shower when she'd heard the approaching truck, had quickly pulled on dark leggings and a snuggly green sweater and stepped into wellies by the door to go out and meet them.

Just the act of stepping out of the castle, hair free and catching the breeze, made her feel some ownership. Never had she felt so invested in a property she'd wanted to buy until now. Even the fact that, should she win, she'd be taking Finn's childhood home away from him, didn't bother her overmuch. He hadn't lived here for well over three decades. And he seemed to want the place more for its potential in gaining him a script sale than anything.

It took about an hour for them to carry in all the supplies to the ballroom. The crew of three men did not set up anything. They weren't paid to do that. Taking the invoice, and explaining Miranda's sudden medical condition, Allie promised to send the bill to her daughter so it would be taken care of.

She tucked the invoice behind the list on the clipboard. Then she marked off the few items they'd accomplished on the list. There were still so many things remaining. Miranda would be in no condition to do any of this.

A text pinged on her phone. From Dorothy: Taking Mum

home with me this afternoon to rest and recuperate. She's doing very well. Will check in after we get her settled.

Good for her. Only a couple of days in the hospital, and now a stay with her daughter's family. That was the best place for Miranda to be right now. She texted back that she and Finn were ticking the preconvention tasks off the list. Then she quickly checked for flower delivery in Edinburgh, where Dorothy lived. Within ten minutes she'd ordered a lovely bouquet to be delivered. Miranda deserved a bit of cheering up.

Plus, it didn't hurt to butter up the woman she was trying to buy the castle from.

Oh, Allie. Had she just thought that? She wasn't that kind of person. Apparently, the competition with Finn had brought that out of her.

Her pencil paused by the item: *trim hedgerow.* Finn had spent some time wandering along the stretch that bordered the west edge of the property. He'd mentioned calling his dad to take a look at it. She had faith that he would.

After a quick trip to her room—now that she wasn't rushed—she pulled her loose hair into a ponytail to keep it out of her eyes and returned to the ballroom with clipboard in hand. Miranda had sketched out a seating arrangement.

There were one hundred and sixty chairs that had to be squeezed into the ballroom. It required skill to make it work and leave room for walking around and areas all around the circumference, including leaving the hearth area untouched, as Miranda had planned. That was to be her stage area where the microphone and speakers were placed. The sound system sat in a large box near the hearth. She didn't touch the electronics; not her forte. She also noted something about a projector and screen, but that hadn't been delivered with the chairs.

When finished, and happy with the militant placement of the chairs, Allie relaxed on the sofa before the hearth and wished she could flick a switch to produce fire. She loved a gas-powered fireplace and vacillated on whether to install one here.

If she got the place.

Finn was determined to win. So was she. He also seemed determined to get her to reprise her role as Madeline Williams. Could she be a carrot to lure in a film company? She found that unlikely.

What was clear was that Finn didn't seem dialed in to her feelings toward him. The feelings she'd *once* held for him. He hadn't known what they'd had while filming for six years?

She'd had to walk away from their moon-gazing last night and that sweet handhold, because to stay and wade through those memories may have seen her in tears.

Her infatuation with the man had set her memory to something more romantic than it had been. She had fallen in love with the *idea* of the man, half real, half a larger-than-life character. A highlander, for heaven's sake, who was part fairy. A literal romance hero who had worn a kilt and had all the muscles (so many shirtless scenes) and said all the right things when the heroine needed to hear them.

The series writers had created a romantic mood and setting, utilizing the delicate line between emotion and drama. Every scripted word she'd spoken had reverberated inside her, become her. When Allie, acting as Madeline, had kissed Connor MacKenzie, in that moment it had been real. A real kiss that she'd felt to her bones. And when Madeline had fallen in love with Connor, so had Allie.

But that was the crux. Had she fallen in love with the fictional Connor or the real Finn or a mixture of both?

After Finn had stepped off set, she hadn't been able to stop pining over the man, despite during the second season when his date-of-the-weeks began hanging around off-stage, or years later when she'd begun to notice he'd swig whiskey between scenes. During the fifth season the makeup artists had noticed it as well. Dark circles under his eyes from partying.

Shaking her head, Allie brought herself back to the present.

Getting over Finn/Connor had not been easy. And it was obvious to her, even after all these years, she wasn't completely over him.

Her marriage to Jean-Louis had been an experiment to see if she could forget Finn. Well. She hadn't gone into it thinking *experiment*. She had been dazzled by Jean-Louis. Yet in the back of her mind, Finn had remained present. She wondered now if that infatuation had contributed to her failed marriage. A little? The truth of it was that they wanted different things, even before the curveball of no children came into play. Jean-Louis had wanted to dive into the acting lifestyle and immerse himself in Hollywood while she had wanted to run screaming in the opposite direction. And that had nothing to do with Finn.

Yet after the divorce, in the midst of her dark melancholy muddle (as she'd called it), she'd looked up Finn through help from her agent. Had almost called him.

Thank goodness her mom had rescued her from that muddle and she'd gone to the retreat and met Savannah. They'd both just come out of divorces and displayed their broken hearts as if offering it up on their open palms. Together, they'd supported one another when they sought new partners, and consoled when those romances fizzled.

It was all good now. And as for love? Well, she hadn't really worried too much about that for years now. Except there was a part of her where Allie really did want someone in her life. And now that a very particular someone had reappeared, she was confused at what her heart was asking of her. A heart that still lay on her open palms. It wanted her to talk to Finn, get to know him, see if there was another option besides shoving him out of her heart. And yet it also wanted her to stand tall and realize that she had loved a character realized by an egotistic actor. Could Finn ever be real? He was still playing parts. And she only wanted real now.

"Sleeping on the job?"

She smirked at the sound of Finn's voice but didn't stir because the chair cushions had accepted her as one of their own and she could fall asleep here if left alone.

"You set all this up?" He sat on the chair opposite her. His boots were muddy, and she made a point of looking across the floor to his tracks. "Sorry, I'll…"

"I'll get it," she said with annoyance.

"You don't have to do that."

"Honestly, I'm not convinced you won't make more mess trying to clear it up otherwise." She sighed as Finn stood and looked around the ballroom.

"Wow, you did good in here. It's very…militant."

"Thank you." Despite her irritation, her perfectionista beamed inwardly. "How's the hedgerow coming along?"

He hummed in thought. "I'm waiting on a call from Dad so I mucked out the stable instead."

It was then Allie realized the mud on his boots might be more than dirt. But she also knew there were no animals on the estate. "What was there to muck?"

"Not much, but I did discover a family of squirrels in the hayloft. They're awfully cute." He tugged out his phone. "Do you want to take a look?"

"No, I'd rather just take care of the mud." She stood and he tucked away his phone. She strolled out toward the kitchen and he followed. "Will you take those boots off outside and leave them out there?"

"Yes, Mum." He left and she heard the side door open and shut.

Allie checked herself. She'd deserved the *mum* accusation. That wasn't her MO. Just being in the same room as Finn seemed to flip her *normal* on its head. She'd apologize.

But first, this mess. With a shake of her head she filled a mop bucket with hot soapy water.

Finn signed for a package the delivery man dropped off, then with a side excursion around the back of the castle to collect some of the white lily of the valley blooming in a little garden, he returned to find Allie emptying a bucket of dirty water into the sink.

What an oaf. He needed to start looking beyond himself. His agent had said much the same. *If you want to get work again, McGregor, start acting like you're not the only man in the room. The oxygen must be shared.*

That comment had cut deep.

If he wanted to sell this project, he'd have to make some changes. Starting with his massive ego. Despite him acting affronted by Allie's mention of it, he knew it existed. It had been honed by his years of standing before an admiring crowd and insinuating their adoration into his veins. Of becoming accustomed to seeing his face on billboards, online and in Times Square. He *expected* that adoration. And when patrons in a restaurant did not turn and gawk at him, it hurt him in a manner that—it felt silly to consider it now.

Those stares and promotional blasts never felt like validation. At least it hadn't lately. Would having this castle *really* catch a producer's interest despite a script that he wasn't sure would ever meet his standards? It had been rewritten three times, and he still had a list of changes despite sending it around for reading. His role had to be made larger and not so secondary.

But then, if Allie wouldn't consider reprising her role, did he really want to go ahead without her? He'd considered making her death a major plot line. But now that he'd stepped back into her life, he did want to work with her again. How to convince her to give it another shot?

What was he doing here? Mucking a stable and trimming hedgerows wasn't increasing his chances at gaining another movie role. And plucking flowers… He wobbled the handful he held. A few bits of dirt fell from one stalk which he'd completely uprooted.

Was he trying to charm the girl? If he could get on her good side, she might change her mind and decide acting was for her, after all?

Or was it something more than coaxing her back under the limelight? Something personal. Maybe even, he sought an intimacy they'd never had while filming.

Why couldn't he keep his priorities straight?

Allie set the bucket on the floor, squeezed out a cloth over the sink, then nodded at him. "Don't tell me you've been mucking about in the garden. Let me see your shoes."

He lifted one leg high enough to reveal he had taken off his shoes and wore but wool socks. He wouldn't make the *mum* comment again. That had been a dig she hadn't deserved.

"I left the dirt outside this time." With a glance behind him, he noted a few sprinkles of dirt fallen from the roots. Oops. "I thought these would brighten things up a bit?"

He handed her the flowers. She examined them, finding the roots were now clean of dirt (he'd have to backtrack, clean up the trail he'd left) and nodded. "Apology accepted." She turned to open cupboards and discovered a vase, which she filled with water. "What's in the box?"

"It's a delivery." He set the box on the counter near the sink. "Have you heard more from Dorothy? How has Miranda settled in?"

"I was going to check in with her in a bit. I'm sure she's very busy making room for her mom and tending to her."

"From a printing company." Finn read the address label on the box.

"Might be something for the event. There's a note on the list that says 'pick up standees on the twelfth,' which is today. It's got a hardware store listed."

"That's in Portree. We can make another trip in to pick up whatever the standees might be. I talked to my friend Crispin while I was mucking the—er, scooting out squirrels from the hayloft. He's tossing a party tomorrow at his family's manor. Fancy shindig. Thought I'd pick up something more appropriate than jeans to wear to it. It's a wedding celebration. Always a good time. And we Scotsmen like to dig out our kilts for a bash."

She fussed with the flowers in the vase.

"Do you want to come along? Lots of school friends and their wives and tons of food."

Her eyebrow lifted. "I can never say no to food."

That had been an easy win. That he had no intention of arguing. "Brilliant. We'll ride in to do some shopping in a bit?"

"Sounds like a plan. Will my red suit work for the party?"

"It sure will. Maybe…"

"Too fussy?"

He shrugged. She had worn the suit like a queen. But for a wedding he wasn't sure what the female dress code should be. "You look great in anything you wear. Like a silver goddess."

Another eyebrow lift. "Thanks, but I'll take a look in some shops when we're in town and see what they have. Will you bring that box into the ballroom?"

"On my way." Finn headed toward the ballroom where he set the box on one of the tables set up inside the doorway.

Silver goddess? He was talking like a teenager speaking to his crush. And he felt like it too. His heart was beating and his hands—they were sweaty! Finn never felt awkward around a woman. He was smooth and knew a wink or a few complimentary words would have them in his arms and his bed if he desired.

Allie was different. He didn't want her to swoon over him like the fangirls and women he'd dated, not that she was likely to anyway! He'd grown out of that surface need for constant fawning attention.

Really.

Mostly.

But he did want Allie. And in a manner that surprised him. He wanted her to like him. To accept him. To be a friend. And even more, he wanted to know if she felt as attracted to him as he did to her. And that had nothing to do with convincing her to reprise her role in his project.

They had a date for a party. Life was looking up.

CHAPTER NINE

ANOTHER RIDE ON the back of Finn's motorbike into Portree had Allie considering getting a Vespa to scoot around her place back in Arizona. Or maybe even after she won the castle here. It could happen. She would think positive thoughts and manifest it. Her mother would be so proud.

After stopping for sweet treats at a local bakery, the twosome strolled down the street, eating and pointing out the buildings they remembered from when they were filming, noting which had repainted or changed to completely different shops.

"Spent some good times in that pub," Finn said after a bite of his doughnut (no frosting, the heathen). "I lost quite a bit of cash to one of our costars playing darts."

Allie had rarely joined in on the cast's pub trips and Finn had certainly never encouraged her to. Usually after a long day of filming she'd crashed in her trailer.

"You ever hear from the cast?" One last bite of the chocolate croissant and she wiped flakes across the thighs of her jeans.

"I did a flick with Owen about ten years ago."

"Oh, right, was that *Catastrophe*?"

"Yeah, my biggest grossing film besides the *Code Grey* series. I suppose you didn't see it?"

She had mentioned to him she rarely watched television, let alone found the time to sit in a movie theater.

"I did see it streaming a few years after release. I love that you saved the cat at the end."

"That damned cat." Finn mocked a shudder. "I was about ready to strangle the critter for all the scratches I suffered. It was not well-trained. But never kill the kids or the animals is a sound rule to live by in the movie industry."

"Yes, I felt the horse death scene in our series in a visceral way. Even though it was a fake horse!"

"That's what made you a great actress. Your emotions show in every movement and expression you make. Whoa!"

A group of women darted out from a café and one of them stopped abruptly before Finn and Allie. Eyes wide, her hands fisted in glee before her. Behind her, two other women held the same looks of adoration.

"You're Finn McGregor!" she announced on a squeal.

He glanced to Allie. Was that a hint of annoyance in the flinch at the corner of his eye? Impossible.

"I am." He took the woman's hand and shook it, but before he could let go, she hugged him fiercely.

Allie stepped back, giving them the distance required for the twisting, squealing bear hug that would see Finn deflated and lying on the ground soon enough if he weren't released.

"I love you so much!" the woman declared. Then, seeming to realize she still held him captive, she jumped back. The women behind her added, "We've seen all your movies. Who would have thought when we came to the Isle of Skye, we'd run into its hometown hero!"

"Well, I wouldn't go so far as hero, ladies." Finn crossed his arms, which surprised Allie. The classic "stay away" move.

None of the women acknowledged her. Which she was thankful for.

But maybe…just a little jealous they hadn't recognized her?

"Can we get your autograph?" one of them pleaded.

While Finn asked them about their trip and scribbled his

signature on their slips of paper, Allie wandered down the street toward the hardware shop.

"I'm the only one for you," sounded across the street.

Allie turned to see the women clapping and swooning over the famous line that Connor MacKenzie had always said to Madeline, the woman he loved. There was a time she'd believed that line. Had wished it were true.

Had she really been so naive and easily malleable that she'd thought Finn could *really* fall in love with her? Yes, she had been.

But through many conversations with Savannah, her mom, and the gratifying process of building her a business and coming into her own power, she'd erased that silly desire. Now it was only a haunt.

A persistent haunt.

Fine! Those feelings had not been completely erased. But she knew better than to allow her heart to get bruised once again.

All of a sudden Finn was by her side and hooked his arm in hers. His bright smile wiggled the heart lying on her palm she'd forgotten to tuck back in her chest. Okay, so she didn't *need* Finn McGregor but she certainly didn't mind spending an afternoon with him.

"You didn't feel the need to rescue me?" he asked.

"Oh, please, Connor MacKenzie would never allow a woman to rescue him."

"I'll give you that. But this guy, the mere mortal who is not half fairy, was nearly crushed to death by fan enthusiasm. I think I cracked a rib."

"You'll survive. I initially thought you were annoyed by the women."

"I actually was, strange as that sounds. When you stepped away, I felt as though they'd forced you from me. I…felt your loss."

That was a weird thing to say.

"I would have rather continued walking alongside you, talking about nothing and everything, than sign autographs is what I mean."

"Oh." Feeling some satisfaction in knowing she'd been his focus, she decided to accept that and not overthink it. The man was still a rogue. And he *had* signed their autographs.

"Do you see that?" He pointed across the street to a tartan shop. "That's new."

"You want to check it out while I stop in the thrift shop? I haven't forgotten your invite to the wedding party."

"Nor have I." His eyes twinkled. "You go for it. I'll meet you in the hardware shop in ten."

She wandered ahead to the thrift shop, led by the window display of colorful dresses. The cobalt one called to her. The wrap dress was nothing stunning, but it fit her like a glove. Much as she enjoyed neutrals, bright colors lit up her face and gave her a healthy glow. Ten minutes later she walked out with a bag on her arm and a swing to her hips.

She stopped before the hardware store just as Finn called from across the street. A thud in Allie's chest felt as though her heart were trying to escape again. "Heaven above."

The man was wearing a kilt. And he looked—*whew*—damn good. Not an official Highlander's kilt with yards of pleated fabric, it was a pull-on in brown suede. It fell to just below his knees where an enticing peek of dark-haired legs stopped at his socks.

"What do you think?" He splayed his arms as he approached her.

"Where'd you get that nice tan on your legs?" *And really, Allie, stop staring!*

"Remnants from a shoot in the Bahamas months ago. I see you found something?"

"I did. Nothing fancy, that's for sure. Is that what you're wearing?" It wasn't over the top as far as kilts went, casual even.

"I am. And you could wear Miranda's rain slicker and look stunning."

"Well, I..." Really? The compliment warmed her soul, and that annoyed her. What was with these reemerging feelings toward Finn?

"Let's go inside."

Saved by his suggestion, she followed him into the hardware store. The walls and aisles were covered with tools, containers, stacked wood, clothing, food, electrical and farm supplies. It had everything. The clerk at the counter asked if he could help them.

"We're here to pick up an order for Miranda Donaldson. Some sort of standee?"

"Oh, aye. Hang out for a bit. I've to go get it in the back."

Allie thanked the man, then sidled up alongside Finn, who studied a display of pocket knives. It was just the kilt, she reasoned with her inner swooning heart. Not the entire package of a man with twinkling eyes, a killer smile and a Scottish brogue that could summon any woman to curl at his feet. "Can you imagine the swoons if you'd been wearing that kilt when those women recognized you?"

"You think? You should have stuck around," he said. "They would have wanted your autograph."

"They had no clue who I was. Or that I was even with you. They were blinded by the bright glow of *People*'s sexiest man of the year."

"Twice," he said with a raise of two fingers.

Allie turned to hide the rolling of her eyes.

"I saw that. I know awards and all those accolades are just self-congratulating bullshit. But it does look good on a man's résumé."

"The sexy title was well-deserved," she offered. "But I

think you look much sexier now that you've allowed the gray to filter in around your face."

"Did you just give me another compliment?"

Oh, how his eyes matched the sparkle of his smile. The struggle to put her heart back behind her rib cage was real. "I suppose."

"Allie, I know we had a bad relationship twenty-five years ago. But can you cut me some slack? I am a different person now. We know so much about one another. We get along. I sort of thought last night's dinner was a date?"

Really? A date? Was he joking? The one thing she'd dreamed about while filming with him was to date him, to become his girlfriend, to have him love her as much as she had loved him. But could she really hold the past against him now? Hadn't she promised herself she was letting all that go?

"I can go with the date label." Because it sounded much better than friend zone.

"Good. Then that means tomorrow night will be date number two, aye?"

Cheeky of him. But she had agreed to go along with him so she couldn't claim ignorance.

"Here you go!" The clerk placed a large item on the floor before the checkout counter.

Allie took one look at the life-size standee of her and Finn wearing their *Clan MacKenzie* costumes and posed in the classic romance-couple clinch and shook her head. "Oh, my God."

They hadn't a means to get the standee home with the motorbike, so Finn had raced back to the castle, located the keys to Miranda's pickup truck and returned in good time to have the hardware clerk help him heft the awkward standee board in the flatbed and secure it with a few straps.

In that time Allie had disappeared. The clerk hadn't a clue where she'd gone.

Finn had laughed at her reaction to the standee. It *was* kind of funny. He was used to marketing and promotion and seeing his face on billboards. This was nothing. But also nostalgic to see himself in the kilt and Allie in that outfit with her researcher utility belt circling her hips.

Just when he thought he'd have to honk the horn while driving down the main street and call out her name, she appeared wielding a bag of groceries. A baguette stuck out of it, along with carrot fronds and other veggies.

He climbed behind the wheel and nodded to her. "Couldn't bear to stand next to yourself for long, eh?"

"That thing is…"

"Ah, come on, Allie, it's just for fun. I bet Miranda was over the moon about it."

"She is such a sweet lady. Fine. I'll suffer the indignity of having to stare at my younger self for a day."

"What if we could go back in time? Tell our younger selves one thing?"

"Oh?" She set the groceries on the truck floor before her. "I don't know. What would you tell yourself?"

"To hold tight to my roots. To never forget that I'm just a lad from Isle of Skye and not anyone special."

"But you are special. You're a very talented actor."

"Thank you, but you know what I mean. I do have a big ego." He did not miss the subtle nod of her head. "But you know, spending time with you centers me?"

"I'm not doing anything to bring that on."

"Exactly. You're just you, and that's what I strive for. I've gotta be me." He fired up the ignition. "So. What would you tell your younger self?"

"Probably to ask for equal pay on my contracts."

"Ooh, good one. There's still a wage gap in Hollywood. Kind of sad. But it's not only the entertainment industry."

"That's why I have Glamcations. I like being my own boss and setting my own wage."

"You've got it all. But are you happy?"

Allie's lips parted as she assessed him. Beyond her outer calm and seeming contentedness he did sense there was something not completely whole. Like him, she sought something. Or maybe struggled with something.

She nodded. "Happy as a person can be. What about you?"

"The truth? I'd be happiest to have a real companion. Someone to care for and walk through the rest of my life with."

She tilted her head, considering. He'd never told anyone that dream he'd held for years. Movie stars were expected to live large and allow the whole world to peer into their every waking moment. He guarded the little wedge of personal life he did have well.

"I'm good being alone," she finally responded. But it didn't feel genuine. Had she just lied to him? No one should ever be completely alone. Even when surrounded by the media, a working crew or fans, Finn knew that feeling.

"Right then." He shifted into gear and pulled down the main street toward their destination. "But in case you decide alone isn't all it's cut out to be?" he said with a wink her way. "I'm the only one for you."

He caught her suppressing a laugh, a tight close of her eyelids. *Yeah, she thought it was funny. Maybe?*

But *could* she be the one for him? They certainly already knew their way around one another's bodies. How weird would it be to have an intimate relationship now? With no cameras to record their every move?

Very nice, he thought to himself. And yet, that sort of intimacy was not the most important on his list. It was that dream of family. It suddenly nudged at him with a relentless elbow.

CHAPTER TEN

THEY LEFT THE standee in the truck bed because they'd gotten home after dark and decided the logistics of carrying it in would best be handled in daylight. Allie heated a delicious tomato pea soup for them she'd gotten at a deli, then when finished eating, she went upstairs to wash up.

As she strolled down the second-floor hallway, she ran her fingers along the old cut-velvet wallpaper. Remnants from Victorian times? There were no family photos hung or artwork on the walls. But there was a curious amount of small taxidermied animals stuck here and there within the entire castle. This floor had only been used for filming in Madeline and Finn's bedroom, which Miranda had kept unchanged and unused.

Avoiding that room, even though she was coming to terms with the memories, she was suddenly compelled by a bigger curiosity and wandered toward the end of the long hallway toward the tower room door. That room had been blocked off when filming. Apparently, it had been used for storage and the crew hadn't thought it would make a good filming location.

"You missed your stop!" Finn called from down the hallway.

"I, uh…" Caught! But not going to apologize for it. She gestured ahead. "I was going to sneak up to the tower room and check it out. I've never been up there."

"Can I come along?" He rushed to join her. She'd never become accustomed to seeing the man in a kilt. It screamed "I dare you not to look." And she failed every time.

"I suppose you've been up there?" She tried the doorknob and it opened to a dark cold gush of air.

Finn reached over the threshold and flicked on a light switch. "Of course. Used to be my mum's crafty room. I snuck up there a few times during filming but it was stuffed with packing boxes and holiday decorations from the previous owners. Go ahead. Let's check it out."

Following the call of the unknown, Allie walked up the curving stairs, marveling at the curved wood railing that Finn explained had been hand-carved when the castle had been built in the eighteenth century. She breathed in the cold dry air. Smelled old, and like…memories?

At the top of the stairs, the door swung inward to a large round room that sported paned windows at each of the compass points. A large round tapestry rug lay on the center of the floor. A few boxes stacked against the wall, but otherwise bare of furnishings.

"Haven't seen it this empty. Ever," Finn commented.

Allie strolled to one of the windows. She guessed the moon was visible from another window so she walked the circle to the next and spied the golden scythe over the sea. "So, what's a crafty room?"

"Ah. Me mam was a crafty woman. She had all sorts of hobbies. Knitting, sewing, painting. Her easel stood between those two windows, and a cabinet filled with all colors of paint was over there. And before that wall were stacks of fabrics and wool tucked into little cubbies. She'd spend a lot of time up here. Made all my clothes when I was a kid."

"That's cool. I bet you got teased for the homemade couture though."

"You guessed it." Finn's smile briefly burst but too quickly softened. "I spent many an hour up here, dazzled by all the art supplies. Mum allowed me to touch them. I was so careful, running my fingertips over their glossy packaging, reading the color names like ochre and sunflower and persimmon and puce. They seemed magical to me." He wandered to the center of the carpet and spread out his hands as if to measure something. "There used to be a massive round ottoman right here. It was a rusty orange color. Had big heavy tassels around the edge. My ship's ballasts."

"Your…" Allie joined his side and imagined the big piece of furniture he described "…ship?"

"Oh, aye." He sat on the rug and patted it for her to sit beside him. "I just wanted to be around Mum, yeah? She'd never say no when I asked, but I knew she was busy so I occupied myself. Sometimes I'd lay on the ottoman and read." He leaned back and lay his head down on the rug. "My favorites were adventure stories about pirates. And other times the ottoman was my ship. I was the dread pirate McGregor."

Enthralled by his childhood memories, told in that heightened Scottish brogue that seemed to have taken him over since arriving, Allie lay back beside him.

"I'd sail the treacherous waters while Mum painted daisies and cats. I had a peg leg, you know?"

"Is that so? I suppose that is standard pirate gear."

"You know it. Every so often Mum would turn around and find me splayed across the ottoman. She'd ask what I was doing. I'd say 'I'm in a whale's belly, Mum. It ate my ship.' She'd never laugh. Just turn back to her work and say 'Good then, you're warm and safe there.'"

Allie smiled at Finn's soft laughter. The origins of a future actor sprouted right here in this tower room? For sure.

"Or sometimes I'd tell her I'd been forced to walk the plank and I was laying at the bottom of the sea and the starfish were nibbling at my toes and my peg."

Turning to her side, Allie met Finn's gaze. "You've always had that creative spark in you. You were destined to become an actor."

"I suppose so. Some days I used to sail my ship through the

clouds. And other times I would slip off the ottoman crust of a big pizza and swim through the tomato sauce of the floor."

He turned to face the ceiling. Like a switch thrown, levity seemed to spill from his smile as it straightened. Finn sat up and wrapped his arms around his knees.

Allie propped up onto her elbows.

"After Mum died," he said, "Da was inconsolable. My Aunt Jody, his sister, came to stay with us. Made sure I was fed and my clothes were washed. She planned Mum's funeral."

Allie sat up and took his hand, pressing a kiss to the side of it. Nothing else to do in the presence of another's grief. Just being there was the best thing. She'd learned that from years of her association with women's cancer recovery groups.

Finn sighed. "Days after her funeral I came up here to lay on the ottoman. I wanted to hear Mum's voice asking me, 'What are you doing, lad?' I would have said, 'I'm lying on my ship's broken stern. Floating in the black sea under a million stars.'"

He tilted his head against hers. "It took a long time to get to the point where I could step off that floating detritus. I know she's in a better place after struggling with the cancer for so long."

Such a horrible thing he had to go through. Allie had not yet lost a close family member. She didn't know how to relate. But from some of the conversations she'd had with the brave women who rented Glamcations, she'd listened to their stories of struggle, suffering and sometimes defeat with disease. Grief was a very personal thing. It should always be honored.

"Thank you for telling me that," she said quietly. "For letting me into your heart."

Finn exhaled and stretched back his shoulders. "Whew! Don't know where that came from."

"From here." She pressed her palm over his heart.

He clasped his hand over hers. "I've never told that to anyone. It feels…a relief to put it out there. And I'm good now. Every movie I make is for Mum. I know she's watching over me."

"Is it…okay if I give you a hug?"

"I'd like that."

She wrapped her arms about his back, pulling him against her. He relaxed, tilting his head against hers and squeezing as gently as she did to him. The moment was sad but she couldn't help linger in his warmth, and the sure structure of his body. It had been a while since she'd hugged a man. And it admonished that part of her that insisted she shove him away. Finn didn't need her to push him away.

Could they ever sever their connection? Why did she require that slash?

He slowly melted away from her to study her gaze. "That was nice. I needed that."

She pushed back a scruff of hair over his ear that their hug had mussed. "I did too. This room holds some wonderful memories for you."

She almost hated that she might win the bid and take it away from him. Almost.

"Well! Didn't think to end this day on such a somber note."

"It's okay, Finn. Let's head down."

Once back at her bedroom door, Finn brushed her cheek with a kiss. She sensed he was still deep in his feels so didn't take it as anything more than chaste. And when he stumbled for something else to say, she bid him good-night with a squeeze of his hand.

Alone in her room, she undressed and pulled on a cozy nightgown.

"Alone," she whispered with a glance in the direction of his room.

The two of them, in this big old castle. Set in their ways. Determined to best the other and walk away the winner. So close, yet still so far away.

Never had she felt the immense weight of her aloneness until now.

CHAPTER ELEVEN

THE NEXT MORNING they managed to heft the life-size standee of their embrace into the ballroom. Allie stepped back beside Finn, who held a thumb and finger to his chin in contemplation over the atrocity. Flashes of her days working the red carpet, attending endless press junkets and smiling for what had seemed thousands of cameras instilled a deep ache in her chest. Not a warm feeling. More like heartburn.

"Remember that outfit?" he asked.

"Of course I do." The cotton shirt, skirt and petticoats had been historically accurate. Their costume designer had won an Emmy for her work on the series. "It weighed twenty pounds, and with the utility belt and heavy wool shawl I was always wearing, it was so cumbersome. And if we filmed on a misty day, it was never completely dry."

"Moist," Finn deadpanned.

Allie chuckled. "Definitely."

"Remember when they were doing publicity shots for the first season?" he asked.

"Before we'd even started filming."

"Right, and they hadn't fitted your outfit yet. So I had to hold you in a romantic pose while also holding together the back of your loose shirt so it would look good. Ha!"

"You had it easy with the kilt."

"I like a proper kilt. Very functional. But I wasn't allowed to go commando. Remember that stupid skintight modesty garment they made me wear? Can't be showing the danglers on national telly."

"And yet we women can flash everyone with our breasts. Such a double standard."

"No doubt about that." He rapped the standee wistfully. "He was a handsome fellow."

"He still is," she offered without thinking. But then she'd done it. She'd let her emotions pry past the memories and reveal themselves. "Well, I mean…"

"Come on." He nudged her arm with an elbow. "That younger Finn was more handsome."

Did he not see it?

"He was full of himself and pumped up on ego," she said.

Finn mocked affront, but then nodded. "Guilty. But that young lad has learned. Mellowed over the years."

"Exactly. And…" She allowed herself the luxury of taking him in without the mutinous feeling that she was doing anything wrong. After he'd opened up to her last night, she was learning Finn was a real person and just as needy as she could be. "He's grown into himself. He's more appealing for the life that has crinkled across his forehead and at the corners of his eyes. Very handsome."

"Why thank you."

That he didn't try to joke his way out of the compliment showed her he had matured and changed. It was refreshing.

"I'd say the same for her." He pointed to her younger, slimmer, more naive self. "Still gorgeous. Still so kind and energetic. The new hair color is stunning. Like precious metal crowning a goddess."

Allie burst into laughter.

"What?"

"What movie was that line from?" she asked through fading laughter.

"That wasn't a line. Allie, you are a stunning woman. And

if I can take a compliment… Egotistical, self-aggrandizing me. Then you can do the same. You're beautiful."

"Whatever." She'd had enough of this exercise in trying to outdo one another with compliments. Turning, she strolled across the ballroom.

"You are!"

"Mm-hmm," she muttered to herself. Was the man angling to get on her good side? He already was. *Damn her!* But it hadn't felt like overt flirtation.

Why *didn't* he flirt with her?

Oh, Allie, why are you acting like a teenager who seeks the eye of a cute guy?

On the other hand, there was nothing wrong with flirtation. She'd stopped feeding her need to always be what others expected years ago. Allegra Stark did nothing to please anyone or to receive a positive nod. If she wanted to look the fool flirting with a man she'd once drooled over, she would. And she wouldn't label it foolish. Just…fun.

She left the ballroom and decided to check in with Savannah.

Her best friend answered after one ring. "How's it going? Did you win the bid?"

"Won't be announced until the convention. Miranda is recovering at her daughter's home right now. She'll be returning here in a few days to look over what we've done."

"So funny that you got trapped into fixups and repairs. We don't need the property that badly, Allie."

"I know, but… Savannah, I think I might want this place for myself."

"Oh?"

"Don't worry, I won't use Glamcations' funds if I decide on that. I have to win the bid first. And even then, it's just a fantasy. It is a big place for one person."

"If there were two people, it would be more manageable."

"You mean me and you?"

Savannah's laughter was full-bodied and deep. Just like her personality. "Darling, please, don't tell me you haven't tapped that handsome Scot yet."

"Savannah!"

"I know, you two were never meant to be. But what if you were? I saw his last movie. The man's still got it. He's so sexy."

"He is—"

"Yes! I knew it."

"You know nothing, Savannah. We're just…" *Friends* felt like the wrong word. They were growing closer. And that part of her that wanted to let her hair down and just…see what might happen was rising to the fore. "Tell me not to do anything foolish, Savannah."

"Oh. Wow. So it is serious."

Allie could but sigh. Was it? What was going on with her heart? One minute she hated herself for loving the man, the next she was floating on a broken ship's hull amidst an ocean of memory.

"I would never tell you what to do, Allie sweetie, you know that. And if you want to buy the place for yourself, I'm very cool with that. With me located in Arizona, I could cover our properties in the States, and you could handle Europe from the Isle of Skye. It would be a perfect situation."

She hadn't thought that far ahead, but it would be perfect. Especially since Savannah did not like to fly overseas. With her inner ear issues, the woman could barely handle a four-hour flight to New York without getting sick and suffering a spinning head for days after landing.

"Or maybe if I moved in…" Allie said, working through the angles and also avoiding discussing Finn "…and lived in one half of the castle, and designated the other half for Glamcations. It's large enough. It could be very workable."

"I do like that idea. Where would Finn sleep?"

"Not going to answer that one."

"Then I'll make my own conclusions. So the convention is in a few days? Call me as soon as you know who won. Love you!"

"Love you back." Allie clicked off and tucked away her phone.

She did like the idea of living on-site while also hosting guests. And Finn, well, he could sleep wherever he liked.

Maybe even…

"Are you really going there?" she chastised her wanting heart.

Her heart answered back with a resounding, *Yes*.

CHAPTER TWELVE

ALLIE HAD ASKED Finn to drive them to the party in the rental car. She wasn't precious about her looks, but she did want her hair to hold the curls she'd put in it for more than ten minutes. Wearing a helmet was not conducive to remaining party ready.

The blue wrap dress was nothing fancy, but elegant enough for a wedding party. Scrunching her fingers in her long loose curls, she remembered Finn had called her a silver goddess. The fine silveriness of her hair was the universe's apology for making her go gray so early. This was her blonde era. (And don't try to convince her otherwise.) Finishing with a dash of red lipstick, she then skipped down the stairs to meet Finn outside.

Half an hour later they parked before a mansion that put the Donaldson castle to shame. It looked like something a billionaire would own, replete with a dealership-worthy line of flashy sports cars parked out front.

"This looks like a fancy shindig." Allie stood there in the cool night air, staring at the grand stairs leading to the front doors festooned with thousands of red and white roses and fairy lights. "I'm underdressed."

"Nonsense." Finn offered her his arm. The suede kilt, along with a crisp white shirt, made him the definition of dapper. If a little too sexy. "You look like a movie star."

No movie star sequins or diamonds for her tonight. Or

ever, truth be told. "I reserve the right to dodge out if I feel uncomfortable."

"Of course. You can take the car back on your own if you get spooked by some old biddy's diamond tiara."

"There's going to be tiaras?"

"Allie." He bent to meet her gaze. The caress of his hand along her arm was unexpected but also calming. And it felt… unscripted. Caring. "Are you nervous?"

"I hadn't expected so much…grandeur. You know that's not my scene."

"The MacCreavys may look flashy but underneath all the sparkle there's haggis, plaid and barrels of aged whisky. That's what their family does is distill the whisky. Don't worry." He squeezed her hand. "This bunch is fun. Me and Crispin, the father of the bride, go way back. We used to party all night, sleep all day."

"How does partying and whisky play in with your sobriety?"

"You worried about me?"

Was she? Memories of him drinking on set were among the ones she never cared to relive.

"I wouldn't set foot inside if I didn't know I couldn't handle it," he offered. "I'm good, Allie. Come on. Time to begin date number two."

That word *date* still weirded her out. Was he joking? Did he understand that was all she'd ever wanted from him? And to hear it now…? Well.

Don't read anything into it, Allie. You've also been thinking about flirting with him. Have fun tonight!

The grand foyer led them into a massive ballroom, three times the size of the castle's ballroom. Music blasted through speakers, lights flashed. The rose-festooned decorations perfumed everything. Most were dancing or milling in groups.

Diamonds and sequins flickered everywhere. Gold and red streamers and balloons advertised congratulations.

"McGregor!"

Finn was greeted by a hearty man-hug from someone about his height and age. He wore a tartan kilt with all the add-ons, including tasseled sporran and Balmoral bonnet. "You look good, you gnarly old beast. Saw you on the telly not long ago. Still disarming bombs and hanging from helicopters?"

"Whenever they'll pay me to do it. Crispin, this is Allegra Stark. Allie, Crispin MacCreavy, my best mate from school."

"Ah, such a lovely lass." He took Allie in from head to toe. "Like a silver fairy danced in from the stones. Grab a pint and let me introduce you around, will you?"

"Will do." Finn slapped him across the shoulder as the man was obviously making the rounds greeting people. "Bar's over there." He nodded toward the far wall and took Allie's hand. Once there, he ordered nonalcoholic beer for himself. "What about you?"

Allie perused the shelves behind the bar, not sure what she was in the mood for. When a glint of red caught her eye, she studied the tall vials a group of women at the bar were tilting back. "What are those?"

The bartender leaned forward, "The bride's special. Cherry kisses." Before she could ask for one, he turned and pulled out a cold can of NA beer from a cooler for Finn, snapped the top open and handed it to him. Then he poured a vial of the cherry kiss for Allie. And another. "One for each hand." His wink was just flirtatious enough for her to wink back.

"Two-fisting it tonight, eh?" Finn smiled. "I'll have to keep an eye on you."

"I'm sure they're a whole lot of syrup and soda. Are you going to join your friend?"

"I do want to catch up with Crispy. Let's walk around a bit, and I'll see if I recognize more faces. I don't want to leave you alone."

"Don't worry about me. You've got some catching up to do. And the introvert in me doesn't mind people-watching. I might park myself at one of those high tables over there and take it all in. Go ahead," she encouraged. "We'll dance later, yes?"

"Honestly?"

"Finn."

"All right, all right. But I won't forget you promised me a dance." He tipped his can to one of the vials she held, then took off, only to be accosted by another man his age who also wore a kilt.

Allie wandered to a high table, on the other side of a trio of women tilting back the cherry kisses. Sliding onto a stool, she took in the virtual wonderland of kilts. On men of all ages and sizes. There were sexy hints of leg everywhere. If there was one men's fashion choice all women could agree on, she felt sure it was a kilt.

"Nice." With a tilt of one of the vials to toast the field of kilts, she took a sip. Very sweet. A strong cherry flavor with a hint of chocolate. Little alcohol that she could detect. The first vial went down quickly. And as her eyes took in the room, finally landing on the bride, who wore a tartan gown, the second vial went down.

A group of teenage girls moved in on her table, attention on their phones and giggles as they shared photos. One of them looked her over and said, "Your hair is so pretty!"

Allie stroked her hair. "Thank you."

"It's just like my grandmama's." She beamed guilelessly as the other girls giggled and tugged her back to their phone screens.

Grandmama? Ouch.

"Oh, I'm not a…" Allie sucked in a breath as it was apparent the girl was not interested in whatever flimsy excuse for vanity she could offer.

Slipping from the stool, she started a slow wander around the perimeter of the dance floor. Along the way, she set the empty vials on the bar, and they were immediately replaced with two more. "Oh, no, I can't."

The bartender did like to wink at her.

Very well. She could hardly refuse when he'd already poured. Grandma material? Never!

Turning, she spied Finn gesticulating wildly as he talked to a half circle of men and women. A little jump. And then some sort of jig move. What was he talking about? And dare she join him? Just to…slide her palm against his and hold his hand. Lean against him. Take in the electric charm of Finn McGregor.

Sure, so much charm, but she had seen a part of him last night she'd never thought to experience. That intimate moment in the tower room when he'd told her about his mom. It was rare a man opened his heart to a woman like that. At least from her personal experience. She wanted to be closer to him. To stand beside him and just…be.

Why not? Independent woman here. Who did whatever she damn well pleased. And this girl didn't have to worry about grandchildren giggling in her wake. Setting the empty drink vials on a silver bar caddy, Allie went to claim the sexiest man of the year—twice over—for a dance.

Allie was feeling her oats. They'd been on the dance floor for quite a few dances and she showed no sign of slowing down. The current song blasted a rallying call to *get drunk, get laid*. She sang along with everyone else. Jumping, pumping her fist, dancing around him as they matched the beat. Finn had not seen her so loose and carefree.

He suspected those red drinks had something to do with it. She'd even danced with the groom, and the bride. All the friends he'd talked to thought she was lovely and most had suggested he settle down and make her an honest woman.

He knew what that meant. His friends were small-town workers who were impressed by his stardom but didn't need that sort of extravagant life for themselves. Simple family, simple job, simple lifestyle. That made for their happiness. And…he was feeling that simple happiness right now.

Allie spun before him and signaled she needed a break. He followed her to the bar where they slid onto stools. A long strand of silver spilled across her face. He stroked it aside and over her ear. Lost in her iceberg eyes, he could but grin. In his happy place.

"Finn, are you flirting with me?" she slurred. Perhaps she was more drunk than he'd first assessed.

"Aye, no one else in this room I'd rather flirt with." He nodded to the bartender. "Two waters, please!"

"Water?" She took his hand, shaking her head. "I need another of those cherry things. They're like punch, Finn. Probably full of sugar."

"How many have you had?"

"Two?" She shrugged. Her entire body wobbled on the stool. "Eight?"

The bartender set water before Finn and another vial before Allie.

"Oh, no." Finn shoved the vial away. "She's had enough."

"Spoil sport." She pouted.

"Let the lady live it up," the bartender argued.

"Seriously? Give it to someone who isn't already in her cups." He was no fan of a bartender who encouraged over-drinking.

"What?" Allie leaned forward, her smile slippery. "You going to call me Granny too?"

"Granny? Where did that one come from?"

"Stupid silly girls. They'll be wishing for my lush, beautiful, loooong hair when theirs starts to thin."

Now she was surfing in waters he couldn't begin to navigate. "I think it's time me and your gorgeous head of hair head for the castle."

She laid her head on the bar. "I could take a nap."

"I think you're done for the night."

"Don't want to spoil your fun. You stay and party with your friends. I'll drive home on my own."

"No driving for you, dear one. Come on."

Wrapping one of her arms around his shoulder, he managed to make an exit while also calling to his friends to have a good night.

The ride home had him wishing that he'd stopped her from drinking so much. She sat quietly as the car took the single-track road. Eyes closed. Smile fixed. In a happy place? Very well, so an occasional letting down of one's hair was never a bad thing. Had someone called her Granny? Idiots.

Now if it had been him in her position—no, never again. He'd done the twelve steps. He even caught a meeting whenever he was close to one. He never wanted to go back to the Finn McGregor who would yell at his costars and demand he be listened to. Booze had made him annoying and entitled.

Apparently, Allie still thought he was entitled.

He was. But he was learning that it didn't get him where he wanted so perhaps it was time to let it all fall away. Only a fool would hold to the belief that he could forever headline a movie as the handsome young action-adventure hero. Age happened. And he wasn't inclined to a facelift (much as it had already been suggested; many times).

"I can do this," he muttered.

Allie giggled. "You want to *do* me?"

He parked before the castle and turned off the engine.

"You heard me wrong, my pretty lass with the goddess hair. How are you feeling?"

"Tonight was…" she sighed and hugged herself "…a blast."

"It was. I could have danced with you until the sun rose."

"Nothing more than dancing?" She leaned toward him, a pout on her lips. "You know kilts do it for me?"

"I think they do it for all women." Finn pushed a thick hank of hair from her face. She giggled again and her head dropped onto his thigh. He carefully lifted her up by the shoulders and tilted her back onto the passenger side.

"You hold steady. I'll run around and help you out."

"Aye, aye, dread pirate McGregor!"

Smirking, he couldn't be upset for having allowed her into that memory. She would guard it well and not try to sell it to some tabloid. He lifted her into his arms and carried her inside. All the way up to her bedroom. (He'd check later for mud left in his wake.)

Setting her on the bed, she rolled to her stomach, arms up over her head and face down. Blowing out an exhausted breath, Finn collapsed beside her and groaned.

"Why are *you* groaning?" she muttered from her motionless position. "I'm the one who's drunk. My god, I've never been so drunk. This pirate ship is going down!"

"Oh, Allie, I am an old dread pirate now. I should not be carrying a pretty woman up so many stairs. I can't do that kind of physical stuff anymore."

Moments of silence passed as he counted his pounding heartbeats. Truly, was he so out of shape?

And then… "You think I'm pretty?"

Finn smiled. "Aye. You're the prettiest lass in all of Scotland. All the men were asking about you tonight. They think I should keep you. What do you think of that?"

No response. He didn't hear snoring, but he could guess she had passed out.

"I thought it was an intriguing suggestion," he continued. "But I know you can find someone better than Finn Mc-Gregor to make you happy. Still." He rapped his chest. "How many of those prospects could sling you over his shoulder and carry you up a flight of stairs at this age? The old pirate still has it, even if *it* hurts."

Still no response, but he did hear her soft breathing. Probably a good thing she hadn't heard what he'd just said.

In truth, Allegra Stark was too good for him. She'd achieved business success, seemed happy mentally and obviously didn't need a man to take care of her.

Yet for some reason he now found himself chasing after a dream that had blossomed and wilted long ago. He could have had her then.

Would anything ever be enough for him? He wasn't stupid. He knew his leading man appeal had waned. Yet there were parts out there for him. Juicy, meaty roles that would give him satisfaction. A new kind of satisfaction for a job that he had to accept must change and alter with his accumulating years.

Maybe he needed to step back and take a wide view of it all.

With luck, Allie would be in that view, and she wouldn't try to step out of frame.

CHAPTER THIRTEEN

REMARKABLY, ALLIE FELT not terrible the next morning as she nursed a glass of orange juice by the kitchen counter. Finn was out back doing something, and she was glad for a few moments of peace to sit in the sunlight.

He had carried her in last night and put her to bed. And she couldn't recall if she'd made a move on him. Or vice versa. She knew she got frisky when she drank. Her husband had said as much. But she'd been fully clothed this morning so...

She would not overanalyze what could no longer be changed. And really? No regrets. Save that she should have never gone beyond cherry kiss number three. Or four. Or... she may have had a dozen. Usually she was so good at stopping when she achieved a mellow relaxation. It had been that comment about being a grandmother that had pushed her over the edge. And coming from mere teenagers. Why had she let it bother her so much? She was perfectly adjusted regarding her wrinkles and silver hair.

Possibly, the fact that she could never become a grandmother in actuality...

With a sigh, she shook her head. No need to dwell on it. Despite her slip into inebriation, she did recall much merriment. Dancing with Finn. Dancing with everyone. She would move onward.

But maybe a little slower today. While she didn't have a

hangover, her brain was a little muggy. Maybe head out for that walk she'd been meaning to take since arriving. After... a nap. Yes, that sounded good.

Finn hung up and tucked away his phone. Allie had been inside all morning. When he'd gone in for lunch, he'd peeked in her room and saw she was napping. He had an idea of what the woman might need, so he'd arranged for that to happen very soon.

Wandering inside the castle, he heard some commotion in the ballroom and found Allie wielding a broom.

"How are you feeling?"

She set the broom against the stone wall and put her hands to her hips. Even on the day after a good drunk she looked nothing less than gorgeous. "Just taking the day easy. No raging hangover. Thank goodness. I, uh... Thank you for bringing me up to my room last night. I'm a little humiliated that you had to—did you actually sling me over your shoulder?"

"Told you I could do that. You weren't going to get to bed by crawling. I didn't mind."

"You're too kind. I suppose all your friends think I'm a lush."

Finn chuckled. "You didn't take a census of the room as we left. You were the least drunk of the crew. Don't worry about it, Allie. You gotta let your hair down once in a while."

"Yeah? If I ever get drunk again, it'll be too soon. I don't know what was in those cherry kisses, but—whew!"

"Vodka."

"Really? I can't handle vodka."

"Obviously. But hey, you're not an arrogant drunk, like I used to be. You like to dance and let it all hang out. You've got a freak flag, Allie. Last night you let it fly."

"Oh, mercy." She pressed her loose fists to her mouth in a moment of panic. "Did I do anything embarrassing?"

"You mean like flashing your boobs?"

"What?"

Before she could think the worst, he rescued her. "Don't worry. You didn't perform a strip show. But you did talk to everyone in the place and invited them all to stay at *your* castle."

"Oh, bother. Sorry."

"No need to apologize for having a good time. And if I win the castle, I promise to honor your free stays to any who come to claim them." He smiled at her thoughtfully.

"*If* you win." She shoved her hands in the back pockets of her jeans. "So what's up for you today?"

"My dad called. He's going to stop in to help me with the hedge tomorrow. Until then, I might try my hand at installing the sound system that's been sitting there in a box." His phone pinged and he checked the text. "As for you…"

"As for me?"

"I've got a surprise."

"A—oh, I don't know, Finn."

"Don't worry. It doesn't involve any heavy lifting, dancing or even use of your brain. In fact, I want to pamper you today."

"Pamper me?" She stroked her lips, a nervous reaction as her hand fluttered away and across her stomach.

"Yes. You're all about pampering other women. I'm going to guess you ignore yourself. So… I hope you don't mind but… I hired a masseuse to come in and treat you this afternoon."

"A…" She winced, but then tilted her head in thought. "Really?"

He nodded, hoping she'd be okay with it. "She just texted me that she's arrived. I should go out and help bring in her stuff. If…that's okay with you?"

With a heavy sigh, she nodded. "Sounds good."

"All right!" Finn clapped and headed toward the side door. "Why don't you head up to your room? I'll send her your way."

Once the masseuse was all set up in Allie's bedroom, Finn left the women to themselves and went down to tackle the sound equipment. But also, he needed to check on the pantry's potato supply.

This. Was. Heaven.

As the masseuse's hands glided over her oil-slicked skin, Allie sank deeper into a mindless vanilla-scented bliss. That Finn had thought to do this was the nicest thing a man had ever done for her. Jean-Louis had never even brought her flowers.

When finished, she chatted with the masseuse, got her card and promised she would call her. No way would she *not* hire someone with hands of gold like hers. After a hot shower, and feeling like a wilted plastic bag—but a happy wilt of plastic—Allie dressed in leggings and a sweater and wandered downstairs, following the warm savory scent of...

"Baked potatoes?"

She wandered into the kitchen to find Finn setting a pan on the counter and wielding a knife. "Take a seat," he directed. "I made you a snack."

"A snack?" She hadn't eaten all day, beyond the orange juice this morning. And, well, she was hungry after that heavenly massage.

"How was it?" he asked.

"Utter bliss. Thank you."

"You're welcome. Mm, I could lick you like ice cream."

"Wha—?"

Finn looked up from what he was doing with a knife and fork. "What did I just say? Oh. You smell like vanilla."

"Uh, okay." But really? That was his first thought at smelling her? *Hmm... Nice.* "The masseuse was so talented I took her information. When I get this castle, she'll be the first person I call with a job offer."

"When you get the castle?"

She shrugged and propped her elbows on the table. "I'm hopeful."

Finn set a plate before her and a fork. "Jacket potato. Hot from the oven."

"Are you kidding me?"

"I don't think so." He seemed genuinely confused. "What's wrong?"

Wrong? The man had just set a baked potato before her. Sliced down the middle. Squeezed open and fluffed. And covered with oozing, melting golden butter. A potato. She did recall telling him her love language was potatoes. What fantasy had she walked into today?

"Allie?"

"There's nothing wrong. It's..." She could cry, the moment was so perfect. So thoughtful. "Thank you."

"Great. I'll leave you to enjoy it. I've almost got the speakers working. If you hear some music blaring, that means I get a gold star."

He left her leaning over the potato, breathing in the buttery goodness as if it were oxygen.

What had she done to deserve such a kind gesture? She'd gotten drunk. Had probably humiliated him in front of his friends (despite him saying otherwise). And now he'd given her things that any woman would dream to receive from a man. The consideration and knowing that she needed a little tender loving care after a good drunk.

"A potato," she said, her lower lip wobbling. Potatoes made everything better.

Digging in with her fork, she savored the first bite. A potato baked for her by a man she admired. Nothing tasted better.

Was it necessary? The pushing aside of all memories about Finn?

Another bite of potato had her rolling her eyes in bliss. Even better than the massage.

"Oh, that man."

While she was a big girl who could buy herself flowers and book her own massage any time she desired, the thoughtfulness of Finn's gift defeated that final thread of resistance she had spun in her quest to leave the past in the past.

CHAPTER FOURTEEN

THE NEXT MORNING a neighbor knocked on the door. The woman offered Allie a dozen eggs and fresh milk from their cow. She'd wanted info about Miranda and Allie had filled her in on the little she knew and thanked her profusely for the food.

Finn was the master with eggs, so she'd stick to basics and boil them. Finding a portion of salted ham in the fridge she decided it had best be used before it spoiled. She intended to replace all the groceries as they used them and was keeping a list.

She didn't mind cooking for Finn. He deserved it, the sweetheart he was being to her lately. She wondered suddenly why he seemed so down on himself regarding his career. He had deemed himself handsome in standee form. But she could sense the subtle doubt just beneath his surface. It almost read to her like grief. Finn wore a surface sheen she knew came from being an actor. He portrayed an image he wanted others to see. But the glimpses she'd seen of the real man under that facade made her want to pull him close and tell him it was going to be all right.

She wanted it to be right for him. She'd want that much for anyone.

However, owning this castle wasn't going to alter those deep emotional needs for him. Winning the castle may nudge a producer toward taking on his project, but ultimately, Finn would still be in the same headspace. Emotions dug into one's bones and clung. And the only way through them was to face them.

On the other hand there were some deep childhood memories here in the castle that he deserved to have, and own.

She fished the eggs from the boiling water and held them under cold water. He had pampered her so perfectly. But when was the last time Finn McGregor had been pampered? Why didn't more men believe they deserved that?

"I knew I smelled something delicious." Finn wandered in and grabbed a piece of toast from the toaster. He took a bite of the dry warm bread.

"The butter dish is on the table, next to your juice," she said.

He wandered over and sat before the place setting she'd made for him. "Ham and…?"

"Boiled eggs. It's the only kind I can make without screwing up." She placed an egg beside some ham on a plate for Finn, then handed it to him. "I was just thinking how men deserve as much pampering as we women," she said as she dished up her own plate. "Glamcations focuses mainly on woman. Perhaps it's time we added a Guycations option? Do you think men would like that?"

Finn smacked the egg against his plate and peeled away the shell. "Are Scottish midges insufferable? I mean, but I don't think that word would attract too many of us. Pampering. It's…girlie. Like pink fingernails and hair curlers and gossiping about boys."

He had a point. "How about…rugged retreats?"

"Now you're talking."

"Doesn't sound very relaxing though. The point of Glamcations is to relax while being treated well. Having all your worries whisked away."

"On behalf of we men, the idea of meditating while some-

one gongs on a crystal bowl is…as they say nowadays…
cringe. But put us in a boat on a serene lake filled with fish?
Now that's relaxing."

"I may need to bring in the male perspective for this one.
Well. It was just a thought. We do quite well catering to
women."

"There could be a whole untapped market of hardworking blue-collar men out there who are probably hungry for
a good fishing trip."

"That market is already covered."

"You have a point. But the pampering aspect does appeal."

"Massages. Meditation. Hot yoga?"

"I'd do some yoga if you asked."

"You would?"

He winked over a bite of smashed egg on toast. "Aye, you
could ask me anything, Allie, and I'd do it."

Now that was a practiced line. And yet Allie cautioned
herself from expecting the usual from him. What was wrong
with a little flutter of her freak flag? With engaging the man
and making an active step toward friendship or…something
more? He had been calling their outings dates. So…

"What if I asked you to help me clean the bathroom connected to the ballroom today?"

Flirtation level? Total failure. But slightly freakish, if truth
be told.

Finn set down his fork and sipped his juice before placing
his palms on the table as if to counter her offer. "What if I
said I'll call a cleaning crew to come in and give the ballroom and bathroom a good once-over—on my tab—while
we take a hike off the property?"

He was so much better at this. And a hike? She'd yet to
venture out, as planned. "You win. You think you can find
someone to come in today?"

"I'm on it." He tugged out his phone. "I'll bring in a cleaning crew and..."

"Was your dad going to stop and help with the hedge?"

"Aye, later today, so we'll get to that walk straight away."

She collected their plates to set in the sink. "I'm going to find some hiking boots. See you in a bit."

Allie motioned to Finn that she was going to walk ahead as he took a call. He nodded and put up his hand, fingers splayed. Five minutes and he'd catch up, so she wandered ahead, assuming it was his agent. The grass was slick under her boots, still wet from the morning dew.

The fairy pools were a big draw on the Isle of Skye. They were a tourist attraction, however those particular pools were not anywhere near the castle. A similar smaller pool sat at the edge of the property. It didn't flow from a river, as the others did, but was served by an inlet from the sea. The series had filmed here often. Allie had fond memories of the standing stone that marked the pool and the lush bluebells that carpeted the banks.

She couldn't imagine wanting to sell such a gorgeous property. This was a dream. The air was salty and crisp. The sky a hazy blue but still better than pollution-clogged city skies. And on most days a person could spy seals or even dolphins swimming in the sound. Such wonders!

Of course if Miranda wanted to travel it made sense to sell. The castle was too large for one person anyway. And now she would have the aftermath of her heart attack to deal with.

Approaching the bank of the fairy pool she stopped to smooth her palm over the large standing stone. Only as wide as a broad-shouldered man, yet twice as tall. About four feet up from the ground circled a smoothened groove rubbed down over the centuries by hands such as hers.

The pool was clear as day and tinted a green as pale and

clear as Finn's eyes. Ochre rocks hugged the opposite side of the pool and Allie imagined the colorful pebbles coating the bottom, at most two-feet deep in places, were fairy glitter.

Yes, she did believe in fairies.

The banks were grassy and... Her boot heel slipped and before she could fathom that she was falling, she knelt in the water on hands and knees.

After a quick assessment she didn't feel any pain or injuries. It had been a clean slide. An embarrassing one at that. Looking around to ensure she was the only one about, Allie shook her head and pushed herself upright to stand at the edge of the cool pool. She was soaked up to her knees and elbows.

"Not the way I'd intended this hike to go."

Finn spied the standing stone and then noticed Allie. In the water? He hurried his steps but paused on the bank. "Allie?"

Standing to her knees in the water, she waved him off. "I'd forgotten how slick these banks can be." She held out her arms and looked over her body.

"Hang on. I'll help you out."

"No!" She put up a hand. "That'll end in both of us taking a bath. I can manage."

She navigated to a stone at the bank and, using her hands to grip the grass, walked her way up, and he was able to reach and give her a firm hold as she found purchase.

Leaning against the standing stone, Finn said, "Oh, Scotland, you are so moist!" he announced in his best Miranda impersonation.

"We probably shouldn't be joking about a woman who has just suffered a heart attack." Allie squeezed the water from the hem of her leggings, then tugged off her boots and drenched socks to reveal bare toes.

"You're right. That was crass."

"But it *is* moist." She tilted one boot to pour out the water. "Weren't there steps to get into the water when we filmed?"

"Those were added for our safety and presumably removed after we wrapped filming."

"Whew! Well, the fairies didn't rescue me."

"This fairy would have if you'd have let him." He cast her a smile and this time she cared little if it was a patented charm. She'd fallen. Hook, line and fairy-pool eyes. "I do recall I've rescued you from near drowning before."

"You've saved drowning associates twice, in fact."

He nodded, recalling they had filmed a drowning scene in the first season and then in one of the later seasons he'd rescued one of his cousins from a watery end. Filming had always presented him with physical challenges, and when given an option to use a stuntman, more often than not he'd done his own stunts. The accomplishments fed his ego. And he was younger then. Nowadays? He left everything for the stunt people.

"I also rescued you from being trampled by wild horses."

"Ever the hero." She tilted her head briefly to his shoulder, then pulled off her other boot to empty it. "I recall I saved you from some sort of flu-like sickness."

"Oh, aye. I suffered terribly for days as you tended me."

She chuckled. "You play sick well."

"And you play the compassionate heroine well. Remember the brigands from the pirate ship?"

"They would have raped me if you'd not shown up with the entire Clan MacKenzie to overtake their ship and slay the dread pirate captain."

"Some of those plot lines got out of hand."

"Kind of reminds me now of the dread pirate McGregor."

"Aye, my lass. I would have sailed up on my velvet ottoman and defeated the brigands with a squirt of me mam's oil paints."

She laughed and leaned her back against the standing stone. Her bare toes wiggled, catching his eye.

He'd played with those very toes in one of their more intimate scenes. Hell, he'd touched most parts of Allie's body. At the time he'd had to focus and remind himself a dozen crew members were also watching. Had he fallen in love with her back then? He'd not thought so, but…maybe?

"I watched you give birth to our son," he said with the reverence he'd felt during that scene.

It had almost felt real. Allie had been coached on how to enact the birthing process, as had he. And when they'd brought in a crew member's newborn baby boy for him to hold, swaddled in soft linen, he'd been so fearful he might drop it. The tears of awe had been real, and that had been an episode for which he'd been nominated for a Golden Globe. Really it had been Allie who'd deserved the award, but there he'd been, hogging the limelight as usual.

Allie's release of breath surprised him. He looked to her to find her eyelids closed tight. She clasped her arms tight across her chest. A strand of her hair stuck to her cheek and he brushed it over her shoulder. "Allie?"

"I always wanted to have kids," she said. "But Jean-Louis did not."

"I'm sorry."

She shrugged. "It wasn't meant to be."

He knew she'd not been married since her divorce. Had faded from public view. And he understood now that the public life hadn't been for her. "What about having kids on your own? Adopting?"

"No. I thought long and hard about adopting as a single parent, but ultimately, I believe a child should be raised by two parents, or at least that should be the plan from the outset. As for having one myself… I, uh…well I can't physically carry a child. Infertility. It's a deep longing that I had to slowly rise out of."

"I'm so sorry, Allie. I shouldn't have pried."

"You're not prying. And I don't mind sharing this with you. I've dealt with it. Grieved it. And then once Glamcations got off the ground, I knew I'd not have the time to devote to raising a child. I accepted my path to happiness was going to be different than the one I anticipated as a little girl." She straightened her body, seeming to shuck off whatever darkness had swept over her. "What about you?"

"Me? Kids? I'm too busy with my career to be a proper dad."

She nodded. "It's not an easy business to raise a child in."

Finn smoothed a hand across her back. "I'm sorry you weren't able to have the children you wished for. I think you would be an awesome mother."

She nodded. Closed her eyes. And a tear spilled down her cheek.

Finn had touched something in her so tender it made him wonder if he should leave her to her privacy. But in his next thought he couldn't imagine walking away when she must feel vulnerable. As he had felt the other night in the tower room.

He hugged her, and she laid her head on his shoulder. Holding her did something crazy to his insides. It lit them up and set them on fire, and then settled them to a cozy warmth.

And it felt real. Not like a script he was meant to emote and dramatically bring to life. This was just he and Allie. A woman he had pushed out of his emotional sphere because he hadn't known how to embrace a true relationship when they'd first come together for filming. And now? He didn't want to push; he wanted to pull her closer.

"I'm here for you," he said softly.

And he meant it.

* * *

Standing in Finn's embrace sparked so many old feelings in Allie. She started to shove them back, but then paused. Because the old feelings were tinged with something new. And…inviting.

It was okay to allow Finn to stay in her heart. He held a cozy place there. One filled with dancing and laughing over a shared joke, eating together and even a newfound trust found after a night of flying her freak flag.

"What are you thinking about?" he asked.

About allowing you to stay in my heart.

Instead she checked herself and asked, "Did you find a cleaning crew to come do the bathrooms?"

"You're thinking about bathrooms? Here I thought we just had a moment."

She still wasn't ready to let him in, was she? Not really. Sure, she was softening to his charm, but she hadn't forgotten the past. She parted from him and shoved her hands in her back pockets. "We've had so many moments, Finn. The rescues, the adventures, the childbirth. How can we ever know what's real?"

He nodded and bowed his head. "I know what you mean. But you know what, Allie? I want whatever this is to be real. Even if it's just a few days of learning to be friends. Or maybe something more."

"What do you mean by something more?"

"You know what I mean."

She did. And…she wasn't against that. But she wasn't sure she believed it was possible. Not when she was so set in her ways. Was it ever really in her cards to find that happy-ever-after? Most especially with someone who lived his life following scripts?

"We're both at weird places right now," she said. "I tend to follow life where it leads me."

"What if it leads you to me?"

"It already has, by some Miranda-manufactured coincidence. Must be the fairy magic, eh?"

"Aye." He took her hand. "Is this okay?"

She looked down at their clasped hands. Nodded. For now she could be okay with it.

He squeezed her hand. When he suggested they head back because of her wet leggings, she shook her head. They'd already begun to dry and she wanted to enjoy the early sunshine. They strolled along the cliff, pausing every now and then to look over the sound. Emerald waters flashing with silver caps and deep shadows. A diving cormorant's splash punctuated the still morning. No dolphin sightings though.

After about half an hour Allie realized she was still holding Finn's hand. This was nice. She didn't want to question anything but whether the sunshine would last or if the rain might begin. Just…be in the moment.

"So what's your next project?" she asked. "You mentioned something about a porn star?"

"I'm going to pass on that one. It's not in my realm of understanding."

"I don't know."

He gaped as if she'd just accused him of being lascivious.

"I don't mean it that way, Finn. Seems the way for some of Hollywood's aging stars to gain new fame. Play bald and ugly, mentally unstable, real and edgy, revealing their true selves that lurks beneath the sheen of makeup."

"I get that, but I'm not keen on the fake penis."

"Really? There's a prosthetic involved?"

He nodded.

"Yikes. But wait. Aren't you okay with the full monty? Didn't you do that for one of your movies?"

"Two of them. And, yes, I have no problem flashing my family jewels. But wearing a big fake one? That's just…"

"Cringe?"

"Exactly."

Their laughter echoed across the sound. They wandered in the direction of the castle while a flock of seagulls called from nearby.

"Fair enough," Allie said. "Two movies, eh? Which one did I miss?"

"I'll never tell."

"That's okay, there's a site online that details which actors flash which body parts in which movie. And they even give the exact time stamp it happens."

"I'm going to set aside the concern that you know so much about such a site. You don't need to look it up if you're interested in an update on any of my body parts."

What was he implying?

"Sorry, that was not what it sounded like. Eh. Maybe a little. Allie, I want to kiss you."

"Oh?" *A kiss wouldn't be terrible.*

What was she thinking? Of course she'd like to kiss him!

"You're thinking about it too much." Finn searched her gaze. "That doesn't weigh well in my favor."

When her phone jangled, she quickly tugged it out of her jacket pocket. Not saved by the bell. Maybe a little. Strange nervous energy shot through her veins.

"It's Dorothy," she said to him as she pressed Accept. "How's Miranda?"

They spoke as they wandered toward the firepit behind the castle. Dorothy detailed they'd gotten her mother set up in the guest room and she was doing very well, if exhausted. She was excited for the convention though, and wanted to return to the castle the day before the event to ensure everything was in order.

After she hung up Finn asked, "How's she doing?"

"They've got her set up in their home for her recovery.

Though she's very tired and uses a wheelchair to get around. The doctors are pleased."

"Do you think the convention should still go on?"

"I was thinking the same but Dorothy said Miranda is insistent it takes place. It would lift her mother's spirits. So…"

"Then we've two days to make this place perfect for Miranda."

"I'm in." She lifted her fist.

Finn met it with a fist bump. "The show must go on!"

And in the next moment they both quieted. Eyes dancing. A little smirk on Finn's face. The suggestion for a kiss had been interrupted.

Yet the moment had passed.

With hope, it would return.

When a horn honked, Finn turned to wave. "That's my da!"

CHAPTER FIFTEEN

FINN WENT AROUND front to welcome his dad and Allie slipped inside, wanting to give them the reunion they deserved. When they didn't come inside, she assumed they'd headed out to the hedgerow. Pleased that job would get ticked off the list, she had decided to do a little baking. Partially to satisfy a craving, but also she wanted a treat for Miranda when she arrived home.

While the last batch of mini pumpkin muffins baked in the oven, she peered out the window to see Finn and his dad working on the hedgerow. She would go out to say hi soon. She'd met Sean twice while filming and had found him engaging and kind. He possessed the bright green eyes of a Hollywood movie star, like his son, and carried himself with a sense of gravitas that never overwhelmed his charm.

Being a hedgelayer was an amazing job that didn't just involve trimming hedges. He actually wove fences and barriers with the branches of established trees and shrubs and created intricate artwork. She'd noticed a lot of such work on her journey from the main island and to the castle. The craftsmanship was truly remarkable.

After placing some muffins in a metal tin to take out back for the men, along with a container of fresh icy water, she was interrupted by the arrival of the cleaning crew. Getting them set up in the bathrooms and directing them where they needed to cover in the rest of the castle, she then grabbed her treats and headed outside.

A fine mist dusted her face and hair, which she had pulled into a loose braid and flipped forward over a shoulder. The sun was high and the air warm, so she left her jacket inside and even wore a cotton blouse instead of a sweater. Still, it was always wise to wear her muck boots. And after slipping into the fairy pool, well…

Finn waved and came to take the food from her. "It's Allie, Da!" he called.

The old man whose hair was white as snow looked up from his work. An effusive grin burst onto his face. He shed his gloves and scrambled over to her. Following close behind, an aging yellow retriever seemed to take each step with care.

"Allegra Stark!" He met her with a generous bear hug, which she sank into gratefully. He smelled of fresh-cut wood and sea salt. A girl could get lost in such a warm embrace and never wish to surface. "It's good to see you, lass."

He held her at arm's length and looked her over. "I see we're doing the same hair color now. But look, you haven't aged a day."

"Oh, you're such a teaser, Mr. McGregor."

"It's Sean to you, lass. You're family, you know that."

His warmth and comforting presence was just the same as it had been all those years ago. He offered a kind of familial and respectful presence that was rare and should always be cherished.

"What sort of treats did you bring us then?"

"Muffins fresh from the oven." She walked over to the hedge and studied the intricate weaving that bent from the ground at a forty-five degree angle to form a sturdy wall against even the most aggressive deer or ewe. "This is so beautiful." She turned to Finn, half a muffin in his mouth. "Did you do this?"

"I've been supervising, mostly. Da's the real genius."

"Do you want me to show you how it's done?" Sean asked

as he popped a tiny muffin in his mouth. "Och, those are tasty. Give me three more, boy."

Finn offered his dad the entire tin.

"There's more inside," Allie offered. "And I'd love to watch you work."

For the next hour Allie listened as Sean explained his craft, cutting, bending and weaving the vicious blackthorn branches into a literal work of art. She donned Finn's heavy leather gloves and tried it herself, finding it took a firm hand and muscle.

"You've a career as a hedgelayer ahead of you, lass." Sean's smile was a drug of which she couldn't get enough. Real truth, compassion and an all-around kindness in his eyes. And his heart.

When her phone pinged, she read the text. "The cleaning crew has a few questions so I'd better run back inside. I'll make us supper if you're going to be here all day?"

"You won't be able to get rid of me now that you've hooked me with those tiny treats." Sean winked at her. Like father, like son? Most likely. "We'll need to do some catching up!" he called as she wandered back to the castle.

Having never known her father—her mother had honestly told her he'd been a one-night stand she hadn't cared to make a life with—Allie had a tendency to soak in the attentions of older men who showed her a care. Sean was one of the best. A fine example of a man. And Finn had followed very closely, she decided. Sure, he'd had some pitfalls along his path.

"He's a good man," she muttered to herself as she entered the boot room. "And…it feels different this time around."

And not a bad different at that.

Later that evening they built a bonfire in the firepit. After a meal of fried potatoes, sausage links and toasted bread, they all wandered out to warm up before the fire.

Finn poked the blaze with a long stick, his gaze flickering with flames, transfixed.

Sean sat on a folding chair beside Allie. He leaned closer and said, "He always did like to play with fire. Would stand as if bewitched before the flames." He chuckled, then gave his trusty dog, Bones, a pat on the head. "So how have you been, lass? I followed your career until you slipped out of sight."

"Acting was not the best fit for me. I tried my hand at marriage. It didn't last. So then I focused on taking care of others. Or at least, giving others an experience. Did Finn tell you about Glamcations?"

"Pampering women and charity? Sounds like you're doing a good thing. And you want to fix up the castle for such use?"

"It would be perfect for a getaway. But I do understand that it would also serve Finn's plans. As well, this was his childhood home."

"Eh." Sean dismissed that with a gesture. "He's enough on his plate. He doesn't need another castle."

"Another?"

Sean shrugged. "He did own the one in East Lothian but he let that one go. Offered it to me. I'm not much for big places anymore. I like my tidy cottage on the shore. That and my dog. We do well together, me and Bones."

The dog looked up at his person, unconditional love in its tired eyes, before laying its head back down.

"A simple life," Allie said. "I like that."

Allie closed her eyes and settled deeper into the old chair cushion.

"I always knew you and Finn would get together some day," Sean waxed.

Allie opened one eye to see him smile widely at her. "We're not together."

"Well. You are. You just don't know it yet." He chuckled. "I knew from the day I met you that you were the one for my son."

She'd never heard such a thing from him. And he *still* believed it? The man had no clue how she and Finn had changed over the years. They hadn't been meant for one another when filming. Why now?

Why not, Allie? Weren't you going to embrace what life brought your way? The good man, remember?

"Don't try to convince me otherwise," he offered. "You're good for my boy. And while I suspect no man may be good enough for you, he'll do. You need him as much as he needs you."

"Mr. McGregor—"

"Uh." He raised an admonishing hand.

"Sean." She glanced to the fire. Finn still stood before the flames. Unaware of their conversation? She hoped so. The crackle of the flames was loud. "I've given up on love."

Though inwardly she cringed at that surprising statement. What was wrong with love? Not a thing when it came at the right time, and with the right person. And she knew it was real. A lot to ask. Yet she had grown closer to Finn in the past few days.

Wasn't enough to start something lasting though.

Sean slapped a hand over hers, startling her. When he gave it a squeeze, she wanted to tug away. To run from anything that wanted to convince her that happiness came only as a result of love. But she didn't pull away because she knew better. Everything he was saying was probably true. As he'd stated, she just didn't know it yet.

"You're not the type of woman to give up on anything, lass. I know you."

He didn't, really.

"Finn's had his struggles with finding his place in a relationship, but if I know one thing, he's found his way back to something good." Another of the infamous McGregor men's winks was aimed her way.

Allie sighed but didn't protest. She'd let it hang. No sense in arguing with the man. She didn't want to hurt his feelings. And she'd be damned if part of her didn't wish for the same. Spending time with Finn these past few days had not been so terrible as she'd expected. In fact, she'd settled into a sort of cozy companionship with him. He was there but not. Close when she felt the desire to chat with another person. But he allowed her the space she had earned and cherished as an independent woman.

"Allie, Da, look at that!"

On the cliff overlooking the sea stood a deer with a massive antler rack, silhouetted against the deep cobalt sky. Allie joined Finn beside the blazing flames. "That's like a fantasy image."

Looking aside, she saw in his gaze a softening. An unspoken question. *Can we?* But then with a glance to his dad, Finn lifted his chin, and instead of kissing her, he pulled her to his side and hugged her as they watched the deer hold a pose for them to admire.

"I should be heading home." Sean stood and Bones slowly rose. The aging dog must have loved the warmth of the fire. "It's been a day."

"It's late," Finn said. "There's another guest room you can use."

Sean waved a dismissive hand. "I won't be an imposition. And who said I'm going back to the mainland?" With a wink to Allie, he patted his thigh and Bones followed him around the side of the castle.

"I'll go see him off." Finn quick-stepped it after his dad.

Allie picked up the designated fire stick and poked down the logs into the ashy pit. The fire would only burn for another hour if they didn't stoke it. She sat again and looked for the deer but it had gone.

Cozy nights like this made her wish the castle already belonged to her. And that she would make it a home instead of a vacation property. This life felt perfect to her. An escape from the bustle of reality. But nothing ever came so easily. And really, Finn deserved the place more than she did. He had an emotional connection to the place, from the memories of his mom to the very hedge he'd helped his dad tend over the years.

Or had he told her about his mom to appeal to her compassion? To make her want to hand him the win?

She shook her head. No, that didn't seem like Finn.

Finn walked his dad to the waiting truck out in front of the castle. Before he could stop himself, he said what he'd been feeling when standing before the fire. "I wish we were closer, Da."

"Aye, the distance is a bother. You can call me more, you know. And not just when you need help with a hedge."

"Sorry about that. I've been busy, but…not really. Haven't worked for months. Not sure when the next job will come."

"Allie told me you want the castle for a filming location?"

"Well, I thought before I came here that packaging the castle along with the script for a sequel would help."

Though he knew he'd given up on that the moment he'd looked into Allie's iceberg eyes and felt his heart open to her once again.

He opened the side door and waited for Bones to make his slow and lumbering way up inside. "I probably shouldn't ever have tried to buy the castle."

"Why not?"

"The fact that this used to be my home doesn't even draw me. Sure, it holds memories, but I've kept the good ones close. Here." He patted his heart. "Allie deserves this castle more than I do. And me. I'm…at a crossroads. Maybe I don't need what I want? But I want what I can't have?"

"She's the one for you, son."

Finn closed the door behind the dog. "You think?"

His dad eyed him seriously. "You know."

That look was always the "listen well and do not think to do the opposite" look his dad would employ. Finn had never dared to disobey. "I do. But she doesn't know that."

"I think she does. There's something keeping her from you."

Finn leaned against the side of his dad's truck. "Do you think I made a mistake in keeping her at a distance when we were filming? In not trying to make a go of it with the two of us?"

"It may have been the best thing you could have done for the both of you. Especially with your drinking issues."

"It's been twelve years since I've taken a sip," Finn said.

"I'm proud of you, son. It takes a strong man to defeat such a devil as that. As for you and Allie? Love isn't always easy. Now comes the hard part."

The hard part. Right. The part where he had to step outside of his fictional world of accolades and ego brushers and learn to function in the real world. With a real woman. "It always looked easy with you and Mum."

"Aye, it was. Mostly. Still is. I talk to her every morning. Tell her how I'm going about my day. She'll love hearing about my day with you."

"Tell her I was thinking of her the other day, sitting in her crafty room."

Sean glanced toward the tower room. "She used to sit up there and stare out at the moon. I'd find her illuminated by moonlight as if a magical being."

"She was magic, Da."

Sean bowed his head and nodded, "That she was." Bones pawed on the truck window and Sean rapped it gently. "You think you can manage the rest of the hedge? Just a bit of trimming left."

"I can. But you can come back tomorrow if you want to. I know you'll be stopping into the inn in Portree. Is Shirley still there?"

His dad's snicker was accompanied by a shaking head. "You know too much, Finn."

"Sure, but I didn't give you a hard time about your lover in front of Allie."

"Fair enough." Sean clamped a hand on Finn's shoulder, then pulled him in for a hug. "Love you, boy."

"I love you too, Da. Thanks for today."

"Let's not make it years between visits from now on, aye?"

"I promise. If I get the castle, I'll be here all the time, eh."

"But if Allie gets it, you could be here as well." With an affectionate punch to Finn's shoulder, Sean climbed into the truck and took off.

Finn rubbed his arm, more surprised by the hug than the fake punch. "Now comes the hard part, eh?"

Never in his real—not fictional—life had he fought hard to keep a woman. Hadn't the desire. But he did know that he and Allie were meant for one another. In his very bones he felt that.

So, it was time to get his act together and fight.

CHAPTER SIXTEEN

THE HEDGEROW WAS LOVELY. Allie strode by it, hands in her pockets, determined to look over the land as a buyer.

The castle was set on a large lot, and with a neighbor on one side and a nature preserve on the other, there was little worry of someone building close. Miranda had mentioned the occasional hiker would stray onto the land since there were no fences other than the hedgerow and there was the right to roam, which allowed for hikers not in the know—and even in the know—to cross private property. She didn't mind that, and with a gentle word explaining they'd walked onto private property, there were never any random campsites being set up.

Tourists came from all over the world to hike the Isle of Skye trails, one of the most beautiful of the almost eight hundred Scottish islands. It was crazy to imagine, but less than a hundred of those islands were actually inhabited.

Skye was the second largest island. The Red and Black Cuillin mountain ranges appealed to Allie, even though she had no desire to climb them. She recalled seeing snow on the mountaintops during some rare filming excursions in the winter months. (They'd filmed the majority of the winter scenes in Canada. Go figure.) She could live here. Even the cooler temperatures didn't bother her. A steady sixty to seventy degrees in the summer was not a hardship. Though the winds could be annoying. And the midges would never allow a person to forget their existence.

If she were ever to live here, she may want to learn rudimentary Gaelic. It was used by some of the locals. Such a musical language.

What was she doing? Imagining a life here on the island? She'd only come to buy a castle and add it to her vacation roster. Of course that would involve staying here while fixing up the castle for use. But that didn't mean she had to live here forever.

Had Sean's suggestion regarding her and his son gotten into her head? Staying here, whether for a few months or longer, had nothing to do with Finn.

Though it could.

Reaching the crest of hill that looked over the sea, she sat on a large boulder facing the sun. A cormorant, which she recalled some crew member calling a sea raven, made a guttural sort of clucking. She caught the skitter of a red squirrel that disappeared into a scruffy patch of brush. No trees up here. It was an outlook that offered a view of the heavens down to the sea.

"I want to live here," she announced to the universe. Her mom had taught her to put her desires into words in order to manifest them.

Yet this remote location would never serve her heart well. Sure, the nearest town was a twenty-minute motorbike ride away. But the castle truly was too big for one person to live in. It craved the laughter and wonder of vacationers enjoying a welcome change from their erratic lifestyle. It could become a place of emotional healing for some.

Allie had thought to find such emotional healing by coming here. To once and for all bury the heartache she'd experienced while filming on this very site. Instead she'd been forced to face it head-on in the form of the one man who had broken her heart. He hadn't known he'd done so. And he had apologized for their lack of friendship.

Wrapping her arms about her bent legs she squeezed. Hugging herself was never as gratifying as receiving one from another person. Finn's hug yesterday had mined deep into her bones and stirred up that desire again…

Had Sean McGregor's silly suggestion that they belonged together some truth to it? Why did the idea of running into Finn's arms feel so appealing? Like first love filling her lungs and making her laugh and sigh in silly waves. It felt good being with Finn. And so different from when she'd secretly loved him long ago. This time around he reciprocated her attention. And that was something she'd never thought to receive from him.

"He has changed," she mused to herself. "More calm, not quite so egotistic and seems to really listen."

Still handsome as ever. And the patented McGregor men's wink was not something a woman could walk away from without a slight wobble to her step.

"There you are!"

Closing her eyes to the welcome sound of Finn's voice, Allie smiled to think that perhaps the universe was nudging her toward something she would be wise to pay attention to.

"Wanted to catch a moment to myself," she said.

Sliding over, she patted the rock and he settled beside her, shoulder to shoulder.

"Thank you," he said quietly.

"For what?"

"For being so nice to my da. He really likes you."

"I love your dad. He's one of the kindest men I've ever known. Wish I could see him more often."

"If you move into the castle, I'm sure he'd stop by all the time. He, uh…thinks we should be a thing."

"He told me that." She glanced to Finn who had fixed his

gaze on the horizon. "I told him he didn't know what he was talking about."

"Huh. I kind of thought you were starting to sweeten toward me."

She was. Had been all along. Or maybe this time it was real and she was starting to embrace that. "I like you, Finn. But your dad sees us as…"

"As a pair. Just…imagine it for a moment, Allie. The two of us, sharing this castle, this life. We wouldn't have to be married or anything silly like that."

"You think marriage is silly?"

"For us? At our ages? Maybe a little. I've nothing against the institution. Never tried it so I suppose I can't speak good or ill against it. I like the idea of being in a relationship where two people respect one another, are there for one another, but don't need the other. If you can understand that?"

"I do." He was talking her language. First potatoes and now the truth about a real adult relationship? The man really had matured. "So that's what you see for us? You've got dreams."

"Maybe, but they won't happen unless you allow them to. And we're going to have to do a whole lot of making out to get there."

"You think sex makes for a relationship?"

"Who's talking about sex?" He leaned back on his elbows, stretching out his legs before him. "I just want to kiss you."

Cheeky. And yet. "I hardly think a few kisses are the basis for a lasting relationship."

"Well, but I've got you thinking about us in terms of a relationship. Score one for me."

His smile wasn't even that annoying übercharm smile. A visceral reality had formed between the two of them. Solid. Real. Trusting.

So Allie leaned down and kissed him. Mouths pressing

softly, testing one another, then deciding it was okay to linger, to breathe in one another. Nothing urgent or deep. Simple. So remarkably easy kissing Finn. *I'm the only one for you.*

"That was…different," he said as they parted. "Better."

"Than what?"

"Than when we used to kiss on command for the camera." He stroked her jaw, eyes taking in her face. "I like having you to myself. Not having to perform. Do you know I'm not sure I've ever kissed a woman without performing?"

"That seems awfully unfair to the woman."

"Right? But, Allie, my entire life has been an act. At times I don't know how to turn it off."

"Then how do I know *this* isn't an act?"

"Because—" he took her hand and pressed it over his chest where his heart thundered "—my heart's never been privy to a kiss before. It's telling me to be honest with you. To not let this one be another performance. Can you trust me?"

"I think I do," came out in a breathy hush of hope.

"Do you still want to kick me out of your memories?"

She bowed her head to his chest, then rolled to her back to lay beside him and look up at the sun-bleached sky. "I may have been overzealous in wanting to erase the past."

"The past can never be erased. It's been done and experienced. It should be honored. But we've moved on. We've only got right now. And the past should never be invited to now."

"You think?"

"I think." He rolled to his side, leaning up on an elbow. "Can we kiss again?"

"Please."

Allie closed her eyes to the sunlight to experience the delicious joy of Finn's kiss. The brief thought that she should be perfect, turning her head the right angle because a film crew was watching, was vanquished as he pulled her against his body. The kiss touched a passion they had never manufactured for film. It permeated her soul. She clung to him, taking what she'd always wanted. Something real and true.

An ebb in their connection did not part them, but they only took a moment to feel one another's heartbeats, to meet in their new reality of honesty and trust. And then the kiss deepened. It demanded they not ignore the other. That they take what they believed they deserved. And she did.

And when Finn parted from her, he stared into her eyes, his head blocking the sunlight. His smile was that famous McGregor charm but this time it was only for her. "That felt like a first kiss."

"I think so." She pushed up to sit beside him and he clasped her hand as she tilted her head onto his shoulder. The first of so many more?

Yes, please.

"The day can't get much better," he said. "A first kiss. And now sitting on a big rock on the edge of the Sound of Raasay with a pretty girl."

"With Miranda coming home tomorrow, I wonder should we pack up and rent some rooms in Portree?"

"Now who's talking about sex?"

"I didn't mean it—well. We *are* adults. We can do whatever we wish. But I was thinking more on the lines that Miranda doesn't need the worry of houseguests."

"Good call. Will her daughter be staying?"

"Dorothy intends to stay a few weeks or so after the convention to go through the house with her mom and decide what needs to be packed and what can be sold."

"You're always considering the welfare of others. You're a good one, Allie."

"Meanwhile, my own welfare wonders what the heck I'm up to at all times."

Finn laughed. "You seem to have it all together. You've got the perfect life."

"And you don't?"

"It's better than most. I'm not afraid to admit I've got certain privileges because of my job and the income it's brought to me. However I've got my issues. But you? I can look over your life and see you've got it all. You didn't allow Hollywood to break you."

Allie pulled her hand from his abruptly. The intimate moment suddenly wilted. His comment gripped at her very soul. Forced her back to the past they'd just begun to walk away from.

Hollywood hadn't broken her? On the contrary. "You don't know that."

"I think I do. Look at you. A smart, brilliant businesswoman buying up castles and properties across the world to enhance the lives of others. That's something amazing. You don't think so?"

"I am in a good place right now. On paper. Financially. But my heart?"

She winced. Shivered. She hadn't a jacket and the day had chilled considerably. Could she really go there and expose her heart upon her palm to Finn? She wanted someone to know she wasn't right, had never been right. And desperately wanted to find that right.

"Allie?" Sunlight sparkled in his fairy-pool eyes. How quickly her body imagined itself back in a place where things between them had been so hard to decipher.

"Finn…" Why was she feeling nerves? She was in her fifties. She had become that strong woman he admired. She could handle anything that came her way. But it had been a long time since her heart had exercised that same resilient strength. And right now the hapless organ was wobbling between new adventure and old anxieties.

"When we were filming," she started. "Well. I appreciated your apology about us never being friends. I could have used a friend on set. But even more…" A sigh was unavoidable. "Finn, the truth of it is that I was in love with you. For real."

He tilted his head. Was he really surprised at the confession?

"It wasn't acting for me. Every kiss meant something to me. When we filmed those close-ups of staring into one another's eyes and sharing those looks—those were real to me."

"They meant something to me too, Allie."

"Maybe. But you were able to pull away and walk it off. Me? I couldn't do that. After 'cut' was called, you'd leave the set and I'd be sitting there trying to find a headspace that wouldn't have me crying or yelling after you, why don't you love me? I know it sounds crazy. I wasn't able to separate the character from the emotions."

"I'm sorry, Allie. I never knew it was that serious for you."

"It was. And I came here to close that chapter on my life for good. But I never expected the very man I wanted to push out of my heart would be here. Or that I've found myself actually racing toward him—you—as if this is a new and exciting adventure. It's really messing with me."

"You know what I've never been able to understand, Allie?"

"What's that?"

"I never understood what you saw in me and, to be honest, I still don't. Look at you. You're in such a great space mentally and work-wise. And here I am, the man who is on a desperate quest to keep his sagging career alive by acquiring a stupid old castle. Always thinking only of myself. You deserve someone giving and—there is that ego of mine you keep reminding me about. How could I ever be good enough for you?"

"Don't be so hard on yourself, Finn. You are a good man. And…it's not so much the validation of another job you're searching for, I think it's that ingrained quest for adoration that keeps you searching."

He sighed heavily. "You're not wrong. Just never heard it put so bluntly like that."

"I'm sorry. It's what I've observed. You do like the adulation."

"It's what's kept me going for decades. But believe me, I can relate to your escaping that early on. When fame struck, I grabbed it and consumed it like a beast. I wouldn't have dated me, if given the chance. So…"

"You don't need to worry about me, Finn."

He was right, in his weird sort of way. Why had she begun to think dating him was a good thing? To indulge in the fantasy she'd once lived daily? Because he'd been calling them dates. Leading her down a path he wasn't even invested in?

Finn had changed in many ways, but he still seemed to cling to some values she couldn't connect to. And probably he didn't even know how to do love and romance. "This… whatever we have right now, is my problem. I'll deal with it."

"I just worry I'd mess everything up for you, Allie."

She heaved out a breath. "Honestly, Finn, don't worry about it." Seriously. He could not be the man for her if he didn't even know himself. How had she ever let things go this far?

"I'm just trying to be honest about how I feel," he said. "I know a lot more now about myself. And I wasn't Mr. Spectacular back then. At least not when it came to relationships."

"Sure, I get that. But what do you really expect me to do with what you're saying? You lead us to this point and then you turn around and shrug it off. It's not fair."

"I'm sorry you see it that way."

She frowned. "One minute you tell me you want a relationship with me, the next you're telling me you'd still run from me. And that kiss—what did it even mean? And besides that, we are rivals for the castle. This can't end well."

"That kiss was real, Allie."

"How can you be so sure? You. A man who acts out fiction for a living."

The sound of a horn honking alerted them to a truck driving toward the castle.

"Must be the caterer. The list noted they'll be bringing in the refrigerated goods today. Allie, I know what I felt when we kissed. And we... I want us to have a relationship. A real one." He huffed and shook his head. "Why is this such a challenge?"

"Exactly," she said. "You'd better go meet the delivery truck."

"This conversation is not over."

"Don't worry about it, Finn. We're good."

As friends. They could never be a *we*. Because if he wasn't willing to step up to the challenge, then—much as she wanted him to be—he was not the man for her.

CHAPTER SEVENTEEN

IT WAS THE middle of the night. Allie sat on a window well placed at the landing halfway up to the second floor, watching the sight outside the window. After the caterer had left, she and Finn had dined on some of the samples they'd provided and then both had quietly went about their own thing. She'd retired to her room early, not sure a conversation with Finn was what she wanted right now. But she hadn't been able to sleep. Which is why she'd wandered out for a snack and gotten waylaid by what she saw outside.

Truthfully? Their conversation was not over. And she didn't want it to be over. She…wanted Finn in her life. Kicking him to the curb didn't seem feasible anymore. Not to her heart. But she still struggled with not knowing exactly where his heart was with her. The ineffable *knowing* she wanted to feel was missing.

He had said he wanted them to have a real relationship. Oh! Did the man realize how he confused her with his indecisiveness?

She startled at a noise behind her.

"Sorry." The landing was illuminated by moonlight, but she finally saw Finn's face as he stepped onto the top step and walked over to her. He wore striped pajama bottoms and a loose cotton robe that revealed a glimpse of the lightly haired chest she'd once explored intimately.

"Why are you sneaking about at midnight?" she asked with a tint of anger over him scaring her.

"I wasn't sneaking. I was being stealthy." He took a bite of one of the pumpkin muffins he held in each hand. "Had a craving for a midnight snack. What are you doing here? I didn't see you coming down."

"I…" she chuckled "…had the same urge for a snack but got distracted by that down there." She pointed out the window toward the ground and Finn knelt one knee on the ledge where she sat and peered out. "See them?"

"Fireflies. I used to chase them all the time when I was a kid."

"But look closer."

He took another bite of his muffin and peered outside more intently. She would not be distracted by his bare chest. But the man had not gotten flabby, that was for sure.

"Ah. A wee fox is playing with the bobbling lights. Isn't that enchanting." He sat opposite her, putting up his legs. Their toes, both sets bare, were but inches from one another. "Mind if I join you?"

"You can do as you wish."

"Allie, please don't hold a grudge against me. I don't want us to do this."

"I'm sorry, I just…" *What about that relationship? You were so close to being open to it.* "You're right. I am holding a weird sort of grudge. You've done absolutely nothing wrong. I just need to get straight in my head how I feel about you."

"I vote for liking Finn McGregor."

"I do too." His face brightened behind another bite of muffin. "But it's not that simple. And don't tell me it can be."

"I won't. I haven't been clear on what I expect between the two of us. Not really sure what that should be, but I do know whatever is going on between us? I like it."

She did too. Oh, how her plans to forget him had been foiled. "Do you have two muffins?"

He held up the other that he hadn't bitten into yet, a big grin on his face.

"Give me that."

He studied the uneaten muffin. To give up his booty? Or to share? Finally, he leaned forward and handed it to her. She took a bite.

"With Miranda returning tomorrow," she said, "I should touch up the guest room on the main floor. Dorothy said she doesn't want her mom having to deal with stairs."

"The grounds are looking tip-top shape. We work well together, Allie."

"We do."

"I thought you were going to get in my way that first day I arrived to make a bid. Keep me from getting something I needed."

She waited for more but he looked down through the window. So she prompted, "But?"

He shrugged. "I like you in my way."

"Even if you don't get what you think you need?"

"Honestly? I may have everything I need at this very moment." With that, he stood, kissed her on the head, then headed up the stairs to his room.

Such a dramatic exit. The actor's momentous departure. The cliffhanger. The "what happens next?" moment.

He had everything he needed? Did that include her?

Did he have her?

Taking another bite of the muffin, she refocused on the fireflies below. Enchanting, indeed. And, yes, he could have her. Because she needed him. And it was time to stop her inner battle against him. The McGregor charm had reeled her in. And despite her misgivings, she wanted him. Right now.

If only for the night.

"Wait for me!" she called and hustled to catch up to him. Finn waited at the top of the stairs, his face in shadow but his smile a beacon.

Allie tilted onto her tiptoes and kissed him. The kiss was urgent. Deep. Wanting. "Can we spend the night together?"

He took her hand. "Come with me."

Once in Finn's room Allie pulled off her sweater and walked toward him. He stood before the window, silhouetted by the moonlight. When she began to think that they'd been here so many times before—as actors—she shoved that thought away. This was now. Not then.

"This is not an act," she said, tucking her fingers into his waistband.

"Never." He cupped her cheek and kissed her. "This is real."

CHAPTER EIGHTEEN

ALLIE BLINKED AT the bright sunlight that beamed through the window. She loved Scottish mornings. The sun always managed to sneak in before the sky decided whether to bring on the clouds, rain or both. The line of Finn's shoulder partially blocked her view.

She touched his firm, muscled back. The skin so warm. It had been years since she'd made love with a man. Not because she hadn't dated—she fit in dating here and there—but because she hadn't been compelled to take it to that next level. One of trust and intimacy. Sex meant something to her. And, yes, it could be a quickie that brought the date to a satisfying end because that was what she wanted. Or even an impulsive desire to sleep with a man with whom she had once been infatuated.

But more so now she desired touch, the panting breaths measuring one another's desire, the slow glide of a kiss across her skin. The waking next to the other person in the morning because last night had been more than surface and the answer to a mere need.

She took her hand away from his back. So that was where she was with Finn? Last night she'd wanted to be with him. She'd asked, and he had answered. No concern for what it would mean regarding their future.

This had been the first time they'd stripped naked, without a camera crew filming them, and truly stepped into one another's space and shared. It felt immense. But she cautioned herself not to slide down the hill and splash too deeply into the water. She wasn't a naive young woman. She had established a routine, manners, was set in her ways. She knew what she wanted…

A companion. But more so, someone to share her life. To accept her where she was at, independent yet still in her own way slightly needy.

But she also knew Finn did not live in the same world as she did. His life was engineered by movie scripts and jetting across the world to meet filming schedules. His very nature demanded he feed the creative beast that gave him his success. Acknowledgment. Validation. He could never settle alongside her and simply be.

Did she want that from him? Actually, no. She didn't require a man to move in with her, spend 24/7 with her, marry her. At this point in her life she enjoyed her freedom and personal space. To allow another to intrude on those carefully curated boundaries would be a challenge. She wanted a lover. That could mean someone who lived elsewhere and whom she saw every now and then. (More than that. Often.) But only if it was real.

Finn rolled to his back, scruffed a palm over his face, then turned a smile to her. He winked. Oh, that McGregor charm.

She nuzzled her face against his shoulder without saying a word. Could they be real? Dare she want more than a fly-in lover?

"Can we stay like this all day?" he whispered.

She smirked against his skin. "I wish. Dorothy and Miranda will arrive soon. I'd like to get out and take a walk before then."

Sitting up, she eyed her clothing on the floor. She glanced back to Finn. His smile owned her. She bowed to kiss him on the forehead, then brushed her lips over his. "See you in a bit?"

"You've seen my bits. You want more?"

Laughter was easy. She stood and pulled on her sweater and leggings. "You are incorrigible. But I like that about you."

"I like that you like something about me."

"I like a lot about you, Finn."

Miranda and Dorothy arrived an hour later. Allie was out walking the cliff, watching the seals swish and splash below. Finn burned the last of the clippings from the trimmed hedgerows, and a constant plume of white smoke drifted toward the clouds.

As she headed toward the castle to greet the women, Finn reached out and pulled her to him. Landing in his embrace felt like the most natural place to be. No more longing. Wondering if he would ever notice her and reciprocate her feelings. She'd won his interest. Now, what to do with that win?

"You'll be reprising your role tomorrow," he said. "How do you feel about that?"

"I hadn't looked at it that way. It's only for an hour or so. I'm good with it."

"I still can't convince you to consider taking a small part if the project gets sold?"

She shook her head, spun from his embrace and called as she walked away, "I'm sure you'll find someone who can take my place!"

"You're irreplaceable, Allie!"

She could read that statement two ways. As an actress or…in his life? More and more she tilted toward allowing him full access to her life.

An SUV parked before the castle. Allie didn't want to get in the women's way. This was a personal family matter. But Miranda had insisted, by text as they were driving here, she and Finn continue their stay since the convention was tomorrow.

Before heading inside, she veered toward the little garden with the lily of the valley. The bouquet Finn had given her needed freshening. Bent over, she spied Finn making his way inside through the boot room. As eager to greet the women as she? The man was far more compassionate than he believed.

When a fox scampered across the back of the garden plot, she pulled out her phone to snap a few photos. To remember her time spent here in Scotland. Because…maybe the castle really should go to the man who had started his life here. Had memories here. She could visit him. Have an affair? It wasn't out of her realm of possibility. But she wouldn't want to be caught visiting if they filmed the new series here.

Or would she? The idea of reprising her role wasn't so offensive to her now that she considered it. It wouldn't have to be large. Just a few cameos?

Oh, what was she doing? No. Absolutely no more acting for her.

With a decisive nod, she watched the fox scamper off.

Leaving her boots in the coatroom, Allie wandered toward the kitchen. The sound of Dorothy's laughter rang. And with it came Finn's deep chuckle. She spied Miranda in a wheelchair, a blanket across her lap, a big smile on her face. When the woman sighted Allie, she gestured for her to join them.

"It's so good to see you smiling," Allie offered, going over to give Miranda a hug. "You've so many of these lilies. We've been enjoying them every day." She did a switch-out on the flower vase and placed it in the center of the table. "How are you feeling, Miranda?"

"Quite well, considering. Could use a nap. But sit with us a moment." Miranda's speech was slower, measuring her words, perhaps simply exhaustion. "Finn told us about your fall into the fairy pond."

"Oh, dear." Allie cast Finn a glance.

He shrugged. "It made them laugh?"

"It feels good to laugh," Miranda said.

Allie clasped her hand as she sat beside her. "You've been so generous to us. A little laughter over my fall is warranted."

"And you two have been so brilliant helping us as you have. The convention is going to be a success," Dorothy announced as she got up to fill her teacup with hot water. "And Mum is well enough to make an appearance. But we'll need to keep an eye on you so you don't get overworked," she said affectionately to her mother.

"I'll be fine. Just a little slower is all." Her expression softened and Allie could see she was exhausted. "I'm quite excited to pack up and move on from this place, actually. Staying with Dorothy and my grandkids these past few days has lightened my wounded heart."

"The kids love having Gammy stay with us. The guestroom is yours as long as you need it, Mum. Even longer. You won't be world-traveling for a while, I imagine."

"Oh, I'll be up and about in no time. A little physical therapy, and then I'm off," Miranda declared with a whisper of her usual gaiety.

"Where do you plan to travel first?" Allie said.

"Greece, of course. I want to soak in the blue water and find myself a sexy Greek man to tickle my fancy."

"Mum!"

Miranda chuckled at her daughter's outrage. With a shrug, she then yawned.

Allie asked, "Do you want me to bring you to your room for a little rest?"

"I'll do it." Dorothy manned her mother's wheelchair. "The two of you have done so much to pretty up the castle and the grounds. I really appreciate all of it. Did you notice the hedgerows when we drove up, Mum?"

"Did I? Beautiful!"

"That's thanks to me da," Finn provided.

"You'll have to invite him to the convention," Dorothy said. "So we can thank him properly. Oh, and I picked up the costumes on the way here. They're out in the trunk if you'll fetch them."

She passed them her keys and Miranda waved as her daughter wheeled her out of the kitchen.

Allie set down her teacup and sought Finn's gaze. "Costumes?"

He pressed a palm over his heart and mocked a dramatic wince. "Not sure I've the strength for it."

She could guess at what the costumes might be, and for whom. Had she really just spent over a week at this place, tidying, gardening, fixing just to win a bid? And now she would don a costume and play a role to ensure that win?

She took in Finn's charming smile. It said so many things, not the least that they were good with one another. Perhaps she'd had ulterior motives all along. Like welcoming him back into her heart.

"Shall we get it over with?" Finn gestured toward the door.

"Do we have to?"

"I thought you wanted to ingratiate yourself to Miranda so you could win the castle?"

"I did. We both are. But really? Costumes?"

He hooked an arm, indicating she should join in. "We're in it to win it?"

With a shake of her head, she took his arm and they wandered outside. Gray clouds softened the sky and they walked right into a cloud of midges. Running and laughing to escape the tiny horde, they reached Dorothy's car. Finn corralled her into his arms and kissed her. With a glance to the castle windows to check they weren't being watched, he kissed her again. Long. Lingering. A few giggles punctuated shorter kisses because it felt so new, sweet and yet also daring and like…finally.

Allie pulled him to her, taking everything she'd ever wanted from him. Kissing him without an audience was a new experience. As had been having real sex with him. Just the two of them. In a big bed. Alone. Together.

Don't fall in love again, whispered in her thoughts.

Too late, she whispered back.

"Kissing you is better than any award or accolade I've ever received," he said, stepping back to touch the car. The hatchback trunk opened to reveal two large costume boxes. They had seen the sort while filming. Pulling them out indicated their heft.

"Tell me these are not what I think they are?" Allie asked as she spat at a midge and then wrangled her arms about a box.

Finn, doing the same, joined her as they wandered back inside. "These are not what you think they are." He set his box down once inside the boot room. "But."

She nodded. "Don't even say it. I know. I…know."

After trying on the costume in her room, Allie pulled on her clothes and as she did the purple fairy stone fell from the pocket where she'd tucked it. Warm in her palm, it reminded that the past could return. And be welcomed. And even be a little magical.

On a whim she decided that maybe Finn might like a little magic before their big performance tomorrow. Intending to give him the fairy stone, she snuck down the hallway toward his room. His door was barely open. She lifted her hand to knock when she heard his voice. Talking to someone on the phone?

"I've got Allegra Stark as well. She'll reprise her role. Listen, Howard, if the studio wants the script, then I can bring whatever you need for it to you on a silver platter."

Allie gasped, clutching the stone to her chest.

Finn was making promises that he couldn't possibly make happen. She'd told him she wasn't interested in reprising her role.

Had he been getting close to her to achieve that end? Had he been using her emotions to soften her, butter her up and make her agree to act in the sequel? Was she a bargaining chip to sell the script?

Her newly hopeful heart tore in two. She'd allowed herself to be open to him. To welcome him back into her heart. And he'd hurt her. Again. She let the fairy stone drop to the floor and walked away soundlessly.

CHAPTER NINETEEN

FINN HUNG UP after talking to not the head of the studio but an underling, a mere assistant. A third studio had passed on the script. Not even the prospect of the castle had influenced them to buy. Or that he might be able to get Allegra Stark in a reprisal of her role.

The reason this time? The series was old and today's viewers wanted new. Sure, the dramatic series format was popular, but the most popular were not straight historicals. They wanted dragons, demons, apocalypses and more.

He could work with that. Weren't fairies fantasy enough? He could up the fantastical quotient. No wings in the original series. But now? Bring on the CGI.

He sat on the end of his bed where sunlight beamed and lay back, spreading his arms across the counterpane.

Three noes did not mean he'd never find a *yes*. But it was disheartening as hell.

At the moment the only other standing job offer was for the porn star Dirk Swagger. He did understand that he could make it a meaty role, as Allie had explained. But still, he didn't identify in any way with the porn-star character. Even the emotional part about changing his life and…

"Not fitting in anymore," Finn muttered with a shake of his head.

It suddenly hit him. He *was* Dirk Swagger. He was the once-famous actor at the top of his game now stumbling through life trying to find his way. To cling to the remnants of his fame. To just be noticed. And loved.

He whistled in amazement. How crazy was it that it just hit him now? Take out the porn and make it action adventure and they were literally the same actor.

Should he consider taking this role? Could it be his greatest role ever? If he mined his own emotional struggle, he could make it so. Maybe it was time to try something new as Allie had suggested? Polish up the tarnish of aging out of action/adventure that he'd felt settle onto his shoulders.

Much as he tried to embrace that idea, the cringe factor still made him—cringe.

To be really honest with himself? Acting wasn't fun anymore. Not even when he was hanging from a cable before a green screen pretending to cling to a precarious cliff edge. Somewhere along the line he'd lost the thrill of the new and unique. Of telling a story that no one had seen before. All the stories he'd been cast in lately were the same. Just plug in a different hero, setting and romantic interest.

No, that wasn't completely true. There were still great movies being made. And they were great because the people behind them believed in the story.

When had he stopped believing?

After he'd gotten sober, he'd been cast in the *Code Grey* movies. The high point of his career. But eight years had passed since the fourth movie had been filmed, and the producers decided Jack Greystone's story had been told. He'd been getting action parts since then, but the production budget had been half or even a quarter of what he was used to. And some had even gone direct to streaming, not even hitting the big screen.

It had been a culmination of small letdowns over the past half a decade that had challenged his beliefs and made him question his own talent. Made him hungry for the eager fans, the obsessive paparazzi, even a glowing review in a major publication and not some side note stating that Finn McGregor was acting in B movies.

"B movies," he muttered with distaste.

The Dirk Swagger inside him had to accept that he had aged out of the roles he loved to play and needed to look toward something different if he wanted to remain in the business. And he did want to continue acting. In the right role. That he could believe in.

In reality he'd give up on selling the damned script if only Allie would give him that look again. The one that said "I trust you and feel safe with you." The one that he now knew she had never faked when they'd been filming. She'd been in love with him.

There was a reason they'd walked back into one another's lives. He believed that. And making love with her had not been just one night for him. They'd begun something here at this castle that held so many memories for him. Could he claim his bonny lass?

"I'm the only one for you."

He smirked and shook his head. Cheesy line. But still. His dad thought they were meant for one another. And Sean McGregor never got a thing wrong.

"Where's Dorothy?" Allie asked from the depths of name stickers.

After a light lunch Miranda had insisted they write all the convention attendees' names in calligraphy on name tags. That would take a lot of effort and time they didn't have. So Allie had looked up a program online to print the names in a fancy font. Now she had merely to separate the perforated tags on the printed roll while Miranda sipped lemon tea and supervised.

"She's gone out to the shed in search of Finn."

"Did she need help with something?"

Miranda chuckled. "Oh, no, she's set on flirting with him. She may be decades younger but she's a good eye for a handsome lad."

Smiling to herself, Allie began to alphabetize the name tags.

"Are you jealous?" Miranda proposed over the rim of her teacup.

"Why would I be?" And *how* could she be after what she'd heard Finn telling someone on the phone about her agreeing to reprise her role?

Miranda set down her teacup with a clink and a wobble. Allie dashed to catch the cup before it tilted on its side.

"Thank you," Miranda said. "I'm still a little shaky after what I've been through."

"You're doing well. You were very lucky."

"Yes, if one can call having a heart attack before two people they admire lucky."

"Oh, Miranda, you mustn't be embarrassed in any way."

"I am. A little. But I also know how lucky I was the two of you were here when it happened. But enough about me." She rubbed her palms together gleefully. "I've seen the way Finn looks at you. He's sweet on you, I *know* it." She looked at Allie meaningfully.

Allie tapped the pile of *S* names. She didn't want to have this conversation. Not with a woman who headed the *Clan MacKenzie* fan club and had detailed and kept notes on their every move through the years. Was all information she gleaned eventually disclosed in the newsletter?

"You two have become close, I see," Miranda announced with a glee that touched on her usual busybody self.

And while it was heartening to see a flicker of the woman's usual vim glitter in her eyes, Allie didn't want to encourage her. Especially when close to two-hundred fans were due to arrive tomorrow morning. It was time for some PR control. "It's not like that."

"Oh, I think it is. You two have always been meant for one another."

"That was fiction," Allie said firmly as she distracted herself from meeting Miranda's gaze by starting the *T* pile. "Real life isn't scripted."

And yet Sean McGregor had said much the same to her the other night. She'd allowed herself to believe in the fantasy. To open her heart to Finn.

What a fool.

"That's what makes it so special," Miranda said. "And interesting. One day you're thrilled to be standing in your own home with two of your most beloved television characters. The next moment you're sprawled on the floor, fighting for your life. Unscripted."

"Exactly. That one didn't go so well, did it?"

"On the contrary. It was a means for the two of you to come together. Spend time alone together..."

Yes, and to realize she could never have what she shouldn't want. Finn had been using her as a means to gain a producer's attention. That was the truth. As well, she'd wondered if he'd told her about his mom to appeal to her compassion regarding his winning the castle. The man was so...calculating.

Quickly going through *T* and then *U*, she then leaned back in her chair. The expectant glee on Miranda's face was enough to break her heart. If there were a way to fulfill the woman's fantasy of her and Finn getting back together, Allie would...well...

"I think you already love him," Miranda noted with a conspiratorial tone.

Already? Or once had? Or...still did?

It was complicated. And as much as she had opened her heart to a new beginning, she knew Finn could never be true. He'd not asked if it was okay to use her name as a bargaining chip.

It had been good while it lasted.

"No." Allie stood and stretched. She needed to get away from this conversation. Miranda could finish the rest of the alphabet.

"I've seen it since I returned. The way you look at him," Miranda persisted. "You love him."

"I will never love Finn." Allie announced the bold lie as only an actress could. "I, uh…need some air."

With that, she took off toward the boot room. Stuffing her feet into her wellies and grabbing a rain slicker, she headed outside.

Finn stepped back from the wall where he'd tucked away after overhearing Miranda tell Allie she loved him. He'd been about to walk in and tell them the parking signs were all in place for the event. But then he'd heard Allie say she would never love him.

His heart dropped. He should have burst into her room earlier and told her he did love her the moment he'd been thinking about it. Then she may have thought differently before replying to Miranda. But at the same time he knew Allie was lying.

She had to be. They'd shared so much these past few days. Had grown closer. Had shared their most intimate secrets with one another. He'd kissed her under the moonlight. They'd made love. Had it all been a lie?

CHAPTER TWENTY

ALLIE MARCHED TOWARD the pond, lured by the stoic solidness of the standing stone. Yes, marching was her go-to means to running away from a problem. She didn't scream, yell or even accuse. It was feet on the ground, moving swiftly.

As if that could take her away from the issue.

She was not in love with Finn. They could never be good together.

Well.

"No." Shaking her head, she carefully navigated to the pond's edge and sat far enough away so that she wouldn't slide in, but close enough to jump in if she wanted to. Not that she would. Maybe? Could a dunk in the fairy pool soak her with some magic to change her life?

She didn't need change, she needed…who knew anymore? Her indecisiveness was driving her crazy. What had happened to the strong, confident woman who had come into her own?

Finn McGregor, that's what had happened. They had grown close in the days they'd spent here at the castle. Had learned things about one another, personal, private things one only shared with someone they trusted. She'd even set aside her desire to erase him from memory. But after hearing his phone conversation…

Just one mention, Allie. You should ask him about it. Confront him before you go off the hook and turn this into a disaster of a romance.

True. A smart woman would talk to him about what she had heard. Not make assumptions.

Allie gripped the cool grass. Right now, she needed to be angry. Fly that freak flag that had surprised Finn so much. Because she wasn't always the calm, cool businesswoman. She had feelings. A heart! She might tell herself that she was all for leaving Finn in the past but deep down she knew that was a stupid piece of emotional armor she wore to protect herself from getting hurt again.

She'd been so mad at him for not knowing what he wanted from her. But if she were honest with herself, maybe she didn't know what she wanted either. Even from this castle. If she did win it, would she rehab it and transform it into a fabulous vacation spot? Or would she move in and settle herself, become the old woman in the castle with few friends, but an abundant garden with veggies to gift to the townsfolk. And mind the fairies, will you?

A kooky fantasy. But she wasn't entirely set against it. Glamcations could be run from anywhere.

Now she slipped off her boots and inched forward to dangle her bare toes in the cool water. If there were any fairy magic at all in this pond, she wished for a clear vision of her future. For a knowing. To simply be at peace with whatever it was her heart chose for her.

I've got Allegra Stark as well. She'll reprise her role.

How could he say that she would act in the sequel when she had plainly told him she would never act again?

"Careful you don't slide in," Finn's voice called as he approached.

Always there whether she needed him or hated him.

Allie closed her eyes, feet still in the water. She didn't hate him. But she didn't particularly like him right now either. "Would you just…go away."

He squatted beside her. "Really? That's what we're doing now?"

"I came out here to be alone."

"Very well." He stood. "I overheard you talking to Miranda just now," he said softly. "So I don't want to bother you overmuch, but…" His heavy sigh hurt her heart. "You do alone very well, Allegra. And maybe a real relationship is something you don't actually want. With anyone. But I'm willing to give it a go. You just have to let me in."

"I…" She didn't say *don't want you* because that would be a lie. "I have let you in."

"Eh." He wobbled his hand between them.

"Finn, I heard your phone conversation. Are you telling producers that I'm willing to reprise my role as Madeline Williams?"

"Oh, well, I, uh…" He winced. "Honestly? It was a brag that I was hopeful for but knew might never come true. A third studio passed on the script. And they gave me the news via some pitiful underling. It was a moment of desperation. I said it because I wanted it to happen. I'm sorry. I had no right."

"You didn't. And I would never consider the role. I thought I'd made that clear."

"You did. I'm sorry, Madeline, it was just something I said in the heat of the moment."

"What?" Allie fisted her hands at her thighs. "Did you just call me Madeline?"

"I, uh…" He winced. "Sorry. That—I know you're Allie."

"You don't even know what's real between us, Finn. You never have!"

"Allie, please, you just mentioned the character name and it was zinging around in my head. I know your name! And we've become close. You know we have! Something has changed between us."

"It's never going to change. You're...who you are. I'm... not willing to change to accommodate what you think you want, fictional or real."

"I'm not asking you to change—"

And she was growing frustrated by this roundabout conversation that never seemed to resolve. "Listen, it's not as if we're going to pledge ourselves to one another within the next twenty-four hours and ride off into the sunset. You have your life. I have mine. We'll be going our own ways soon."

"So you *do* love me?"

Why was he so insistent she confirm that to him?

He shoved a hand in his pants pocket. "Look, it's a lot to ask. I know that. I'll let you think about it. I just wanted to come out here and—"

"Tell me how I feel?" She silently admonished herself for her terse tone.

"I suppose. No. I mean... I've always loved you as a person, Allie. We were tossed into the wild and crazy world of filmmaking together. We didn't do that right. Or maybe we did. I don't know. I protected my heart at the time, but I should have been more protective of yours as well. I'll never stop apologizing for that. But just know that this time around I'm coming to you with a lot of self-awareness and...there's no one else, Allie." He tugged something out of his pocket and handed it to her. The purple fairy crystal. "I want to be with you."

He toed the base of the standing stone, hands in his pockets. Then, he turned and wandered off. Like a boy who'd just opened his heart to the girl and been refused.

The crystal wobbled on Allie's palm.

She hadn't refused him. But she hadn't embraced him either.

He'd called her Madeline.

Of course she knew it had been a slip of the tongue. But still.

Clasping the crystal to her heart, she watched Finn stride toward the castle. A lump formed at the base of her throat. She wanted to shout a swear word, and then cry at the same time.

Could it work? Could they be together?

Every molecule of her being seemed to activate to move her legs, to follow him. Run after him and beg for his attention. If he wanted to give love a chance between the two of them, then she would be a fool not to try. Because maybe, just maybe, he was the one for her.

Pressing the fairy stone to her heart, she whispered, "Do I dare?"

CHAPTER TWENTY-ONE

AFTER SUPPER SERVED by Dorothy (which Allie took in her room, claiming she had some business calls to make), Miranda had asked Finn to cue up the music for tomorrow's event. Tucked in the wheelchair with a tartan blanket and fuzzy bedroom slippers, he could feel the woman's exhaustion radiate from her. But he could also read the excitement in her eyes. This was something she'd wanted for a long time. Even a medical emergency wasn't going to keep her from participating.

At least someone was feeling a modicum of joy.

Allie had literally told him to leave her alone. Why was she the one set against them now when initially she'd been harboring a long-held love for him? What had he done to change her mind about him? What she'd overheard during his phone conversation had been a stupid man trying desperately to toss out one last hook to grab a producer.

Way to make her even more resistant by calling her Madeline. Idiot.

It was time to set aside the script and rethink what he really wanted in his career. If he couldn't have Allie alongside him if the sequel ever did sell, he didn't want anything to do with it.

In truth, all he really wanted right now was Allie. Her trust. Her respect. Her attention. But he may have just destroyed any chance of that ever happening. His dad had been wrong. Allie and he were not meant for one another.

"Let's hear a few songs," Miranda prompted, stirring him from his desolate muddling.

With a nod, he scrolled on his phone. Miranda had curated a playlist from episodes of the show. One song had become famous, winning a Grammy for film scoring. He cued it up and adjusted the volume and balance between the speakers. It began with a haunting drumbeat and deep cello background. Then a fiddle danced in, performing a technique that emulated a Scottish bagpipe. Slowly the melody rose. A soft bagpipe wavered around it all.

Miranda closed her eyes, head nodding as the music crescendoed into an orchestral marvel. It had been the theme for Connor and Madeline's wedding celebration. They'd gaily reeled down the center of the ballroom, surrounded by their television family clapping and making merry.

"The way you two danced," Miranda said with reverence. "It was so joyous. And romantic."

Romance felt unreachable now. Yet it was all that he desired with Allie.

"We practiced for days to get that dance right. I'd never danced in my life. We had to learn a reel, a grand march and then this slower dance for the bride and groom. Though I recall Allie was a natural. So graceful."

At the time he hadn't known what he could have had. Pitiful. And yet, he'd the sense not to hurt her. Because he had cared about her. Maybe even loved her. Though at the time he was too young and set on dazzling every woman who looked at him to recognize a genuine love. Now he would never win her trust because she felt he had hurt her.

"Would you two dance for us tomorrow? It would be like acting," Miranda pleaded. "Not that *you'll* be acting. I know that much, don't I?" she winked.

Cheeky woman. But not wrong.

One last dance? How sweet would that be? A memory to tuck away after the two of them appeared at the convention, learned who won the bid, then ultimately walked away from one another.

"I would be happy to. But you'll have to ask Allie. I won't ask her to do anything that would make her uncomfortable."

"Oh. Have you two had a falling out? She seemed set against anything remotely related to love between the two of you when I spoke to her earlier. It's not right. The two of you…"

Finn winced and turned down the music. "We were probably never meant to be."

"You don't believe that."

He shook his head and squatted before Miranda's wheelchair. He tapped her hand and she took his in a clasp. "No, I don't believe that. But she does."

"I'll talk to her."

"Please, don't do any such thing. Allie's life is hers to direct. And… I'm not the one for her. That was a role I played. We both played." *I was in love with you. For real.* Such a fool that he'd not seen her truth then. "If I'm not a part of that life, then so be it."

"That's too sad."

He patted Miranda's hand. "I know you wanted us to become a thing when you invited us here."

"Maybe."

She could play coy but he had figured that one out the moment he'd looked into Allie's eyes and seen her surprise. Neither had expected to see the other again. Miranda had played this well.

"I don't mind your well-meaning plan to reunite us," he offered, standing. "It was good seeing Allie after so long.

She's actually made me rethink some of the things I want from my career."

"Is that so?"

"I'm not so happy with acting lately. Maybe it's time I started making a life. Noticing things beyond my tight circle. Have a family."

"With children?"

He chuckled. "I'm a bit too old for nappies and chasing after a toddler. Family is someone with whom I can share my life. Hold close and know I'm safe. Make memories. You've a wonderful family with your daughter and grandchildren."

"I'm blessed. You are as well… Oh. You do love her," she reiterated.

He nodded. "I do."

"Then it will end well."

From her mouth to…whoever might listen. Finn tapped the phone screen to replay the dance. He could listen to this song over and over. It had such a yearning emotional undertone to it. One of the sound technicians had once referred to it as a rallying cry to romantic hearts. He'd never understood that.

Until now. Allie had touched his heart, softened it, embraced it and made it whole. Or almost whole. He would never feel that fullness if she were not in his life.

Out of the corner of his eye he saw a flash of silver hair. Finn slapped a hand over his fluttering heart. Allie wandered into the ballroom. She set a box of goody bags on a table and walked over to them. "I remember that song."

"Your wedding song," Miranda said with a glance to Finn.

The sparkle in her eyes was what had made Finn's ego soar through the years. That unconditional devotion from a person who called themselves a fan. But he understood it wasn't tangible or real. The only real thing in his life had silver hair and iceberg eyes.

"I'm a bit tuckered," Miranda said. "Going to see to another nap." She wheeled out of the room as the drumbeat began the promontory march.

Finn held out his hand for Allie. "Would you do me the honor?"

She stared at his hand for a long time. To refuse him now would be the arrow to his heart. He expected it. She didn't owe him a thing. Allegra Stark was her own woman. Set in her ways. Able. Independent. She didn't need him.

He needed her.

So when she nodded, it was as though she'd just caressed his bruised heart. Offered him some hope. If only for a moment.

For one last dance.

Her hand slid into his and the memory of the dance overtook his muscles. Finn bowed to her. Raising their clasped hands above their heads, they stepped toward one another. They walked slowly in a circle and then turned to walk down the aisle between the militant rows of chairs. He couldn't recall all the steps, but it was mostly walking until they got to the rise in the orchestral accompaniment and then he remembered he'd taken her in his arms and spun her.

There was no room for a spin, but he'd be damned if he wouldn't show her how he felt about her now. Finn turned Allie under his arm and then pulled her to his chest. Hands clasped near their thighs, they swayed. So much in her iceberg eyes. Cold yet warm when he held her. A goddess.

When the orchestral melody once again drifted away to the single violin and drumbeat he bowed to kiss her. He wouldn't ask anything with this kiss. It was already all out there. She knew where he stood. She'd told Miranda they couldn't be. He had to accept that. But not without this last kiss.

No resistance on her part. He wouldn't read that as promising. Didn't want to get his hopes up. But when he parted, she stepped back, tugging her hands from his. Bittersweet. She was the one thing that gave him life. Made his heart sing.

"I'm glad we got to dance once again," he said. He stroked her hair. "I know Miranda will ask us to dance tomorrow."

"Then it was good we got in some practice."

"Allie…"

With a sudden tilt onto her tiptoes, she kissed him. He couldn't decipher what she asked in this kiss but he sensed she asked something. Dare he wonder if her heart had changed in his favor?

"I don't want to talk about it anymore," she said. "We've said it all."

"I, uh…" He touched his lips. She was still there. How to process that kiss?

"I'll see you bright and early tomorrow." She stepped away and rubbed a palm over her shoulder.

"The spotlight calls?"

"One last bow," she said.

"Aye." His heart stopped beating. Shaken. Rejected. "One last bow."

CHAPTER TWENTY-TWO

THE CASTLE BUSTLED with excited convention goers. The schedule of events went from eleven to four. Most activities would take place inside the ballroom. Some speakers. A video presentation of fans' memories over the years. Assorted games. Miranda wanted Finn and Allie to make their surprise appearance around three o'clock, which was an hour from now.

They'd kept to the upper rooms all day, wanting to keep out of sight at Miranda's request. Allie had paced, wondering if she should talk to Finn before they had to pull on their roles, bow and then…walk away from one another. Ultimately, she'd kept busy by reviewing Glamcations' invoices and sending out necessary emails to their accountant, tax preparer and others a business owner couldn't avoid having on her team.

That busy work hadn't kept her thoughts from straying. Finn didn't understand how her heart had been tossed and tumbled since reuniting with him. He'd used her in a desperate ploy to try and convince a studio to buy his project? Understandable. Not acceptable. But ultimately? She forgave him.

She picked up the fairy stone he'd given her. Maybe there was some magic in this prop? It kept pulling them toward one another.

Why *did* she have to be so hard-nosed about something she wanted? She wanted Finn. The past two decades she'd never let him go. And now that she had him, she was making excuses to shove him aside. That was idiotic. Why not give him a chance?

She could summon no strong argument against another chance.

But after all the business had been taken care of, she padded quietly past Finn's door and down the hallway toward the tower room door. It would provide a quiet place to reflect about the time she'd spent here and to prepare for an afternoon of craziness.

Last night after they'd danced, Finn had wanted to hold Allie and never let go. She hadn't said anything like "I love you" or "let's do this" or even "we can work," and he hadn't asked.

So now, alone in his room as he dressed, when his phone buzzed and he saw it was his agent, he let it go to voicemail. However he cautioned himself against tossing it all aside. It could feel important a week from now when he was back in New York, Allie nowhere to be seen, his fingers hovering over the screen in wait of him calling his agent back to accept the Dirk Swagger job.

But he couldn't know that would happen. And he actually didn't want to look beyond the moment. So he wouldn't. Today was for the fans of *Clan Mackenzie*. He and Allie were the surprise. The secrecy and big reveal felt silly to Finn, but he didn't mind. It was a show-business tactic. Miranda had been kind to them. The very least he could do was don this kilt and put on a show.

Kneeling on the floor, he carefully folded the plaid fabric he'd laid out. The costume was a reproduction of the kilt he'd worn for the show. He'd known how to fold and put on a kilt since he was a boy. Sean McGregor would never allow his son to not learn such a thing. It was a manner of pride for a Scotsman. And while the tartan pattern was MacKenzie, he had the McGregor plaid at his Inverness home in a closet somewhere. He pulled it out for award shows. The "what's under your kilt?" jokes never bothered him.

Wouldn't they like to know?

According to Allie, there was a website that detailed exactly where a curious fan *could* learn what was under his kilt. Some people had far too much time on their hands.

He stood, wrapped the fabric around his hips with the pleats in the back, tied the straps and fitted the belt high around his waist, adjusting the folds. A fur-rimmed sporran with metal detailing was next; he hung it from its chain under the belt just below his naval, ensuring it didn't hang too low. Can't have it banging his jewels. The sporran could fit his phone inside but…he tossed the phone on his bed. It would destroy the historical look.

Tugging on dark socks, he realized he should have brogues for the more formal look but all he had were the hiking boots. The look was as good as it was going to get.

He looked damn good. He would feel even better if he'd woken alongside Allie this morning.

The night they'd made love had been real. No acting whatsoever. For once, he'd shoved aside the actor and let out Finn. That guy didn't usually get to come out much. Yet he'd had free reign here at the castle. Working with his dad. Hiking the grounds alongside his silver siren. Taking in a party with old friends. And even cooking for Allie. Who would have thought potatoes were her love language? He'd felt it all in his heart, his very bones. So much so he couldn't even summon a worry over the recent rejection. And he didn't worry about the results of the bid either.

Come what may.

Miranda was going to announce who had won the castle at the close of the convention. A little dramatic, and he preferred that announcement to take place off camera, but again, he wasn't going to argue with a woman who had suffered a heart attack. This convention meant the world to

Miranda. The fans down below wanted to feel something in their shared love for a story and its characters.

And he was more than happy to make it happen for them.

Now, how to make things go the way he desired in his personal life.

A knock on his door was followed by Dorothy calling for him.

"Be right down," he called.

He wished he could talk to Allie before they stepped on the stage, but maybe this was for the best. In a way it felt as though he were going to meet his bride waiting at the end of the aisle. Silly. She'd never marry him. And…well, he'd never thought to marry only because he'd never thought to find *the one*.

I'm the only one for you.

Might she believe that?

Dorothy had directed Allie and Finn to wait outside the ballroom until Miranda announced their surprise guests. Allie smoothed a hand down her long cotton skirts as she approached Finn. The style was reminiscent of the Gibson girl, with sleeker lines. The corset was snug, and she'd had to tie it a bit looser than she recalled doing so long ago beneath her fitted white cotton shirt. She'd forgone the heavy woollen shawl because—so hot. Around her waist she'd belted the expedition bag she's always worn in the show. The leather satchel with various pouches and pockets had carried her pens, paper, some herbal remedies (for tending wounds on the go) and of course snacks (something craft services had made to look old-timey). Now it held the fairy stone.

When Finn turned around, his jaw dropped open at her approach. "You look amazing. That costume! You look just like you did then."

"Save the gray hair and wrinkles?"

"What wrinkles? And the satchel. I remember you would never go on camera without it."

"My superhero utility belt of sorts." She patted the leather belt. "It makes the outfit."

"No, you make the outfit." He leaned in and when it looked as though he would kiss her, she pulled away. "Allie?"

"Don't, Finn. The other night was wonderful but—"

"I'm sorry for calling you Madeline. And for pretending you'd want to reprise your role. I suppose I still hoped you might, but it was wrong of me. I really am sorry."

"I know that. You were doing what you needed to do to get a producer's attention. It's just…" Now was not the time to discuss this, yet it seemed he wasn't going to let it go. And, damn it, her heart demanded they get things straight. "We don't even live in the same country."

"I spend a lot of time in the States. Allie, I know we need to talk about this more and there's so much to be said, but… I want you to know…"

"Two minutes, guys!" Dorothy called from somewhere down the hallway.

Finn took her hands. "Allie, I love you."

"You…" Her heart stopped beating. Sound focused intensely on the two of them. The flash in Finn's green eyes held her captivated. But she couldn't have heard him correctly. "What did you say?"

"I love you."

"But you…didn't…" *say it in all the time we've spent here.* And processing something she'd wanted to hear from him for so long felt almost impossible. She couldn't be sure if the thudding in her ears was her heartbeats or if she'd stopped breathing and she would drop any second now. "Finn, I'm…"

"You said you once loved me."

She could but nod. Once? Or always?

"Do you love me now, Allie? Can you possibly see beyond the idiotic things I've done?"

Allie couldn't find her voice. Her center had been rocked off-kilter. He loved her.

Dorothy marched toward them, a headset strapped from ear to ear and her mother's clipboard in hand. "You two look great! Let's move to the door so you're ready to enter when Mum calls you out."

Finn loved her. And she hadn't the time to respond. Or to even consider what her response might be. As Dorothy gave her a gentle shove to move, Allie let go of Finn's hand and followed. She looked back. He nodded and winked.

He was the only one for her.

And she did know what her response should be.

Dorothy stopped her at the door and made an adjustment to Allie's hair, which she'd braided down the side to fall forward over her shoulder. "You two walk out, wave, let everyone *oooh* and *ahhh* over you. We'll take a few questions and then we'll have an autographing session over on the west side of the ballroom."

"Sounds good," Finn said. His hand slid to Allie's back. She leaned into his touch, feeling a nervous need for protection. "I got you," he said as Dorothy moved away. "You good?"

She nodded. She was good.

"Finn, I…"

"Yes?"

She had to put it out there. "I never stopped loving you. But I don't want my heart to be hurt again."

He moved close, his cheek hugging hers as he whispered aside her ear, "I promise to be true to you. Will you give me a chance?"

"I… I will. But we would have to take things slow."

"Of course. We'll do this however you want to do it. But I'll fly anywhere to be with you. Anytime."

Miranda announced them to wild cheers and whistles from the crowd.

Finn pulled back, his gaze intent on hers. He'd made her a promise that she wanted to hold in her heart. To know it would never be broken.

"Time to take a dive!" Dorothy prompted. "Let's go!"

Yes, anywhere, anytime.

And together Allie and Finn took the stage.

CHAPTER TWENTY-THREE

IT WAS A weird feeling taking the stage. Holding Finn's hand returned her to those days they'd faked it for the crowd, putting on their smiles and acting all the way through interviews and photo shoots. But it was different now. *I love you*.

And she loved him. The real Finn McGregor.

The audience stood and clapped and cheered. Photos were taken. Excitement was so palpable that Allie's smile was real. She and Finn waved. They stood there and took it in, as did their fans. So strange that these people still held a place in their hearts for the series after so many years. And not so strange.

It was time to allow her heart to gracefully accept the experience and treasure it.

Finn leaned close and said over the roar of the crowd, "Crazy, huh?" He squeezed her hand. "I want to do something."

"What's that?" she asked, barely able to hear her own voice.

"I want to kiss you."

Oh. Uh. More acting? Just when she'd started to believe they were real? "For them?"

He turned her to face him amidst renewed applause. And in that moment all sound faded, leaving her standing before a man with whom she had fallen in love.

"For us," Finn said. "Always and only for us." With a smirk, he offered, "But also for them."

For us. Yes, she wanted that. And yes, she could play a role for the onlookers, knowing in her heart it was more for her. For the two of them.

Remembering what she'd placed in her leather belt, she pulled it out and held it between the two of them. The fairy stone. The crowd cheered wildly.

Finn took the fairy stone from her. Then he swept her against his chest, and as he bowed over her, whistles and hoots rose from the crowd. It was a silly gesture. It was a deeply resonating act of claiming one another for all to see. Not an act. This was real.

And she was all in.

They assumed a stage kiss, mouths touching but not moving, her back arched as Finn leaned over her, holding her firm. Always secure. And in the last seconds, when she sensed he would pull away, his hand caressed her cheek and the kiss grew real. Behind his hand, only for the two of them, they kissed.It sealed the promise he had given her.

As they straightened, a bow felt necessary. It hadn't been an act. It had never been an act. Yet they hadn't been meant for one another. Until now.

A steady drumbeat suddenly sounded through the speakers, frisking the crowd to another hearty cheer. Their fictional wedding song. The one that they'd danced to yesterday. And so many years ago. It was a nostalgic call to those emotions she'd once felt. Emotions she had learned to embrace and treat with respect. Because they were her reality.

Finn bowed regally before her and offered his hand. "Shall we?"

She curtsied and took his hand. They began a slow circle, lifting their entwined hands above one another's head. Nothing felt more right than this moment. The clothing wasn't hers, but the memories were. And the love, well…

Finn McGregor was the only one for her.

* * *

The dance segued into a grand march down the center aisle of chairs, which was joined by the entire crowd. Allie and Finn graciously danced with the exuberant fans for a few more songs. It was fun. And she couldn't deny her genuine happiness. When the music stopped, Dorothy appeared up front by the microphone. Everyone filed to their seats and she and Finn stood off to the side near the hearth.

Finn hugged her against him and kissed the top of her head. "Having a good time?"

"I am."

"Same. This stay has changed my life," he ended on a whisper as Dorothy began to speak.

"A big thanks to Allegra Stark and Finn McGregor for graciously appearing today. As you all know, this convention is a bittersweet goodbye to the castle. My mother suffered a heart attack a week ago. And as you've seen throughout the day, she's been in and out. Resting, but also, no one could keep her away from you lovely folk."

The crowd cheered as Miranda, sitting in the wheelchair and wrapped with a tartan blanket, waved and threw kisses to them.

"Now let me tell you the reason Finn and Allie are really here," Dorothy said. "My mother is selling the castle so she can travel. She invited them both to bid on the castle. And on the evening they arrived, each presented her with sealed bids that she only opened a few minutes ago. And now my mother wishes to announce who has won the bid."

More applause as Dorothy handed the microphone to her mum who stood and thanked everyone for coming and gave a little speech about her plans to travel after a full recovery spent with her daughter in Edinburgh.

"I thought I'd open the bids, see an obvious winner and then, well..." Miranda paused for dramatic effect. "I knew

I'd make a decision based on who I most believed would serve this castle well. Preserve the memory of a lovely television series we all adore, but also make it their own, use it in a manner perhaps I never dreamed of."

Allie looked to Finn. She had no idea who the winner would be, but right now she didn't care. This had been Finn's home. If anyone deserved it, he did. She'd actually gotten the prize in her new relationship with Finn. Anything beyond that was icing on the cake.

He kissed the top of her head and squeezed her hand.

"I have the bids right here." Miranda waved the two slips of paper. "I won't reveal how much each bid. Allie's bid is this one." She waved one slip. "And Finn's... Well, Finn's has been superseded by the request he made of me some days ago now." She glanced over to them and nodded to Finn, who offered a shrugging confirmation. Allie frowned. What was he up to?

"Finn has withdrawn his bid with the declaration that he wishes for Allie to have the castle. And so it will be. It turns out the decision was an easy one after all, at least for me."

Allie turned a gaping glance to Finn. He shrugged.

"And so the castle goes to Allegra Stark!" Miranda announced to renewed cheers.

"You..." Allie clutched the front of Finn's shirt. "But...you wanted this castle? All your childhood memories?"

"I still have them. Right here." He slapped his chest. "Maybe I've known all along that I have all that I need. It just took you to make me really believe and understand that."

"But the script. The producers."

"It'll play out the way it's intended. With or without the castle or the return of beloved characters. I like your idea for this place much better anyway. And I'll want to contribute so you can offer it for charitable stays. I can't wait to see how you refurbish the place. Are you happy?"

She nodded. She was happy to have won the bid. But more so, happy to know that what she'd felt growing between them this past week had been real, after all. He was the only one for her.

"Go on and shake Miranda's hand." He nudged her toward the stage, where Allie bent to hug the seated Miranda. And then, to renewed applause, Finn leaned over and handed Miranda the fairy stone.

A Q&A and autographing session closed out the day. Finn and Allie sat at a table talking to each attendee, signing T-shirts, glossies, set shots, books and all the related merchandise. Someone had even brought an unopened box of chocolate biscuits that had been marketed under the *Clan MacKenzie* brand around season four. The winner of the standee had them autograph that.

Miranda had turned in hours ago. She'd soldiered through the day. Had taken a nap around the lunch hour. Had stood and walked a bit during the games portion. Her wish had been granted.

It was dark by the time the last person left. Dorothy had pushed a broom down the aisle in the ballroom, then decided it was worth it to call in a cleaning crew in the morning. She ordered takeaway from a local restaurant, and now Finn and Allie sat out back before the bonfire, still in their costumes, finishing off the pizza.

"So what's your schedule for fixing the place up?" Finn asked, his gaze fixated on the flames before them.

"Dorothy intends to move her mother's things out over the next month, and then I'm free to step in. Of course we'll need to go through all the legal stuff. It'll take a few months to get plans drawn up and to hire contractors. But I'm thinking I may move in as soon as possible. I love it here."

"I do too. You're lucky. You've found peace."

"You haven't?"

"I have come to terms with the fact I'm no longer the leading man. But I could be a different kind of leading man. I'm going to be choosy about my next project."

"No Dirk Swagger?"

"I don't think so. The role has got to call to me. And while I'm waiting around for the perfect project, I think it's time I started living a real life."

"I think your life is pretty real."

"Aye, but you know acting. That's not real. I've missed out on family, kids, having a dog."

"You could have a dog. Kids too."

"Honestly, I couldn't imagine enjoying that at this point in my life. Like you, I ended up on a different path. But I am going to look into a dog. I like mastiffs, but a man shouldn't be welcoming one of those into his New York penthouse. I'll need some land for it to run free."

"You can manage that. If you want…" She reached out and clasped his hand. Fire glowed across his face and his eyes twinkled. "You could visit me here. Often."

"I was hoping you'd extend an invitation. But merely visits?" He screwed up his mouth and gave her his best pout. "I thought we'd begun something."

"We have. We—but what about if the script does sell? Or if you accept another role?"

"Then I'll plant myself on the film location and do my job. But as for my home base…" He kissed her hand. "It's not my place to ask…"

"Ask me," she said. Her heart thundered in anticipation of so much. A new beginning. A satisfying ending. An adventure that promised love and that connection she'd pined for.

"Can we…live together?" he finally asked. "Will you share your peace with me?"

It wasn't a proposal. And she hadn't wanted that from

him. But she was more than willing to make room in her life for real love.

"I'd like that. But understand, I'm still my own woman."

"Of course. I know you're not the sort of woman who needs a man. You're very smart, Allie. You can take care of yourself. But can you fit me into your perfect life somewhere?"

She got up and stepped over to sit on his lap. Watching the flames flicker in his eyes, she nodded. "You fit here." She patted her chest. "And you're right. I don't *need* a man. But I do want you."

"You do?"

She kissed him. "I do."

EPILOGUE

One year later...

ALLIE STEPPED INTO her muck boots which sat outside on a scruffy rug. She pressed a hand over her forehead to block the high noon sunshine, yet smiled because the day was bright, her spring tulips were blossoming and the air was not terribly moist.

She and Finn would forever laugh over that word.

Finn had moved in a month after she had, and he'd stayed with her the entire time while refurbishments were completed. She'd made up half the castle for guests and kept the other half for her private quarters.

Her and Finn's private quarters, that is. They'd spent every day together, hiking the island, laughing, dancing and making love. The word *marriage* had not been uttered. She didn't want that. Their relationship was solid, and it felt forever.

Picking up a basket that she intended to place some cut tulips in for a bouquet, she stepped out and spied the hefty bulk of fur and lolling tongue leading his master back toward the castle. Finn had adopted a mastiff and named him Jack after his most famous role.

Finn lumbered down the hill toward her and she quickened her steps to meet him halfway. Stepping into his embrace, she devoured his kiss as Jack nudged their thighs for attention. They'd mastered the ability to kiss while being accosted by two hundred pounds of dog.

"Soon enough you'll have Allie all to yourself, Jack," Finn admonished the dog, who did favor Allie because she gave the best behind-the-ear scratches.

"Another week?" She clasped Finn's hand and led him toward the tulip garden.

"I'm already dreading being away from you."

He'd taken a role that began filming in Iceland, of all places. But as luck would have it, Allie had her eye on a property in Reykjavik for Glamcations, and intended to visit it in a few weeks. Their schedules were almost synched.

"I'll visit you on set," she said. She didn't mind at all that he'd taken the role. Acting made Finn who he was. And he needed this role about a lone icebreaker who fights the elements when trapped in a storm to learn that he could be fulfilled by the less-flashy roles. "Isn't the ice melting there right now?"

"It is, but we'll be trekking northward for the outdoor scenes. I've to stock up on some thermal underwear."

"Well, I'd be there to keep you warm, but I wouldn't want to distract you."

"Distract me all you like." He kissed the side of her neck, which was about her favorite place for him to touch her. Giddy goose shivers! "The first booking arrives tonight?"

"Yes. A trio of women who have come for the hiking and soul renewal."

"Bring on the crystals and masseuse."

"Silly man, you love our masseuse." They'd hired the same massage therapist Finn had hired to pamper Allie, and she'd come in a few times to treat them both as a couple.

"Money can buy happiness."

"What about love?"

"Love comes from here." He patted his chest, which

alerted Jack, who jumped up for a full-body hug and top-pled a chuckling Finn to the ground.

Allie laughed and bent to cut some flowers.

"Aren't you going to help me?" Finn called.

"You've got this, dread pirate McGregor. Show him who's the boss!"

Amidst a tumble of fur and flailing limbs, the twosome play-wrestled on the ground. It felt perfect to Allie. Her heart, no longer exposed on her splayed palms, had been hugged and cherished and put in a safe place. Forever in Finn's arms.

* * * * *

If you enjoyed this story, check out these
other great reads from Michele Renae

Jet-Set Nights with Her Enemy
Billion-Dollar Nights in the Castle
Cinderella's One-Night Surprise
Faking It with the Boss

All available now!

MILLS & BOON®

Coming next month

BRIDESMAID'S FAST-TRACK FLING
Elle Brown

Nikos swallowed a laugh.

'A race,' he repeated. 'Yes. A Grand Prix. You're not a racing fan, huh?'

Olivia shrugged. 'No. I'm not much of a sports fan in general. I'll go to a baseball game, but that's more for the vibes.'

A look of horrified comprehension washed over her face. 'Oh, I see your shirt. I'm so sorry. You live here. I bet you're a big fan. I'm not trying to be rude. I'm sure it's a really cool sport. A great time. No offense.'

'None taken.' He smiled. 'But back to your cookies. I've got a bike. We can get around the barricades.'

'A bike, huh?' She tilted her head.

Say yes, say yes, his heart thudded.

Unbidden, he imagined her arms encircling his body...

She blushed as if she could read his thoughts. Or was she having similar thoughts of her own? Either way, she didn't appear to be put off, which was encouraging. But he still wasn't sure she would accept. There was uncertainty, and he wasn't used to uncertainty with women. This was a challenge. He liked challenges.

Continue reading

BRIDESMAID'S FAST-TRACK FLING
Elle Brown

Available next month
millsandboon.co.uk

COMING SOON!

We really hope you enjoyed reading this book.
If you're looking for more romance
be sure to head to the shops when
new books are available on

Thursday 15th January

To see which titles are coming soon, please visit
millsandboon.co.uk/nextmonth

MILLS & BOON

LET'S TALK

Romance

For exclusive extracts, competitions and special offers, find us online:

- **f** MillsandBoon
- **X** @MillsandBoon
- **○** @MillsandBoonUK
- **♪** @MillsandBoonUK

Get in touch on 01413 063 232